More Praise for *American Gospel*

"*American Gospel* is a stunningly rich and complex experience of Place. Behind the urban development plan of Baltimore's Highlandtown neighborhood, the novel vividly immerses readers into the everyday lives of its affected residents. For each character, Jeffra's dazzling prose evokes a longing for connection, peace, and belonging, culminating in a deep meditation on the meaning of home."
—Junse Kim

"Equal parts tender and fierce, Miah Jeffra's *American Gospel* is an uncompromising portrait of Baltimore and the people who call it home—a portrait framed by three finely wrought characters whose voices converge into a vibrant polyphony that reminds us of the inherent beauty in our brokenness."
—Zak Salih

"I wish I could go back in time and give my younger selves Jeffa's character Peter Cryer. In *American Gospel*, the corruption and violence—both personal and political—is only half the story. The other half probes into big questions about family, place, and history. Jeffra's ensemble cast is fully realized, each of the main characters attempts to love one another through their complications and contradictions. Queer, poetic and deeply reflective, Jeffra's gorgeous prose portrays the Cryer family and Baltimore in all their struggles and gritty glory."
—Matthew Clark Davison

"*American Gospel* is ambitious and fresh. I like and then despise and then like again several of the characters, which is real life. This is a complex and honest novel. Wonderful."
—Felice Picano

Additional Praise for Miah Jeffra

"Jeffra is a master of writing that stands out in how unflinchingly it inhabits and experiments with abstract ideas." —*San Francisco Chronicle*

"Jeffra's love for language and humanity is evident in his work, yet he demands us to face the ugliness of our society, even in the most likeable of characters. I am deeply impressed by this writer." —Randall Kenan

"Miah Jeffra is a true original, and a talent to watch." —Dan Chaon

"Jeffra compassionately and unflinchingly depicts an array of desperate characters as they try to attain the lives they've always dreamed of." —*Publishers Weekly*

"Both tough and tender, sometimes laugh-out-loud funny and other times direly serious, Miah Jeffra flips the script on danger and sexuality. Moving between critical, narrative, lyrical modes Jeffra illuminates and entertains." —Kazim Ali

"Is Miah Jeffra a philosopher? Is he, perhaps, a prophet? Is Miah Jeffra…a loud, queer pop lit voice for the new dawning? The author proves that he is all these things and more." —*Lambda Literary Review*

"Miah Jeffra is that rare writer who's as committed to the individual sentence as much as he is to developing a bold, animated vision." —Paul Lisicky

"Jeffra is a hyperrealist, and his stories vibrate with pain and love." —Maxine Chernoff

"Brilliant and daring, full of horror and tenderness, Miah Jeffra gives us the American stories we need to be reading." —Andrew Sean Greer

"Miah Jeffra writes somewhere between a scream and a growl…here is a writer who grabs the reader by the balls in all the ways one hopes to be testicularly taken." —DA Powell

"Miah Jeffra is one of the most interesting writers working today—the electric, eclectic way Jeffra straddles and subverts genres." —Chanan Tigay

"Miah Jeffra does not use his imagination to protect himself or to protect us. Instead, he gives us stories of reckless tenderness and anger and sorrow and lust—that overflow with images of wonder and desire. How wonderful!" —Robert Glück

AMERICAN GOSPEL

a novel in three parts

Miah Jeffra

www.blacklawrence.com

Executive Editor: Diane Goettel
Cover Design: Matthew Revert and Jared Shaffer
Cover Art: "1423 Mosher Street, 2011 & 2020" by Ben Marcin
Book Design: Amy Freels

Baltimore
Words and Music by Randy Newman
Copyright © 1977 SIX PICTURES MUSIC
All Rights Administered by UNIVERSAL TUNES All Rights Reserved Used by *Permission*
Reprinted by Permission of Hal Leonard LLC

Published 2023 by Black Lawrence Press.
Printed in the United States.

for my mother,
and for the Colorado River

Stories about places are makeshift things. They are composed with the world's debris.

—*Michel de Certeau, "Walking in the City"*

Get my sister Sandy
And my little brother Ray
Buy a big old wagon
Gonna haul us all away.

—*Nina Simone, "Baltimore"*

I

Fear at the Table
Makes For a Heavy Load

Prelude

February

These men will not matter in the end, but the story begins with them, in a boardroom, in a hush. They all knew it was a hush because they could hear it, the audible pause in wait, the music rest, the preparation for the pounding notes of new decision. A photograph would pick up no hesitation, no anxiety, only the smooth wide smiles of people who know business, the khaki casualness of it, the whiteness of it, the teeth of it. The men knew this was a skill to their profession, something taught and drilled with the diligence and precision of Japanese Noh. This performance, of course, was confidence, an unquestioning belief in what is being sold.

Between them all, on the 16th floor of a glass building towering over Baltimore's Inner Harbor, white pages gleamed from the table.

MacAllister, the developer, relished in the cleanliness of the contract, the crisp bold serif font, the fine paper, the flush lines of black to white. He knew the men saw his good side, all of them slightly tilted sideways to fit tightly in the circle around the table. They were standing, the discussion done, negotiation sealed by the readiness of straight legs, the standing over of something, yes, the final glance of predators standing over prey. MacAllister had made the kill, 126 pages of gleaming white.

The rest were admiring the catch, aware they looked like idiots in their hovering. But they didn't want to miss this moment either, wanted to take a photograph with their mind's eye, document the time when they participated in something out of the ordinary, part of something that would fill their names into ledgers to be read, newspapers, legacy. They would Google themselves and this moment would be the first item listed on the pulsing screen, the keywords *deal, real estate, revitalization, urban renaissance*, and, perhaps, *Baltimore.*

Beyond the meeting room on the 16th floor—dark wood table, gray and burgundy accents—the city was well in movement. Buses screeched their wheels, cars blared with impatience, harbor taxis clanged their bells, lipped against the loading dock. Heels clicked cold asphalt, volume determinant of ambition. Names called out across streets, into the wind. All the sound colluded in its rise high above the Inner Harbor, until it could be mistaken for the ocean, a shore of concrete, brick and glass, one edge of the world. Steam hissed out of potholes, synchronized white plumes dynamizing Charles Street, Light Street, Pratt Street, Gay Street, the pillowy display above revealing nothing of the seething below, in the gray and brown belly of Baltimore.

The men in the boardroom, however, heard none of these sounds, or perhaps heard selected sounds—the ding of elevator doors closing to rise, the snap of briefcases when emptied, the *ka-ching!* of cash registers—all very resolute sounds that signify the endings of things for most, and the beginnings of things for them.

None of these men really knew each other. They knew *of* each other, knew what each other worked for, signified, represented, pretended to be. They had done various one-on-ones in coffee shops, donut shops, barber shops. Some worked in the same building, none worked in this one. Two of them had their sons baptized at St. Paul's Cathedral, not at the same time, without either attending the other's. Some were childless. One knew that another was from Butcher's Hill, that his son went to St. Mary's, but he didn't know that his son's history teacher, Brother Thomas Manilli, would be in this very same building days later, receiving the deed to his dead mother's house, the house that stood across the street from one of the men's favorite restaurants in Little Italy, which was co-owned by another of these men. No one knew MacAllister had gone to Archbishop Curley High School, but if he told them he would have discovered that one of the others went there at the same time, that they had Biology together forty-one years ago. The oldest one there had slept with the youngest one's fiancée years before they'd met.

There were some less impressed with the deal. They were the smaller politicians, the neighborhood councilmen, the ones who were less visible but more connected to Highlandtown. And the farther one was removed from the neighborhood, the more triumphant they parted the circle. This is where the neighborhood councilmen gave themselves away; they were the only ones left staring at the document, the finality of it. The others had already begun the resounding handshakes, the clap of the palms, the slip and grip.

MacAllister remained close to the contract as he shook the hands, slapped the shoulders, slicked the grin that all men envied. After all, it was *his* kill, and anyone desperate enough would evade protocol, maybe try and take a bite. He would guard the bounty until all had left the circle. He prided himself on his thoroughness.

MacAllister held little reservation with the deal. His wife wasn't too pleased, but that's because she didn't know what it took to make things happen. She was full of what-ifs and might-its—*What if the people who live there can't find a new place to live?*—but he knew that nothing is ever accomplished with doubt, nothing that can be carved into legacy, anyway. How could anything progress with that kind of questioning? He knew the Crabtown deal was good for his family *and* for the city. How often does one get to contribute to both?

Over the years, he'd watched Baltimore fall into ruin. He'd watched whole areas become impossible to live in, to even drive through. The drug-addled streets, the lurking black eyes of vacant rowhouses, the rabid air of whole districts. He had stopped attending Orioles games, never venturing close to Memorial Park, until they built Camden Yards, of course. What he had loved as a child—the streets lined with vendors, the crowded sidewalks, families having picnics in Druid Hill Park and snacking on their stoops—was gone. He despised the city now, how it allowed itself to get so tarnished, a beautiful young woman going the way of a whore. How could his wife be opposed to bringing back the city they loved? Yes, there would be people affected—and his intent was never to push those folks out—but no move towards progress is perfect. There will always be externalities, as they say in business. MacAllister learned long ago to keep focus on the big picture.

They broke from the circle. Some were grabbing iced tea, chips and crab dip at the refreshment table by the window, looking out over the street to the harbor, smiles lingering. They turned to one another and began the small talk, the human part, the return to self, that ritual of transformation after catharsis. This is where the glimpses of their lives colored in the black and white singularity of the business deal, the where-are-they-froms and are-they-marrieds. Many of them had already asked those questions before, at city meet-and-greets, campaign dinners, charity events. It was acceptable to forget. *So many people. You know how it is.*

MacAllister wondered which of them would be the first to question the project once the afterglow faded. He wished he had an instrument that could bore into the solid knot of their gut, examine how tight it really was, where there was chance for fray. He didn't worry about the investors, or the park designer; this was sure-fire for them. But the politicians. They didn't have any goal as fixed as profit. Their goals were not as predictable. And the means were a little questionable if not aligned with the outcome. Oh, the means of things. Isn't that where suffering resides? But there must be suffering to usher positive change. These men knew this, had read their Marx and Machiavelli, had learned to look away when it was important. But the politicians. They knew they'd have to answer to the means, not these men with the higher thread counts and silver belt buckles. The means have faces that can yell and spit and cry, can seethe, even erupt.

For now, though, the men were solid, pumped, the swell of impending success anchoring their movements.

This is big!

That neighborhood will clean up!

It's going to be like Six Flags!

Like Disneyland! Only in the city!

A Baltimore-themed park! A better version of itself!

So clever!

New jobs!

At that moment, in Highlandtown, where the theme park's grand entrance would be, a gaggle of squirmy seventh graders were learning fractions in their King Middle School classroom. At that moment, in Highlandtown, the spot designated for the Star Spangled Music Hall was a plague of seagulls tearing apart a grease-soaked paper bag in a Roy Rogers parking lot. At that moment, in Highlandtown, Peter Cryer was emptying buckets of mayonnaise into a condiment bin, inside the same Roy Rogers, one that MacAllister had already bought and where the Old Bay Resort Hotel would stand within the year. At that moment, in Highlandtown, on the future site of Hush Puppies, the kiddie section of the park, Peter's mother, Ruth Anne, stood in the corner of her small living room in her small rowhouse, one scheduled to be demolished by the end of the year, her fingers clenched around an official Orioles baseball bat, fearing the shadows outside the front door, fearing the shadows would be the strong arms of her estranged husband, ones that could wrap around her torso and drag her across a room, that could squeeze her skull like a water balloon. At that moment, in Highlandtown, on the same block that Crabtown's signature roller coaster would be erected, a small young woman was being beaten to death by her tweaked-out boyfriend, her baby-daddy, twenty-eight blows, four of them to the head. She had hid his glass pipe under the sink as a loving suggestion. The screams that emanated from the dilapidated rowhouse could have been the sounds of a thrill ride, long and looping, sharp and falling, the low moans of the finish.

MacAllister's shirt fluttered, as if he could sense the crime, could sense the life exhale from that woman's body. But change does that—a fluttering. He continued to smile and shake. He knew there was good in what he was doing, felt it in his fingers. He was cleaning up the city. Crabtown would help bring people back to the Baltimore he loved, the only way that was certain. Look at what South Street Seaport did for Manhattan, and didn't the West Edmonton Mall revive an entire part of Canada? And Disneyworld? It made a whole city from scratch.

So why did he feel like he was falling, as if the window glass he leaned against suddenly dissolved in the salty air?

He put his hands in his pockets, rocked on his heels, and smiled. His gaze fixed back on the conference table, the contract, neatly wrapped in Velobinder, something that made sense to these men. They caught his gaze, and they all followed it, and nodded almost imperceptibly, like a secret had passed among them.

That ended the meeting. Moving forward. They grabbed for their coats, started to bundle up against the city outside, even smaller talk now, the weather kind, all of them stealing quick glances at MacAllister, to make sure of something, all looking for the same word.

"Gentlemen," he said, and they all felt better.

Their story ends here, at the beginning. This is common: the rich begin the story, and the poor bring up the rear.

1

Ruth

I know Isaac called last night, could tell from the breathing and nothing else.

I check to make sure Peter locked the door. He did. But before I walk away, I find myself checking again.

Peter probably thought I was asleep, that I was heavy to the pillow, thought he could sneak out the house, grab my truck, rev and take off, like I was in some kind of coma. Course not. I wasn't asleep. Not with that puke calling me and just breathing. I could almost feel the heat of that mouth, even through the phone. But Peter didn't know Isaac called. Peter thought he could just skip out like I wouldn't know. Teenagers think they're so clever. Think their mothers were never teenagers.

All I want is for the night to go away, for the dark to go away, for Isaac to go away. And I don't even know where he is. And I want to know, to know where not to be. Isaac. My *husband*. Isn't that something? "Never do it twice," Mama said. That's about all the advice she got right.

The doorframe is chipped, and the layers of paint show just how many times people have moved into this rowhouse. Layers of white, beige, light blue, brown, beige, white, off-white, white. Little chips revealing the years, the different moves, the different families. We've only been here six months, another coat of paint sealing up the windowpanes, making the door stick in the summer. Been here a couple months longer than the place on the west side, and a couple months longer than the place before that.

A memory shouldn't be clearer than the event itself. I guess that's what they call a haunting. My head always plays the look of Isaac when he came home that one day, rushed right to me and picked me up by the neck, that vein popping out on his forehead. His blond hair sweaty and stuck to his forehead. He was so angry. And angry at what? I wasn't cheating, I wasn't lying, I wasn't talking shit to people, or telling them about the drinking.

I replay that day all the time to figure it out—did I say something that morning? Did a co-worker of his feed him a line of bull? He just came in the front door, went straight to me and started beating me to Kingdom come. It's been two years now, and I'm still asking the same questions, playing the same memories like the record player done skipped and all you got is the one bad song on the LP. The look in him, the heat in his face. *I'm gonna kill you bitch*, with all the growl in his throat like phlegm was the devil churning his guts. The world closing up around me, blurring out, his hand crushing my throat, his one single hand killing me easy, and only his mean, mean face, the big clenching jaw, the vein, the liquor smell in his unwashed hair, wanting me dead, *You been fucking tar when I'm working? You like fucking tar, don't you? You miss fucking tar?* There's nothing as scary as seeing someone you love be like that, someone that shares a bed with you. Shared, I mean.

If Peter hadn't walked in and screamed, I don't know if Isaac would have let me go. And when he did I grabbed anything I could to get between us. Chair, water pitcher, brass bookend. Peter screaming, glass breaking, and when he charged towards Peter I went all crazy and took that ceramic jar to his head. Isaac ran out, *Bitch, you fucking bitch*, out of the house, out of what I hoped was a home for a family. I bet those little spots of blood that followed him out the door are still there in that Cherry Hill apartment.

Did I lock the door? Christ.

I close my eyes and go back to the daydream, a better record done skipped, of those Tennessee foothills, the chimneys puffing smoke in winter around each slope of the holler, the snow white and clean, rounding up the hills, rounding down the valleys, like some whipped peaks in the meringue. Me as a pale little stick of a thing, bright red curly hair getting tangled up with twigs and crepe myrtle leaves, without men to worry about. Something so clean and simple about the place. There weren't trucks out there choking up dirt and salt to clear the streets, no gutters and trash cans. Everything had clear lines and clear colors, not the grubby blur of the city. The green was grass green, the blue was sky blue. Colors weren't confused, and they just were what they were in Tennessee. But here in Baltimore, they're all mixed up—a slate-brown and dirt-gray.

But this is where we gotta be for now, what with Peter going to that good private school for free. Besides, Appalachia country is no place for a boy like him.

I spend what's left of the night biting the plum polish right off my nails, drifting in and out, fingers bleeding on my pillow, waiting for the day to come up. The whole idea of daylight is what I wait for now, the clear and safe, things being seen. God knows I haven't been sleeping, with Isaac being around, maybe around, maybe not. Which is it? And when I get up on these days, it's everything just to pee, get the hair out of my face. I don't get up to shower in the morning anymore, because I know I won't take one. Too tired by the time I finally pass out to the time I have to wake up. I have to give it my all to tug my clothes off, put on new ones, get the brush in my hair. If my fingers get tangled in one of the knots, I'll just pull them out and leave it there.

I could feel the spread of Isaac's lips through the damned receiver, almost feel his beer breath on my ear. I called him a puke into the phone and slammed it down.

If Granny knew I was behaving this way, she'd say, "Child, who pissed in your boots?" and then I'd smile and say, "I don't have no boots, Granny." She'd say, "That's cause women are too dangerous with the boots" and then plop some sausage gravy on a plate and slide it to me. "Need some grease in that gut, make your hair shiny." God damn I miss her. She was simple and clear as day, like you could see through right to her heart.

Isaac wants to get me. Two years of running, and he's still hell-bent. If Joby was alive and around for all of this he would have screamed at me for staying with Isaac in the first place—*What's wrong with you, Ma?*

Why did I stay with him, Joby? Why didn't I follow you out the night he attacked you? I remember the way Isaac came home that evening, too, in his bodyguard uniform with the shirttails all out of his pants. He was drunk already, his face sweaty, eyes swimming like eggs in a bowl of water. He had found out that you'd been stealing money from his sock drawer. Why did you think you could get away with that, Joby? Huh? Why were you always doing shit like that? Not that it mattered—it coulda been anything that set him off. But that night, it was the money. You and Peter playing video games, and he got across that living room faster than I ever seen him move, and he grabbed the front of your t-shirt and threw you to the ground before you even knew he was home. I remember how big Peter's eyes were, him climbing backwards up the back of the couch. How easy it was for Isaac to throw you like that, like you weren't already becoming a man yourself, like you weren't close to being as tall as him. How Isaac kept spitting *You think you can take my money? You think you can take my money?*

I knew he didn't like you, but I never thought he would be like that. Not like that, Joby. That was the worst he'd been, up until the last time he went after me. I didn't know, Joby. I didn't know.

Why didn't I grab Peter and follow you right out the door that night? You looked at us, just before you closed the door, before you left. You looked at both me and Peter like it was the last look you'd ever give. Through all your I-don't-give-a-shit attitude and hard-ass face, I saw the little boy in you, like you hoped to be picked next for the little league team. You wanted us to come with you. You wanted us to leave, too. If I would have, things would be different. You'd be alive.

I want to check on Peter, just to get a good look at something I can see, but I already know he's gone, Lord knows where, and whatever he's doing gets later and later, into the night. I'm not ready to figure that one out yet, but it sits in front of me, stares at me in the dark so I can't see where it's looking. I wish I could tell Peter sorry for all this and everything, for the running every few months, for the shitty apartments, for Joby leaving, for me staying with Isaac too long. But Peter and I don't say sorry to each other. I've wanted to say it many times, probably him too. When we're supposed to say it, like over dinner or after we see a really good movie that makes us cry, we'll get quiet with each other, like it's a ghost of a word or something. Like you can love some people, really love them with your whole heart, but never tell them. You can tell others, but not them. The word don't fit somehow. Me and Peter, that ghost word is *sorry*.

I stub my toe on that exposed nail again, walking into the basement. All it would take is a good hammering, but I never get around to it. I never get around. I go down there in the musty dark and lay on some laundry in front of the old dented washer. It feels good. The towels have been here awhile. I smell the peach of my lotion, the mushroom of Peter's dirty underwear. When Peter was a baby, Joby used to take his diapers off him and flick at his doo-lolly. "Pe-ter's lit-tle ding-a-ling, Pe-ter's lit-tle ding-a-ling." It was downright nasty but I couldn't help laugh. Joby was barely out of diapers himself, then. Oh, Joby, sometimes I see you in the corners of the day when I smell a pot pie or mustard, or when I see those braids of yours you loved to wear so much on some other kid.

I jerk up in the dark to the front door slowly being closed, which just makes it creak longer and louder than if Peter were to do it fast. Part of me wants to yell up the stairs, make him know I know he's been sneaking off in the night. But why? Anything a kid doing this late ain't anything I'm ready to hear about, not right now. And, Peter? Well, if he can't tell me what it is he's doing, then it's probably something I don't want to know. I have a feeling he's a fairy, but that's not my business, and it's not what gets me, either. It's that he's out there in the night, and Isaac could be out there, too. And he knows what Isaac can do, has seen it for himself. Teenagers are the dumbest things, thinking they're so clever.

His footsteps try to make no sound, back up to his room. No mind, though. I sigh the relief. Peter is home, and he's safe. But how was I supposed to be calm with him gone? I have been hugging the laundry pile like it's the last dance at the party. I sit up but that's it for a while, the mound of clothes some kind of comfort. The dark and the quiet and me sitting on the floor and not sleeping all jumps right in the pit of my gut, and it's a cold kind of hurt, not knowing what to do but knowing you need to do something.

How did you get here, Ruth Anne?

The front door is locked. I know it, dammit, but I have to check. Children never know the danger of the world and swing safety willy-nilly like their dangly arms, nothing careful. I stay there a moment, looking out into the night, Patterson Park, downtown beyond. The park is dark and still. All sorts of things happening there—hand jobs behind trees, kids selling drugs, spray-painting on walls—but whoever is doing it keeps to themselves. I pull down on my oversized t-shirt and touch the Celtic knot around my neck.

In the winter, the park's branches look like crooked old fingers pointing in the night, accusing me of something. In the warm months they are large and full, all over and out, but now there's a wickedness to them. They reach out to nothing. They seem all forgotten, shrunk like the way shame does you, just out there in the open. The trees, I mean.

Down the street, south towards Eastern Avenue, cars glide through the wet of the road, one by one. Up the street, there is nothing at all, no movement, no light, just the neighborhood of Ellwood. Cars are asleep and all the windows are shut and locked. At any moment it could become all craziness, silent then screaming, calm then storm. All those police raids recently... the last one only two blocks up... creeping closer. The blue lights flashed everywhere, bouncing off the faces of the five men they threw in the wagon. Women all around them cried and got in the way, their ass squeezing out of their Spandex leggings, and that's only what I saw. Who knows what they got in trouble for, probably selling drugs, or hurting people because of drugs. Everyone north of Patterson Ave acts like a bunch of animals. I don't even walk their way in the *day*-time. Peter and Joby's father from up that way. He said it wasn't always bad like that.

The skyscrapers can only be seen from our rowhouse in winter, the buildings straight ahead, beyond the other side of the park, couldn't be any more than a couple miles away. Their lights wink like stars through the layers of branches—orange, white, and yellow. When they were still little kids, I would tell Joby and Peter that when you go far away from cities and look up at the sky, you can see bands of stars, and if you look long enough just after it snows, the band will have rainbows in it, a star for every color. Joby snorted and said, "Yeah right, Ma." Peter kept his neck craned to the sky like he was trying to see through the smog and into what I was telling them. I didn't know if he believed in what I said, or if he just wanted to. Hard to tell with Peter.

Sometimes I know in my gut that Isaac will end me. How crazy is that, Ruth Anne, some crazy shit to admit to yourself? Mama would probably think it was punishment for marrying twice, or maybe it was for first marrying Abe. But look how that turned out—punishment enough. Hell, what if she's right? Maybe it's what I deserve for losing Joby.

The purple lines of dawn peek through the thin clouds, and I find myself thinking of when Isaac was just a strong man, and not strong in the way he became, when he would touch my back as we walked through a crowd, when he carried me up the stairs after I fell asleep on the couch. I love a strong man. And maybe that is the shit of it all, that what I like so much can get so bad. It always ends up that way. All my men have been that: strong in the shoulders and arms, but weak in the head.

My first husband, Abe—Joby and Peter's father—was strong too, but never once took a hand to me. In the beginning he was a real gentleman and took me ice skating (a Black man ice skating still makes me laugh), kissed me under the monument in the middle of Charles Street the day he proposed, people around making all kinds of sweet faces, his pride in me so clear. *My bride, my bride, my bride.* He would swing me up on his arms every time we came in that first apartment of ours, even when I got heavy with Joby. He would kiss my belly, cup my breasts, lay on my legs when he came home from the spice factory, smelling like cinnamon and sweat. He would make love to me, real soft not to upset the baby.

He would play with Joby's feet until the boy be a worm in hot ashes, giggling something awful.

Abe was a real gentleman, then, before the factory closed and the drink opened him up, brought out the dark part. With men, you don't want to see that much of them. A strong man keeps what's really in there away from anyone seeing, whatever it is. But the drink opened them both, Abe and Isaac, and they let it all out. Abe only did it in words, the yelling and crying about how he was a nothing, a nothing of a man, walking through the rooms with his chin raised up like a question and dropped down like a sorry, rubbing the top of his head, those words over and over. It was so pathetic to watch him cry all the time.

Isaac got weak in a different way, weak but really strong in his hands— few words, mostly hands, the slaps and grips and punches.

Glass breaks somewhere outside. I jerk my neck to see where the commotion's coming from. Isaac could be anywhere, and my knees do their shaking, getting all flush-like. What will he do to me this time? Will he show up, stand across the street so he doesn't violate the restraining order? Or park his car in the alley behind our house and just sit there? Or will this be the time he rushes me, right when I'm thinking the craziness is all over, like he's given up, and I let my shoulders down? I whip around to get behind the door. I think of grabbing the bat in the closet, and that's when I see a streak fly across the sidewalk in front of my porch. Her legs are pushing hard and fast, her tits bouncing all over the place as she runs. A bottle crashes close to a small car, right in front of my neighbor's stoop. "Bitch!" comes from a low voice somewhere I can't see. Not Isaac, and I let up in my shoulders. The "bitch" is out of sight, too. It's just one of those hooligans who lives up the street.

I yell into the dark, "No need for that, now," but not the way I wanted it to sound—full and strong, like I got some authority, like Granny. Granny would stand at the farmhouse screen door with her big legs and say the same thing when me and the cousins started acting up in the front yard, the thick summer heating our tempers, and our arms be right at our sides in a split. I don't know why I yell. It's not like a damn soul gonna heed my voice, all nose and no chest. Maybe I want the last word. I put the baseball bat back in the closet.

I slip back in the bed, bunch the duvet around me. The sun peeks through, dead flies on the window sill. No Isaac. Least not until tomorrow night.

Or the next, or the next.

The nights are getting harder. It might be time to move again, just so I can get some sleep.

I hear the floor above me creaking around. Peter, where have you been?

2

Peter

On my way to school, I notice there are more stray cats scurrying around the neighborhood than human beings—screeching, clawing commas within an empty sentence. They stop and preen amongst the cavities of the city—orange and gray flashes in the shadows of all the gutted rowhomes, half of them long-abandoned, their doors and windows pulled out. All that's left of them are brick skeletons. This nonsense wouldn't happen in Manhattan or San Francisco. You rent a place, you get a house with windows, and you're guaranteed a door. Streets wouldn't be this hollow, anyway.

The sidewalk is dug up with an arrowed sign saying "Detour", pointing right back from where I came, and little orange plastic fences surround what was the grass of Patterson Park. I'll have to go the long way. Equipment piles dot the park and the sidewalk. No one is around with all the construction blocking every which way, even more barren than normal.

And now this walk to school is even lonelier. Despite the apocalyptic setting, I used to look forward to it, back when I started St. Mary's and Ma required Joby to escort me. Joby always complained, but would shoot me a grin like enjoying the walk was our little secret.

And we'd walk through this shitty neighborhood near the school, through the trash and shattered glass and the cats leaping among the rowhouse cavities, him telling me about whatever girl he was hitting up, me telling him about the books I was reading.

And he always kept watch, would keep his head high, scanning the street while I rambled on about Cervantes or Cisneros. I pretended not to notice.

Even after I began sophomore year—and felt old enough to walk in the neighborhood alone—Joby would accompany me. The talk moved from girls and books to Isaac—how much of an asshole he was, how Ma had such bad taste in men, how shitty he treated us. Joby hated him, and his face would freeze in this gritted-teeth pose as we ambled past the bombed-out alleys, the shifty-eyed corner boys that Joby told me never to stare at. He'd say, "You pretend you can't see them, they pretend they can't see you."

The one time I ever interacted with cops in this neighborhood they weren't going after those corner boys at all, but stopped me and Joby. We were close to the school and Joby had his hand on my shoulders in that protective big brother way, when a cop car crept alongside us as we walked. It trailed us like that for maybe a full block. Joby's body tensed up, muscles in his neck ribboning, and his gaze shot steadily forward. At one point the cop leaned his head out the window: "Hey, kid." It took me a moment to realize he was talking to me.

"Yeah?" I said.

"Everything OK?"

I didn't know what he meant. Did I look upset? Was something happening that made me look distressed? I was telling Joby about what new asshole thing Tony Farissi had said to me in Biology class the day before. "Yeah, officer."

The cop then looked to Joby, with a much gruffer voice. "What are you doing with this kid, here?"

Joby knew something I didn't, because he sort of laughed to himself before he looked at the cop, and spoke strangely, annunciating every syllable with exaggerating clarity, like he was practicing a reading in public. "I'm walking my brother to school."

The cop seemed confused for a moment, scanned Joby, then me, then back to Joby. Then to me, "Is that true, son? This your brother?"

"Yes, sir."

The cop then said to Joby, "That better be true." Then added, "I'm watching you." He pointed his peace fingers at his eyes, then pivoted them at Joby, and drove off.

Joby muttered under his breath a slew of curses, eyeing the cop car as it turned down a side street.

"What?" I said.

"That cop probably thought you white."

"Why?"

Joby snorted. He stuffed his hands in his pants pockets.

"He's a cop. He's making sure we're safe," I said.

Joby laughed, and it was so bitter, like the way most adults sounded when they laughed.

*

The school is huge compared to all the small loneliness of the neighborhood, a six-story beaux-arts graystone palace rising atop a soft slope. It looks so out of place, a diamond in the rough, as they say.

I hop the stone steps leading to the grotto and then farther up to the main building. There are still fallen leaves confusing the steps, shredded and dulled in the corners. It's freezing around the grotto, the ancient trees making their own cathedral hall, drinking the sun and keeping it from warming my head.

The statue of Mary is flaking, her former white communing with grimy nature. She stands almost at eye level with me, more a glorious peer than a divinity. Her chipped head is tilted to the left, flat and plain, eyes deceiving, looking down while simultaneously looking straight out. I never knew if that was a mistake, or if the sculptor wanted me to feel humbled as Mary listened to my thoughts. I never do. She is soft and quiet, unwearied. I talk to her sometimes. I know it's ridiculous talking to a statue, but that's it— no judgment, no response. Everyone else has a fucking opinion.

I like sharing with her the fantasies I have about Jude, and getting graphic is entertaining, every gory detail. The way I graze up his white legs with one single finger, along his calf, under his athletic shorts, the receding blond hair on his thigh, until I almost get to, almost get to, almost get to. I know she loves it. I mean, it's the Immaculate Virgin. Someone's got to tell her what she's missing.

The grotto is mine. No one else stops here. Students keep walking up the path, not even noticing that Mary waits for them, or that I visit her a lot before school. They all run around oblivious to her, to me. They're only responsible for their football helmets, math homework, and being stupid.

"I hate them, Mary. I mean, Joe walked endlessly to find a place for you to have a kid that wasn't even his. That's sacrifice. And all these ass-holes run around talking about the lunch special in the cafeteria like it's the only news in the world."

She listens to me, unmoving. I grab a bit of crabgrass from the crevices of the stones.

"You'd be disappointed with me if you knew what I did, Mary."

She waits.

"I fucked Grant again." I can't help but laugh. It sounds so funny coming out of my mouth.

"I know, I promised I would quit playing with daddies," brushing leaves away from her base. "But they're more fun than twinks on the apps." Which is true. God, the apps. Painfully dull exchanges of *hey-hey-what's up?-nothing much hbu-pics?* and then flexy torsos and dicks and blurry shots of buttholes. "There's no fun in all that, Mary. No eye contact across a room, no body language, no seduction. It's all so transactional." *Grindr, Scruff, Squirt, Wild, Tapdat*, whatever. An endless litany of unimaginative names that hint at the destination and not the journey. "Besides, Grant can pick me up while he fucks me."

I hold her shoulder to keep myself up, I'm laughing so hard.

"But don't worry, I won't get pregnant, if that's what you're thinking."

I look up at her. Her eyes look down at me. Tough crowd. Ah, she's laughing on the inside.

The rest of the school is where I feel wet and heavy. I am reminded of thickness, the suffocating. The huge stone building looms over me, judges me, reminds me of the very same words I share with Mary, and now renders them shameful. I cannot ignore the awe I feel every time I walk from the grotto to the main building's entrance. I grow smaller, shrink into the last thought, the forgotten final dot of a correction pen. St. Mary's. The more I trek this route, the more needlessly poetic I make my suffering.

I near the doors that from far away seem to appear as only ominous slabs of dark wood. But with each step I begin to recognize the familiar slopes and crevices that only nature or an artist can fashion—one with fury, the other with care. The artist, whether paid or inspired, chose depictions of the Crusades—overdressed men on horses, valiant and determined, a shield with engraved Latin in one hand and a cross held like a sword in the other. Who in their right mind would engrave Crusaders on the front door of a place of learning? A place where you get suspended for fighting! And here, the great murderers of the western world parade themselves. Hooray for Christianity! Bash those heads in, rape those innocent virgins, take the children! I imagine what they'd have done to me. I, their fodder with which they started fires and burned cities to the ground. Lighting my hair and throwing my diseased body into a pitted pile of waste, my class-non-mates waving their fists and spitting as I burn. Aid in the demise of Sodom! That would be a rightful way to die. A more purposeful way to live.

I crack me up.

The main corridor is echoing layers of conversation over shrieking, the clanging of locker doors, dress shoes scuffling, tapping, scuffing dull linoleum. I stare down the hall, brimming with adolescence, the smell of young body odor reminiscent of re-heated pizza, hormones. I imagine oil, dripping from their pores, slow at first, watching the broth fall and burst on the floor and ooze into a thin, slick sheen, then steadily getting heavier and heavier, until the entire main hall of St. Mary's is covered an inch thick in young males' greasy gunk. They start to labor in their movement, slipping a little here, catching a little there, some lose footing, until there is nothing but a dense pit of slipping, stumbling mass faltering in its own pubescence. I navigate through the entanglement, but without so much as a slip. In fact, these pimple-faced cherubs are parting the hall as I walk by. They don't want to share their puerile body-fest with a salacious sex-leper. I rip my rainbow "H" off my lapel and stretch it up to the sky. The only perk for my destiny is a clear hall to walk through. An empty hall here, and in my heart, and everywhere else. The demons applaud, louder and louder and louder and louder.

I head to homeroom. Lots of shuffling. I get ready for the onslaught. I look for Jude. He's doodling on his desk, Tony Farissi and Jimmy Wilkinson crowded around him. Jimmy sees me first.

"Aaaaaaaaaaaah. Petey is back." He punches my shoulder. "Had a nice vacation, there, Petey?"

My desk is next to Jude's.

"Hey," Jude says. He's wearing the tighter black button-up, the one that shows the steady slope of his shoulders.

"You wore that for my homecoming?"

Jude doesn't hear me. No one does.

Jimmy's eyes are expectant. "So, why were you suspended, Petey?"

Tony rolls his bulging pussy glassy eyeballs. "Don't interview him like he's a fucking celebrity."

Tony was always skinny and pimply, and only recently bulked up, puberty finally giving him a break. Baseball helped. He is nowhere near handsome, but ever since he grew some manhood in him, he's been more forceful in his annoyance. At least it's better than before, when he would make the basest cracks in his broken voice, his neck so skinny and his head so big it seemed it would loll right off. We were friends for maybe three days in ninth grade, just when everyone started figuring out who was destined to be friends, nemeses, the whole works—High School Soc 101—but we've been enemies ever since.

I turn back to Jude, who's still doodling. I fish into my pack. "I got the new remastered Juju." He looks up. "The sound is super clear."

"You fucker. It just came out Tuesday."

I pull the LP out and dangle it in front of him. Grant's brother manages a record store that specializes in rare vinyl. Fucking him is good for something. Well, two things. I obviously share none of these details with this crew.

"Let me see." He snatches it from me, his eyes happy. They are pale today. He must be tired.

He reads the back, opens it up muttering, "Shit. I need to get this."

"You can borrow mine for a while. I also have this Bauhaus bootleg."

"For real?" His eyes widen, and I can't help but show teeth. "Thanks, man. I'll give 'em back."

"Whenever."

Jude keeps reading. He's lost in it. His hair wasn't brushed this morning. It strings out like horsehair, not a wild Arabian mane but a malnourished Clydesdale. My fingers would tangle in it as I grabbed and rode along the beach, or into the sunset.

"How's your boy Janke?" Jimmy grins. "Seen him yet?"

"Not yet."

Tony spits a look at Jimmy. "Shut the fuck up, Jimmy. Christ!"

"You shouldn't use words like *Christ*, Tony," I say.

He looks at me with hate. This mutual hate has lasted years, from the latter days of our freshman homeroom, when he sat in front of me. He turned around and asked me, "Are you actually Black?" The question felt like an insult, somehow, so I responded in the calm sharp delivery I was newly practicing, "Are you fat?" He then called me a faggot, I gave him the finger, and now the antagonism was crusted into tradition, an institution of its own, he spewing out mostly true epithets, and I calmly undermining them. Ping-pong.

I turn back to Jude, who still reads the liner notes. We could listen to the album together, in a quiet, dimly lit room, my head resting at the bottom of his belly. "What are you doing after yearbook?"

"Going to Fell's Point. There's a free show at the 8 X 10."

"What time?"

Tony answers deadpan, "Nine." He doesn't even need to threaten me with the curt syllable. I wouldn't be able to go anyway.

The bell rings. Everyone drops into their desks. I look to Jude for some kind of sympathy. He just keeps looking at the liner notes, only his eyes stay fixed.

Tony Farissi sucks.

The administrative offices are tucked in the quiet hip of the school, linked by a paneled hallway with a red carpet that is off limits unless we have an appointment. I pass by the class portraits of all the graduating seniors before me. The hall is long, and the pictures gradually become more and more strange. The bowl cuts of the nineties and oughts. The orange air and bushy hair of the seventies and eighties. The crooked smiles and wild eyes of the sixties. The change from color to black and white, and crisper uniforms. And so on. Decades become more indistinct as clothes become less comfortable-looking. The pictures begin to fade as time raises up the particles of the young men, rendering them faceless. The ones from the nineteenth century have practically disintegrated. Even a photograph cannot survive the paling of time.

The principal's office is to the left, just in front of the chapel. I walk across the red carpet. The wood around me needs polishing. In the doorway, Mrs. Bell, the secretary, is busy eating her pencil. She expects me. I look at her with wide eyes.

"Not too bad. They all just sat down," she grins.

I walk into the back room. The conference table is too large for a meeting this size.

"Peter."

"Good morning Principal Dell. Good morning, all."

I opt for the chair directly across Father Mike, one of five sitting around the conference table. Brother Thomas is not here. *Fuck*. He's my biggest advocate. This could be bad for me. Once I sit down, I feel swallowed in the formality.

Principal Dell folds his hands and begins the meeting in good cinematic style with a gruff clearing of the throat. "Mr. Janke isn't sitting in on this meeting. He told me he will talk to you later, in private."

I nod my head. Dell always sounds like he's forcing his voice to be that low. I imagine him practicing in the bathroom mirror, his hairy gut hanging out of an old pair of BVDs that fit him two decades ago. He leans back in his chair. "How was the time off?"

How do I answer that? It was a suspension, not a sabbatical. *Oh, darling, I ambled along the river's edge and skipped rocks in my petticoat.* What did I do? I stayed at home and watched YouTube videos on me and Ma's computer and delighted in not having to be in school.

I say, "Thoughtful."

"Good." His lips purse in fear of some thought he wants to vocalize, but censors. The quiet conflict makes him look stupid. A fish. "Good."

Brother August leans in. His mouth looks funny with the puckering of his lips. "Peter, we've been discussing your career here at St. Mary's, and we want your perspective."

Dr. Ducee interjects with his flailing, nasal, intensely proper voice and pointing finger. "We cannot deny your caliber as a student. You are one of the top in your class. And congratulations on your SAT scores."

I don't know if he wants me to say thank you. I nod. Even his compliment is drenched in attack.

"But that is not the only requirement for being a successful student at this institution." Point point point. "Strength of character is another essential ingredient. Respect and honor." Point point. "And your gestures toward Mr. Janke were anything but honorable."

My lip twitches. I'm a rabid dog, taking a bite out of his emaciated leg, slurping up the blood of his ripped muscle while his eyes scream, paralyzed, in horror. I pull his flapping skin left to right, back and forth, and watch him jerk uncontrollably, a puppet with an epileptic master.

I put my fingers to my mouth, and feign scratching, hide the twitching. Out of the corner of my eye I see Brother Saul trying not to smirk.

Father Mike asks me with sincerity, "What made you say those things to Mr. Janke?"

I feel like every word I say right now will drip with insincerity, so I first paint a troubled look and appear almost speechless. Then, "We were having a disagreement, on transubstantiation." That is the truth, so the words sound appropriate.

Father Mike repeats the word to himself. There is a pause between us.

Dell's voice booms, drowns out Father Mike's. "Peter, you called him—the exact words—an imbecile."

The exact words were "imbecilic sheep", but I don't correct Principal Dell. I nod.

"This is your second altercation with Mr. Janke in three months. Not to mention your other suspension last semester. All arguments, with teachers. Were they all about trans…"

"No," I say. "It wasn't really the subject that…"

"Do you have a personal problem with Mr. Janke?"

The question tightens me. "No." Should I make this meeting a plea for my case or keep listening and nodding? "Not really."

Brother August and Dell lean forward. "What do you mean?"

I sweat. The pause feels long. Their faces are getting farther and farther away, and I see them climbing onto the table and crawling across as the table gets longer. They move too slow. My throat fills with thoughts, a mob of words. No no no. The words expand like sponges to water and I wheeze, which ones, which ones. I am brittle nails scaling concrete. Here it comes.

"I believe his views are too strictly orthodox to be instructing an upper level Religion class."

The table has a faint carving of the old familiar suggestion etched crudely, right under Dr. Ducee's ragged knuckle.

"Do you believe that is case for you to make insult to your teacher, a difference in opinion?" August has a patient face, but I see its confusion in the wrinkled skin between his eyebrows. Is there a name for that spot?

"No."

"Then why did you?"

"Mr. Janke would not accept my opinion. He said it was heresy."

"What is your opinion?" Now Father Mike is leaning forward. Why even have a table? Why not huddle around the delinquent, drop him in a cauldron, and make grunt-speak?

Dr. Ducee puts his hand up in protest and looks to Dell. "Though it is interesting, we didn't come here to discuss Peter's position on religious tradition. We came to discuss his behavior."

I sneak my hand into my pants and rub my fingers in the sweaty crease between my leg and balls. Who will I shake hands with first?

Dell lifts up his shoulders. The hairy mole on his left cheek is dancing as he speaks. "Peter, your academic standing naturally makes you a peer leader. I believe with that comes an inherent responsibility to be a conscientious human being." There is pause for effect. He definitely practiced this monologue, this is what he really wants to say. "The younger scholarship kids are looking up to you, and the faculty wants to see them following those who exemplify a good Catholic life." When he says "scholarship kids" I know what he really means. Of the small handful of Black and Brown kids at St. Mary's, most are part of the scholarship program. We're called *freebies* by assholes like Tony Farissi. "Your recent outbursts could have consequences that go beyond you. Don't you want to set an example for the kids like you?" The mole is really a little gorilla begging for a banana, or maybe relocation.

"Peter, you need to respect other people's opinions and refrain from insulting your teachers." Brother Saul talks with a campfire in his throat, a little mumble in the lips. His words do not command attention in a room with so many egos. His eyes stay focused on the tabletop. I feel respected when he talks to me, but he's also not that bright. He probably feels boosted somehow in my affinity for him, poor guy.

Dell sucks in a lot of air. This is the dramatic moment. His lips part to freeze time and heighten anxiety, the way a principal is supposed to. "We don't have much time. Look. You can't afford any more trouble at this school from now until graduation. If you receive one more suspension, one more demerit, even a legitimate complaint by any of the faculty, you will lose your scholarship, and you may be expelled. Usually, someone with your disciplinary record would have been asked to leave after this last situation. But like I said, you are a good student, and we're taking that into account."

The sudden worry almost surprises me. I take little breaths. Losing the scholarship would mean being kicked out would mean no graduation would mean no college would mean no getting out of this choking, tight little Baltimore life, all this bullshit and brick. I need college to get out of here.

"I'm sorry," I say, and there's even some sincerity to it.

"I think we all know that. Let's just be responsible for ourselves and enjoy the rest of the semester."

I nod. A pain shoots down my shoulder and up the back of my head.

The meeting begins to shuffle around, and Dr. Ducee is the first to rise. Everyone follows. As he walks by me, he says, "I think we are being more than fair, Mr. Cryer."

I extend my ball-sweat hand, and he looks pleasantly surprised and shakes it. I had to do it. He continues forward to the door. Dell and August nod their head and move into their adjacent offices almost in sync.

I slowly get up. I can't feel the pins and needles in my legs, but I know they are there, my stomach a cavern. I need to install bars on my mouth, like the rowhouse windows along Eastern Avenue. My tongue is a sharp one that flicks quick, painful things.

I manage to walk stiffly to the hallway, on the red carpet. Father Mike touches my rigid shoulder. "It will be all right. Just play it cool." He begins to scurry away with his rabbit legs, but turns. "Oh, Peter, I would still like to hear your views on Transubstantiation." I nod, and he shrinks down the corridor. I almost feel sorry that I never will oblige. He's not worth the time, an unnecessary trifle.

But Dell is not. He might be a moron, but he sticks to his word. The way he even says *expulsion* is full of dark spots. I need to play beatific angel from now on out. If I fuck up, that's it, everything else is fucked, too. And not even the ones who like me—Brother Thomas, Brother Saul—could help me then.

The old men's variously bent frames take their time crossing the red carpet and disappear behind the photographs.

Time to be a good boy, Peter. At least only be naughty outside of school.

3

Thomas

The clock teased me last night, declaring how often I woke up: 1:15, 1:53, 2:10am ... its green neon a taunting specter. I should have turned it around; I needed to hide the time. What I really needed was sleep. I have school today, beginning my lecture on The Battle of Tours and the Frankish-Muslim conflicts, which a bunch of teenagers only find interesting when I can manage a spirited charisma, wave my arms around and perform historical figures with accents. Yesterday's phone call from the hospital, however, took hold of my mind.

I was finishing notes from fourth and fifth period classes when my cell lit up. Someone from Mercy Hospital. My mother had an unexpected aneurism and soon after fell into a coma. She was currently hooked to life support, on which she was entirely reliant to maintain her vitals.

The woman's voice on the other end was kind yet firm. "Your mother listed you as her health care surrogate."

"What does that mean?" I asked.

"You make decisions regarding her care moving forward, since she is incapacitated."

"Decisions?" I tried to envision my mother in a hospital bed, what she looked like in the years—six, maybe seven—since I'd seen her last, if her hair splayed on the hospital pillow, if she still kept it tight to her head in a bun or if in indolence let it grow. Did she have any social life left that would make her mindful of her hair, at all?

"Mr. Manilli, the hospital recommends your mother be taken off life support. Even before she slipped into the coma, she demonstrated no capacity to breathe on her own, and even if she were to recover that ability, she is technically brain dead. Of course, that is your choice."

"What did my mother want? Can you adhere to whatever her wishes were?"

"She did not leave instructions. Only that you were to be the health care surrogate."

"I wasn't in close contact with her. Might there be someone else more suited to make this decision?"

"I'm sorry, Mr. Manilli. It must be you, I'm afraid. And the decision needs to be made as soon as possible. I understand this must be difficult for you."

I pulled on the buttons of my shirt.

"I am currently at work. May I call you back?"

"Please do so soon. The hospital doesn't want to place on you any extra financial or emotional burden."

And so, the muck-like coffee that I'm chugging this morning is only giving me jitters and not gumption. I think to cancel my final periods, just for the break, for the reprieve. It's not as if the students will glean anything from me in my half-awake state. And I'm sure they won't mind skipping the module on Charles Martel. In a nutshell: Chucky killed a piss-load of milkmaids during the battle and blew his nose on their *jupes*. Their hands smell of cow tit, their lips of his groin. Next lesson.

Of course, that's not what we can teach them. Can we, Chucky?

Decisions.

"Thomas." August says my name with a sing-song cadence as he enters the teacher's lounge. After all these years, I understand that to be the signal for some sort of admonishment. I grip my coffee mug, my hairy knuckles paling against the ceramic.

"August."

He flounces over to the faculty mailboxes. The fabric of his black shirt—the one all of us in the order wear—stretches awkwardly across his back, pinches above his love handles. "We didn't see you in Peter Cryer's disciplinary follow-up. I thought you were out sick or something."

"No, I'm here."

He performs a dramatic turn to face me. "Are you?"

"What?"

"Sick."

"No. I…"

"Did you forget about the meeting?"

"No. Not exactly."

"Then, why weren't you there? Everyone else was there."

"Sorry."

"We'll still need your input, to share with Peter. It's a shame you weren't there, you know, for context, to inform your statement."

"Does it matter?" I ask, staring at the whitish film forming on top of my cooling coffee.

"What do you mean 'does it matter'? This boy has a record of demerits, even a prior suspension. I would think so."

"I mean, does it *really* matter? He's in high school."

"Thomas, I'm going to forget you said that," August says, and flits out of the lounge.

I realize that I have lived with August in the rectory longer than I've lived with anyone, more than I did my father, certainly longer than my mother. Aren't I more qualified to be *his* health care surrogate? Was my mother so alone that she would bequeath such responsibility to the son she abandoned? How lonely was she? Did she choose loneliness?

Mercy hospital calls again. Instead of answering I watch the ten numbers glow on my cell phone screen until they stop. I finish the last of my coffee, take a deep breath and stand up, readying myself for the second half of the school day.

Periods four and five stretch long during my lectures, one a recap of Medieval European wars, the other early colonial American expansion. I can't help but see similarities—the urgent need to gobble up land in the name of God. I ask the students what they think about the role of the Church in these scenarios, but I'm met with only shrugs, half-answers that half-heartedly support the Church's efforts. Perhaps they are worried I'm asking them a trick question and they defer to their institutional allegiance, the one I represent to them. Times haven't changed at all, have they?

I stare out the window of the teacher's lounge, the gray winter hovering over the city, hoping to summon insight, a direction in which to move, but nothing comes. Absolutely nothing.

*

After dinner, after all of us in the rectory have turned in for the night, I take out my phone and listen to Mercy Hospital's voicemail.

"We really need an answer concerning your mother, Mr. Manilli. Let us know how we can help you and your family in this rather difficult time."

Yes, take these vague images of her out of my head, the ones of her when I was small, looking down at me with the sky surrounding her head, the ones of her smoking with her back to me, the seams of her stockings a perfect vertical line from skirt to shoe heel. These images are all vague, of this woman whom I hardly knew, who abandoned me and my father when I barely started school—maybe five, maybe six years old? There was no sit-down, no living room announcement. I didn't even see her leave, so sometime between then and now I fabricated a scene that filled in my absence of a memory: her waiting for a taxi on the front porch as rain pattered the aluminum gutters, her chestnut hair smoothly pulled into a soft bun, the navy pencil skirt she often wore, looking out to the road, fearing we would return home before she could escape. Escape us. And now, she is dying.

Family. That word. The more you say it the more unfamiliar it sounds. And that was my family, perhaps. People who came and went, migrated through time and space without settling into anything resolute, a series of blurs. My mother left. My father died young. His family loved me at arm's length.

Once I joined the order, all those years ago, the elders warned me that my family would most likely distance themselves. Though a respected vocation, giving up the earthly pleasures would be perceived by most as somehow unnatural, they said. They prepared me for the response. This would be easy for me, I thought. I had no siblings, my father had died when I was no older than my students, and my mother had long been gone. After joining the order, once I had my first encounters with the little extended family I knew on my father's side, they did look and treat me differently, something between perverse fascination and veneration. Lots of polite silences. I was no longer someone you could tease, no longer a man of casual banter; I became more a curiosity than a cousin. I have been wedged out. Maybe that has made it easier to stay in the order, even once my exuberance for the life waned. Yes, I must admit that it has waned.

I hear Brother August next door, snoring.

I push the covers off and slip out into the hallway, dark and still. The kitchen hums, the fridge packed with leftovers from a church banquet.

"Couldn't sleep?" a round voice comes from my left. Brother Simon. I notice his black hair is getting just a wee bit gray at the temples, though he's a good ten or so years younger than me, the baby of the rectory, really. "Me neither." He bends his slight, slender back into the fridge, and with long fingers pulls out a carrot cake cube. "Don't tell Father Mike," he says, winks, and gobbles it up.

"Why can't you sleep?" I ask.

"Too much on my mind." He stops chewing, looks at me, "I'm sure you understand."

"Sure." I stare at my feet.

His attempt to smile is fooled by the bits of cake in his teeth. "One of the reasons I joined the order was that I always felt too much, for everything. It kind of pulled me places, couldn't concentrate, you know?"

I nod. It doesn't seem necessary to ask him what he means.

"That development proposal passed."

"Crabtown?"

"It got the greenlight. Fast. They're not wasting any time. It's going to change things, I think, a lot."

"Maybe for the better," I say. "It'll bring some activity, at least more than all the drug dealing."

"A theme park in East Baltimore. It'll bring money, sure. But for *whom* is what makes it so suspect."

"I'm sad they're not preserving some of the architecture," I say. Most of the rowhouses there had that charming turn-of-the-century frankness, the flat brick fronts adorned only with a marble stoop, plain windows, and a red door, built by industrious immigrants who struggled between their European practicality and New World ambition. It's an America that seems to be fading. A shame they don't respect the spirit that built this city, at one time the second city of America, second to only New York.

"That's your concern?" Simon's face flares in incredulity, but then settles quickly. "Something about it doesn't make sense. All these councilmen say it's a clean-up. Who cleans up with a bulldozer? It's like washing dishes by smashing them on the floor."

"It's pretty rough around here. It could use some cleaning up."

"That doesn't make me feel better." He picks at the Formica counter. "I went to one of the neighborhood council meetings last week. Some resident advocates said the city hasn't even found new assignments for all the public housing tenants. There's a lot of people worried. They see things differently than you do." He leans in closer, a whisper. "Thomas, have you ever noticed we have no Blacks in the order here? We had Douglas, but that was years ago…" he says to a memory.

"He went to St. Louis, right?"

"I wonder if he felt out of place."

"With us?"

"Us. Maybe the order. Catholicism. I don't know, but I can see what these people are thinking in the neighborhood. Everything else is being bought for pennies or condemned, except our school, and the way the architects have even negotiated Crabtown to fit us in? We are wedged into the side of this park." He laughs, "Father Mike might be administering Communion under a big Mickey Mouse sign. I don't know, it feels problematic."

I try to reassure him. "But we're a school. Everywhere needs schools."

"King Middle is a school too, Thomas, and that's being razed. The city condemned it, they're going to bus the kids north."

"King has problems, though. The metal detectors, that poor kid who got shot in the cafeteria?"

"You're right, but this is a problem, too. A real problem." Simon's eyes disappear into the problem, which I'm rather unclear about in my sleepless state.

Once upon a time I might have thought *too* much about King Middle, the residents of the neighborhood, the lot of it. I'm surprised I haven't thought about it much at all. I stare into the back of my head, at the newspaper articles in the past months, the signs, all of it vague and existing without urgency. The amusement park—Crabtown—will break ground later this year. I recall editorials blasting various government agencies, raising big questions like "Where will the people go?"

Simon's shoulders soften, head tilts, a well-rehearsed yet somehow genuine gesture. It brings me out of my brief trance. "How are you? You seem troubled," he says.

I tell him about my mother, the hospital's recommendation.

"Well, you know the stance of the Church. How do you feel about that?"

"I don't know," I say.

"We have a duty to preserve life," he says.

"Yes, I'm aware, Simon."

"But we also have a commitment to personal dignity."

"That is true."

"What does that mean to you, Thomas?"

"I don't know at the moment."

"If only decisions could be so easy," he says.

"Yes," I say.

"What are you going to do?" Simon asks.

"I don't know. I suppose I need to do something."

"Yes, you do," Simon says, with what I detect is a hint of judgement. I wonder what he is getting at here, but I'm too tired to ask.

"I should sleep. I need to be ready for the kids tomorrow."

"You love teaching our students." Simon's voice is resonant and nurturing, like a back rub. The order looks for voices like this, a bonus. I bet he practices in front of the mirror. I can see him doing that. He's very popular at St. Mary's, especially with the cooing mothers.

He's right, though. I do love the students. They give me something urgent to think about, beyond chapel and the drudgery of rectory meetings, the details of our dying order. I can focus on something outside of my own life. Everything is new for them, and everything is same for me. Except for my mother. Dying. A different sort of death.

I nod, staring at my feet.

"But Thomas, it seems like you need to decide this quickly. What are you going to do?"

I feel slow to respond, as if the question is not intended for me. Not only Simon's question, but the hospital's. It's like asking a vegan which salami he prefers. It doesn't feel connected to the reality, at least not mine. And yet it is my mother. It is about the end of her life. I am her son. The feeling of flatness is what has me concerned. Shouldn't I be able to summon my empathy, my concern for the welfare of others, for her? Why hasn't the impulse surfaced? Or, maybe this numbness, this failure to act, is uniquely about her and I, this particular mother and son—the estrangement—that flattens whatever urgency her death might bring. There wasn't much between us, except for questions. Answers that now I will never get, but that I feared to seek, anyway.

"I need to be doing something."

He laughs. "Have you been praying?"

"Probably not enough." I refrain from telling him that I haven't prayed in weeks, maybe months.

Simon leans in, as if he really does want to help me, as if he really is willing to listen. "He helped me through both my grandparents. I couldn't have done it without Him."

"Simon?" I surprise myself with the way I say his name, like pouncing on an escaping rat, like jumping into a pool of cold water before I think about how it'll feel. "Do you…" I feel as if I should trust asking this question. This is my rectory brother, a member of my extended religious family. No matter how strong the faith, there is always doubt, especially in times like these. Do we always know to consult with God in times of indecision, in times of duress? Maybe Simon would appreciate the question.

But I can't. There is just enough time to reason, and to fear reproach. Besides, I don't know where the indecision truly comes from.

Once upon a time, I felt like I chose this life. The impression of passion, of vocation, pressed resolutely in my mind, I recall. I felt like I was entering into a home. Now, I can't remember why, or even when that choice was made, or even if that recollection is true. Is that what we all experience with our choices? Does the reasoning fade, like all memory? "I'm…tired," is all I say.

"There's nothing like sleep to clear your thoughts." His face reads like a Hallmark card, pink with affected sincerity. I nod, look down at my feet.

He steps closer to me. "If there's anything I can do…" And cups my shoulder.

I walk back to my room, de-robe, drop into bed, pull the covers over my hairy middle-aged Sicilian gut. I look at the clock.

Tomorrow will get my blood flowing, I'm sure. If I could only get some sleep. I remember Ruth Anne Cryer telling me once during one of our many coffee shop chats that the worst thing to do on a sleepless night is to pray. She then let out that snorty laugh of hers, slapped her lean, freckled thigh, of which her wrap dress had slid off to reveal only a small soft peek above the knee.

I turn on my back and stare at a water stain.

I haven't talked to God in months, about my numbness, about my growing ambivalence with the order, and now this decision concerning my mother. Why is that? What's more disturbing is that even with this realization, I feel no rising inclination to do so.

*

The next morning is cold yet clear, some sun to brighten up the string of gloomy days.

The corridors are full of students—locker door slams, jocular chatter, general jangly adolescence. The high ceilings and stone walls of the school give these sounds the effect of a museum lobby, or even the vestibule of a civic hall. The din is vigorous, familiar, and pushes me out of my circling thoughts. Entering St. Mary's is always a welcome pivot.

About halfway down the longest corridor, between the admin offices and my classroom, I notice a disturbance amongst all of the backpacks and legs swarming the halls. An unusual half-circle has formed, bottlenecking the typical movement of bodies. I walk closer. Beyond the amphitheatre of teens two freshmen are facing each other, taking turns leaning forward and yelling, then backing up, fingers flicking as they spit indiscernible epithets. The beginnings of a fight. They inch closer to one another with each exchange, back and forth, back and forth, until they are within shoving distance, which the shorter boy takes advantage of. Napoleon Complex. The push is merely a step in the escalation, not harmful. The taller kid throws his backpack to the ground and replies with something more intentional. I squeeze into the inner circle. The spectators grin and whoop, their pubescence crackling, jumping circuit. Circus Maximus. Lions and Christians. Weegee's photograph, "Their First Murder."

"Gentlemen!" I yell, as the shorter boy throws an awkward punch. They don't seem to hear me. The punch makes contact with the taller kid's shoulder.

"Gentlemen," I repeat. A few of the onlookers turn towards me briefly, but resume their gawking at the scuffle. The fighters don't even hesitate. The taller one punches with more gusto, and lands his fist deeply into the shorter boy's stomach. The shorter boy doubles and then without hesitation rams his head into the taller one. They're both on the floor, rolling around gracelessly. That dirty linoleum floor.

I lower and yell out to the fracas, "Hey!"

Just as the shorter boy scores an effective elbow to the taller boy's jaw, Father Mike out of nowhere rushes into circle, grabs the taller boy by the collar and throws him against the wall of onlookers. He runs into the center of the circle and extends his arms in a T between the fight. "Enough!" he bellows. I marvel at his agility, his force, despite being older and shorter than me.

The boys stop, huffing, shrugging off the hands of students half-heartedly trying to calm them down, their new obligation now that authority has shown up. Brother Simon appears as well, ready to act, with a very similar wild and electric face to the adolescent spectators.

Father Mike nods at Simon, barks at the boys, "Go to the office." Simon tells the fighters to grab their backpacks and follow him, which they do.

Father Mike turns to me. "Who started the fight, Thomas?"

I pull on the buttons of my shirt. "Does it matter?"

"Of course it does."

"It's over, though. No one's hurt," I say.

"We have to assign responsibility. Who started the fight?"

"Can't we just let this one go? Just this once," I ask. I'm so...tired.

He leans into me, away from the remaining circle of curious boys. "What kind of example are we setting if we don't?"

"Will a lesson be learned, Mike? Really?"

His face is creased with bewilderment. "You need to take action, Thomas. You witnessed the fight."

"Fine." I throw my hands up. "It doesn't matter who started it. Give them both goddamn demerits." I move out of the circle.

I hear "Thomas!?" behind me.

I head towards my classroom. I have only a few minutes left to write out the long vocabulary list for my first period lesson, jot down the announcements for homeroom. My mother, in a hospital bed, and I determine her fate.

August appears out of nowhere. "Thomas!"

"August, I don't have time right now."

"Peter Cryer. You need to weigh in. We're submitting his report today, before the weekend."

"I can't talk about this right now."

"I know you favor Peter but that's exactly why you need to make a statement."

"Then you know my position."

"It needs to come from you, Thomas."

The weight, the judgment of his words fills me with anger. I swing my door open with too much force. The door slams loudly against the inside wall. "Why do you need me? Huh?" August's eyes are anime-wide. "You don't need me!" My voice cracks and I feel both of our embarrassment, but I am too heated to acknowledge it. I escape into my classroom.

*

I head to Mercy right after the final bell rings. I don't dare entertain my after-teaching ritual of getting coffee in the faculty lounge, especially since August has probably told the whole order about my blow-up. I don't want to face an inquisition. Fuck it.

The third call from the hospital came in the morning while I was teaching, and judging from the cold, curt tone of the administrator, the mention of "costly for you" and "you will give us no choice but," I had to do something. Fuck it.

Mercy is between St. Paul and Light Streets in downtown just north of the Inner Harbor, a modern high-rise building with brick accents, a feeble attempt to straddle the historical architecture and the metal-and-glass skyscrapers erected in the seventies and eighties.

The front desk informs me that my mother is in the Critical Care Unit. I pass by the gift shop on the way to the elevators. Should I get flowers? A balloon? I realize as I'm scoping the shelves that I have no idea what types of flowers she prefers, or if she likes them at all. I settle on a card with a soft-focus rose—her name is Rosa—and storybook gold cursive that opens to the message "Get well soon." And then I realize how ridiculous the gift is, how ridiculous this all is.

At the admin desk on my mother's floor I am greeted by a pensive-faced woman with disheveled curly black hair. Her smile is tired but friendly. I wonder if this is the woman who left me the messages. I wonder what she thinks of me not answering. *How could he not respond to requests regarding his mother's fate? What kind of son is he?* The possibility of admonishment has me hesitate to approach.

"Hi, I'm Thomas Manilli. I believe my mother is here?"

The woman looks up my name. "Oh yes. We've been trying to contact you."

"Yes, I'm sorry about that."

She explains what I already know, about my mother's condition, the hospital's suggestion to remove her from life support, the cost of keeping her on it.

"I know this must be difficult."

What this woman doesn't know is that the difficulty isn't what she may believe it to be. I stare at my feet. I have this overwhelming sense of paralysis. What I want is to escape, to leave this hospital, to leave everything, and let the world move without me, at least for a while, to watch it rotate while I view from my bed, floating in space. Was this the same feeling my mother had all those years ago, when she walked out on my father and me?

"Can I see her?"

My mother's room is full of sterile surfaces and beeping devices, beige curtains drawn between patients. She is on the window side of the room, dim winter light peeking through the blinds and casting lines onto her slack face. Her hair is not in the tight bun I've seen her wear before, but is wispy, dry, the gray extending two inches from her head before meeting the black dye of the rest. The color is gone from her lips, which in the few times I saw her were always adorned with rose-colored lipstick. Maybe roses were her favorite flower. Rosa.

I stare at her with nothing but wonder. Where was she when her brain exploded? Was she in her house? I try to remember the layout, the arrangement of her kitchen, her living room. Maybe it has changed. Was she alone? And then I get this overwhelming feeling that she was, that she has been alone for years. She has been alone, even though I've been so proximal for years, no more than two miles away. And yet she may as well have lived across the continent, on another planet. What flashed before her in those moments before she collapsed? Did an image of me appear? Does she regret leaving her only son so long ago? Did she even love me?

I leave the room, exit the floor, the hospital, and turn left, away from the lot where my car is parked. The cold air is refreshing. I walk up St. Paul Street, pass alongside the large, stately rowhouses, these grander than most of the city, wide and multi-storied with ornate cornices, built to house the tycoons, the families of entrepreneurs prior to the urban boom of the early 1900s. The trees splay over the street in a nurturing canopy. How lovely it would be to live here, a vestige of gentility.

I understand that my paralysis has nothing to do with the conflicting ethics of my mother's circumstance. I realize I'm not tortured about my mother's dignity. I'm also not vehement about the sanctity of life. In both cases, I don't know how those would be measured—her dignity, her life. I know nothing about it. What about her life did she value? Obviously not me. Was there something of value to her? Was life itself valuable to her? Or, maybe she was done living it. I just don't know. I can't know. She gave me no way to know.

I call the hospital as I pick up the pace back to my car.

"I cannot make this decision."

"Mr. Manilli…"

"I will not."

"Are you abdicating your rights as surrogate, Mr. Manilli?"

"Yes."

"If that is the case, the hospital will make the choice they think is best for your mother."

"Yes."

"This is a recorded call. Are you absolutely sure this is your choice?"

"I can't."

"Have you said your good-byes, then? Do you want…"

"Don't make me say another word." I hang up before I hear a response.

4

Ruth

From my bedroom, I hear Peter close the front door, on his way to school. I listen to his feet on the sidewalk, strain my ears when it gets softer and softer. I check my cell phone. No calls. I'm so tired. I have to work—that side job bookkeeping for Mr. Pass—but I also know I can't be alone. I make myself some coffee.

Sarah is usually home on Mondays. She picks up on the fourth ring, her hello all full of snot.

"It's me, girl. Why you not up yet?"

"Who said I had to be up at the ass-crack of dawn?" Sarah asks.

"Hasn't Eddie left for work?"

"Yeah, but we weren't getting along last night, so I didn't make him breakfast." My sister's and Eddie's fights are nothing, but they have them a lot. There is nothing like hitting going on, but Sarah's Tennessee rattlesnake tongue can make Eddie speechless some nights. He's a good man, and he loves my sister. I know she knows it, but I wish she didn't wave it in his face like she did. And I know: after one of those good yellings, he's going to go off to work one day and never come back.

"Is he all right?" I ask.

"Why you asking me? Let me tell you what that puke said to me last night. He come home from Danny's—that pool hall on the corner, you know—and said he saw Delia hanging out with that Sammy character…you know Sammy. He had the balls to say to me—his exact words—that she was acting like a tramp. Can you believe it?"

"Sarah, Delia has been dressing pretty hoochie-coo, lately."

"He has no right to say anything about my child, Ruth. It's not his to say."

"He takes care of yours like they're his own."

I hear Sarah light a cigarette, take a full puff, and let it out slow before talking.

"What are you calling so early for? I hope not trying to make me think all sensible." Her laugh is throaty and deep. I always liked it over mine.

"Are you gonna be home today? This afternoon?"

"Uh-uh. I have to go into work. I'm taking off Friday for Delia's baby shower, so…You know that girl bought all this frilly glitter shit at that Walmart on Ordnance Road like she had any money at all. For the party? And here I am thinking that a shower is supposed to be paid for by, you know, her friends, right? Bunch of peroxided sluts."

I close my eyes. Sarah takes another deep puff and blows it into the receiver. "Need help with something?" she asks.

"No, no. I just wanted some company. I thought we could take a look at the sink, too." My eyes stare heavy into the rim of the coffee mug.

"Sorry, girl. Maybe I could come back home for lunch and swing by then. It won't take long to fix that hose. It's still leaking, right? It never takes long to fix a *hose*." She laughs, choking on smoke. "Ruth Anne, why aren't you laughing? That was funny." I hear her suck. "Something wrong?"

"No, I just…is Delia working today?" I say it weak, and that gets me.

"She as hell better be. That girl needs to stop laying on her back, you know what I mean?"

My mouth goes molasses. Who else can I call?

"After she has this baby, and even after she tells me she done spreading her shit all over town, I'm going to give that girl a bit of reckoning…Ruth, what's wrong? I can hear you fidgeting through the damn phone."

I stick my finger in the coffee, feel the heat of it. Sarah would only say that I was paranoid and scared and acting like I had no guts. She goaded me like that when we were kids, made me jump off the oak by Marley Creek and break my arm, play Evel Knievel on my bike and bust my chin. I didn't learn, neither. Every time, I would be suckered into her shenanigans and pay for it later. Nothing changes.

"Ruth, is it Fuckwad again?" She sighs real exaggerated.

"Sarah, I'm just saying hello."

"Did he call you? Did he send an email?"

"He called but didn't say anything."

"What you mean 'he didn't say anything'?"

I pulled out a cigarette of my own. "He just breathed."

"How you know it was him?" Sarah asks.

"It was him."

"Did his name come up on the caller ID?"

"No Sarah, I just know it was him."

"Oh, girl. I know that man was a son-of-a-bitch, but you have got to stop looking over your shoulder. Breathing? Even if it was him, don't you know he's just being an asshole? He's a *man*, Ruth Anne. He's just pissing on what he thinks is still his territory." Sarah has been spilling this lecture now for over a year. Thinks that Isaac is toying with me, that he's keeping me afraid as a way of keeping tabs on me. And every time the subject comes up she says the same damn thing. If I didn't want the company I'd hang up now. She's my only family left in Baltimore, besides Peter.

"Well, I'm not gonna pretend it's all hunky-dory."

"What you want me to do, Ruth? You want me to come down there? Sit around and wait for him to show? You wanna watch YouTube videos together and learn karate?"

That's exactly what I want, but Sarah is saying it like she's making fun of me, like we're little girls back in Tennessee all over again, and I'm not wanting to cross the rocky river on a shaky log.

"No. Nothing. It's nothing." I don't need her telling me what a pansy-ass I am. I have taken care of myself 'til now. I can certainly do it today.

Drinking the coffee wakes me up, gives me gumption. I didn't even drink coffee until I married Isaac. Peter and Joby's father didn't drink it, and I was too young before that. Isaac drank it every morning, before he went off to work, the bodyguard job. He would sweat after one cup, the pits of his shirt a dark circle, but he would always drink another one, anyway. At first I would keep with my glass of milk, but I began liking the smell of the Sanka, and I could feel close to Isaac those mornings when we drank it together. Those mornings were as happy as it got, talking about the future—the house we would buy one day, a small Victorian farmhouse on the Eastern Shore, if we just saved enough, and maybe even having another baby before it was too late. But then the beer replaced the Sanka, and those mornings were done.

*

I don't want to be in the house alone, so I look in next door at Mrs. Gabriel. She's in her kitchen, as usual.

"Morning, hon. You hungry? There's biscuits under that cloth there."

I take one, hot and fluffy. The woman is always cooking something, this time some kind of casserole. She is a little thing, a full head shorter than me and looking like she don't eat a spoon of what she cooks. I wonder where the food goes, cause she's an old widow and lives alone, yet whips up full meals fit for a family. Sometimes she'll knock on the door with a wrapped-up meatloaf, or some corned beef hash, once even a pile of damn good fried chicken. We'll chat for a few minutes about the weather and our children, then she'll go back in her kitchen to cook desserts. I don't talk to her too often, but I've learned just enough to like her a whole lot. She keeps to herself.

"I saw your boy leave this morning. I feel he's gotten taller just in the time you've been here, Ruth." She laughs.

"Hopefully he's done growing, Mrs. Gabriel. I can't buy that boy pants every three months. He'll just have to wear highwaters like it's the style."

"He's a perfect string bean, what he is."

"Looks like he doesn't eat, huh?"

"All boys like that at his age. Mine were tall, too, though you couldn't tell by looking at me." She laughs again, and cups her face in her hand. The bottoms of her hands are almost as white as mine, though she's way darker than Peter, almost as dark as Abe. She puts her face in those hands in a way that looks real natural and elegant. "My, oh my," she says.

I smile. Such a nice face for an old woman.

"He goes to the Catholic school up there north of the park, that right?"

I want to roll my eyes just thinking about it. Catholic school. I don't know what mumbo-jumbo they teach him in that place. I'm not a religious person. Never had the need to worship something I couldn't see. I went to church when I was a kid, but I did that for Daddy, who loved God almost as much as he loved me and Sarah.

I nod. "That's right. St. Mary's."

"Beautiful building, with all those trees and stone pathways."

I never feel right with Peter's school. The first time I ever set foot in any high school was when I registered Joby for ninth grade. Not like he stayed there long, anyway. Joby wasn't much for school, though he was smart, like heart-smart, could read a person like a restaurant menu. But Peter was way different from his brother. He wanted to go to a *Catholic* school, said they were the best. I looked at him like he was made of marigolds. *Where are we going to get that kind of money?* Mind you, the public high school was full of hooligans. They even had metal detectors in the lobby. But a private school, a *Catholic* school? Sure enough, he took some test and aced it. Got a scholarship that pays the whole thing. I'd tell Mrs. Gabriel, but I'm not one to play the horn. Besides, it was all Peter. He spoke for himself. And funny, because Joby couldn't speak for himself at all; a lot of silence and lots of doing were what he was about. He spoke with his actions, and his body looked it, all lean and muscled, a real handsome kid, if his face didn't look confused all the time. And Peter, skinny and freckly he was so light, but you could tell in his nose and hair he had Abe in him. Not much of a body that does things at all, but he got enough voice for both of the boys. I see that good sometimes, bad other times. I wonder if Peter got the voice for them both, and Joby got the body.

Peter was always pretending to read when he was a little bitty thing, a book in his lap, using his finger to trace over words and telling some story. And he would get mad if you told him that wasn't what the book said. Three years old, getting pissy over a book. That type of thing hasn't changed in him at all. He learns a new word every day it seems. So many words. Course—sometimes—he doesn't have a lick of sense.

By the time I say bye to Mrs. Gabriel and get back to the house, the morning is half over. I grab my coffee cup and pour out what's left, turn the water back on and grab me more Sanka Fresh Pack. Sanka isn't quite as strong as the other mixes, but it's twenty cents cheaper at Giant, and I like going there because the deli guy winks at me and always adds more to my bologna stack after he weighs and stickers it. I wear my sundresses into the store and try to get the best deal. I know that I look good in anything that shows off my figure, even after having the boys. Peter, when he goes with me, rolls his eyes and says 'Ma-a' in his nasal voice and turns his head. But I always catch him grinning. I don't need to see his face to know that.

I go downstairs and fetch Mr. Pass' folders. It's so dark down there and the day seems to be coming out nice, so I decide to work up in the kitchen, at least until Mrs. Gabriel leaves. When the water comes to a boil, I pour it in my mug. I drink mine just with sugar, just like Daddy. I remember making his coffee for him in the morning, his hairy belly squeezing in between the chair and the table. He was a character when he woke up, and would try to grab my nose and step on my feet. I thought it was the funniest thing and I'd squeal and make all kinds of raucous. Mama would just stand still against the stove, ignoring us, pressing on the scrapple until it screamed in the fryer. If it wasn't for Daddy teaching me, I would never've been doing Mr. Pass' books. I got an ease with numbers. Always did. Daddy would get me counting how much he sold every day, counting the money and making weekly reports. The little vegetable stand he set up in front of the farm was the only thing that made any money for us, which he said was because of my math skills, and what Mama said made him a sorry excuse of a man. Mr. Pass was a good friend of Daddy's over at the Kennicott Copper plant. He really helped us out after Daddy died, real nice man.

Which makes me feel bad that I'm late on finishing his books, but I don't think he'll mind all that much. I can do no wrong in his eyes, especially since I always catch them resting on my boobs. But that's the way it's been since I was twelve or so. I bloomed before most of the other girls, and he always would say so.

"Wow, Ruth Anne, you get bigger every time I see you," his eyes never leaving the top seam of my dress. At fourteen, I noticed one was bigger than the other, and I wondered if he noticed it too. I could never tell. He was too cross-eyed. I thought it kind of sweet, in the way that a child spitting up is sweet.

Mr. Pass wasn't the only one who stared at them, either. By thirteen, I already knew that boys were looking at me, and I started giving them permission by lingering longer over the bank counter or letting them lightly brush up against me in the lunchroom. I saw what it did, and that was when I got a knowing of what being a woman was. The boys would stutter and sweat. The men would nibble on me with their eyes and give me presents. I preferred the men. Mr. Pass would come over for dinner, a bottle of wine in one hand, a package in the other. It would be a music box, or glass bead earrings, or a set of perfume and brushes. "For my little girl," he'd say, his old foggy breath grazing the bottom of my crucifix.

There were more. Many of Daddy's worker friends from Kennicott, oil-stained fingernails and hairy faces, would give me picked flowers and wet kisses on the cheek, making sure to tongue away the winter chap. I delighted in their care of the details, which normally didn't seem a worry for them. It excited me to know I made them stand up straighter, speak more polite, have manners.

I soon learned that going beyond the lingering and sweet glances only made a fool of me. I had thought by giving more I would get more, but it didn't work that way. And it all makes sense when you think about it. The more you give, the more is taken *from* you. That's all that's guaranteed.

It was one of Daddy's worker friends, Hollar McCoy. Big burlap hands and a nose like a zucchini, dirt behind his ears and in the top folds of his eyes. He was nothing better than the rest of them, only his staring always held on a little longer and it turned the game on me. I would start sweating. It was all dangerous in my head, and at first I was a worm in hot ashes, not knowing what to do around him. He knew what I was playing. I think all of Daddy's friends did, only he made sure to let me know that he knew I was playing it, and that drove me crazy. It was a fight for something I couldn't see, but was important somehow. Except I lost.

It was getting cool, and the leaves were starting to turn, but Daddy invited some of the boys over for barbecue. We hadn't been in Baltimore more than a year—since Daddy lost the farm—but he made friends easy at the copper plant. And the house in Dundalk had just enough yard for folks. He entertained almost every weekend to get from spending time with Mama alone. She was sweet as bee's legs when we had company, and charmed the boys with her sensible hair style and red velvet cake. They would always come over with a cooler full of beer and macaroni salad and a deck of cards. This time they brought a rusty metal drum to build a fire.

After everyone had ripped apart the spicy chicken and cornbread and were near swimming with Coors, a few started to play cards, some helped Mama in the kitchen. I was in the back yard cleaning up when Hollar offered to help. I knew then that he was up to something, cause Daddy often came home yelling about how Hollar McCoy was the laziest son of a bitch that ever lived and wouldn't lift a finger unless a hot poker was stuffed up his butt. I was already feeling dangerous by letting him be out there with me. The dying fire in the drum had our skins glowing.

What he said wasn't really something to recall. I don't even know if I remember truthfully, cause he caught me with his eyes, a little close together and round, and they were doing all the talking. While he said whatever he was saying he kept those eyes on me, and then would get too close where his chest would surround my face. He was tall and it was easy to see the muscles on his hairy arms. He didn't even smell good, but something strong and almost a smell pulled me close. As our cleaning up went on, I wouldn't step back at all when he brushed against my dress or touched my hand. His own hands were large, my two fingers making his one.

We did it behind the shed.

Now, I never thought that what happened with Hollar was love, by no means. I was a smart girl, and I knew that love didn't do it behind a shed so quickly and so without looking at me. Hollar had licked my neck and my stomach and other places, but not once did he look at me. So, I knew it wasn't love. I didn't start stalking him or calling him at work. Matter of fact, I never searched him out to do it again or nothing. If he wasn't already giving me flowers before, I wouldn't have expected them, neither. But that's the thing, he did stop giving me flowers. And when Daddy brought him over he didn't even kiss my cheek or tell me how good I smelled or nothing. He didn't say two words to me. I would keep looking at him to even see if he would sneak me a wink or something—maybe he was just nervous about being found out. But, nothing.

A few months later at a birthday party for Patty Crouch, wife of Bean-pole, while I was throwing kindling in the woodstove, he came in to get a beer from the fridge and it was just the two of us. I said, "Hello, Hollar. How you doing?"

He pulled up from the glow of the fridge light with his beer and looked straight at me, only this wasn't the same look he'd given me before we did our business behind the shed. It was a look of pure mean, the middle of his upper lip pulling to his nose. It was the meanest look I think I had ever seen, like he was in the presence of some god-awful abomination. And all he said was, "I don't need no whore talking to me."

He closed the fridge, hocked up snot into the sink, and walked out.

I couldn't move for a while. I didn't know where to move to, or what to think or nothing. I couldn't have made a choice right then if my ass were on fire. I was just stunned, and cold, even though I was right by the woodstove. That was that. I gave too much, and that much was taken. Simple math. And that cold fourteen-year-old me thought right then— remembering Mama and the way her hands would curl into fists at her side when Daddy told a joke and laughed—I guess I'm a woman now.

I take the pot off the stove and reach for a spoon, but my cell rings again.

This time it's not breathing. Isaac's clear voice is not much more than a whisper but feels like a megaphone. That old voice that could whisper in my ear, fill me up in the night. The voice that could also slam me around the room, make me bite my lip miles away. Now, the voice of all that was shameful in my life.

I stand up and flatten my hand on the table. I want it to be a fist, in his face.

"What you want, Isaac?"

"I just wanted to see how you're doing."

"Not much can damn-well change since yesterday. I know it was you who called." I shake a little with this kind of talk. It feels like a scare on my tongue, dangerous.

"What are you talking about, Ruth?"

"How'd you get my number?"

"Numbers are easy to find."

My heart stops for only a second. I remember what Sarah told me before—*act like you don't give a shit, Ruth Anne. If you don't care, he won't either.* I breathe deep. I play my voice bored. "What you want?"

"I stopped drinking, Ruth Anne."

"Well, good for you."

"I thought you'd like to know."

"What you want, Isaac?"

"I wondered if I could come over."

"No."

"It wouldn't take me long. I think you still got some of my things."

"I threw them all away long ago, Isaac."

"Now, I know you wouldn't do that. Come on, Ruth, I know you."

"You're not allowed on my property. I'll call the police."

"I'm just thinking a short visit, that's all."

"No."

"It would only take me a minute to get there."

I hang up, the whole damn world in my throat. I pace the kitchen. I call 911.

"My husband's threatening to come over...no, he doesn't live with me anymore...I got a restraining order...he said in a minute...no, he didn't threaten me, but he said ... I understand, but he implies things without saying them ... he leaves me messages, sometimes, or stands across the street, or ... I have a kid, and ... but it might be too late ... yes, I've called before ... no, he doesn't always show, but sometimes ... yes, ma'am ... I get that, but ... you can't send one? ... It'll be too late, then."

I hang up, wondering why I even still call the police, run to my room and grab a shirt and some jeans, grab my shoes, Mr. Pass' books, reach for my keys and run out the door. Better to just leave. I'm not sure where I'm going yet, but I already feel safer with the mid-morning air cooling the sweat on my neck.

5

Peter

Eastern Avenue looks more appealing at night than in the day. You can't see all the trash lying around, the cockroaches and bottles, the leak of cars, the weeds in divorced sidewalks, the crooked walk of old women wearing colors that don't exist anymore—on their dress, on their face, in their hair. At night, there is only the glint of all this. The white of eyeballs, the shine of beer cans, neon signs, silver cars, gold teeth. And the women are inside, watching TV, complaining about their backs, telling their same stories over and over again, slapping their blue thighs, potato chips crumbled in the corners of their mouths.

Benny's Lounge is nestled between a corner grocery and a window replacement service. I wonder if Benny is really the owner's name. I always think to ask, but never do. The fag website said the bar has been here for over five decades, so Benny would have to be ancient. The idea of an eighty-year-old fag creeps me out, cuz *fag* makes me think *dick*, and *old* makes me think *splotchy-saggy*.

The first time I came here I was expecting something conspicuous, an overwhelming swirl of color, hysterical music laughing through the walls, the door not unlike the entrance to Hell or Heaven, perhaps a combination of both. Instead, it is the same Baltimore brick, same slapped-up mortar, normal, disappointing, with the word *Benny's* over the door. I say at least dress it up, this harem of O-mouthed shame and guilt—give it a little pizzazz if it's pulling me away from piety and into grabbing hands and grinning teeth. At least do that much. Not blend in, of all things. It should clearly announce the sin I'll be committing. A neon sign that followed you around with a blinking arrow. *Sinner. Sinner. Sinner.* That would be awesome—give some jazz to the place I escape from my shitty little Baltimore life, from Ma, from her chain-smoking and shaky fingers. Licked to the window is a small sticker of a Bud Light bottle shimmering at the end of a rainbow.

Inside: dark wood, a pool table, beer paraphernalia cluttering the walls, nothing mysterious or fanciful. The patrons, mostly middle-aged men, are hunched on stools. Some talk to the bartender, some to the guy next to them, most are looking at the mirror behind the bar—or at the mixed kid, at least half their age, who has just billowed in from the cold. I pretend not to notice them, look innocent, my eyes searching for Grant.

He's talking to one of his friends, I can't remember. Robert? Richard? Something very Accountant. His clothes are very Accountant. Grant is brighter, if not obvious, sea-green button-up that stands out on his dark arms, tight jeans. Closely-cropped fade on a square head, thin sideburns slice down to his big ears that stick out a little too far. He's talking to Accountant but his arm is resting on some white guy I don't know, younger, still way older than me, but good-looking, crispy, chipper-as-fuck blond. Grant knew I was meeting him tonight.

He sees me, nods his head in that cocksure way, that dusty confidence of tenure. I grin, so that he thinks I'm flattered, when really it's pity. This is as far as Grant will climb in the social chain, a big slab of beef hung on a small rack. That's why he preys on the likes of me. I score him points. He lowers his head to blond guy in secret alliance as I walk over. "Peter," he says, kissing my neck with his full lips, "you look cute."

"Nothing is cute in this place." My eyes fix on blond guy.

"Peter, Adam. Adam, Peter."

"Nice to meet you," says blond guy. He's a total queen. All high-pitched and vocal fry, the tip of his tongue poking between his teeth, the words 'meet you' a nasal squealing luge. I imagine him on the home page of some fag website, on his knees with his back to its devoted view-ers, craning his neck around, offering them that fake gay smile—the too-wide eyes and the too-white teeth—spreading his shaved ass-cheeks apart, his perky pink flower. A banner blazes 'enter at risk' at the top of the website. He's the kind of faggot that dates Black guys because he thinks they all have big dicks.

I give him a nod, really give it to him. "I've never seen you in here before."

Grant laughs. "You sound like you're a regular."

"I've been here enough to know I've never seen Adam," I say.

"A tally of the human inventory," the bartender says. Grant's sideburns grin even when he doesn't.

Adam says, "I live in Mount Vernon. So…" He folds his hands in his lap, smiling. Yes, the fake gay smile.

"Mount Vernon is really nice," I say, looking at Grant.

"How old are you, Peter?" Adam asks. "Like, fourteen?" He laughs. So do the guys next to him. So does the Accountant.

I hear from one of the indistinguishable heads lining the bar around us, "As long as they got fur, I'll make 'em purr." A ring of guffaws.

Another one slobbers out, "Shit, they don't even need that." Guffaw, guffaw, guffaw. Oh, so funny. Hairy beached whales shaking their bellies, sexualizing under-agers while slurping beer. It's not ideal, but it's what I got for now. High school doesn't allow much in the way of same-sex escapade. And in my all-boys Catholic school, even if they wanted to, they aren't doing it yet. They gotta keep it real *bro* for now.

But not here, at least. I look at Adam. "I'm old enough to be fucking Grant."

The men roar with hee-haw, slapping Grant merrily on the back. He's a little pissed, but grins. I see pride in the pulsing of his temple. He begins to say something, raises his finger, but laughs. "You want a beer?"

"I don't drink in a place dirtier than my thoughts."

*

I follow Grant in the truck, as usual. He doesn't like driving all the way back to the bar after we're done, so I sneak out, grab Ma's keys, and pray she doesn't wake up. I call these rendezvous "truck and fuck."

Grant's apartment is small and unimaginative, on the third floor of a converted hospital in Canton. On his bedroom wall he has a poster for some movie called *The Goonies* and a calendar with skinny twinks from, like, Eastern Europe or something, some corny shit. They recline back on rickety futons with their dicks pointing to the ceiling, and yet beam this innocent wide-eyed face like they're sitting on Santa's lap. February's is a shaggy-blond pouty number bent over for a spanking.

The mirror on the far wall shows my hair out of control, as usual, a deep impression in my head wherever I favor it while I sleep, or in this case hanging with Grant in his bed. I pull at the tight curls, a little too loose to be a fro, tinged with Ma's red, the color of the freckles all over my face that have given me hell since I was a kid. I remember some girl in second grade said to me on the playground, with the certainty of news anchor, "Black people don't have freckles."

I spread out on the bed. Grant's singing through the shower spray behind the bathroom door. John Legend. I remain still so I can feel him, my hands on my stomach. The streetlight dyes my skin orange in the dark room. The hair on my thin legs has grown darker and darker and further up, I've noticed. So has the hair around my belly. I swirl it around my index finger, pulling a few strands knotted together by dried cum—his or mine, I like to think both.

I wish it was Jude's cum, that I was in Jude's bed right now, listening to him sing in the shower. That would feel different, laying here and all, because what we'd been doing is making love. The two of us, the same age, at the same school, like some gay-coming-of-age movie that I used to sneak and stream on the public library's computers. That cheesy-ass moment when they realize without saying it that they are both homos and love each other? Cue the piano. But I guess that's why I love those movies, because when I watched them I'd swell with so much feeling, had to hide my face with my hands. I bet it won't seem so cheesy when it's me in that moment. Besides, Jude and I would be fresh about it, indy-style, like *My Own Private Idaho*. And Jude would be singing something cooler, The Faint or Velvet Underground. I look for other cum spots and peel. Little flakes of manna.

Grant's somewhere between forty and forty-five, I guess, but looks good for his age. He walks out of the bathroom, towel low around his waist, where I can see the outline of him pushing against the terrycloth. He's unbelievably sexy like this. His skin looks darker than usual when he's wet, almost more blue than black; Sudanese father, he says. Dark hair curls all over his chest, shoulders, stomach. It's a little flabby, but it doesn't stick out further than his pecs. He told me the rule. *Chest must come out further than the stomach.* I imagine him at fifty-five, sixty, stomach pooching out from all those Coronas, resorting to chest implants in panic, pooch getting bigger and bigger, injecting more and more silicone. But for now, Grant is good, definitely good enough.

And, it's not like Jude is rushing to get my pants off. He's never once returned my steady gaze when I got bold enough in Chemistry. Or when I keep my hand just a bit too long on his shoulder when greeting him in homeroom. I think he's gay; he just doesn't know it yet. It's not that I've seen him check out any guys at school, but I haven't seen him check out any girls, either. So, one day he'll figure it out; he'll *see* me. It will take an eternity, though, if ever, before we get naked together. I might as well have some fun in the meantime, right? You know, before I settle down and move into a tract home in Crofton and have, like, ten thousand of his babies. They'd be so striking—my redbone skin and his gray wolf-eyes, a soft combination of my kinky curls and his silky straight hair.

Whatever. I can't wait for love just to get laid. Grant's a good place-holder. Better than anyone else I've met at Benny's, anyway.

Of course, that really isn't anything to be proud of. Jerome wanted the lights off because he thought his skin looked jaundiced. He was right, when I was in a bad mood. We only did it twice. And my first, Gary, was simply unpleasant to look at. He had a sweaty lip and dumb eyes and a long comb-over. He made a deep guttural wheezy grunt during the deed, like an ogre with asthma. But he was grateful. Besides, it'll all be good storytelling in college, when I tell the privileged coeds in the dorms that I used to score ass at a divey gay bar when I was barely driving.

I tried doing the internet thing, the apps, ugh. One time I met a jocky college guy at his dorm room—I can't even remember his name: Brad? Chad? Brett? Hunter?—but it was so technical. He sent me pictures of his dick, then his face, then directions to the Hopkins campus. He had posters of Escher and Jim Morrison on his wall. College guy opened the door, said hi, took his clothes off, and looked at me like *what you waiting for?* He was really cute and all, with a tight chestnut curl that bounced above his left eye, but there was nothing *but* the sex. I mean, we spoke maybe three sentences each, and they certainly weren't loaded with anything like meaning. And that's not what it's all about, at all, even when I know it's just a hook-up. What I like is the play, the eyes, the dance, the game. The tension in the romance, or whatever. The anticipation is fun, to be wanted. Not to be had, but *wanted*. Even poor middle-aged Gary, with the sweat flattening those eight long wisps of hair to his spotty forehead, knew this, was more exciting than college guy.

If only Jude would let me in, maybe I'd know the whole deal, the sex and the romance and everything else. I would get to see someone I could call my boyfriend every day, in school, in class, after class, hold hands, all that shit. We'd be able to fuck in the daylight. I've always wanted to do that. And I will do that, with Jude. Of course, I'd have to tell him I liked him.

I can imagine saying to him, during homeroom, like really matter-of-fact, "Jude, I think it's time you know that I'm in love with you, so I can know what it's like to have sex in the daylight." What would those gray wolf-eyes do then? Open wide in shock? Narrow in confusion? What if they dropped to half-lids, and he quietly took my hand in his under the classroom desk?

My *boyfriend*. That sounds so lame, but man I'd like to call him that. Or, better yet, my *lover*. That sounds more like *want* than *have*.

"What are you laughing at?" Grant asks, walking over to the closet.

"Nothing. What are you doing?"

62 AMERICAN GOSPEL

"Getting ready for bed. Work in the morning."

"It's not too late," I say. I stand on my knees and show him I'd like to do it again.

"I can't. Not tonight. And you got school."

"Aw, Daddy, can't we go around the carousel one more time?" I push out my bottom lip.

"Don't call me that."

"Oh, sorry. Get into bed, *papa*."

"You think you're so funny." He keeps fumbling around, not looking at me. I lean my back on my heels and trace my fingers on my nipples.

"I *am* funny. Hey."

He stops and looks at me, his eyes moving past my body. "Peter, stop that. What do you want?"

"You know what I want." I leave my tongue gliding over my teeth for effect.

"You're not right," he says, shakes his head.

"I've left later than this on school nights."

"Tomorrow's important." He puts on a t-shirt that makes his arms look good.

I honestly don't know why tomorrow would be important for him. I don't even know what he does for a living. We never talk about it. Of course, the impulse is to ask him now, but something has me hesitate, a knowledge or familiarity that would give us a kind of weight that isn't there yet, somehow, that feels more in the real world than what we're doing. I'd like to know, though, to have something shared between us, a kind of *how was your day at the office, dear* kind of thing. Maybe Grant avoids that altogether, and that's why he hooks up with boys half his age. Maybe he wants no questions. Well, fuck that. I ask anyway.

"Bidding on a project," he answers. "A big demolition, a whole bunch of blocks in Highlandtown. Big money."

"You destroy things for a living?"

His face sours, "Well, yeah, when you put it like that, but only stuff that no one wants, I guess. This is a real big project."

"That's where I live. Are you bulldozing my house?" I stick my hip out, rest my hand on it, and grin, but I feel this slight tinge of ire that curls my lip. He has no idea I live in Highlandtown; we never talked about that, either. I didn't know what he did for a living, he doesn't know where I live. How many times have we hung out?

"Maybe," he says, rummaging in his chest of drawers—answering the question, but not responding to me.

"What are they blowing up?"

"We're not blowing anything up. A middle school, a lot of houses, most of 'em are all abandoned and fucked up, though."

"Definitely sounds like my hood. What are they building?"

"Some kind of amusement park or something."

"In Highlandtown? Are you sure? What kind? Like Six Flags?" I can't imagine anyone building anything like that, or anything else in my neighborhood. It's a bunch of old boarded-up brick rowhomes and streetlights, nothing else. How would an amusement park fit in? Images of lunging roller coasters winding between alleyways, water rides carrying brown bags of Old English—and the guys on benches that guzzle it—through the gutters, an arched neon entrance butting right to my front door. I could step outside and in seconds flick rubber-bands on a Gravitron.

"I don't know, Peter. I'm just the demo guy, destroying things, right?"

"That's so weird, though. Why would anyone want to *amuse* themselves there? I mean, who thought of this idea?"

"We don't even know what the idea is."

"You said it's an amusement park."

"I said something like that, I don't know. I didn't say I knew for sure." His voice sounds a little squealy.

"Building anything there is weird."

"I need to go to bed."

"So, like what type of amusement park is it?"

"I told you, I don't know."

"But don't you want to? You're tearing stuff down. Don't you wanna know what for?"

"I don't need to know, Peter. I'm the demo guy."

"But aren't you even curious?"

"I need to go to bed."

"Fine."

I slip off and look for my clothes. I intentionally leave one sock. I like this tradition—the idea of one of his other trophy tricks raking the renegade sock while searching for the lube, wondering who it belongs to, the magma of jealousy churning. I slip on my pants, he walks into the bathroom. I throw on my shirt and lie back on the bed and announce, "I have an important day, too. Another day in high school." He tries to look busy, goes to his dresser, opens the top drawer where he keeps his condoms.

"I hate school. A masquerade of talking assholes dressed up as teachers and students. Dr. Ducee is a shit stain, actually, not really an asshole…he is only the rub against it. That's even more pathetic. Catholic school is pathetic. Maybe I should drop out and get my GED. I could just get a job, something simple for now, not worry about anything. Maybe bar-back at Benny's. Wouldn't that be funny? I could pop the top on your Corona." I wait for him to laugh. He likes the way I talk, the way I play with words. He's said so before. *Peter, you're funny for a kid,* he's said to me. This time, though, he makes no sound, like he doesn't even hear me, and keeps circling the room. I lean forward, and give my best downward dog, long arms and ass up. Nothing from him. "What are you looking for?"

"Huh? What are you doing?" He looks confused.

"I'm talking to you. What are you looking for?"

"Nothing. You should go."

"I know. I'm leaving." I grab my coat and pull on my shoes, my left foot sockless. "Hey, what are you doing Thursday? After work. I know you go to Benny's a lot, but I was…"

"I don't go to Benny's *that* much."

"No, I mean, you know, on Thursdays. I was thinking maybe we could go out."

"You can't go anywhere. You're seventeen." He says it as much to himself as he does to me.

"I'm eighteen."

"Peter..."

"And I'm not talking a bar or anything. I mean, like a restaurant."

"I saw your ID. You're seventeen."

"What difference does it make?"

He walks to the front door. "It means you're a minor."

"So, who gives a shit? Who would report us?"

"Your parents?" He also doesn't know that it's only my mother, that my father left before I could know him, before I could care.

"My *mother* doesn't have a clue. She doesn't even know about me."

"She can find out."

"It doesn't matter. I'm going to be eighteen in, like, five months."

"Peter. That's not the..."

"Just a restaurant, or maybe the park, then." I hear myself pleading, like hanging off the edge of a cheap hotel balcony. I don't like it. It's separate, not really my voice, not coming from me. Both of us are speaking outside ourselves, ventriloquists trapped in a conversation without puppets.

"Peter. You're a seventeen-year-old dude. Why do you want to go out on a date?"

"I don't know." I want to say *because that's what people do*, but I don't really know why it's important to me. It's not like I want to marry him. Maybe it would be nice to hang out with someone who knows I'm a homo, to have a friend in the daylight, to have a reason to stay out of the house while Ma freaks out—*once again*—about Isaac, or Joby, or the rent money, everything. I want to be anywhere but that house.

"You shouldn't be thinking about, you know, romance," he says with the affected sound of a father.

"What should I be thinking about?" Politics. Armageddon. Mountain Dew.

"Fucking," he says, so casually. "You're seventeen. I wasn't thinking about going out to dinner and walking in the park when I was seventeen. Hell, I still don't."

"You've never been on a date?" I ask.

"Well, yeah, but not because I wanted to."

"What do you mean?"

"I don't know."

"You did it just to fuck someone?"

"That sounds a little harsh."

"But that's it." I throw my hands up. "That's it?"

"This is weird." He grabs my shoulders. "You're seventeen. And you're upset about getting laid? What else did you expect? I didn't think you wanted anything…I mean you're…"

"I'M SEVENTEEN! I KNOW! God." I gather up my keys. My nose starts to run.

"We're having fun, right? Why does it need to get weird?" His hands seem uncomfortable with the rest of his body. They flap, like a bird. "Peter. We met at a bar. I've seen you, what, five times? What's that?"

"I don't know."

"People told me you were cool." His hands illustrate 'cool' by cupping them together, as if 'cool' meant a small empty bowl.

"At the bar? What do you mean?"

"Yeah. That you…were cool."

I slit my eyes. He looks blank and stupid.

"I've only fucked a few other guys, Grant. I'm not some prostitute."

"There's nothing wrong with that, anyway. What's wrong with having sex?"

"Nothing. I don't know. Something, when that's it."

"You sound like a woman," he says.

I bite down hard on my teeth, and want to break them. I see Ma running around the house, checking that windows are locked, making frantic phone calls, scared all the time.

A loose "fuck you" and I'm walking towards the door. The walls are melting into my face and I hear my heartbeat, louder than everything else. I open the door. He raises his voice from behind, "Why are you being such a little bitch!?"

I spin, fire red, blistering, spitting, not caring that I'm up in his face, "CAUSE I'm SEVEN-"

"Hey!"

I feel the soft and hard of his push, and then the whir of the hallway and I fall down.

From the floor I watch his elbow disappear behind the door and a "Jesus-fucking-Christ" sharpened by nervous laughter. It slams shut. I dart around, grab my keys. I instinctively touch my chest, even though it doesn't hurt. I jump and run. I want air. The elevator would take too long. I run to the stairwell. I rush the door, pull it open. I hear him laughing behind me in the hall, the whole floor, cackle in the carpet, the wallpaper. I run the steps to the lobby and outside.

The city is loud, orange and black. I want it around me. It's cold. I must have dropped my coat. *You sound like a woman.* My underwear is crumpled, cutting my ass. The cold stings my face. I can't hide my nose. I feel messy. The air makes it better. It makes me solid, firming my skin, shrinking my throbbing head. The harbor water comforts me, smells like fish. I turn the corner. The truck is alone, under a streetlight. The street is empty. I am the only one, the only one stupid enough to be here. I feel the sticky when I sit, the failure. Just leave, get as far away from this, leave before it lingers. Even as I drive away, with all the singing of Canton, above the bells of the harbor taxis, the rattling of the truck, I still hear laughing.

Hurry up and realize you love me, Jude. I don't want to do this forever.

6

Thomas

My mother left me everything, mostly comprising her house in Little Italy. Was this somehow recompense for walking out on my father and me all those years ago? Or, was she following tradition begrudgingly since I was the only child, the next of kin? In my small, familiar classroom, the questions seem to crowd around me. I didn't have to know her well to feel the absence now. However, the absence is strange—not a loss so much as a reminder of a thing that wasn't really there. The rare times I'd seen her these past twenty-odd years, I noticed her age, her oldness. She moved deliberately, like she was aware of her whole body aching. Perhaps most children don't see this because they watch their parents slowly progress through time somewhat regularly. Because we had only in my adulthood reunited—though that would be an overstatement for what we had done—perhaps I saw the age more clearly. She went from a young mommy to an old mother, with not much significance or memories made of the forty years between.

Of course, it could have been the bay water, all those crabs she ate, that everyone eats in this town. Another vague memory of her from childhood, before she left. Her sitting at a picnic table with a mountain of steamed crabs, smearing Old Bay on her fingers, sucking out meat from tiny claws, picking, pulling, cracking. Drinking beer, her face stained orange, her breath, the crab guts, dead yellow, like dried mustard, everywhere. She couldn't get enough of that shit coming out of the bay—her or my father—the dirty nasty bay. The great delicacy of Baltimore: barely steamed crustaceans, bottom feeders that eat anything, including trash, being fished out of the most polluted water in the country. And they wonder why the city has the absolute worst cancer rate in the nation.

I use the fifteen minutes before next class to call the lawyer. My mother's house is in decent shape, and paid for. I have the option of sprucing it up and selling it for more than it's worth, or as-is for more than it's worth. Of course, the lawyer asks why I'm not planning on keeping it.

"I am a Catholic brother, a clergyman."

The lawyer has no idea what I'm talking about, the voice a patronizing mix of lilts and forced laughter. "A brother?" he says. "Is that like a priest-in-training?"

"Sort of," I tell him. "We can't own property."

"Oh, wow."

"Imagine that," I say.

"Well, what about the money from selling the house . . . can you keep that?"

"Yes."

I hang up the phone and sit at my desk. I pull out my yellow pad, and turn to a random page towards the back. I need to make a list. I could give the money to charity, maybe even to the school. I could turn it over to the rectory and be loved by the brotherhood, install ceiling fans and a dishwasher and other things that hum incessantly. I could take leave and travel for a while, sip afternoon coffee in Rome, feel alone in exotic places, and sip evening wine to alleviate the ache. But I am too mired in history to fully enjoy such present moments. And the order would likely not approve anything for too long, maybe only a couple weeks for "bereavement."

There must be plain old pain somewhere in me, but I don't know where it will come from. My mother is not resolute, my memories of her mostly still, static—like photographs and not videos. Old ones, losing color. The monochrome of my memories of her can't make up their mind whether to reveal themselves in white or black. And pain, pain is something of a color, an orange, a brown, a blazing rust.

I glaze over the choices. I've never had a surplus of money, and I don't know what there is to do with it. The Church takes care of my food, my housing, my expenses. I don't have much, but I want for nothing. And choices. I'm not accustomed to making many, and the ones I do are in the safe confines of a classroom, an institution. This I see as a blessing. Yet, somehow over the years, I feel less and less a part of any real community, like the rectory is more a boarding house than a family of any sort, which is of course how it is understood: a religious family. Perhaps because there are too many of us, and we are all grown men, that family doesn't seem the apropos word to describe us? Or, that I uniquely don't feel a sense of ownership? I'm not really sure. But it's the only home I've known for so long. Maybe that's all home is, a sense of longevity. I'm not sure. That doesn't feel enough, sometimes.

"I thought I might catch you in here." Peter's voice is a muddled mix of oboe and cotton.

"Mr. Cryer. Did you already meet…" I look up to a steadily nodding head, dead weight dropping from side to side. He is not a subtle kid. "And how did it go?"

"If anything else happens, they'll kick me out."

"If it weren't for your grades you'd be…"

"I know." His face looks tired. Worried.

"You'll play it cool," I say.

"Right. I've heard that already." Peter is skinny. Tall and skinny, and looks taller because he is so skinny. And when he makes a big gesture, he resembles a dancing string puppet. This time he rolls his eyes and swings his head far back, nothing subtle about it.

"I just want to get out of here. Four months."

He's been counting down all year. The end of our conversations always conclude with how much time he has left. The repetition gets tiring.

"Have you heard from any schools?"

He shakes his head. "Nothing about *money*." His face is turned down to the edge of my desk. His fat bottom lip drops. The freckles that cover his face look like they're going to fall off, there is so much exaggerated worry.

"It's a little too early for that. You might have to wait a while."

"That's what everyone's saying, but aahhhh…"

I laugh. His big open mouth reminds me of Animal from the Muppets. My laugh is as full as my gut is round. It feels so good to laugh.

Peter first looks at me with suspicion, but then his eyes soften, and he grins. His large mouth spreads wide. And he has his mother's green eyes, which pop out even more because of his darker skin. The red tint to his hair, the eyes, the temper, there is no mistaking at least one half of his ancestry, and Ruth Anne Cryer is a pure Irish looker. If he smiled more, didn't maintain a perpetual scowl, Peter wouldn't be a bad looking kid. I would tell him that, but he would come back with something bleak, something that a bitter comedian would spout between cigarettes. One has to be careful with the boy, which is why he doesn't have many friends. His intelligence intimidates, and it's unfortunate he doesn't use it gracefully. He is a wild kind of smart, too crazy for his age, and can be particularly mean with it. It makes it hard to fit in, and the random uncensored outbursts further alienate him.

"Can I just stay here all day?" There is humor in his voice, but I know he means it.

"Skipping class. That's the way to get on their good side."

"They don't have a good side." His tone is full of meanings, a teenager's grasp at complicated layers. I try to ignore the drama and instead ask him what was said in the meeting.

"Don't you know? I thought they published a newsletter. They said, 'Bad Peter, don't do it again. If you do…'" He brings his finger to his neck and drags it from ear to ear.

"Did you explain yourself? Did you tell them what you told me?"

He shakes his head. "They don't care." I've seen low-budget melodramas from the fifties make it less melodramatic. "Besides, it wouldn't have made a difference."

"Well, that is definitely true. But at least they would've known you weren't merely being an asshole kid."

"You shouldn't say words like 'asshole', Brother Thomas. I'm still impressionable."

It's hard to keep a straight face, but I don't want to indulge him or his coquettish flirtations. I know he's light in the loafers, but talking about or acknowledging it would only create trouble. For him, for me. Definitely for the school. "Wouldn't it have been worthwhile to explain your reason?"

"I didn't have reason. I was pissed off." He stiffens his face.

"You know that's only half true. You were making a sound argument. You just said it a little…forcefully."

He snorts. "And Janke still didn't hear me."

"So why didn't you tell them just that?"

His mouth draws from a simper to an inert thin line, his body still. I continue playfully, "It certainly wouldn't hurt to explain, right?"

"We embrace vows of silence, right, Brother?" His eyes dig into mine. The boy was fierce. Lucky for him, I have as much patience as he has fire.

"That was terrible," I say with a smirk.

He shifts, lightens his voice. "Did you write that recommendation for me?"

"Not yet. I've had…"

"Brother, I need that letter. Sarah Lawrence wanted a third."

"I've been a little busy."

"But most of the deadlines have passed."

"My mother died."

"Oh. Sorry." His eyes look expectantly into mine as if I hadn't yet realized this. "She was old, though, right?"

He becomes aware of the surprise on my face. He picks up on his rudeness and finds an excuse to leave.

At least it wasn't "If there's anything I can do…"

For as abrasive and arrogant as he can be, I still am surprised by what slips out of him. I don't even think he realizes what he says. It's easy to forgive, though, with the life he's been living. Besides, it's refreshing to have a genuine asshole instead of another false sympathizer.

Peter as a freshman was a different story. You could tell it was his first year in Catholic school. It must have been hard for him to walk into an institution so already established with its own culture. The rest of the kids ran around and chattered in orientation, most of them having known each other for several years. There were the kids who came in just for high school, but most had gone to another Catholic school since Kindergarten. These kids were lifers. But Peter was new, and mute. Wide, frightened eyes. I got the feeling that not only was he new to Catholic school, but to the entire faith. Of course, that would be impossible. St. Mary's didn't accept *anyone* who hadn't gone through Confirmation and Communion. Of course not. Why, that would be blasphemy—a non-Catholic accepting the body and blood into his unconfirmed mouth. The whole world would rotate backwards. I'm not sure how he did it, but he got through the gates. He was a regular Galileo.

I watched him close that first year. I had him in U.S. History. Recognizing his intellect was the easy part. Impressive, but unexciting. What I really enjoyed was observing him in the daily Mass. His eyes were alert, watching the ritual unfold as he participated. He picked up on it quickly, the recitation, the songs, the proper placement of hands. The most amusing was him first learning the cues to stand, to kneel. When he was slightly behind, and everyone else would kneel suddenly, he would overcompensate by dropping his body like an elephant, his error bouncing through the empty cavern of the chapel. I used to get a kick out of that.

*

Students hate World History, except for the Great Wars, and when I deliver Ancient and especially Medieval History, it's all snores. And it bothers me—it is my favorite. You would think they'd be fascinated by at least some of the morbidity that went on during the Middle Ages, with the outlaws, ruthlessness, unreasonable violence. Of course, that occurs throughout history, but plagues, Crusades, mysticism, all the unknown?

I wave arms, dress my speech, break chalk as I write on the board in a frantic sweat. Arms up, one, two, one, two. Charlemagne, Black Death, Holy Roman Empire, cha cha cha. And none of them even acknowledge the effort. I guess it's not their job to do so.

If dust is the lingering of dead skin, and odor the uncontained particles of things breaking away and slipping into our nose, why then does my classroom not emit a vibrant, prickly scent? This is a classroom full of uncontained particles of youth, of eruption and growth. Yet, the room smells stale, almost lifeless. Does it have to do with being a History classroom, as if knowledge bears the same physics as all other things, and the ideas from these textbooks and lectures break away, float up and fill the room? Even the light coming through the windows looks like the sepia of old photos.

I have an hour and a half for lunch, so I take my time gathering up papers. I come across the yellow notepad, my list. Again, I stare at it until my vision blurs everything else. Go to Rome. Donate to House. Donate to Charity. I still can't think of anything else. I feel like I'm ruling something out, but I don't know what. And that makes me truly sad, I realize, more than anything else related to my mother.

*

The quiet of the rectory is expected when I come in from the cold. The coat rack is empty save one scarf and one hat. Most of the clerics are still at the school, and the few others that don't teach come later from their respective positions in the Church. I sometimes leave the school as soon as I am finished, just to get these minutes of stillness before everyone comes home, before the clinking of dinner begins, and the recycling of limited conversation stock concludes yet another evening.

The rectory—once one of the aristocratic Carroll family mansions—has a symmetry save one touch of Irish practicality, being that the front door does not open directly onto the main staircase, preventing the winter chill from blowing right up to the second floor every time someone comes in the house. The Carrolls were Irish, of course. Otherwise, the house is pure Georgian order. On either side of the parlor is the dining room and study, and straight back is the main hall, where musical instruments would have been played at one time, but now is solely a library. The kitchen is far down the right wing of the house. It used to be detached for fear of fire, but a hyphen was added that now acts as storage for dinnerware and ceremonial knick-knacks. The other wing houses the private chapel and Father Mike's bedroom. The rest of us sleep in the second floor's eight bedrooms, and three sleep in the old slave quarters on the third. At any given time, while the Carroll family still lived here, half of the second floor bedrooms would be unused, and thirty or so servants working on the estate would cram into the third, nailing blankets to the rafters for privacy.

I hear arguing from somewhere deep in the house, the clipping of words, the steady rise of sound, then silence. I go towards it, in the library, and find Brothers Simon and August standing across a couch, a roll of papers in August's hand. Simon is leaning forward in attack, his slim body pointed and springy. August is defensive, if not a little defeated, his fleshy shoulders close to his ears. They both see me, but Simon keeps his eyes fierce on August.

"Thomas. I'm glad you're here. Simon and I were just discussing that hearing with the developers for Crabtown. They've asked us to send a delegation down to make testimonies."

"No, August, they've asked us to be accomplices in a crime," says Simon, a confident lean in his body. He is obviously angry, the vein on his forehead throbbing blue, disappearing under his thick black hair. The recent promotion to assistant principal has given Simon confidence to become more outspoken than he already was.

I am confused. Hearing, testimonies, delegation. I'm not sure what that has to do with the development. Words I think of for amusement park are family fun, fanny packs, fattening food, stained shirts. Not courtroom jargon. "Why are you two arguing over this?"

Simon scowls at my question, as if, unknowingly, I've sided against him. He folds his arms and turns away.

August comes around with a consoling arm and gives me some background in his teacher voice. The developer for Crabtown is about to begin demolition of six square blocks of rowhouses in Highlandtown's north end, known as Ellwood Park. Our school sits on the edge of this development. The homes apparently were served letters of condemnation, many of them already vacant and boarded up. The demolition begins in several weeks. "There have been a few residents who are a little upset about the amusement park," August says, his fingers forming rabbit ears on the word upset.

"No, August, they're furious," says Simon. "People are being kicked out of their homes."

"Not exactly, Simon. They're given relocation fees," argues August.

Simon slams his palm to his forehead.

Crabtown has been in the works for a while. All of us in the rectory know of it, to some degree. Last year, two youngish men came to present the plan to us, dressed in very sharp gray suits. *Crabtown was to be a 124-acre amusement center that would celebrate Baltimore's heritage, with all rides, stores, and a hotel themed around aspects of the city. Different historical neighborhoods would comprise sections of the park: Fell's Point, Little Italy, Hamden, Bolton Hill, Greektown, even a Highlandtown.* The suits had an arsenal of flowcharts, aerial photographs, digital renderings. These images showed a twisting roller coaster towering over a series of colorful main street-like shops and eateries, other rides and pavilions dotted in between. Some of the areas would show exact replicas of old Baltimore, with actor-peasants ambling on cobblestone walkways in period garb, selling Dippin' Dots out of horse-and-cart buggies.

Their presentation was long, but energetic. It used phrases like *community revitalization* and *urban renaissance*, words like *character* and *safe*. This last word was of particular interest to the lot of us who were there. Two months prior, Father Mike had been mugged outside the rectory. Students reported assaults on their way home from school. Parents were taking their kids out of St. Mary's because "the area was getting too rough." Sirens were more prominent now than ice-cream truck jingles.

We couldn't argue. After a hundred and fifty years of continuous instruction St. Mary's was now in the hood.

The suits promised that the school and rectory would remain. None of us had objections. It seemed like a good idea. Much of the housing in the neighborhood was abandoned anyway.

"The city council asked if we could send some people to give testimonials concerning the current state of the neighborhood," August says, "from people who live in the community."

Simon snorts. "When has the city council ever been concerned enough to inform people they're having a public hearing? And who are you going to send to give testimonials?"

"Why, a couple of *us*, of course. We live in the community, Simon."

"But we aren't the community," says Simon. "The people who are being kicked out should be the ones giving testimonials." Simon runs his fingers in his hair, grabs and pulls. I covet his very black and very thick hair, his lean body, his youthful intensity. I can't help but associate beauty with virtue, even to this day. If that were the case, Simon would be our beacon of morality. He runs every morning, keeps himself groomed meticulously—something most of the order gave up years ago, certainly I.

"Simon, they are not asking us to approve or disapprove of the development. They only want us to make statements describing the current *state* of the neighborhood. We live in it!" August turns to me, softer. "Would you do it with me, Thomas? You know so much about the area, history and all. All you have to do is talk about what you see now, what it used to be. It's not that we have different interests than most people in the neighborhood. We're only sharing what we see every day."

The moulding around the ceiling of the library needs some maintenance. It is original. The tin inlay was probably added later, unless of course the Carroll family was ahead of their time. If I sold my mother's house I could get the moulding of the rectory stripped, bring out the details of the neoclassic lines that have been dulled by years of paint. Restored. History made present. Maybe that would make this place feel more like home.

"That's not what they intend to do, August," says Simon. They're taking advantage of our position in the community. They know what we're going to say. It's manipulation."

"Simon, that is paranoia. Besides, our description of the neighborhood will be no different than anyone else's. No one's going to *praise* it. Thomas, what are you looking at?"

"Huh?"

"Will you come with me?"

"Do I have to?" I ask.

"Well, you and I are the Outreach Committee. We were elected. This is what we're supposed to do."

I pull at the buttons of my shirt. "I don't know what I'd say."

"You don't have to do anything you don't want to," Simon insists.

"Speak on the history of the neighborhood, its glory days, something like that," August says in his cheery Disney voice.

"Okay," I say.

Simon looks at me as if betrayed. "Do you even *have* an opinion on this?"

I shrug. I like Simon. He is young and energetic, and he cares deeply about everything. I think he sees me as an ally in the rectory, if one were to discern sides. I'm not sure why, though. I don't see sides per se. I only see a range of similarity. What is there to be so passionate about against an amusement park? What about all the other impending cataclysms in our immediate future? Global warming, terrorism, nuclear armament? I look at Simon, every muscle activated in his stance towards me. How can he direct so much energy to this, to each of his many concerns? Running, teaching, and this amusement park. Who cares? The thought exhausts me.

Simon sighs. "Do all your choices get made for you, Thomas?"

He exits the room. August watches him leave, remains quiet.

There are many improvements this room could use. I could also refinish the hardwood around the doors and walkways. All of it is so worn out. So worn out.

7

Ruth

I had to come back. When you're not planning to spend the day in town and you run out of the house, you don't bring yourself. Everywhere I went I couldn't get anything done. Mr. Pass' books didn't make any more sense. I forgot my calculator, and when I went into the market I had to choose between that and cigarettes, which I also forgot. There's no way I could've made it without smokes. How embarrassing, not to have enough to get cigarettes *and* a calculator, and a waste that I got nothing done. I don't mean to beat the steering wheel, but that's all I got right now.

Sarah's probably right. The more I think about it, Isaac's just keeping tabs. He didn't come by the house, I bet, which just fires up my gut even more. Besides, it's late afternoon now, and Mrs. Gabriel will be home. I need to get these books done.

I look to make sure she's in her kitchen. She is. She sees me and I wave. She waves back. She touches her apron and comes to the window.

"Warm today for February, isn't it?"

"I know," I say. "I'm used to blizzards this time of year."

"It's that global warming you always hear about. Soon, we'll be cooking like the turkey in my oven." She lays her face in her hand, and smiles. So elegant.

"Has anyone come by my place while I've been out, Mrs. Gabriel?"

"Not that I've seen, Ruth. Expecting someone?"

"No. Not exactly." I haven't told Mrs. Gabriel about Isaac. It doesn't feel right to burden a sweet old woman with my problems, with my stupid mistakes coming back to haunt me.

"Thank you, hon."

I walk over to my front door. I know he's probably not been here, but it don't hurt to check. I look in the mailbox. He's done that before, slipping a message. But it's never nothing threatening. He's too smart for that. He'll just leave a note saying "dropped by to say hi" or "sorry I missed you." Just enough to let us know he's still out there. Just enough to give me the creeps. He's done it so many times, Peter don't even care anymore, and he's the one that used to get all riled up. I would come home from work and he'd be sitting on the couch shaking like a dog shitting peach seeds. But now he says it's just talking. I don't know. Talking at times has rightfully scared the hell out of me.

I put the key in, unlock the door, kick it wide, and move back. Nothing seems upset, from what I see. I leave the door open and wait a moment. I move back, close to the truck. I know I can run if anything. Or jump into the truck. I need a cigarette. I have two left, but smoke the lucky fag, anyway. I puff and wait.

It feels empty. It feels like the house hasn't stirred all day, but I still don't close the door.

I go through every room, slowly. The baseball bat. I check to see if it's propped at the front door—the Negotiator, Sarah calls it. I pick it up on the way in. The kitchen's the only room that gets any light. Clear. And the living room has that wood paneling that chips off where it meets the floor. Peter nags me to ask the landlord if we can tear it off the wall, but I just hate bringing me to the attention of people like that. I go to the closet. I ready the bat and open it quick.

Nothing. It's too small for Isaac's shoulders.

I go to my room. Granny's old bedroom suite looks sad and faded. The carpet has ghost turds. I go to the closet, open it quick. Nothing. I know he's not here. I know. I knew when I walked into the house, my hairs not standing on end. But these days I doubt my guts sometimes.

After you throw the bowling ball you still have to follow through to make sure you hit the pins. I don't have the luxury to put all my trust into my gut. I lower the bat.

I sit on the vanity stool and look in the mirror, the bed behind me. Isaac used to come home from work and walk straight into the bedroom. I would walk in soon after him, knowing, his uniform strewn over the floor, and see him laid out on the bed, naked. He was strong. I would undress quietly, go over to the bed, and straddle him. It was those first seconds he entered me I liked so much. He was strong all over his body. I could feel that inside me. I just wanted a strong man, that's all, a real strong man.

I'm ashamed for even having these good thoughts of him.

The pictures of my children stuck on either side of the mirror are turning orange. Joby's is at least five years old. He still had spots on his face and his nose hadn't gotten broken yet. He grew to look so much like his father, I sometimes called him Abe by accident. Peter's picture looks like me, with a little of Abe's coloring, and the nose. Though he's gotten more of the lines of a man drawn in his face, he's still soft. In this picture you would think it was me when I was young. We are one and the same, me and him. When he was born, I said "This is my child." Something in me knew that so strong then, and he still is. There is no other truth I am more certain.

I hear some rustling coming from the back, the laundry room. My head shoots to attention and I jump up. Maybe he's by the back door. I lift the bat and slowly creep out the bedroom, into and through the kitchen, making sure not to tap against the linoleum with my shoes. I hear the sound again, definitely coming from the back room. I get the bat into swing mode above my shoulder and inch towards the door frame. Goddamn Isaac. I can hit him before he even knows I'm there.

The sound is a grocery bag. The breeze from the open front door is blowing around a goddamn grocery bag.

He's not here. The air doesn't have that terror, and now this cold is in my blood for nothing. I let out my lungs and lower the bat. Christ.

I open the letter that was in the mailbox—the management company that we rent the rowhouse from.

I have paid the rent on time every month, thank you very much, so I know it's nothing like that. But damn if that matters. After all the worry, after thinking I'm too in the open, about how I am going to convince Peter to move again, I get this. A notice. I guess I won't have to convince him of nothing, because we're gonna have to leave anyway. The letter is something about selling the house for that theme park they're building, that they won't be renewing our lease. We have three months. I lean against the wall, tilt my head back, just to feel something solid. It's all too much.

I hate walking up the attic steps to Peter's room, steep and creaky. Isaac isn't here, but I still need to look around. Before I climb them, I close and lock the front door. I know it's in vain, but I bring the bat anyway.

I don't know how Peter can handle it up here, being as tall as he is. It's so cramped and low, even for me. But he chose the place because of this room. If I have to move him around all the time because I'm too dumb to pour piss out of a boot, I might as well let him decide where we go.

And now, he'll have to decide the next place. Three months.

He keeps his room simple. There's no pictures on the walls but a Polaroid of his old girlfriend—Maggie I think her name was—shimmying in a blue dress, sharing tape with his ripped up Hamlet poster. Maggie was a little on the ditzy side, but sweet. The only other picture is on his dresser, of me, him, and Joby. I was smiling in that picture, gleaming so white next to them. Peter was fourteen. Joby was sixteen or seventeen. Peter's beaming right at Joby with the nicest smile, while Joby and me face the camera. It was one of the last ones, before the fight, before Joby left, behind us the stained yellow curtains from the apartment in Cherry Hill. Joby doesn't look like he was selling drugs in this picture—his grin bringing a little mischief, but only in a good-hearted way. It doesn't look like he could say what he said to me that night, that night in the rain, the last I ever saw him alive.

Joby, sometimes I think it's better to pretend you never walked the Earth than to think of what you took away when you left. You somehow take up more space in my heart when you come to me in words, and it takes time to seal that space back up because words are all that's left of you. It's just not enough. Maybe that's why Peter never talks about you. The words. It's better to say no words than to be disappointed with them never being enough.

I spread out on Peter's bed. It smells like his sweat, spicy peaches, and the stuff he puts in his hair, that sheeny stuff that Abe used.

One time when I was a little thing, on the leaning porch of the farmhouse, Granny told me a story about two birds, Pepper and Petunia Parakeet. I'm not sure if I came up with those names myself, or if Granny did, but they are the names I've remembered all my life. I aim to think it was me, cause if Granny ever gave them a name it would be something like Betty and Ernie and they wouldn't be parakeets. They'd be plain and brown and simple, like the fence that surrounded the farm, the jelly jars that lined her cupboards, the hair that was always sticking to her fat face.

Both birds were flying south for the winter, and had been for days. They were too busy playing bird games to notice the tiny bits of frost clinging to the leaves and underneath the rocks, and having too much fun to notice all the other birds had already started flying south. And when they finally did realize it was time to go, they were very late and all alone.

They were flying through a thick, dark forest when they came up to a wizard made of tree bark. He had branches for arms and roots for legs and a crooked little out-of-place branch that poked out for a nose. The birds were hungry, cause it was winter after all, and when they saw the wizard they asked him, "Mr. Wizard, where can we get some worms and potato bugs, some beetles and grasshoppers, cause we haven't eaten in days and we're flying south and just hungry as a hog in a straightjacket."

And the wizard said, "You haven't eaten in days, you say?"

And Pepper and Petunia said, "Oh, yes, a long, long time, and we're so hungry."

The wizard gave them a choice. He said, "I have always wanted a bird as pretty as you both. This is what I offer you: you can either keep on flying over the icy land until you find your worms and potato bugs, or you can stay here with me all winter, in this cage, where I will feed you whenever you desire. Only, you cannot leave the cage. It is up to you."

Now both Pepper and Petunia were tired and very, very hungry, so the idea of having all the food they could ever want all winter long made their beaks water. Petunia flapped her wings, "I think it would be lovely to have ten beetles and twenty potato bugs in one afternoon, and never have to dig in the dirt. Not one day."

But Pepper, as hungry as he was, his beak watering just as much as Petunia's, chirped, "But to be in a cage all day, for all of winter, never to open my wings and fly through the air and play games. I could never do that."

"That is your choice," said the tree wizard.

So Petunia jumped eagerly inside the cage and began to feast on grasshoppers and worms and even more exotic, tasty bugs she had never even heard of. And Pepper bid her farewell and leapt into the cold air, tired and hungry.

He flew and flew, for days and days, but all the ground was icy and there were no worms to be found. And Petunia kept eating and eating, whenever she wanted, all the exotic bugs she could ever desire.

Pepper grew weak with hunger, but his wings were open and the brisk air flowed through his feathers. Petunia kept eating, and her belly swelled with each meal, more and more.

Finally, Pepper grew too weak with hunger and, completely spent, fell from the sky, landing limply on the ground that was still icy, all the worms tucked snugly under the frozen surface, too hard for his beak to break through.

When the last frost had melted, the wizard told Petunia she was free to go, and opened the cage for her. Now, all this time, Petunia had eaten whatever and whenever she wanted, and her belly had swelled to ten times what it used to be. When she jumped from the cage and opened her wings, they couldn't carry the weight of her belly, and she fell like a stone to the ground, and broke her little neck.

After telling the story, Granny asked me which little bird would I want to be. After wrinkling my forehead for a long moment, I told her I wanted to be Pepper. I wanted to be able to fly wherever I wanted and not get all fat like Petunia.

Granny stared out quiet into the hills surrounding the farm. It was getting dark. The scoops of land looked like cookies, the sun a golden and melting chocolate chip. She stared for quite a while before heaving her body in a deep sigh.

I tugged the turkey flap on the bottom of her arm and asked, "What would you do Granny? What bird would you be?"

She breathed in deep the dirt-smelling air, slapped her giant thighs, and said, "Well, I'd be the bird that flew south when she was supposed tuh." She leaned out of the rocking chair, and slowly waddled back in the house.

I feel that story somehow creeping into me something awful. And I still give the wrong answer, even though I know the right one.

8

Peter

I slowly creep over and ease down next to her, careful not to upset the bed too much. She doesn't look comfortable. Her mouth is slack, lips rubbing against my bedspread. Her hair is all over, but it looks beautiful like that. I notice her wrinkles. They don't soften around her eyes the way most people's do when they sleep.

I forget exactly what she looked like when I was younger. I guess the same, but it's hard to notice someone getting older, their skin like the long hand on a clock. Skin can give it away. I think I do remember hers shiny when I was a kid. There was something luminous and honey-like and warm about it. She was always laughing, and her whole face was animated. Not cartoonish or ridiculous, though. All the movements, the twitches, the furrows, the crinkles, the widening, all of them seemed to fit. All smiles and laughing, teasing, and her hair was never still.

She is still beautiful. I can tell by the way men look at her. I'm not sure if she is necessarily defying age, really, or if she has those timeless features, described by fashion magazine writers when referring to "classic" movie starlets. No, she ages, but it's quiet, and only noticeable when you look at her for a long time. That's when you see things: loose eyelids, creases that orbit around her mouth, a subtle pulling down of everything, as if all her worry and sadness clutch the flesh just below her eyes, and dutifully tow.

I love her. I even like her, though most kids my age would never admit that about their parents. Especially when I remember how much she meant to me when I was little. Her craftiness, the little adventures, the memories full of laughter, our bodies akimbo in the spill of our fun. She might make some really bad choices, but she doesn't deserve all that's been thrown at her. I know this. Sometimes I don't want to know this. It's hard to be mad at someone when they're sleeping.

I lower my lips to her ear. Softly, "Ma, why are you on my bed?"

A half realized, "Huh?"

"You're on my bed. What are you doing?"

"Uh."

"Ma, get up. You're going to wake up at three in the morning if you don't get up now."

She takes that deep waking breath, her arms stretching and arcing away from her body, long yawning groans. Her eyes open. "What time is it?"

"8:30pm. What are you doing in my room?"

She sours, picks her head up, looks around. Stops, thinks, nods her head in remembrance.

Her face opens up when she drops her eyes to the bedspread. "I can't believe you still have this thing. I must've made it when your britches were the size of a Barbie doll's."

It's a patchwork butterfly, three sunflowers, a rainbow in the sky. I love this blanket. I remember when she gave it to me. My fifth birthday. The edges are frayed, stains everywhere, but it still keeps me warm in the way I want.

"Ma. You snooping around?"

"There's nothing I should be snooping around for, is it?" She attempts to throw some country guilt, the downward nod and upturned eyes, but her still bleary face looks more intoxicated, if anything. "Besides, it's not you."

I can tell what she means already. "Oh, *God*." I get up, dragging my arms behind me. "What did he want *this* time?"

"Lower your voice, young man."

"Was it a phone call? An email?"

"He called. I think he knows where we live again."

"It's easy to find people these days, Ma."

"I know."

"He'll always know where we are."

"I hate that you're right about that."

"What if he calls you tomorrow?"

"I know."

"Or the next day. Or the next day."

Her lips wrinkle and she speaks deadpan. "He found out my new number. That's something." She has a way of pulling convincing gravity to her voice when she needs it.

"So he found out your new number. So what?"

"So, that's something. And you weren't home." She delivers the last line with more of a slice. I'm not in the mood to indulge her fear. So what? I've been gone a lot, that's true, was probably with Grant on one of my truck and fucks. But I can't stand watching her freak out all the time. The first ten times Isaac called or showed up or got creepy, yes, we both were scared as fuck. We'd jump in the truck and drive off, stay at Aunt Sarah's and keep watch out her living room window. I remember what that asshole could do, what he did to her. But after so many times, over and over, it lost its sting. It's like getting shocked by a faulty electric socket. After a while I stopped feeling it.

Grant. He pushed me out his door. He laughed at me. Maybe Isaac is laughing at Ma, too, in the same way.

"Sometimes he's not putting me on," she says.

"I know," I say, and touch her shoulder.

"I just can't tell this time."

"But you always do this, even when you think he's lying."

The way she says "put me on" sounds so country. So out of place in this brick and cement city. The woman needs to go back to Tennessee where she can say things like "put me on." Maybe that is what she needs, to go back to Tennessee, and take up the fiddle with the rest of her honky family and eat straw and whatever else they do there. That's the great distinction between Ma and me. She is southern to the bone, and me, I'm a northerner. We would have been an awesome Civil War parable. This white woman laying

with a Black man, having two *mullato* kids, and raising them on the cusp
of the Mason-Dixon. Funny how we live in the city that couldn't make up
its mind whose side it wanted to be on. That's Baltimore: a city confused, a
long pit stop in the middle of some journey for both of us. Mine a straight
line up north to New York, hers an ellipsis right back to the South.

"Peter, what do you expect me to do? He's not always full of bull.
You know that."

"Ma, when was the last time he actually *did* anything?"

"I know, but…"

"Can I even remember?" I put my finger to my mouth. "A year? Maybe
longer…"

"Peter." She is focused, staring straight into me. The threshold. I don't
know why I provoke her to this, but I do. I'd never admit it to her, but
I feel the need to. I don't know why exactly. "He said he was coming to
see me. I'm taking no risk."

"You have a restraining order."

"That restraining order don't matter worth bull if he gets here before
the police do."

She's dropped her head. Her thick red hair, this time falling around
her like willow branches. Something like a weary sigh, something elegant. It's not that she is wrong, but I feel it's my job—mine, Aunt Sarah's,
everyone's—to take her mind away from the possibility of Isaac. She'll
get worked up, look out the window every twenty minutes, and the next
thing I know we're moving into a new shitty place, barely able to pay for
the move, everything once again in newspaper and boxes. It's not worth it.
I admit, sometimes Isaac did come around, and sometimes it was creepy,
like the times he'd spend the night in his car just across the street from
our apartment and then drive off in the morning. I get it. But a lot of the
time he was toying with her, a cat pawing a mouse. And it's been *so* long.
It gets tiring. I'm tired of him making her crazy.

She raises her head. "You smell like chicken fry."

"I work at a place that sells fried chicken, Ma."

"How did everything go?" She was exhausted. "You know, at school."

"It's all fine. They slapped me and told me not to do it again."

"You don't sound too upset about it."

"I was."

She gets up, shuffles over to the stairs, turns back. "Peter, your brother's birthday. I'd like you to go with me to put flowers on the grave."

"Ma, not now." I reach for my earbuds to quit the quickly emerging memory of him, because when I hear his name, I see his face, and then I think about what happened to that face, about what I didn't see and can only imagine. Blasting YouTube videos on my cell phone becomes the great neutralizer.

"You never do, Peter."

"I'm tired, Ma."

"It's your brother."

I can't explain to her why I can't talk about him. I don't want her to be haunted by the image of him dead, either, especially how I picture it. I collapse two images of his face: the night he ran away and the composite I created with the little information I knew of his death. Instead of it being only the tear-and-snot streaked face it's also a bloody face, a small bullet hole in the left cheek, like he died the same night he ran away, or something. In a way, I guess he did.

"He's not going to be sad that I didn't make it." I hit play on some Beyoncé and watch her retreat down the stairs, her head dropping with each step. She's dragging the bat behind her. It's so, so sad.

*

Jude looked good in school today. He's getting a little bolder with the dress code. He dyed his hair black. I saw the eyeliner, but I bet no one else did. It was just subtle enough. Fucking idiots can't pick up on a damn thing. I like his hair black. It makes his skin milky, and those clear gray eyes shine that much more, pull me in. How can they not see the eyeliner when surely they're being sucked into those eyes, too? Maybe his eyes are so beautiful they don't care. Not likely. I think they're too stupid to notice anything important at all.

All of him is pretty, and no one knows it like I do. I see him, behind his glasses, the concave slouch, as if pulled forward by his shoulders. It's certainly better than walking around with your chest pushed out like all these other brutes, some kind of grandiose display of maleness—the St. Mary's stance. I've seen actual peacocks with more sex appeal. They might as well kiss their arms, spending more time swelling up with barbells than learning what *narcissistic* means. Jude, though, he's different, he's a natural beauty. The *real* kind. I feel superlative seeing it, the only one who sees it. The only one who can.

I wonder if he's listened to the Bauhaus yet. I had never heard of them before, but Jude was raving about them the week before. So I went to Record and Tape Traders, where Grant's brother works, and asked if they had any rare bootlegs. I listened to it first. It wasn't bad. A little depressing. Joby would have called it honky music and tossed a nod to Ma at the kitchen counter, and we'd crack ourselves up. I keep hearing one of the Bauhaus songs in my head, *The sky's gone out!* I don't know the name but I like it. The sound is sparse and crunchy and reminds me of how I imagine New York City to be—gray, sharp, smart, like Jude's eyes. Maybe I like honky music more than I ever admitted to Joby.

I could just call Jude and ask him, but every time I think it's a good idea, I'm reminded that we aren't that close, really. Maybe he would think it was weird.

There was the time on that field trip to the Smithsonian last spring we sat next to each other on the bus. And then Community Service Week, where we worked together at the Food Bank. We chose the same place, which I prefer to entertain as kismet. But that's the extent of our time spent together outside of school. We've never called each other or spent a casual afternoon together at a coffeeshop. Lately, we've been talking more and more at school, though—that has to mean something. I've been getting into a lot of the music he likes—The Smiths, Depeche Mode, Siouxsie, all these old bands. Sometimes, we'll talk during homeroom. Even my mouth is beginning to relax more when we speak. I used to get dry and jittery, covering up my lips so he wouldn't see them quiver or stick to my teeth, would feel so overwhelmed with him that I had to find an excuse to leave before I exploded. I must have looked ridiculous.

There was one time when he asked if I wanted to go to a record store with him last semester, but I had to work. That's the problem. I'm either working, at school, moving, or on lockdown because Ma thinks Isaac's gone ballistic. I have to sneak out late at night for any social life, and all I've done lately is go to Benny's and fuck men twice my age. How exquisitely romantic.

All I want is to spend time with him away from school, away from all those idiots, away from Tony's constant dogging. I really don't know why Jude relates to that moron. No, I do know. They have a history together. They've been hanging out since freshman year. It's easy to succumb to habit, stick with the same friends, no matter how much you change. In my case, it's become habit not to have them. I haven't cared for most of my available options.

I will call him tonight. I've had his number inked on a napkin yellowing on my dresser since junior year when we were supposed to be in a study group for History. We never had a chance to meet, but he wrote his number down in the cafeteria while I filled my mouth with vegetable medley so my lips wouldn't go into seizure at the sight of the light hairs of his forearm flexing for the scribbled numbers. He smiled at me, his eyes that still gray. I wasn't yet swallowed up by him but, at that point, I was sliding around on the enamel of his teeth.

But 10:15 is too late. I'll probably wake his parents and he'll be irritated because they're yelling at him in his ear while I froth in the other. *Parent.* His father's been dead for five months now, though he's never mentioned it. We learned about it through the scratchy PA system, a sentimental message delivered in Mr. Dell's patronizing inflection, and Jude's empty seat in homeroom for almost two weeks. In Jude's absence, I daydreamed the funeral, the family silences at dinner. I imagined what was happening in Jude's heart, the way his seeing must have been skewed—colors and shape altered by grief. I'm not sure why I was so intoxicated by these thoughts, but I became obsessed. And I didn't know anything about Jude's life outside of school. I never felt the opportunity to inquire. It was after his father died, though, that Jude became increasingly compelling to me. In the thousand times I replayed the fantasy of him crying, suffocated by sorrow, as I sat in my monotonous classes listening to teachers the way Charlie Brown heard his own, I fantasized the vibrant tragedy of Jude. He presented himself as a mythical character, one of elegance and water, of grace and survival, yet made somehow electric and colorful by the harsh universe. It was then I realized we were both beautiful because of the pain we felt.

When Jude finally returned to the tattered ranks of the red carpet hallway, I had already built for him a temple in my mind, and was ready to welcome his weathered face and soothe it with rose water. He came back on a Tuesday, was wearing his hair behind his ears. He didn't look particularly gaunt or walk with a specific hopelessness. His slacks were pressed, his collar ironed. He wasn't dirty. There was nothing in his appearance that looked different except for darker circles around his eyes. All that seemed to notably change was his voice. I never thought that was a place particularly molested by pain. When he spoke now, there was a dignity, a restraint, a refrain from pointless chatter. The boys squawked all around him, cracking on each other's haircuts or clothes or free-throw, and Jude's participation was half-smiles, single-word responses that sounded more like sighs. He still used words like anyone else, and it wasn't like he expanded his vocabulary, but there was something underneath the voice now, like a subliminal message in a record. Pain may not look beautiful, but it sounds beautiful. So when he returned, he wasn't the electric beauty I imagined. Instead, he was a reserved beauty. I was attracted to it just as much, if not more. I wanted his pain. I wanted to be a survivor whose hair was blanched from suffering, whose eyes saw more clearly, whose voice settled into some kind of knowing.

I've been looking at this piece of torn mess-hall napkin for months, the numbers leering at me, intimidating me. Before, I had nothing to call him for. Now, we *talk*. We have music in common. Why wouldn't I call him?

"Hello?" A woman. His mother. She doesn't sound too groggy, but the phone did ring four times. Ma always waits to answer the phone until the sleep has cleared from her throat. She has this phone voice that sounds like Jessica Rabbit from that old cartoon movie, softer and breathy. She is afraid of growing old, I'm sure.

"Mrs. Woolsey? Hi, this is Peter Cryer. I go to school with Jude. May I speak with him?"

I have no idea why I offered my name. Now she knows that I was the one that woke her up in the night. She'll grant me this one allowance, then forbid her son to ever talk to me again. Or maybe we'll be a modern Romeo and Romeo, lovers who both pick up the phone, but always a second too late. A scene in split-screen, hesitating, one picks up, the other drops the receiver, again, again.

"Hello?" His voice on the phone sounds different, heavier, deeper. He probably has a little hair on his chest already. Just a little, just enough to finger through, hair around the nipples.

"Jude? Hey it's Peter."

"Peter? Cryer? Hey."

"I'm just sitting in my room. Thought I'd see what was up?"

The phone already begins to slip in my hand from the sweat.

"How'd you get my phone number?"

In all the rehearsal time spent answering questions I thought he might ask, this one never presented itself. Yes, Jude, I have your number because you gave it to me on a napkin last fall and I have savored it like a gift this entire time. I've cleaned around it for months, memorizing the number without ever realizing. 760-2184 has become something mythical and erotic.

"I was cleaning up my room and found it in a bunch of papers. I just thought I'd call. Have you listened to the Bauhaus yet?"

"That's what I'm doing right now. Weird." He laughs. "It's awesome. Where did you get it?"

I lie and tell him I got it in London. It just comes out, unrehearsed. Fuck.

"What! You went to London? Cool! When? I'm so jealous. What was it like?"

Luckily, I am a geography aficionado, and read travel books all the time. I tell him about Piccadilly Circus, Trafalgar Square, the Tate Gallery, anything I can remember reading. I start describing the streets, the architecture. I even embellish and tell a story about meeting some traveling musicians on the Thames. I'm sure it sounds genuine. His interest does, at least.

"I've always wanted to go to London."

I suddenly feel so shitty for lying. Why, Peter, of all things to begin the first phone conversation with your High School Rom-Com Dreamboat, would it be bullshit? It's so…well…high school rom-com.

London eases on to music, and that's when Jude takes over. Albums, tours, bootlegs, band histories, his knowledge is endless. I largely say "ooh" or "I haven't heard of that" or "wow." I'm okay with that. As we are going back and forth I hear the sediment in his voice. His laughter at my more clever observations is almost velvety. I could lick the breath circling in the back of his throat. Hope is hot. I am full of it and my ears burn.

"Holy shit, how long have we been talking?" he asks.

I look at the clock. Almost 11:30. I tell him. He laughs. I follow, but I don't know why it's funny.

"I have to sleep. Are you going to school tomorrow?"

"Of course," I say.

"Well, with you, one can't be sure." He affects what I take to be a British accent. "I mean, with all your suspensions, playing hooky and such." That warms me, this type of banter. This is what friends do.

I follow suit. "Well, my dear, you will be delighted to know that I will be present in class tomorrow, I couldn't possibly forego American history. So chummy, those Yanks."

"Splendid."

"Splendid."

"Well then, cheerio."

"Jude." I drop the accent and adopt urgency, a little more than I should. Fuck. "There's a band at the Cat's Eye in Fell's Point. They're supposed to be really promising."

"Who?"

I had no idea. I just knew that Cat's Eye had bands play most nights of the week. "It's free."

"I like free. Let's talk tomorrow."

I hang up the phone slowly, and fall on my bed. I shake, but I'm not nervous, at all. I am filled with something else, something like satisfaction, a lightness, too light, as if I have been breathing in pure oxygen. I'm sure it has something to do with my infatuation, but I'm not one of those corny little school kids in the movies who swoon, eyes tilted up to God as if thanking him, *he's so dreamy*. That shit makes me gag. Okay, maybe just a little bit.

I know I feel good. I do feel good.

I stare at the ceiling, draw lines between the little stalactites of plaster. First, constellations, but then more elaborate images after an hour of fixed staring. A giraffe eating leaves, a Christmas tree with devil horns, a lizard on a cross. I catch myself turning the edges of my mouth up a little. I'm going out with Jude soon. I have never been to the Cat's Eye, nor have I traipsed around Fell's Point for absolutely nothing in particular with a friend. Now, I just have to call in to work and put on a death wheeze. It can't be much different than doing it for school.

I remember seeing Jude once last year laying on the grass by the soccer field, reading a book, his eyes glowing like harvest moons through his glasses. I carry this image, and continue it on my ceiling. I add myself to the image. I go over to him quietly, lay down next to him, take off his glasses without saying a word. He looks directly into me, not moving, as I pull the book from his hands, my own confident and snakey. I take his and wrap them around my back and fall into him, scooping against his stomach. His eyes are open. I lower my head to kiss him. This takes an eternity. Every time my lips are about to touch his, I rewind the scene, again, again. I change the scene, make us shirtless, the light hair around the nipples, a little sweat, but never do our lips fully touch. I don't want to imagine that. I want that to happen in real life.

I see us watching an old black and white movie together, probably a Hitchcock, a Hepburn, our limbs tangled into one another. I drop my eyes and watch his chest breathe. I kiss his shoulders. I rest my heavy head in his neck. He smells like eucalyptus and skin.

After all this time, we're finally going to be real friends, going out somewhere, talking on the phone. Talking for over an hour on the phone. This is what I've wanted and now it's happening. I wonder if he's thinking about me right now the way I'm thinking about him. I think he is, whether he admits it to himself or not. I know he's dated one girl before, but so have I. We have to. It's just the way it is. Self-preservation, so you are not fodder for the ridicule, especially at St. Mary's, the Pantheon for oily sports equipment and dude-bro handshakes. It would not surprise me if the faculty started taking turns throwing stones themselves. I wonder if Jude knows about me. Perhaps I should tell him soon.

No. I won't need to. If he feels the same way, I'll know. If not, then it's best if I didn't. At least not yet.

Staring, my ceiling takes on new forms. I never noticed how beautiful it is—the plaster almost glittery in the divots—this last thing I see before falling asleep. At least tonight I know, and I hope my images of Jude and his voice possess my dreams. There is going to be a future with us. I can feel it.

9

Thomas

After school, I take the bus to Little Italy, to Exeter Street. My mother's house is like any rowhouse in the neighborhood, but is unadorned— no plants in the windows or on the stoop. I'm not sure if only I notice, or if everyone does, but the house looks like its occupant has died, that certain mournfulness that even architecture can assume.

As the door creaks open, I become aware of how foreign the house feels, despite its similarity to all the others in Little Italy—three-story brick edifice, narrow in width, marble steps. I have walked through the neighborhood often, have eaten inside at least a half dozen of the trattorias, have visited friends, have walked through so many of these homes; even this one the very few times I met with my mother, and that acknowledgement raps me with a loneliness so sudden it doesn't feel real. I pull on the buttons of my shirt. That last time she invited me to dinner, she seemed more interested in sharing our family history than actually learning about me, where an uncle settled after the Vietnam War, or how many children a cousin had. In fact, of the times I did see her she only asked perfunctory questions about my life in the order, or anything concerning my life—how was teaching, how was attendance at the Church on Sundays? She never asked anything about my father, ever.

The air is thick, muted, light and dust mingling translucence. An old woman's home, her dead skin cells flaking fast in her entropy, shedding into the light, the soft focus at the end of a life. I move through the space museum-like, hands at my sides, quiet and conscious, taking in the artifacts. The furniture is mostly antique, the anachronism of a deco couch, armchairs from the forties, and a mid-century modern coffee table. My mother had to buy all new furniture when she moved back to Baltimore, because she didn't take anything but her clothes when she left us all those years ago. A collection of framed photographs hanging along the stairway wall pulls me further into the room. An assortment of Baltimores appear—different scenes, different decades, different tones of light. A history lesson.

*

Maryland was supposed to be a sanctuary, the one true colony where all walks of life would assemble together, live in towns together, be neighbors, have barbecues on the main drag and play horseshoes, no matter where you went to church. Fights would break out only when the barrels fermented a little too long. The progressive hub of an otherwise vulgar and Puritan New World.

When King Charles granted the colony of Maryland to a Catholic George Calvert, he wasn't thinking utopia. He heard of the natural harbors, the Chesapeake, the profit potential. And Calvert wanted the investment, and a place where he could smoke his opium in peace. 1632. England was mostly Protestant by then. Stones were being thrown. Calvert wanted cover.

His Toleration Act allowed all Christians to do their thing. Supposed to, anyway. 1649. But why would a Puritan move to Maryland when they could practice anywhere else? It became the leftovers colony. Catholics, Anglicans, and Quakers swarmed in.

Irish first, which explains a lot. The city was nothing but brick and bakery, a few scoundrels, some fishing. And then the Germans came, Catholic and industrious ones that saw the potential. Tobacco. Trade. A glorious port. And by 1752, the little town was stamped with German and Irish life. There was one general store, one barber shop, one church, absolutely no school, and three pubs.

Then mills, more bakeries, iron. Revolution. Railroad. And boom: big city.

The potato famine brought more Irish, more Catholics, more beer. And these guys set up shop around the workers' factories and shipbuilding enterprises in Fell's Point and Canton. Among the bistros and boutiques still lingers the stink of smelted metal. Steel, strong and unwavering. It gets in the blood.

It took years of negotiation for these neighborhoods to take part in annexation as the city grew. Reason? The Baltimore blue law. The one that would close down beer gardens and pubs on Sunday. It took almost one hundred years.

Steel.

Italian famine changed things in the 1880s. Hordes of Italians moved into the Catholic-friendly city and set up around the churches in East Baltimore, mainly by President Street Station, just north and west of Fell's Point. They rented from the German/Irish establishment.

Roberto Giuffrida stepped off the boat in 1903. He lost his mother to fever and the rest of his family was dying from the Abruzzo drought. He came to America alone. He was sixteen. The only thing he knew was farming, and so became a fruit vendor on Pratt Street. He shared a room on Fleet with a Russian Jew named Ilia who spoke with fleshy arms. Roberto knew no Russian, Ilia no Italian. They were great friends.

Sometimes my dirty fingernails smell of apricots.

In six months Roberto could speak workers' English. He knew all the words concerning produce and address, and eventually enough to get him a job with the railroad. He worked a lot, since time passed easier that way, and had neither money or looks to woo women, nor the charisma for friends. He played dice with Ilia during holidays and walked the streets at night with their amber candlelight. He had no particular dream. He felt as if he lived in one.

Until the Great Fire the following year, which devastated the city. Half of it was burning up, bricks popping like eggshells against a ceramic bowl. The flames were on their way to the east side, feet away from a bucket line formed at President Street. Roberto saw and felt the fire. It towered above all the buildings in the harbor, and seemed absolute. He prayed to St. Anthony, as did all the Italians.

And then it stopped. The fire went no further than the Jones Falls, right next to President Street. The Italian ghetto was saved. A clean, distinct line divided the city with Roberto's people on the fortunate side. Of course, the Italians took the credit. Roberto, not taking into consideration that the Jones Falls was a river, saw the defeat of the fire as a sign.

He walked up Fawn Street, where he used to peddle apples, waiting for another sign, probably thinking there would be three. He prayed again to St. Anthony, walked on as he waited. It was on Exeter Street, by the corner of Stiles, amidst cobblestone and shuffling apartment houses, that he found it. He heard a woman's voice. *Roberto. Di dentro.* Granted, a little boy with soot on his forehead groaned and scurried over to the woman, but it was enough for Roberto Giuffrida. He decided the neighborhood was good luck, that it could have been the immaculate Virgin who called his name, and chose Exeter to be the street he would make a home and a family. The Virgin had called him to stay. The fire had been very hot.

Many of the immigrant Italians did the same. They bought the homes they were previously renting. And by 1930, the neighborhood was theirs. By 1930, Roberto had a home on Exeter Street and a family, his wife Rosa and four children, all healthy. Ignatius, the oldest, worked on Butcher's Hill. Joseph was in the railyard with his father. Franny sewed soles in shoes. And Michael manipulated schoolgirls with fairly good poetry. Franny was Roberto's favorite.

In 1938, Franny married a half-Italian, half-Polish steel foreman. Rosa approved only because he was Catholic and hadn't lost his job during the Depression. The same was not true for Iggy and Joseph. The slaughterhouse laid off half its workers and the railroad shut down, so the boys went to look for work in Philadelphia. Michael was working on shrimp boats off the coast of Maine.

Franny was the only child left in Baltimore when Roberto died. 1949. Iggy and Joseph both had families in Pennsylvania and Michael had been run over by an ice cream delivery truck ten years before, the details of which were slippery off the tongues of Michael's associates, the clipped monotone syllables that secrecy swears by. The Great War not only changed politics and pocketbooks, but changed the course of luck, as well. Rosa resented the boys for never returning home. When she died the following year, she willed the Exeter house to Franny. Iggy and Joseph never spoke to their sister again. Italians clutch fury the way veins hold blood. Tight and cold. Steel.

Franny had two children. Rosa and Roberto, same as her parents. She refused to give her kids Polish names, living in Little Italy. Her husband put up no fuss. He was a bland constant for her, and doesn't even need a name. She had no respect for him or for any man. She kicked her husband out on the basis of disinterest and made her living in textile services, enough to keep the house and feed her children. They were comfortable without him.

Franny never trusted her son, Roberto. She bombarded him with questions and suspicions, even in his vulnerable years, and took a skillet to his shoulder when he came home late one night covered in mud and wine. She claimed to see a gestating frost in the glass of his dark eyes, like a shark's, and compulsively walked sideways around him. He was gone before finishing ninth grade. Franny never tried to find him. She only expected him to run off, and told her daughter so.

1965. Young Rosa met James Manilli. For Rosa, it wasn't love, but more an obligation to find security, and to please Franny. James was full-blood Italian and a devout Catholic. It was all Franny would tolerate, though still riddled with complaint. They wed in St. Peter's cathedral. Franny didn't throw rice. Rosa didn't want a honeymoon.

Rosa had her first child in 1972. She didn't like the name Thomas, but James insisted. It was his grandfather's name. Rosa found it colorless, but didn't care enough to argue. She didn't want children at all, especially a boy.

The economic decline of the city came, the big dense thud of the steel industry, the competition of other eastern ports, the Great White Flight. The shortage of work made James look elsewhere. 1976, the year Franny died, he was offered an airport job in Anne Arundel County. Though only a handful of miles south of the city, the county was deeply aware and proud of its southern proximity to the Mason-Dixon. This was not the Maryland that fought for the Union. The one hundred years since were only a bitter waiting for some kind of vengeance, a rebuttal, but to what, no one in the county knew anymore. Rosa would have resisted moving there if it wasn't for Thomas and her own minimal job prospects. They moved in summer and the humidity seething off the South River, the punch of horse droppings lingering in the still air, made Rosa immediately hate her new family, her life with husband and child. Though James encouraged her, Rosa never rented out the Exeter house. Steel. Tight and cold.

James thrived while Rosa listened to the radio in the kitchen. She became pregnant again, and the hope that it was a girl was all that kept her from screaming. She explored herbal and physical practices that even she found ridiculous to ensure a little Mary. When she miscarried the baby in second trimester, she blamed it on the South River well-water, on James, on God. Within months she left in the night, moved back up to Baltimore, leaving behind her husband, and leaving behind six-year-old Thomas. That is history, a third-person narrative. Stories in the distance.

My father never remarried. Not that he didn't try. It was simply that no one wanted him. He was too introverted to be seen as anything beyond a mystery to the county women, acted too much a northerner, and didn't make enough money for them to ignore it. Instead, he focused all his attention on me.

There was only one Catholic Church remotely close to us, but my father traveled to it every Sunday, to make sure I was brought up right. Moral integrity. A sense of faith. A sense of commitment. I was ridiculed in school for being Catholic, and that only made me cling to it even more. I read the Bible every night before bed. My father had me recite my own paraphrased versions of the Gospels, of Job, Jeremiah. I relished in the stories, my father's devotion to me.

When he died from cancer, I was sent to an orphanage in Calvert County. I was a young teenager by then, too old to be adopted, and remained there until I finished high school, a good but unremarkable student. It never occurred to me that my mother may have claimed and taken me in, but she didn't, anyway. By that point she was a non-entity, something my father referred to only in fragments, pieces of story that otherwise could not have been told without her being mentioned. He wasn't a vindictive man, and he praised forgiveness. Not once did he defame her in my presence.

That made my mother more of a mystery, and then in the silences of the orphanage a myth, slowly dissolving with time. Some days I would forget her face entirely. I'm sure that disappearing image had something to do with me joining the order; I'm sure that had something to do with my desire to study in Baltimore. However, when I look back on this time in my youth, I can't remember a decision at all. It feels as if I woke up on my last day at the orphanage, packed my bags, and went straight to the order, no struggle, no fanfare.

When I first moved back to the city, I looked her up. She eventually accepted my visit. A tourist pavilion had just opened among the rotting wharfs and warehouses of the Inner Harbor, and my mother was ridiculing the wasted taxpayer money from her stoop. There was tea, and no explanation for her leaving me behind or apology for never writing. The way she talked to me, distant and casual like a boss to an employee, left me no way to ask her, either. Anything.

I saw her only a few more times in all the years we shared the same city, merely a handful of blocks between us. The last time she phoned me for dinner was around seven years ago. I canceled the plans I had already made, and brought roses from the rectory's garden.

She looked a lot thinner than I remembered her last. Her hair was pinned very neatly in classic sixties style, with a flourish of Italian whimsy, the wavy tendrils that framed her face. A lovely woman, in some ways, even in old age, but with a furious mouth, so thin and fierce. She made lasagna. I had questions; my own research left me with many. Records were shoddy in the immigrant neighborhoods. My father hadn't known much. But I didn't have to ask. She told me the history without expression, about her grandfather, the fire, the house, how I have told it. The only moments where she seemed even to be capable of emotion were in her pleading. "Will you remember this? Will you remember it all?" Tugging on my black sleeve too hot to be wearing in the dusty house. She didn't know me well enough to realize that I would remember everything, and that I would write it down. History, that thing that must be written down, must be made precise, that language cannot fail. How else are we to revere it as anything like truth?

I wanted to ask her a lot of whys, but somehow she made it impossible for me to do that. Instead, I spent the following years filling in those blanks.

And now I am looking at where she stood that moment seven years ago when she told me all she needed to, except now I listen not to her voice but to her pictures. The dust motes almost form an outline of her small, slightly bent frame, leaning against the wall between the living and dining room. I can hear her telling me again, "You had a great *grandfather* Roberto and also an *uncle* Roberto. Can you remember? There were two." Her eyes wide. I feared them. I feared her. I fear her still, but I don't know why. I wanted to ask her questions beyond history, questions that pertained to her, my father, our family, but I didn't dare.

I look around the muted living room. Old books, bric-a-brac, some woodcarvings. Lamps, a tea service, tons of slapped up photos. Specks of men and women, this one of young lovers in a park. She has a pensive mouth, he unconsciously parted lips. I hear my mother's voice like a soundtrack, like a recording identifying the young girl as Franny. It also tells me it was probably taken in Patterson Park. I look at another. This one older, the definition slowly peeling away. Again, I hear my mother's voice narrate the still image. The man leaning on the cornerstone is Iggy. She told me he was tall, the tallest of them. He has thin wisps of hair clinging to his temples. I touch my own bald head. This is my great uncle Iggy.

Another picture shows my much younger father towering over a petite, plain woman with heavy lipstick. She stares at the camera as if playing chicken. Between them is a small boy also looking at me. He knows I'm here. He has black hair spilling from under a sailor's hat. That is us. I'm not sure if it's a voice or if I say it, "Us." The edges of the photograph disappear. It is everything I see. The faces of the man and woman, my mother and father, get clearer. Together. They are together, with me, and this must be Baltimore. I can almost see them moving, their eyes looking up, down, to each other. I keep watching myself.

In this picture, I feel the expanse of time, but like it's been collapsed on the head of a pin. All of time is everywhere and also right in front of me, all of it, in this one moment. Now, the little black and white boy, all of it. The whispering of my mother sped up and layered. All this new time, everything at once. A portal. *Will you remember this? Will you remember this?*

Why didn't my mother take an interest in me? What was she, instead of being a mother? History would normally reveal these answers, but nothing I found in the documents of her life come close to convincing. Though I had met her, spoken with her, even touched her—once, on the shoulder—I knew nothing. There was an invisible polarity between us, a force, that kept us apart, two negative magnetic charges. And now I own everything that was part of her. Why would she give me everything of her death and nothing of her life?

I check my watch. 10:17p.m. I keep staring. It can't be right. I've been here for six hours. There is no way. How long was I standing in front of those photographs? It felt like an instant.

Exeter Street is quiet, only a little shuffling. A few windows are flickering blue and white, but most are dark, the occasional car in the distance. The cold air smells like the dew is already on its way.

In this dark stillness of night, being in this house with this woman, my mother who I barely knew, I feel any center within myself disappear. I look out to the street in the direction of the rectory. And thinking of returning there, to the worn familiar sounds of Saul snoring, August yapping, Simon pontificating, I feel a little dread, and I don't want to go back. But I also don't want to stay here, this house that I never felt invited to stay for long. I step out to the front stoop and look around, alone in the night, these narrow streets that my mother saw every day, the people who live around her that I've never met. It's this overwhelming sense of placelessness, like I belong nowhere, and never have.

*

The next evening, August hustles me toward City Hall, his hand pulling my elbow. "We're going to be late." I hear the polyester of his pants rubbing together. He is overweight, like me. He is slightly older, rosy, almost jolly-like. He'd play the Santa at Christmas, perhaps, if we engaged in such ritual. He hops the first set of shallow marble steps in rapid beats. It looks silly. He doesn't want us to appear ambivalent to the Council, walking in late.

Surrounding the steps is a handful of protestors, maybe thirty in all, moving picket-line style with paint-stick and poster board signs that read "Save our School!" and "Don't Kick Me Out (Again)!" I look at the marching oval for anyone I recognize, perhaps a mother of one of the St. Mary's kids or a neighbor. No one. Most of the entourage is on the younger side, maybe mid-thirties or so. One of them catches my eye. She is short with a small frame, wearing an ill-fitting mauve pantsuit. What has me rest my eyes on her isn't what she looks like, however, but how she moves. Her eyes are closed, face tilted upward as if having a conversation with God, and she follows the protest line as if it's the most natural activity in the world. Her sneakers glide over the asphalt. Upon closer look it appears she is singing quietly to herself while the rest of her peers chant, "Housing is a Right!" There's something almost peaceful about this woman in spite of the context of her present action. She is also quite attractive with slender hands gipping her sign, that glide of her body, the serene face as she sings. What song does she play in her mind right now? How does that song change when her troubles become too much?

"Thomas?" August pulls me from my trance with his schoolmarm eyes, as if a pair of bifocals sat right on the edge of his nose. "We're late."

I take one more look at the woman in the picket line, her eyes still closed and she singing softly to herself.

We ascend the remaining steps to City Hall's main entrance.

It's hard to believe that Baltimore almost tore the building down in the seventies. It had many structural problems, piping issues, iron fixtures falling from the domed ceiling, the roof leaking. But what a roof it was, indicative of the period. Like Philly's City Hall, Baltimore built theirs just after the Civil War in the Second Empire style, when the U.S. and France still thought of each other as brothers-in-arms. And though Philly's is larger, this one is a clearer example. It has the mansard roof, the rectangular towers, the long feminine windows. It's beautiful, and looms gracefully as you come to its entrance.

August huffs, winded, "Have you thought about what you're going to say?"

I hadn't. The night before at my mother's house left me exhausted. How the time had disappeared, how the questions of her kept me from sleeping even when I arrived home. Home. It's interesting to me that I would refer to the rectory as home, when I had just left my own mother's. Of course I would consider the rectory home. It was where I had lived for more than two decades. Why did it feel so strange to think of it as one?

August is rambling, as he often does, this time about why the Church and the local government need to cooperate on issues of housing. Something about checks and balances, multiple perspectives. The words mesh as they issue from his mouth so fast that I almost hear another language. His exuberance further exhausts me.

I can't help but think about how many people have died on these steps. Soon after the building was completed, two city officials got into a fight that resulted in a duel, back when government was more openly ferocious, truer to its nature. America was still young, adolescent, idealistic in its violence. A century later, another city official was shot and killed. By then, however, murder was no longer committed through idealism, but through madness, messy and indirect. It was a man who was pissed off that his restaurant was shut down after a regular inspection. He stormed in with a gun and started firing. No one he hit had anything to do with his diner being infested with rats.

I suddenly wonder if my mother ever had to do business here. She could have walked from Exeter Street easily. Did she follow Baltimore politics? Did she ever attend public hearings or concern herself with the changing times? I imagine she didn't. I imagine her political platform ceased at her marble stoop.

"Don't you agree, Thomas?"

"What?"

"About...what I was...Oh, never *mind*," August says in that sing-song voice of his. The demeanor is at once over-the-top and perfectly honest, which makes it forgiving. Most of the order probably has surmised August's story; it's a common one: homosexual abandoning the lay world out of fear. His highly effeminate gestures would have made him an obvious target in his youth, so he couldn't hide effectively in the closet. And I bet a young August figured that with his devotion to the *right thing*, he wouldn't want to live that life at all, fearing the sin itself and not merely the consequences. Despite the controversies within the Catholic Church in Boston and New York, no one in the order has even bristled with concern for him. We know he has too much fear to ever go beyond thoughts, even if he has any.

We push into the cavernous lobby, the dome windows' falling light. August pulls my arm again, up the steps, through hallways.

"Here we are," he says. The room is a stark contrast to the delicate ornaments of the original Victorian architecture. It has fake wood paneling running up the walls, boxy tables, oversized swivel chairs, brass accents. The air is muffled, the carpet worn and brown. The word that comes to mind is institutional, and I wonder what that word meant before the 1970s desecrated interior design. It baffles me how government always seems to ruin art.

There may be a dozen other people here besides the concave line of chairs filled with the Council. They are in two clumps, sitting on opposite sides of the room. They confer with each other in whispers, some have papers. August slips into a row and sits at the edge. He moves with fluid ease, despite his extra pounds. I follow with less grace.

The City Council is all there, fourteen of them, mostly women. I am surprised how young the woman looks in the center, presumably the President. She has on a sharp suit, her hair stylish and voluminous. Her race is difficult to discern, dark skin, slightly pointed nose, full lips. She is a good choice for Council President, as she seems to be Baltimore's demographic map fused into one individual. The other thirteen are smart looking, with sensible haircuts and lots of gray. The tapping of pencils and fingernails makes it seem they are anxious or bored, or both.

The testimonies begin. Each one is a repetition of the other, except that as they progress, all try to trump the other with descriptions that illustrate Highlandtown and Ellwood Park as a little more destitute, more unruly: bathed in squalor, overrun with urban outlaws, a post-apocalyptic war zone, the gates of Hell.

Sisters, who still live in the house where they grew up, detail the gradual fall of the neighborhood from a modest, supportive community of blue-collar dock workers to a patchwork of desolate slums. Both are in their sixties and have massively flappy arms.

"All the kids in the neighborhood would play in Patterson Park at night. Now, I'm afraid to go out my door in the daytime," one of them says.

A middle-aged man with scraggly salt and pepper hair is called on, a plumber raised in Dundalk who now lives close to St. Mary's. He complains about the trash on the streets, overturned wastebaskets, the litter in the park. "They have no respect," he says, as if he is not part of "they." I wonder who constitutes "they," and if anyone here would claim to be "they," even though "they" are the residents of the neighborhood "they" complain about. I wonder if I am "they." To be honest, I'm not sure. I am here to make testimony, to somehow shine a light upon the neighborhood. There is purpose for this. This is City Hall. Purpose. When August asked me to come, I felt obliged as part of the Outreach Committee, and agreed without much question. But now, I am lost on what that obligation is.

Crime is the focus of a family of four, who recall a break-in that occurred one Sunday night. They had been at the movies, when they walked in on two burglars trying to disconnect their living room stereo.

"The two robbers were high out of their minds and attacked me with a bat," says the father. He holds up his left arm to illustrate the break he sustained in the struggle.

I never had any real problems with the neighborhood. It was true that there was a lot of trash on the streets, that some parts were downright eerie in their decrepitude, and I would never go into the park after dark. I just hadn't really cared one way or another, honestly. I was busy at the school, the rest of the time at the rectory. My small concentric life.

St. Mary's was an island. Most of the kids came from elsewhere, and we stayed in the rectory. All these people here? I don't know them. I don't even recognize them. They may live next door, for all I know. Do they know that we are a school? Or is it the big castle, shadowing the neighborhood? They are the serfs of our fiefdom, except we don't collect fees, at least from them.

The best-dressed man in the room reveals himself to be one of the developers for Crabtown, Ponty MacAllister. He says he lives in nearby Federal Hill, and sees what is happening to Highlandtown. Crabtown is his solution.

"Those streets are not going to clean up quick enough, not for us. Instead, we can get rid of the streets, start over, create a new Baltimore that we can be proud of." His perfect row of teeth gleam when his audience claps. Something in me knots up. It has something to do with his smile, his slightly affected Bawlmer accent, the conscious bowing of his head, but it is faint and not as notable as the stains on the carpet. This *carpet*.

August is called for testimony. A sober respect blankets the room as he speaks, their eyes probably focused on his black collar, the curiosity of it. His is the most colorful account of the neighborhood, the one that prompts gasps from the Council, who suddenly listen as if Highlandtown is a remote colonial village that was taken over by native cannibals. August is impressive, phrases like *shadowed abandon* and *deep-rooted disillusionment*. I even forget that he is describing a part of Baltimore, and picture scenes from *Heart of Darkness* as he speaks. The silent nods around me confirm that I may be the only one not fully visualizing the reality.

Then I am called. I don't know what to say. Between all the other
testimonies, there's nothing more to say. I don't like repeating things,
annoyed when others do. Usually that kind of excess is only done for
the speaker's sake, and listeners tune out, grow anxious. At least I do.
I'm a teacher, I know this. I could talk about how this very room has
seen generations of people living in Highlandtown speak their mind
about the neighborhood's condition, that this is what history is, a series
of repeats dressed in different fashion. I could tell them to be proud they
are speaking in a room filled with whispered complaints that came before
them, no matter when the time.

August nudges me with a poke. I stand up. "Hello," I manage. "My
name is Brother Thomas Manilli. I am a teacher at St. Mary's." I feel like
I need to say more about my identity, to assert my credibility, but nothing comes to mind. There isn't anything more, really, and right now that
makes me feel insignificant. What else could I have become? As a boy, I
dreamed of becoming a pilot. I would lay down on a park bench, close
my eyes and stretch arms out, the miniature trees and houses floating
below me. It changed to astronaut when I got a little older, this time
the planet rotating somberly, the stars cradling my weightless and silent
flight. Above all, I fantasized the silence of these occupations. There was
no one around to talk with. I could look around without interruption,
watch everything else move in silence.

"Mr. Manilli?" The attractive councilwoman looks at me curiously. She
is polite. Perhaps she is eager for my testimony. Perhaps she wants another
performance like August's, a portrait of Sodom, frothing bodies, gnashing
limbs, teeth tearing flesh, the virtuous ones walking away tearfully, daring
one another to look back. I would definitely have turned to salt.

"Just say what you know," urges August. I look at him. What do I
know? What do I know about anything? I studied history, because I could
look at it without being in it. I could observe history forever, because it
would never be where I was.

August whispers hoarsely, "What are you doing? The Council is
waiting." He now uses his whole hand to poke me, then looks out to

the room and cocks his head to the side with an embarrassed smile. Now everyone in the room looks at me, expectant, curious. I feel frozen in their anticipation. I lecture for hours a day in front of students, but maybe I'm not startled by them because they aren't anxious for what I have to say. The kids don't even know I'm speaking half the time. Who knows what they're really thinking about in the classroom. I pull at the buttons on my shirt.

"You don't have to provide testimony, Mr. Manilli."

"Oh, for God's sake, Thomas, tell them what we're here for!" He looks like an animation, a red face popping out of the black uniform. I'm annoyed by the interruptions.

"The neighborhood is forgotten. So many things are forgotten," I say, and sit back down.

August doesn't say a word to me as we leave the Council room. I appreciate the silence. In the lobby, MacAllister comes over to August, shakes his hand vigorously. "Thanks for coming today, Brother. It means a lot that you support us." He doesn't look at me at all.

August smiles benevolently. "Whatever we can do to make our city better."

MacAllister is rich. Everything about his face, his shoulders, the press of his clothes, the gracious smile, all signify a man who has lived—if not all, then most of—his life at the top of the hill, looking down. He glides among people without even the brief awkward moments, when a smile is no longer sustainable and the mouth twitches, or a memory floods into the mind's eye and distracts. He is handsome, slender, soft enough and tough enough, and has a good amount of hair. I dislike him.

August and I walk in the winter night, huddling into our coats for the considerable walk home. He is too irritated with me to speak, which I find comforting. I didn't know what to say in front of the Council, because I hadn't thought much about the reason they were assembled. I wasn't even sure why there was a meeting in the first place. Why would people need to make testimony of a neighborhood that you could reasonably figure out by driving though? Was it merely a formality? And what exactly would it influence? Crabtown seemed to already be a done deal, and there appeared to be no other reason for a group of people to denounce the state of the neighborhood.

And honestly, I don't care that much, at least not right now. There is so much more to immediately concern myself with, things that I can actually affect. My mother's house, the students. I need to make a list: Starch my clothes. Set up parent-teacher conferences. Buy beverages for the Sports Boosters meeting.

And what if this amusement park comes? It might give the kids more to be excited about. They could at least play in the dirt during the construction.

When we are back in the neighborhood, near the park, I laugh. August is too angry to ask what I'm laughing about, so I don't share it, either. I realize that this apparent neighborhood testimonial to the City Council only included people whose homes were *not* affected by the proposed demolition, that were safe, and even though the affected area is comprised mostly of low-income Black people, not a single one of the attendees was anything but white.

10

Peter

I feel sexy walking along Eastern with my best shirt and jeans, my hair shellacked to where my curls gleam stiffened wet—no frizzy fro tonight, the red and white lights of cars blinking up the asphalt, slick with the recent drizzle. I should wear socks, but no. The black ones I have to wear all week don't appeal, coming home to find damp sloughed cotton sludged between my toes, dug into my big toenails, syrupy wet rot soaking the air, the stench fastening to your feet, your hands, the inside wall of your nostrils. Besides, I've left so many behind at Grant's these past couple of months. Instead of notches on a bedpost, I count the socks I have left, and calculate.

I take my strides, relaxing into my pendulous legs, letting them lead me. They veer left down Broadway as if programmed. I am clean. I am wearing cologne, Old Spice. Ma gave it to me after one of her boyfriends left it at the house, years ago, nearly full. It smells aggressive. I feel aggressive. The market up ahead is zig-zagged and dotted with specks of people coming and going. The air is fiercely confident and clear, the cold slicing through the broth of smog, making everything in the night look more resolute and alive. There is such a sense of possibility.

I walk by the lemonade stand, but I know I'm early. Ma washing dishes is always the sign of something contentious, and I didn't want to kill my mood by staying there. It would have been silent and weird, and I didn't need that today. I don't need to be thinking about her tonight.

I have been to the Point many times before, but never at night. It is charged with a different kind of energy. In daylight it was just as busy, but it was full of shopping bags, mothers with baby carriages, kids spilling ice cream or pizza slices on the cobblestone, pigeons grouping around old women tossing chunks of sourdough pretzel. Now it is neon, electronica thumping against brick sidewalks, jock rock braying out of windows, competing rhythms, skeins of black polyester, everything slicked back and streamlined, sleeking forward. I hear the muted clinking of silverware from a café behind me, a soft blur of eighty different conversations seeming all to coalesce into one general murmur. There are more attractive people here than I've seen in all of Baltimore. Everything is prickling and excited. It feels right.

I am—my eyes sharpened and walking down the urban runway—cool.

Broadway Market is packed. All the diner stools are fitted with the backs of men and women, chatting amongst each other at almost a scream to best the chaotic sound of business. The Market is an open air series of restaurants and bars and novelty shops, the dinging of a diner bell on one side mingling with the cash register of the general store on the other. I smell a not unpleasant parade of hamburgers, raw fish, andouille, cotton candy, and Old Bay. I wade through the tight crowd to the general store, bumping several people as I slink by. They seem not to mind, and I don't either. It's all wonderfully dizzy here, and I can move undetected while watching it all happen. It's how I imagine New York will be, except there it'll be everywhere, in the subway, on the sidewalks, the alleyways, everywhere.

The water is cold and overstates my shivering. I didn't wear the coat. It's too bulky and makes me look inflated, so I took it off just as I walked out of the house. I could sit in the Market and watch the lemonade stand from the window, but there's not really a place to loiter in here, and I might miss Jude amidst the mass of people scurrying around the square. I decide to just suffer it outside.

"Peter?"

I blink and turn. Jude is looking blank at me, expectant. His recent shower smells of lemon soap and grape shampoo. Everything inside me speeds.

"Hey." I can't tell if I actually say it or think it. Jude doesn't seem to notice one way or the other.

"Sorry I'm late. I had to run errands with my Mom." He rolls his eyes. I join in, but not genuinely. Some of my favorite memories are running errands with Ma, us singing along to her cheesy hair-metal bands at full blast in the truck.

I push forward into the moving crowd. Jude follows. Jude. He's here now, walking behind me, his feet occasionally stepping on my heels, me looking back, him grinning. Somehow it's cinematic, this small moment.

The Cat's Eye looks like Benny's, only without the rainbows and cruisy eyes. The air is shabby, heavy wood tables and chairs lining the walls. Towards the center is a small dance floor, currently set as a music stage. The crowd, mostly teenagers and college students, are jovial and chatting eagerly, all facing the direction of the dance floor/stage while they lift huge mugs of beer to their lips. It's a lot friendlier looking than Benny's, and I assume it's because of the age difference and the fact that there are girls. I hear their high pitched giggling. There is a folding chalkboard that announces three bands playing tonight: The Miscreant Angels, Cellophane Pain, and Gleek. I look back at Jude, displaying the lineup a la Vanna White. He's wearing all black, accentuating his pale and skinny limbs. The eye makeup is noticeably darker, clumpy underneath his bottom lashes. Mascara residue speckles his upper lids and the liner is drawn out in subtle points on either side. It looks a little silly, but I can't help but notice that even in the darkness, the wolf-like quality of his eyes penetrates three-dimensional space, electrifies the air, makes my mouth hang open. He feigns worry and eeks his mouth into a look of distress. I smile wide and try to look cute by bringing my index finger to my lips in a pose of wonder. We walk to one of the few open tables and sit.

"How good could a band called Gleek be?" he says.

"About as good as one called Miscreant Angels." He doesn't have his glasses on. Did he take them off for me? Does he not know I love him with his glasses on? Of course not.

"Yeah, but Cellophane Pain has a nice ring to it. Sounds Goth."

I hope to God it isn't but say, "We have hope."

He's about to say something, but just as he opens his mouth, the bar squeals with feedback and a voice. A lanky guy in his twenties, floppy straw hair and a wirey goatee, who looks like he stepped out of a Seattle grunge band photoshoot, barks jittery at the audience and makes a few official blurbies. He quickly introduces the first band as, much to my disenchantment, Gleek. Jude reassures me with a mocking thumbs up.

Gobs of black hair dye, glinting sweat from remarkably dense and renegade armpit hair, and faces hidden in twisted expression and smeared makeup. Lots of tongue activity. This is Gleek.

They are worse than I anticipate. I can't even make out individual chords in the guitar riffs, and the singer garbles like he's holding down the urge to vomit while repetitively mouthing lines like "you need to eat my shit to love me." I hope he is being figurative. I look at Jude, who is listening with amazingly straight posture. Occasionally, he looks over, making a face and smiling, but continues to watch. I try to concentrate on the performance, but he is sitting slightly in front of me, and I can't help but caress his profile. He has a man's nose, deliberate and straight. His bottom lip is larger, the upper curving at the sides. From this vantage it looks like he's pouting. I just want to grab his face and eat it. As if on cue, he looks back quickly and repeats the look and my whole body flushes and blood floods to my dick. He doesn't notice and swings back to the noise. He starts nodding his head to the drummer's seizures. I worry that the singer's thrashing strands of hair will slap me across the face with flailing perspiration, so I lean back in my chair, resting my back on the wall, now feeling the inconsistent beat in my head as well as hearing it.

I bet Jude would look really good if he cut his hair. It falls a little too limp to really be pretty, though it does look good when he tucks it behind his ears. I also imagine it wouldn't look too bad mopping sweat

off my naked chest. Just as I'm picturing him snacking on my nipples
with his lips, he shoots a glance back again. Startled, leaning back, fearing the visibility of my hard-on, I jerk, and the next thing I know I'm
splayed on the sticky floor, under the table, my legs sticking straight up. It
takes me a second. With what I imagine to be the most ridiculous face of
dumbfounded-ness possible, I turn to see if Jude sees me. He is laughing
hysterically, already reaching his hand down to help me up.

"Are you all right, man?"

"The music rocked me out of my seat." I look down to make sure there
are no remnants of my excitement as Jude pulls me up. His hand is bony
and warm. People around us are chuckling, some of the girls shaping
their mouths in the "O" of staged concern. I'm sure my face is red, but I
laugh along and direct my gaze back to the glorious gutterings of Gleek,
hoping all others will do the same. It takes forever for the heat to leave
my face. I keep staring in the direction of the band, pretending to listen,
but not even absorbing the music enough to cringe. I hardly notice when
they finish their set.

"You want to stay for the other bands?" Jude says with wide eyes.
For a moment I fear he wants to end the night early, but I can tell he's
scheming something.

"What, and miss Cellophane Pain? Of course I want to go."

He grins, a child-like naughtiness, his teeth barely peeking out from
a broad line of lip. "I got something waiting for us in the car. You up for
it?"

Dozens of possibilities present themselves, and I like them all.

"Sure," I say.

The night air hits fierce, and I wish now I had brought my coat.

He says, "The car's not too far. Just around the corner."

The Point is still streaming with people. Their black streaks are desperate against the orangey glow of streetlight. I can tell a lot of them have
sex on the mind. Their eyes are trying too hard to be seductive. Yet, most
of the men have a victorious and cautious hand on the small of a back,
steering strapless girls through the crowd while they glance back with a

counterfeit face. Away they go, being ushered to their next meaningless sexual experience. Fishing on the bay appears plentiful this time of year.

Jude's car is a boxy station wagon, chipped gray, dents refracting the night light. His identity is only stamped on the back window, bumper stickers informing other drivers that he listens to Black Flag, NOFX, and believes in a fish with legs.

"Get in," he says.

The car smells stuffy, so many odors dominated by fast food grease. A pair of air fresheners hang limp as if ashamed of their blatant failure. I adjust the springy seat to give me a little support while Jude stretches over his own, fishing through the flotsam in the back. I try to catch a quick peek of his flesh under the scrunched up shirt, but it's too dark. I've seen his naked stomach before in the locker room when we had gym together, but that's not the same—and since his father's death, he somehow got out of gym the rest of the year. Something about seeing skin when it's not supposed to be seen arouses me a lot more. I've caught myself many times trying to look through the armholes of a guy's shirt in malls or restaurants, and when they raise their arm just so to pass the salt or pay a sales clerk, in that brief moment you see what shouldn't be seen, and they don't know I've seen it. It's even more intense in the summer when they're wearing cut-off khaki shorts and I can view the blanch of their briefs pressing into their pale inner thigh. Sometimes, on rare days, they don't even have underwear on. *Fuck.*

He reemerges with the grin of a game show host. I can almost hear the sparkle in his teeth. In one victorious hand boasts a large bottle, what looks to be reddish. The mischief in his eyes tells me it's alcoholic. He reinforces the identity of the contents by gloriously announcing its name the way a 49er must have announced a golden glint in his sifter. "Mad Dog, 20/20." He unscrews the top and takes a swig, his face only slightly cringing. He thrusts it out to me. I hesitate. "I don't have any cups," he says, and pushes it further into my face.

"Not very sophisticated, are we?" I say, grab it and bring it to my lips. It tastes like fizzy, sugary, cherry-flavored nasty. I swig again to cover up my surprised prune-face and quickly pass it back.

"Oh, a double-hitter, *are we*?" The cockeyed cockney again. He swallows a huge gulp, and "aahhs" with mocking robustness. "It's not too bad. Better than beer."

"Yeah," I say, and take it back.

We don't say anything for a few more rounds, just drinking, almost competing for who can down the most in the shortest time. I hold my own. I'm already feeling a little swirly. I catch myself in the side mirror—round face, broad-ish nose, fleshy, skinny, young. The bad mix of my parents, I guess. I always turn away before I get too ugly.

"That band sucked. What was their name?" he asks.

"Gleek."

He grins around the rim of the bottle, and tips it back, his neck long and exposed. I shift to accommodate the hard-on.

"You know, though, I don't mind seeing shitty bands. I mean, at least they're doing something they really love, you know?" His arm is splayed over the back of my seat, and I can feel the barely heat of his skin, soft on my left ear.

I pass the half-empty bottle. "Is that what you want to do?"

"Be a rock star? Doesn't everybody?"

The Mad Dog makes me feel more confident. There's less time between thought and speak. "Not really. I don't play anything."

Jude kind of snorts, "Neither do I!" He looks at me, his mouth filled with laughter. When I meet his eyes and grin back at him, he releases it. His eyes look watery, making the gray almost float separately from the white. I understand the reference now to "eyes swimming." It's nice. I wonder if mine are doing that. He continues, "But I want to. I'm getting a guitar for my birthday, this year, I think. Gonna start playing."

"What kind of band?" Goth, I figure.

He laughs with a little embarrassment, his cheeks creasing into devastatingly cute dimples. "No. No, I can't tell you."

"Why not?"

He swallows more Mad Dog and hands it to me. I tense up just a little, but his smile is benign and I take the bottle with playful deprecation. I sip. I can feel his eyes on me, regarding me, while I busy myself with the bottle. I feel a little queasy, but warm.

"What about you?" His eyes are sincere, soft on me. His head tilts back on his extended arm, the one that almost touches me. More than anything else in the world at this moment I want to answer his question. I want to tell him everything. I want to answer anything he wants to know.

"What *about* me?"

He is patient. "What do you want to do, you know, when you grow up? The whole career thing."

I have answered the question before, with the circling adults in my family and Ma's acquaintances asking what I know to be a disinterested requisite, but it's always been a *surgeon*, a *congressman*, an *astrophysicist*, a *Harvard professor*. Nothing that I truly want. Jude's eyes are light, and sponge me.

"Well, I've thought seriously about sword dancing on a Tasmanian cruise ship."

He doesn't laugh.

"I don't know. Well, I'm not sure. I mean, something. I don't know."

"No way!" he says, "You're, like, the brainiac!" His face is getting louder and looser. "You're supposed to have it all planned out, right? That's what smart people do."

"*You're* smart."

"But not like *you* smart." He breaks order and takes another drink.

"That's not true, Jude."

"Come on," he says, "I'm sure you've thought about it at least once. Like, what is your dream, what do you dream about?"

I like alcohol. It gives you license to do things you normally couldn't do. I mean, the fact that I can rest my eyes on him and it not freak him out makes me want to be drunk every school-day for the rest of the semester.

"I dream about getting out of St. Mary's, out of my house, and out of fucking Baltimore."

Look at me, Jude. See my intensity, see my anger. I am wounded. Licking wounds is a munificent gesture, preferably the ones on my back. Tongue slowly.

He looks down at his lap. "You hate it here that much?"

I inch a little closer to him, and pick his head up with my pleading. "Don't you?"

"Well…" He looks down again. I take the bottle from him and drink, my eyes never leaving him. I feel I know what he's going to say. I just feel so confident and connected.

He begins to laugh, a little soft at first, but it grows and fills the car.

"You know, really, I fucking hate it. I fucking hate school. God." His laughing shrills into a cackle as he lifts his head and looks out the windshield as if reading a freshly printed *Baltimore Sun* headline.

I feel like I've won something, and laugh along with him.

I yell over the laughter, "It's my mother. She's so…" I cup my hands in a strangle hold. "Aaaahhhh!"

Jude still laughing. "She's that awesome, huh?"

"I love her, actually. She's just…okay, once when I was…twelve, we went to my cousin Billy's wedding. There was a fountain of champagne trickling from the center of the reception hall, right? Ma started drinking from it, and I got upset because, you know those people that come to your classroom and tell you all the bad things that happen and car accidents and it's the path to ultimate failure? Anyway, when I tell her that drinking is bad, she says *really, and how do you know all this?* I told her I had learned it at school, and she asks me *how do I know it's true*, and I said, *you know, cause the teacher said so.* And, see, Ma is so argumentative, so I thought I had actually beat her, you know?

"And then she says *So, I could say the sky was green. Would you believe me?* And the whole time she has this champagne flute in her fingers, God. Well, of course I say no and she asks *why not?* and I tell her I could look outside and check. *Yeah?* she says. *Yeah,* I say.

"Then, she takes her glass and swallows the whole flute in one gulp and hands it to me and tells me to go get two glasses. So, I get them, hand them to her, and she gives me one back and says *cheers* in this all-sinister voice. See, she makes me drink it! Oh, but that's not all. Of course I'm saying no but she gives me this look she has, this stern look, God, and says with this little bratty smirk, *we're finding out if the sky is green.*

"Anyway, I had to, and you know how nasty that stuff is when you're twelve. Well, she made me drink another, and then another. She made me do it three times, but I can't even remember because I was, like, swaying everywhere. And by the end of it, all I can remember is sitting on this barstool next to her, singing 'Chapel of Love' to the bartender. And I threw up on the way home. See, that's my mom."

"What do you mean? That's awesome!"

I open my mouth, close it, and say, "Yeah, I guess so. It can be. She just drives me crazy."

"Moms do that, especially when you're an only child. No one else for them to be motherly with and shit." Jude laughs and pulls on the bottle.

Jude didn't know me before Joby ran away. Such a far-away place in my mind that I remember like a movie playing on a really small TV. I cried so much when he left, I remember that. I searched for him afterward, for weeks, months, through the streets, on the internet. He disappeared, no phone calls, no emails, no contact. I didn't know what happened, it was all mystery. And it didn't make sense. I mean, Joby wasn't an angel. He got into trouble all the time, stealing shit, selling pot. But he was my big brother, and we knew each other. When my father and Ma were fighting, it was me and Joby in the bedroom playing cards. And then when Isaac and Ma were fighting, it was me and Joby walking together in the neighborhood, plotting our exodus together. We were going to drive to New York City in the middle of the night, rent a really dirty warehouse, like in some movie about the urban underbelly. He'd get a job and I'd go to school, and we'd climb to the top of the Statue of Liberty, pull our pants down and moon the city. Yeah, they were just fantasies to make us feel better, but we shared them. He never threatened to leave, and he never threatened to leave without me. And then he did, and was gone. He didn't sit me down and tell me; there was no final moment between us, nothing. He didn't say goodbye. And I looked everywhere for him. For months I ran after him, to find him, bring him back.

And then, we found out he was dead. I cried so much when he ran away, but I didn't cry at all at his funeral. In my mind, he had already left me, was already far gone, and I didn't want to keep crying for someone who didn't even turn around and say goodbye. Joby has become a small hard pit of a thought.

I *am* an only child. But I say nothing to Jude either way.

"Your mom is kind of hot, Peter. A lot of the guys think so," he says laughing.

I've heard this before. Whenever Ma is seen dropping me off, or one of them sees me out with her at the grocery store, there's always a trail of comments the following hours, days. But only from the assholes do I expect such crap.

"Not you, too," I say.

"Oh, don't worry, man. I'm not obsessed with her or anything. Jimmy is, for sure. I just think she's attractive for an older woman, you know? You can't deny she's good looking."

"You say she's attractive, but are you attracted to her?" I ask.

"Oh, God no," he says quickly. He answers a little too quickly, like maybe he doesn't find women attractive, like at all. My leg twitches. He takes another gulp, missing the rim a little and spills down his shirt. He doesn't notice. The bottle is almost empty.

"I'm just saying your mom seems cool, Peter. My mom is the exact opposite. She watches my every move, and has something to say about every fucking one of them."

He dresses his voice in what resembles the evil witch in *The Wizard of Oz*. "Jude, where are you going? Don't you have homework to do? Jude, get off the phone. Why are you always on the phone?" I laugh, and he keeps rolling, "Jude, why don't you do your chores? Why are you so lazy? Are you ever going to give the dog a bath? If your father was here you wouldn't be acting like this."

His eyes dim a little, as if he is surprised by his own last words, as if they escaped without his permission. But he says it. I don't know if it's appropriate, but the Mad Dog surely makes me brave, and I jump at the opportunity after a crossing of silence.

"What happened?"

While Jude was on exemption after his father died, I asked everyone about it. I was obsessed and relentless, and yet no one told me. Jude didn't tell Tony or Jimmy. All of the faculty would say they didn't know, even Principal Dell, who had to know. He had to. They would say there was an accident, there was a family emergency. Not even Brother Thomas would tell me. Instead, he said, "Information presents itself with clarity only after it becomes a part of history. Only then can we make sense of it. Only then should it be told." It sounded like a quote from one of his textbooks.

I search hard in Jude's face. It's quiet. I didn't want to upset him, but I can't let go of my curiosity. He doesn't move, his face nodded in front of the bottle, staring at nothing. I've stepped over a boundary, I'm sure of it, and now I've ruined the whole night because of how much I royally suck, and I know why I have no friends. I've ruined it with him. Words do this to me. I drop my own head.

"I haven't had to answer that," he says.

I'm not sure what that means, and keep from meeting his eyes. I wait for him to order me out of the car and never talk to him again. I imagine slowly obliging, my pathetic face chapping against the night on my lonely walk home, climbing up to my bedroom and finally smothering myself with the hamburger pillow I made in eighth grade Home Ec.

"I'm sorry, Jude."

There is a long pause. I should quietly let myself out to save him the energy of screaming obscenities. I've exhausted him silent.

"No. Nah. That's why I like you. You say what's on your mind." His voice is deeper, the sound sliding around his face. "It's weird. No one's asked me yet."

"Maybe cause they're trying to be cool, you know?" I sound like anything but.

"It's cool." He stares at the dashboard. "He killed himself."

I almost spit out an incredulous *What!?* but nipped it with my teeth and slung it back down my throat.

"It's cool," he says again.

I don't want to say sorry. You see that in every movie on TV. I'm more original than that.

"How'd he do it?"

His head stays down, the hair curtained around his face. I wait for him to hate me. Everything seems to be moving too slow.

He nods up and meets my eyes.

"Pills. He ate a bunch of 'em after work and spent the night in his car behind the office. They found him the next morning. Choked on his own vomit." He rubs his hands together for warmth.

I smell the wet yeast of his breath, feel the feathered kiss of exhaled air, he's so close. His eyes are brilliant with speckled variations of gray glittering in his head, his cheeks both hard and soft, lips like thin lines of candle wax. He is the most beautiful thing I have ever seen. I can't even hold myself together. I want to lay my hands on his pain and have it circulate through me, like a Van de Graaf generator, not to take it away from him, but to feel it, feel it run through me and have me stand on end, to push out of me, everything pushing out of me, everything but him.

He notices the forgotten bottle of Mad Dog, grabs it, and puts it to his lips.

The reveal of pain, with the glow of neon beer lights, inside a piece-of-shit station-wagon. Fuck, Jude Woolsey, I'm so in love with you.

11

Ruth

Today is Joby's birthday, and I want to bring flowers to his grave. His favorite color was red, so I get whatever I can at the Shoppers Food Warehouse—red and white carnations.

I know he won't come with me, but I knock on Peter's door, anyway.

"What, Ma?" I can tell he's laying on his bed, though his door is closed.

"Last chance. It won't take too long."

He doesn't say nothing. I wait just a bit, lay my head on the door a little. Peter's now almost as old as Joby was when he died.

"Alrighty. I thought I'd try just one more time. You're gonna someday want to go, Peter."

Nothing. Well, then. I can't press it. He thinks he has his reasons. Men think they have reasons for their silences. That's what I have to tell myself, at least.

The cemetery is a big flat green square in Anne Arundel County, not too far south. The morning is cold and gray, and there's not much of anyone around. The carnations look real nice in the wrapper.

I can always pick out Joby's grave because I stuck a pinwheel in the ground that spins the colors of the rainbow. It still stands up, even since Valentine's Day, last time I was here. I walk over to the pinwheel, to Joby. Most of the graves have flowers on them. One is empty, though, two spots down. I pull out one of the carnations and place it on the headstone.

Joby Sean Ewing

I hadn't changed the boys' names back to Cryer before Joby ran away. And, it didn't matter much what was on the gravestone. Abe was so upset. I thought it hurt nothing for Joby to keep his name. If Abe ever wanted to visit him here in the cemetery, he would see his name. It might remind the man that he had two sons, that he had a family once. Maybe it would do him some good.

"Hi, Joby." I lay the flowers down. "Happy birthday."

I know it's not like he hears me, but somehow it makes me feel good to say things out loud to him, here. Maybe not as much for him as for me. Who knows?

"Peter says hi," I lie. It doesn't seem like a bad one to tell. Joby would believe it. When they were kids, Peter thought the world of his big brother. Went around dressing like him, talking like him. Tried to play the same sports, though that didn't work out too well. Peter never did have a thing for baseball. He played OK, but he just couldn't commit himself to practice. Joby, though? He loved practice, hardly ever missed one. Made friends with the other boys, and was a natural at the game. The worst thing I ever did was take him out of baseball. When me and Abe split, I just couldn't afford it. Damn, if I don't wish every day I'd figured out some way. How different would things have been?

"Peter's working, getting good grades. He's doing good."

The wind picks up a bit, and the pinwheel is a bunch of color swirling around. I'll pretend that Joby's trying to tell me something.

"I'm proud of him, too."

I sit for a while in the grass, pull the weeds around his headstone. It's nice to sit in silence and talk to him without it turning into the yelling it always became those last couple of years. The quiet time is nice. At first you think cemeteries are going to be creepy, but it's nice here. There's not so much raucous. I must say, it's the most peace I've felt in days.

When I feel the rain starting to come down, I get up, place the flowers a little closer to where my son's chest would be, and run to the truck before I get wet.

*

Rain makes the road glossy on my way to Sarah's in Dundalk. I don't like taking the direct route along the Key Bridge, it's so high, so I go through town and around. Peter gets mad at me taking the extra time, giving me an earful about fear and all, but I'm not the one who's gonna drive off the bridge by accident. All it takes is sneezing hard and jerking the steering wheel, or blowing a tire. Instead, I cross over the drawbridge grates of the Hanover Street Bridge, very low to the water, thank you very much, the factories jutting out on one side, the Locke building, the Baltimore Sun warehouse, and the marsh on the other. Sometimes I'll see a heron standing straight up in the water, white as clean snow, one leg up, beer cans floating around the dainty, lady-like bird, soggy boxes, plastic bobbing like buoys, and I think why in the hell that thing would want to be here, of all places. Why doesn't it use its wings and move to something just a little less god-forsaken?

If I came across Joby again, in the next life or whatever, what would I say to him, what would I allow him to see? The hurt inside my guts, or the thing that makes a good mother, the open arms?

If I was better woman, it would be the good mother one. I still got something to prove. But man, would I like to peel back my skin and show him what he did—look what you did to me, Joby. Look at all the black where pink should be. Parents take on all that load, but what about their children, who have just as much life in them, just as much secret, just as much piss and vinegar? No one can tell me any different. We feel their sting. Can't we be all human with our children? How is a mother different from a woman, anyway?

Every time I turn this corner, in front of the old rowhouse in Cherry Hill, I say good-bye to him, the two words pulling a happiness out of me, "*I am.*" In Hell, he meant, and turned around and disappeared. He said he was in Hell because of me, and then he walked out, and I never saw him again until he was in the coffin.

And I knew it. That night. It was that look he gave me, so sure of himself, of his hate for me. For what? For the times I right smacked him for talking back? For being with Isaac? For telling him to go to Hell? I was angry, Joby. You were stealing and then yelling at me, like I was to blame. You stole from Isaac, and he was so angry and already getting crazy, and I was afraid he would hurt you more than he already had, and I wanted you to stop fighting, but you kept at it. I lost my temper. I said *Go to Hell*. I did. I didn't think you'd believe me. And the way you said *I am*, like it was the last thing you'd ever say, with that look of pure mean that men will only get with a woman. I knew you were gone for good.

When I'm back in Cherry Hill, I can't roll down the street without seeing him, walking the sidewalk, disappearing into our old rowhouse. I see him flash in and out—a turn of neck, unlaced oversized sneakers scraping the sidewalk, a swing of an arm, a finger rubbing a snotty nose—he's in all these things just for a moment, and then vanishes, and none of them add up to make a whole Joby, either. I wish they did.

I can't fully see what he would look like now, if there was a now for him. A man. Would he take after Abe, dark and soft, gaining a little belly in the front, his sides spreading just enough to look funny in khaki pants? No, Joby was mean and lean, and even though he was still sprouting up the last I saw him, it looked like it would stay that way, at least for a while. All he had from his father was color, much darker than Peter. Would he still be wearing the huge white t-shirts that went to his knees, black jeans around his thighs, how he held them up I haven't the slightest? Would he shave his head out of spite for me? His hair was so black and shiny, the Black and Cherokee together, but he said he looked like a pimp if I made him grow it out, or like a sissy boy, like Peter. God, I smacked him for that.

Maybe some pretty girl could have come along and made him forget why he shaved his head, and urged him to grow it out for her. Would he have actually used his smooth talk to make a small fortune for himself, some kind of grown-up version of the schemes he cooked up when he was a little thing? Would he have been living in a house on the water, or a brownstone in Philly, with the pretty girl who made him grow his hair out? All these things could have been.

The grown-up Joby would have obsessed about doing things on his own, his way, that's for sure. Let's say he buys the house, with the young pretty girl (who is not too pretty so he's not worried about her leaving) but he insists on picking the colors for the rooms. She suggests certain kinds of furniture and all, and he even tells her that she can choose, but in the end it is the living room suite that he wanted all along, in his colors. He sees the idea on a home improvement show, and that is the end of the negotiation. He stops only when he has one just like it. The pretty but not too pretty girl will need some patience, or just ignore it for fear of losing him. Lots of girls are like that. They look at their bodies and give up before they've even had the chance to begin. Every day is a day older, and they become a little bit less than whatever they think they were.

If he was still alive and I ever did see him, it would be sudden, that's how it would go down. I would be running to the truck, rain coming down hard, bags of groceries wound around me rushing to somewhere, and he would be there, his white shirt sticking to his dark chest, standing there, staring at me until I kept going my own way, not moving until he knew the sidewalk was only his again. I would have to be in the safety of my truck, looking at him through blurry windows, taking in as much as I could. He would linger, knowing it would haunt me, then disappear all satisfied, around the corner and into my dreams. He always fought for the last impression. He always fought.

My jaw hurts, my nails bitten, chewing myself up like madness, just in the thinking of him. I get to the blood and taste the metal in it.

There's some goodness in all this, to imagine seeing him in such a quick moment, especially seeing him through the windshield, the clear barrier that it is, putting us out in the open and all the while protecting me, or him, both of us. I can handle your face from the windshield, Joby. I can handle you best from behind glass.

*

I get home just in time to find Mrs. Gabriel returning home, too. She is decked out in that very fancy outfit that comes right out of one of those black and white glamour movies that plays on the TV most Sundays. Her face almost disappears behind a big feathery hat and a wrap that I reckon is real fur. She wears those stockings that have that line going up the back of the leg. It looks like a costume, but it's very fancy. I wonder where she goes looking like this. Church? Out for a fine lunch at one of the seafood spots in the Inner Harbor? One morning every week or so she'll gussy herself up and go out, coming home just before supper. She never brings anyone back, and no one picks her up. She'll come home, change back into her apron, and start cooking like she always does.

I never ask her questions, but not like I don't want to. I figure she'd tell me if it was something she wanted to talk about. Peter and I have stood at the window on the days she comes in and tried to figure it out, like the Guess Who? game. We have ideas. I say she's visiting her late husband's grave and wants to look good for him, just the way he loved her most. Peter rolls his eyes and calls me a romantic. He says that she's part of an elite society of dames that secretly run the whole government, and that inside the fur are blueprints of an underground city being built as a shelter for the upcoming nuclear something-or-other. I snort and we giggle. It was becoming ritual for us to watch Mrs. Gabriel in her get-up, but lately it's only me around.

But not today. Peter's in good spirits. He yells out *Hey, Ma* when he sees me. That suits me fine, cause it seemed for a while there we'd never be in the same mood at the same time, let alone the same place. His face is tilted up and bright and open, like he just won a trip to Heaven. He's wearing jeans and a t-shirt that I have no clue why he keeps it's so small, makes him look even skinnier.

"I got some chicken from that KFC down on Ritchie Highway near the cemetery. Might be a little cold now from the drive. I could heat it up, but you know how it does in the nuker. Remember when I tried that one time to cook a whole bird in that damned thing for Thanksgiving? Coulda killed someone with it, hard as it was."

"Good. I'm starving." He drops his butt down in the chair, hand already grabbing a drumstick.

I slip a plate under him. "What's the weekend looking like for you?"

"Oh, you know." His teeth rip half the leg off.

"Well, I dropped off some nice flowers on your brother's grave. It's nice out there, just to sit with him, you know? I arranged them so that they looked better than all his neighbors."

"Good job," his mouth full of meat. I bet he doesn't even hear me, or he's doing that pretend thing he does whenever I mention Joby. It can't be good for him to do this, and I want to say something, but it's tough because he gives me no way to really talk about it without it becoming a big deal, something that upsets me, him, both of us. So, I drop it.

"I just saw Mrs. Gabriel. She was in her movie-star getup."

"Oh, she was?!" Peter picks his neck up from the chicken, leans like he can look straight out the kitchen window into our neighbor's rowhouse. "Was she coming or going?"

"Coming. Do you think it's time we ask her, see who's closer to the truth?" I pick through the day's mail—coupons and junk mail and bills past due—and see a letter from Towson State University. My heart leaps.

"That might kill the mystery," he says. "Let's follow her, see where she goes. We've been saying this for months. We should just do it. *Reconnoiter*."

"Did you make that word up?" I try to hide my excitement, and drop it in front of him. "This came for you."

I put my elbows on the table and rest my chin on my hands, grinning like a fool.

He looks down, already working on the second bite, and grunts with no interest, goes back to the chicken.

"What? It could be a yes letter. Isn't it time for that sort of thing? Even a scholarship, maybe."

He keeps eating.

"Aren't you going to open it?"

"Yeah." Most of the chicken is gone and he starts nibbling on the in-between places.

I keep looking at him. He scrapes his thumbs with his front teeth.

"Peter, what are you waiting for? The price of oil to go down?"

"OK, Ma." He grins at me. "You're more excited than I am." He wipes his hands on his jeans—I don't say anything—and reaches for the envelope, rips it open like a crabshell, pulls out the letter.

"It's two pages. Isn't that good?" I'm tapping my nails. "It doesn't take more than one page to say 'no' now, does it? Don't look at me like I'm sprouting whiskers. Oh, just read it, will ya!"

He grins, and lowers his eyes. I hate waiting and he knows it, and that's why it's taking him for goddamned ever.

"I got in," he says. "It looks like full tuition."

My hands jump up and clap. "Oh, Peter! That's great!"

He shrugs, says "I guess," and reaches in the bucket for a thigh. "It's not the one I want."

Of all the places Peter applied, Towson was the only one in Maryland. "Aunt Ginny's grandson went there, and you know how smart he is."

"Seamus? I wouldn't say he's smart." The way he says smart makes it sound like some dirty disease.

"Peter." I watch him keep eating, as if he already forgot about the letter. My arms can't rest anywhere, so I pick up a piece of chicken to keep them busy. It's lukewarm and greasy. "What's wrong with Towson?"

"Nothing. But it's not the best school. I mean, it's nothing like Columbia or Sarah Lawrence. You know it doesn't even make the second tier in the *World Report*? And it has ten thousand students. Big."

I bite into the sticky breast, wanting to bite down until I chip my teeth. I want to tear the chicken up into shreds and throw it up to the ceiling. It'd probably stick. I chew hard. I don't even notice what the shit tastes like. For Christ's sake. "Why the hell did you apply there if you knew you didn't like it?"

He drops his hands from his face and cocks his head. "What's wrong with you?"

"Nothing. It's just I don't understand why you apply to a college you don't even want to go to, is all. That's paperwork for those teachers, and you're wasting their time."

He laughs. "First of all, Ma, the admissions office does all the work, not the teachers. And I applied because they waived the application fee. It was my fallback."

"Your what?"

"You know, just in case no one else took me."

I say his name, hearing the frustration in my voice, and stop. I bite into my chicken again and chew, staring at the bucket between us, the Colonel smiling like an asshole, feeling Peter's eyes on me. I keep eating.

"What? What, Ma?"

Ever since he started telling me his college lists, his narrowed list, his final list, I get a clenching in my face. One in Maryland, and all the others a million miles away. I wish he would stop looking at me and just eat his damn chicken. But he doesn't.

I drop the breast with a clink of an exposed bone on my plate and look at him. I shouldn't have hesitated.

"I don't see why you feel the need to go so far away for school. What, does it stink around here? What's so bad about Baltimore?" The question feels weak, cause I could come up with a million things, myself. No trees, no fields, no horses. Daddy asked the same thing when he told us about the job at Kennicott after losing the farm. We were all crying, even Mama. "At least there are Catholics there," he said, offering his hands up like they held the proof he was making a lick of sense.

Peter knows how I feel and yet he still looks far off. I'm afraid of what he might say and him saying what he might say could change things in a way I don't know how. The world might just tilt up on its ass, and knowing that twists up my gut. Why did I ever think this goddamn chicken would taste good? It chews like some Crisco forgotten in the freezer.

When I can muster the gumption I look at him. He has softened up, with a real knowing look at me. I know he loves me, and even that hurts. I hate how he just carries my heart whenever he damn well feels like it.

"Ma. It's not… It's… I've never been anywhere else, you know?" His voice is tender and warm. Under other circumstances I'd welcome it. But he's softening a hurt, no matter how much it's me or something else.

"You've been places," I say. "You went to Philly last year for that school field trip. And we went to Virginia Beach when you were little." I hear how puny I sound and wonder why I even say anything.

"Yeah, but I want to *be* someplace different. I want to get to know a whole new place, like New York. Don't you think that's exciting?" His face was bright and in the moment, like he was speaking to himself. Abe would get the same kind of excited when he talked of opening a restaurant or, when I was pregnant with Joby, what kind of father he would be, his nostrils flaring and his wild eyebrows. And what happened with any of that, as much as I loved watching it? I could tell Peter was playing the fantasy in front of him. Full of fantasy, these men. It does sound exciting when they talk like this, but if they put that kind of umph more into what was in front of them than what was far away, we'd all get somewhere.

But I can't lose the feeling that there is more to it. I wanted to leave home when I was young, too, but I had to. I was pregnant, and Abe proposed right after, and Mama suffocated me, and I couldn't have stayed without going crazy. I pick up my plate and walk over to the sink and rinse it off. It feels better over here, so I run the water and start washing the few dishes left from this morning. The Dawn doesn't really smell lemony fresh. I wash slow. My fingers are looking bony these days. I gotta buy some hand cream. There was a coupon in the Pennysaver I could use.

I hear Peter get up behind me. There's more to say, but it feels dangerous, I know it. He knows it, too. And there's not going to be any sorry between us. He's slow to give me his plate, which I take without making eye contact, trying not to give myself away. He stands there a little longer than he needs to, but I keep washing. I don't want to talk anymore. It's all dangerous right now.

He shuffles around the table, doing what sounds like nothing. I turn the spigot off and wipe around the sink. I'm a good housekeeper when I can't talk. After there's nothing left to do without looking ridiculous I rip off a paper towel and dry my hands. I wish he would leave and let me be, even though I don't want to be alone.

But then I turn and he says, "I'm gonna get going, Ma," and I get that cold, sinking feeling. My first thought is that he's going off to college this second, stuffing all his things into a duffel bag and setting off for the University of God Knows Where, to start a completely new life where I'll only see him after he's changed so much I can't even recognize him. He'll probably pierce his ears and wear different clothes and all.

"Where you going?"

"Remember? Jude and I are going to the Point."

"Again?"

"Yeah."

"Why? There's nothing to do there at night but go to bars."

"We're going to hear some music. I told you, remember?"

"Peter, it gets pretty dangerous along there at night."

He looks at me with lowered eyes, the look he got from me, pushing out his pillowy lips, which he got from Abe. "Really? Of all the places in this town?"

"I was thinking we could play a game of Yahtzee or rent a movie or something. You know, celebrate."

"Ma-a."

I feel small and stiff, like when you walk out into a parking lot and think your car's been stolen.

"Don't be out too late, Peter."

He rushes toward me, kisses my cheek in a hurry and turns. "Be home soon."

I watch him close the front door behind him from the kitchen. The air is kind of scary it's so quiet. Even after his body is out of sight I keep staring. The night is really dark, as if all the lights have gone out in the neighborhood. I didn't tell him about the relocation notice, that we'll have to move soon. And then it dawns on me that I won't even need a place for the two of us before long. Peter's going to college, somewhere far from here. In a few months, I'll be looking only for me.

The light from the kitchen starts flickering against the living room wall like it wants to blow. I watch my shadow come and go, spread across the whole wall, disappear, then come back again. I don't know if I have a fresh bulb lying around, and just as I think to look in the basement for one, the light dies.

I call Sarah. "Hey, girl, what you doing?" I try to keep the crying out of my voice. "Can I come over?"

II

The Crust and Sugar Over

Prelude

March

The quietness at the corner of Ellwood and Fairmount felt more like a hush, as if there were stifled whispers behind the facades of the run-down rowhouses that lined the street like a partition of weathered faces—windowless holes in formstone the sockets of eyes blackened by some dark arts priestess—as if there was something to say, but no one dared, even in the open wide light of midday. No pedestrians, no cars, not even a stray dog rifling through the clumps of trash piling in the gutters. And yet, a promise of sound came from somewhere.

MacAllister heard nothing other than the pounding blood in his own head; imminence. The biggest project of his career, one of the biggest in Baltimore history, was about to commence. He knew the bulldozers and hydraulic excavator would be here any minute, to begin the demolition. The first target, a trio of abandoned post-WWI rowhouses declared unfit for restoration by a hand-shaking city council, flanked on one side by a shuttered A&Z convenience store, an alley on the other, and sold to MacAllister by the city for a thousand dollars each.

This beginning was modest, a rather insignificant half-block of the sixty-four planned for demolition, but MacAllister's fingers twitched at the possibility. All projects begin somewhere—a little here, a little more, and then the landscape is transformed. He could picture the fencing edged along the street in this very spot by this time next year, the elevated train peeking above, circling families around the park's perimeter. MacAllister knew the elevations so well; he was currently looking at the back of one of the restaurant complexes, the one that will serve crab bisque in a bread bowl with a handful of hush puppies dipped in honey butter, crabbie mac and cheese, and fried bay shrimp.

This block was relatively easy. Over half of the dwellings were already empty, and it was quick to declare eminent domain on the three rowhouses in this parcel. Only one had a tenant living in it, and the landlords, an elderly couple who lived in Dundalk the past thirty-seven years, said they were too scared to ever go check on the place, anyway, and hadn't for years. Luckily for them, the tenant they rented to was a quiet old widower who kept to himself, a handyman in his own right, not a complainer, who wanted to return to his childhood neighborhood after he lost his wife to cancer, to spend his last years where he began, who felt the shape of life was a circle, so that death knew exactly where you were. Unfortunately, now the tenant would have to figure out how to get the angel's attention when the time came to move on.

MacAllister, however, was optimistic. The relocation offer was more money than the man had probably ever seen in his own hands, certainly more than his Social Security monthlies, enough to find a nice modern one-bedroom apartment in a safer part of town, or a modest unit in a retirement community. Mr. Jackson, the tenant, would never have to bend down to fix the toilet or clear the gutters of dead leaves again. The convenience would be welcome for a man in his 80s. Surely this was a win for Mr. Jackson, as much as for anyone else.

A few other homes in the plan were already vacated, as well, the eminent domain letters sent out two months prior, and over six dozen returned relocation offers already signed on his secretary's desk. MacAllister had to wait for clusters of homes to come empty before he could begin the good work. This corner was the first.

The elderly couple from Dundalk, Mr. and Mrs. Reginald James, had bought their rowhouse with the accrued savings of twelve years of marriage. It was Reggie's promise to Ida when he proposed, that they would live and make a family in a home of their very own. Their families moved to Baltimore from different parts of the South when both Reggie and Ida were kids, escaping the heat and poverty of Jim Crow. They grew up in Poppleton—on the west side—but that was already becoming dangerous when they fell in love in high school. So, once possible they crossed into East Baltimore, and soon had three children, one after the other, and bought the corner rowhouse on Fairmount, with its three small but cheerful bedrooms, with its growing community of young Black families, with its huge park that the kids could walk to on Saturday afternoons. And, times were good. For a while.

But why would you want to stay somewhere that saw your family fall apart? Their oldest boy was killed in Vietnam, and the youngest boy got hooked on the drugs that came around just after the war. And the gangs, and their friends moving away for much the same reasons, it was all too much to stay. The park that they watched their kids play in as children became a battleground for a war Reggie and Ida didn't understand, an invisible enemy, that appeared in only details: layoff letters, red lines drawn, a grocery store closing, an assassination, the glint of a smoking gun barrel retreating into shadows, a crack pipe, a freeway built, a dream deferred. It was time to go.

MacAllister surveyed the empty lots, the vacant rowhouses, the rows of decrepitude. He marveled over what some of the newspaper and blog articles were accusing Crabtown of—gentrification, opportunism, even ethnic cleansing. One of the writers went so far as to suggest that MacAllister was making profit off of institutional racism. He balked at that blog post, the comments underneath that declared him a bigot, a white supremacist.

They had no right, he thought. This had nothing to do with race. *Look at this place!* If the people who lived here took better care of their neighborhood, no one would have thought to renew the district at all. There was nothing left here to gentrify. The corner was gone, already. *What part of this would anyone want to preserve?*

In the still morning air, MacAllister wondered what would become of Mr. Jackson. He never met him, but remembered Jackson's returned relocation letter—the signature careful and sophisticated, supremely legible (unlike his own) and definitely far more deliberate scrawl than any of his children. Even though the corner rowhouse had been occupied by this old, poor man, MacAllister imagined the interior threadbare but neat, arranged just so for an uncluttered evening that retired up the stairs to a restful solitude. How this man, any man, could have found peace in this broken-down, drug-addled pocket of the city was beyond him. Yes, Mr. Jackson deserved something better than this. MacAllister felt confident he was providing that opportunity. Maybe Mr. Jackson felt some relief, and this thought warmed MacAllister in the places the morning had chilled him most.

When a cloud moved along and released the sunlight to hit the alley-facing side of Mr. Jackson's rowhouse—formerly Mr. and Mrs. Reginald James' rowhouse, and of course someone's rowhouse before that and before that—MacAllister noticed something scribbled along the wall. Graffiti, he thought, and walked into the alley, careful to avoid the paper and glass detritus splayed along the asphalt. At least he wouldn't have to pay to remove paint, which costs a fortune when tacked on brick. There was more than one deliberate scrawl lining the wall. The first was in bold blocky lines the color of red Haribo gummy bears. It read *Future Site of Grab-town*. MacAllister wondered just for a second if it was a mistake. Someone misspelled the word, or perhaps it had more to do with the imprecision of spray paint, that the G was merely a struggle with the nozzle, a change in letter due to a gaffe of a wrist.

Then, MacAllister noticed the second scribbling, this one less pronounced. Simple thin black slits of language, curved as if made in haste: *Whitey Making Balti-LESS*. MacAllister's lower back tensed. Underneath the writing was a crude yet discernable figure, outlined in the same speedy black lines—however the head and hands of the figure were filled in with a bright white and two blue dots made for eyes. And, around its neck, was a noose.

MacAllister darted his eyes around the alley, patted his wallet pocket, and scurried back out to Fairmount Avenue—still bright, still empty. He tried to calm his breathing. Almost at the same moment he thought to wait in his car, he heard the familiar rumble of an approaching bulldozer. Though it was quite cold, MacAllister pulled at the front of his shirt to air the sweat out and sighed with relief.

The closer the equipment came, the louder the sound, the better MacAllister felt. He turned to face the bulldozer leading the other demo gear up the block, and prepared his teeth for the greeting. He waved, hoping it looked more like a hello than a signal for help.

"Hello, fellas," he said to the men once they all arrived and got out of their trucks and machinery. They wore the orange vests of construction that rhymed with his own royal blue dress shirt. His wife insisted he buy the shirt, said it made his eyes pop.

The men nodded or mumbled responses. MacAllister ran to his car and pulled out the clipboard with instructions for the demolition. He sidled next to the foreman, a broad-chested man whose features were large, particularly his ears, which stuck almost straight out. When MacAllister handed the man the clipboard he almost balked at the size of his hands, almost twice as large as his own. He tried to blink away the vulnerability.

"This is the first demo for the whole project."

The foreman nodded. "I heard." His voice was deep and rumbling, like the bulldozer.

MacAllister leaned into the clipboard. "We'll need to complete it before Saturday. Less noise complaints. And can you make sure…"

Something whizzed by their faces, and they pulled back instinctively, the foreman's reflexes more agile than his own, both following the crash farther along the street, a large brown glass bottle, shards still frisking along the asphalt.

"What the fuck," the foreman exclaimed. The other men looked around towards a possible source of the bottle. Nothing else seemed to be moving on the street—no retreating footfall, no squeal of car wheels, no slam of windowpanes. These burly, muscled men wandered their eyes like children gazing at stars. One of them shrugged his shoulders while another mumbled "sheeeeet" as the others laughed nervously. They all looked to

MacAllister, who was masking his alarm with a long cough—not only the alarm of the bottle thrown, but the anger of the one who threw it. Was the anger about change? Was it about Mr. Jackson? MacAllister tried to picture Mr. Jackson in his new apartment, in his new retirement community. Wasn't this best for him in the long run? To be safe? Whoever threw that bottle wasn't thinking about that, and maybe that's exactly what Mr. Jackson needs to be spared from. Doesn't everyone want to feel safe?

MacAllister pulled his square head up straight, then smiled, that smooth white look of success he had perfected over the years, and nodded slightly at the foreman.

"What's your name, foreman?"

"Grant, sir."

"Well, Grant?" MacAllister looked out at the other men with a slight grin.

"Yes, sir?"

"Let's tear this shit down."

12

Peter

The night is smudged newspaper and bitingly cold, the tips of people's columned angers snapping the extremities of the nightwalkers. It continues to rain. Jude's station wagon is welcoming when we climb in. The smells are familiar now and the passenger seat is like any favorite spot. It shapes to my preference.

Tonight was the 8 X 10, a dingy black square as small as its name. I had been asking people all night if it referred to dimensions or a photograph. Either way, the place evoked a languid coziness that made both meanings appropriate. Jude said he had been coming here for two years. I had never been, and he appeared excited about sharing the place. There was only one performer tonight, a local girl, all piano and vocals. It was really intense performing, and I was surprised I had never heard of her. Her songs make fun of the Church. I was grinning and swaying in my seat. Jude didn't like it so much.

"It felt too personal," he said as we walked out.

"How can anything be too personal?"

"I don't know, but it was. I felt like I wasn't supposed to be there, or something, looking at her."

That was one of the reasons I liked it so much. I could glimpse into these perverse private cavities of this woman I had never met before, try on her fears and fantasies like dress slacks in Marshall's. It did feel a little naughty, but that's what made it so great. She was allowing me to peek without overtly giving me permission. Once things are safe and public, they're no longer nearly as thrilling.

"I think I want to be a writer," I say, after Jude passes me the ceremonial bottle. This time it's Cisco, a red, punchy, and overly sweet confection. I down it with the promise of being swirly.

"When did you decide that?" Jude says, taking the bottle from me.

"I just did." I smile.

"You'd probably make a good writer. You know a lot of words that I don't." His clothes weren't as dark tonight. He was wearing a gray sweater and jeans.

"Yeah, I love them. Sometimes they can almost be…erotic."

Jude sprays out his mouthful of liquor. "What? Words? You're weird, Peter."

"You don't think words can be erotic?"

"Not really."

I lean into him. "Have you ever thought about the word…predilection? What about perspicuous? Or…dipthong…that's a good one."

"I never even heard those words before," he laughs.

"You don't have to know what they mean. Listen to how they sound. *Dip-thong.*"

Jude looks serious into my eyes for seconds, sending heat through my thighs…then starts boisterously laughing. Some of his spit hits my face. I don't wipe it away. His gaze gets really lazy-dreamy.

"What?" I ask.

"You are messed up, Cryer." I force a sheepish smile, but am hurt by his use of my last name, the common masculinity of it, the distance of locker-room talk.

He leans back into the seat, looking out the windshield. I follow in my own seat, wishing the space between us to evaporate. I try to figure out a sensible reason why I should be folded into his lap, my head resting on his chest. The car is parked in front of Henderson's Wharf, little lights bobbing to and fro with the will of the water.

I wait for the alcohol to beef up my confidence, my stare, before I turn toward him, so I drink fast and keep my gaze forward.

We drink in silence for a while, and yet it is not uncomfortable. It's crazy—I have known Jude for four years now, had classes with him every year, we were on yearbook together, and I didn't know him a fraction as well as I do now, after a few nights in this car, drinking, listening to music. Alcohol is an amazing substance. It breaks down walls. It allows people to be intimate, to settle into each other so quickly, so honestly. If he and I ever mutually fall in love, it will be in this car. We could make love in this car, we could drive away together in this car. It could send us on a new life, altogether. I could straddle him while we coast down an interstate in the middle of nowhere, Nebraska. The sky would be huge.

"Whoa, what you thinking about there, Peter?" His eyes and grin are looking straight at my crotch. I look down, but I know it's there. I take a drink of the Cisco. He laughs.

"He has a mind of his own, that one," I say in what I think is my best Texan accent.

He laughs. "Mine, too, man. But why in the most random moment, like in the middle of, like, History class, you know? I'm not thinking about anything, you know, and there sure isn't anything around me making it happen..." He laughs again. I can tell how nervous he is talking about it. It's cute, but also annoying. He's obviously never been with a guy before. I guess I'll have to teach him *every*thing I know.

I lean towards him, just a little, only enough to send pulses up my legs and not enough for him to notice. "It's amazing how fast it grows, huh?"

"You mean like puberty, or when it gets hard?" His laughter is nervous, unsteady. Funny how we act when we want to talk about something but aren't supposed to. It's so exposing, yet opportune. Maybe this is the time, or the beginning to what will be the time, a window.

I lean a little bit closer, and make my voice breathier. "Both. Sure. It happens fast. I love mine. It's nice."

"If you do say so yourself," and covers his mouth with booze.

"Yeah," I say.

After a small pause, half-laughing, "So, did you get lucky, like, get your Dad's genes? You know, like what they say about Black guys?"

I lean a little closer, the hard-on at full force. God, I love alcohol. I can stare right at Jude without him getting weird, he can ask indirectly how big my cock is, and I'm not even annoyed that he just chalked me up to a stereotype.

I stay in the Texan voice for safety, "Y'wanna see it?" My arteries are all syncopated drumbeats but I keep my gaze calm.

"Funny," he snorts, and the needle on the record player loses track just like that, the harsh rip sliding along the plastic, and I sink back into my chair. I don't know how much longer I can control myself, honestly.

We sit and drink for a little while longer. The moon is large and crescent-shaped as it rises over the boats in the Northwest Harbor. The faint sound of the rain in the bay is comforting, the winter equivalent to the lustful summer songs of crickets. It would be nice to have a warm day dry out my shoes and coat, but this is the weather I like best. Cold and rainy. The loner-ness, everything in silhouette.

"Peter?"

"Yeah?"

Come on.

"Do you think of dying a lot?" Jude is looking straight ahead. The bottle is half-empty, so I pull myself to my side, and rest back in the seat with a full view of his profile. I like this, this safe place to look at him so directly. He doesn't seem to even notice. I feel like we're now in a clichéd movie—I mean, his question, ugh—but we *are* teenagers. We're supposed to talk about shit like this. And of course I've thought about it. After reading *Frankenstein* last year for Brit Lit I couldn't keep from staring in dark corners, imagining animation, the doctor's mourning for his mother, for his own mortality. Of course I think about death. I have wondered what Joby's last thoughts were before he died. That moment before. I wonder what he felt, and if he knew it was going to happen, if he had a moment to think about Ma or me, or if it happened instantly and without anything to signify the finality of it, like the goodbye I never got from him.

"Sometimes."

"I think of it a lot."

"You're supposed to. You're Goth."

"I am not!"

"Uh, long black hair, mascara around your eyes. Sorry, honey, you're Goth."

He looks at me incredulously, and snorts.

"What?" I ask.

He keeps his gaze a little longer, a little furrowed, scrutinizing, then turns back forward.

"And you don't even need that shit around your eyes. They're beautiful on their own," I brave.

His head tilts, but not all the way, towards me. "My eyes?"

"Yeah. They're like a wolf." I try to look as delicious as I can on my side.

"A wolf," he says into the air. He takes a swig and hands it to me. I get a good gulp in and pass it back.

There is a long pause. I can tell he's getting drunk. "I think about it a lot since, you know." His profile almost glows with the moon shining in through the window, hair frizzy around his temple catching the light. He still needs a haircut. "I try to think of the end, the nothing after it. That nothing."

"You don't believe in any kind of afterlife?"

He shakes his head. "Do you?"

"I think so," I say.

"Wow."

"What?"

"I guess I thought you'd be a…" He flips his hand like it'll help him retrieve the word.

"Atheist?"

"Yeah."

"I don't think so," I say. I know what I am. But a conversation about it would just be too cliché: teenager, drinking, spirituality. I've seen this movie. I want *Peter and Jude* to be something different, an atmospheric indie film that resolves itself of all the great questions in the quiet space of two people, in subtle hand gestures, in glances, not saccharine dialogue.

"Are you religious, Peter?"

I shake my head slow, like I could be forgetting something. He quickly gets exhausted asking questions, so I sit up. I give him a tiny piece. "You know how in Physics Mr. Barrier talks about the properties of energy?"

He nods at the windshield.

"There is a fixed amount of energy in the natural world that keeps getting bounced around and passed through different forms of matter... well, the point being energy can't be destroyed. And then I think about all the ideas inside our heads... and dreams, fantasies, our imagination... they are bits of energy currently existing in the form of thought. They are electrical impulses, right? We've learned that even at school. So when our body dies, where does that energy go? Somewhere. Maybe some trickles off into the form of a... tree, and some joins the wind, and maybe some becomes part of a new life, maybe a new baby on the other side of the planet. But it goes somewhere, right? It can't *cease.*"

He smiles, and sighs.

"What?" I ask.

"You're fucking smart, Peter. I never listened that much in Barrier's class."

My thighs and cheeks warm. I can handle this part of the cliché. "So are you," and look at him. The moment deserves eye contact. "I wouldn't hang out with you if I didn't think so."

"Have you ever thought about killing yourself?" His Adam's apple moves up and down a few times. Jude, an island in the middle of something vaster than an ocean. My sight of him seems to back up, space posits some extra matter in between our two bodies. It's desperate. Okay, so I like this movie; it's different when you're one of the actors playing the role.

"Have *you?*" My voice sounds far and tinny.

He nods.

I sit up. "How often?"

He reclines into the sexy pose of raising his arms and resting them over his head. I can't help but savor the little bit of flesh peeking below the bottom hem of his shirt, the casual vulnerability of it.

"Every day, I'd say," he says.

"Like, what?"

He shrugs. "Ways to do it. What would happen."

"I wonder who would be at my funeral, sometimes," I add, after a moment.

"How would you do it, if you had to?" he asks.

I think for only about two seconds. "Like *Thelma and Louise*. Did you see that?"

He shakes his head.

"Well, it's this old movie about these two women who basically go on this cross-country crime spree in a convertible. When they get cornered by the cops in, somewhere in the middle of a desert like Arizona or Nevada, they grip each other's hand, and just drive off a cliff together."

"Shit," he says. "That's how you'd go?"

I nod. "With a bang. And it would have to be a cool fucking car. Not a station wagon."

He laughs. I join. Then he says, isolated, "Spicy." I'm not sure if he means the suicide fantasy or me. I choose to think the latter.

"I always thought of cutting my wrists," he says. "They say it doesn't hurt, but you don't cut across, you cut down. And you sit in a tub of warm water so you don't stop bleeding." He gives a visual with his own arm. It spooks me.

"Have you really thought about doing it?" I ask.

"I don't know." He picks up the near empty bottle of Cisco, gulps down the rest, and burps. "Have you?"

"What?"

"Thought about it?"

"Well, I mean, yeah," I say. "But it's when I'm pissed off with my mom about something and, I don't know, I imagine it as a vengeance thing. Not for real."

"You wouldn't ever really do it?" he asks.

"No," I reply. I'm surprised by my own conviction. My first thought is Ma, and I am flooded by love for her. "I couldn't do that to Ruth Anne."

"Your mother?"

"Yeah. She doesn't deserve another...she doesn't deserve that."

Just thinking about killing myself makes me curl up. The thought of ending abruptly and consciously seems ridiculous, anyway. I can try to be sensitive to it, but it's so clearly stupid I won't wrap any reason around it. It makes me a little angry with Jude. It's one thing to be full of pain. That's attractive. Being suicidal is different. It's not nearly as glamorous.

I wonder who the first suicide was. There's probably a biblical story. There's one for every human transgression. But really, who was the first to think they could take their own life, and then actually do it? A moron. There's a lot of those in the Bible, too.

I see movement out the corner of my eye. It's Jude, turning towards me, lifting up his sweater. It looks like he might take it off. It catches me so off guard I almost hide my face. This is it. Of course it would happen when I least expected. I didn't think talk of death would spur the moment, but I'm not discriminating. He's taking off his shirt, an offering. He knew I wanted it but he knew he had to make the first move. I think about how the first touch will feel, the kiss to follow.

His face disappears into the knit, his sweater raised up to his armpits, dark and damp hairs against his pale, pale skin. And then I see why he has lifted his shirt, what he wants to show me. It's not the moment, not at all. There is a streetmap on his flesh, bisecting lines curving through skin like paper. Cuts, thin cuts slashed across his stomach, random and various shades of red and pink. The violence behind them frightens me more than the marks thermselves, vignettes of something sharp gliding across his body. His face is nervous, but thin set and still, another red slash.

"Did you?"

He nods.

"Why?" I ask.

He shakes his head. I want to take him in and rest his body on mine. I want to trace each line with my finger, on his stomach, and have it read as something, like a sentence, an explanation. I want to trace over this pain and draw it into my finger, have it trail into my hand, my arm, my shoulder, have it sit unknown in my heart.

"I haven't done it for a while, about two weeks," he says, and lowers his shirt. "I don't know why I ever did it. Isn't that weird? I don't know why."

I don't know, either, but I keep my eyes soft and unflinching. I wonder if he'll let me touch him now, in this uncovering. I remember a scene in a western where a man has been shot in the gut with a pistol. He shows the wound to an overly dressed woman who recoils at first, but then settles in close to the cowboy, and proceeds to suck the bullet out. I think that licking someone's wounds is a show of respect in some countries.

"I always got really…tight, I don't know…right before I did it, like frustrated, but I didn't know what for, you know?"

I want to see them again, all this pain traveling on his stomach. "How many are there?"

He instinctively lifts. "I don't know, I guess…"

But I start counting. I actually touch his skin, at moments lightly graze the flesh with my fingers. He doesn't move. Twenty-three… twenty-four… twenty-five. Some creep up onto his chest, so I pull his sweater up higher to count them. He's so thin, his chest as flat as his stomach, a boy's body. His nipples are dark. I can't help but feel powerful, almost like I'm undressing him for bed, for me. He doesn't wince or pull back. "Thirty-one," I say.

"I don't know why. Don't tell anyone," he says.

I nod. "With a knife?"

He nods.

"Did it hurt?"

"Not really. It stung, but they're not deep. I don't know. They're not deep."

Bloodletting. I remember reading that doctors used to believe that by bleeding a patient, the aspects of illness would seep out, as well. Germs would be carried with the current—bacteria, viruses, tainted blood. Perhaps it is only logical to believe feeling can physically escape through the veins as well; that releasing pent-up emotion with blood would ease its high-pitched cry; that pain generates itself like all other material in the body. All things have physical property: blood, energy, sadness, the memory of death.

When I fantasize about Jude, I think of cupping the pain, holding it in my hands and squeezing, keeping it together and solid—a maintenance rather than a release. I hold it like a heart, a beautiful throbbing organ, a cradled baby, snug against my chest, firm in my embrace. I want it to go nowhere.

13

Thomas

Ruth Cryer has me meet her at Funk's on Fleet Street. Part of our ritual meetups is to find a different place each time. I've never been to Funk's, this *organic urban coffeehouse*.

The building itself is nineteenth century, probably one of the old tenement houses built by the Poles, before the urban reform and building regulations. This street, especially this close to Broadway, saw the first wave of refugees from famined Europe. I'm sure many people died in this room, now thickened with chicory and incense.

Ruth is wearing something that shows her knees. It sways across the bottoms of her thighs as she swishes in through the heavy door. She giggles without needing to. A tilted head and lots of teeth.

"Have you been waiting long?" She kisses my cheek. Her hair is damp. I smell her shampoo. Lavender.

"What will you have?"

"Tom."

"Coffee, tea, or…"

"Tom, how many times will I argue with you?"

"Infinitely, hoping I could have the pleasure. Honey or sugar?" I welcome the chance to get up and do something. I order her a cappuccino, knowing it won't taste nearly as rich in this hip rip-off than it would down the street at one of the Little Italy eateries. It makes me angry giving the pierced mouth and choppy dyed black hair my four dollars for something lesser than I want Ruth Cryer to have. I know she won't know the difference, but that is exactly why I'm angry.

"Peter got his first college letter." She sips the oversized ceramic. It grotesquely resembles Carmen Miranda's headgear, a big strawberry and kiwis. It makes her hands look spindly, lithe.

"Which one?"

"Towson."

"Full ride?"

"Pardon?"

"Did he receive a full scholarship?"

"He did." I see the pride in her eyes, but she also lowers the cup hard to the table.

"I figured." I put my hand on hers, smiling. "And that is only the beginning."

Her skin has a softness, even on her knuckles, that I wouldn't expect, even when her fingers are curled.

"You think he'll get that kind of money from all the schools, even the ones in New York?"

"He'll get something, for sure," I say.

"Some of them cost more than a house."

"They're the best."

"The best." She repeats the words like it's a song title she hasn't heard since she was a teenager.

Her nostrils flare and her hands retreat out of sight as she sits back in her chair.

"Well, it needs to be a full scholarship, and that's it." Her voice mirrors the slight trembling of her lip. She feels it and covers her mouth with the coffee mug. I quietly sit back, knowing neither support nor recourse make things better. I know she will appreciate me for keeping silent. I am not interested in being Ruth Anne's advisor, the role I so readily assume in most of my interactions with people. It's not that I feel uncomfortable in the role, like I do with old school friends. It's not that I feel fraudulent in her presence, as I do on occasion with those whom I believe to be wiser than me. With Ruth Anne, I want to listen only, to her soft drawl, the way her words assemble together like curly-cues. I don't want her to look up to me, but at me.

This, she does. "He didn't want it." She wants me to understand, and I do.

"Ruth."

"I know."

"Towson isn't a bad school, but…"

"I don't get it, Thomas. What makes a school good or bad? Aren't they all good? It's college."

"Some offer more."

"What? More education? I tell myself, how can you learn something *better*. Columbus sailed the ocean blue in 1492. How can you learn that better?" Her eyes drop, and she picks at a slight chip above her glazed banana handle.

"Ruth. I can't tell if you mean what you're saying." I try to grin. My lips stick to my teeth.

She props her elbow on the table and cups one side of her face in her hand. Her pinky slides back and forth over her top lip. Her eyes glaze shallow. The other fingers rest on her high cheekbone. Cherokee and Irish, like so many beautiful women between here and Georgia. She has freckles that collect below her nails, like constellations.

"Why is it so important to leave, Thomas? This is where his family is. I mean, I'm not making honey for this city, but this is where the family came to. And we're here, together. Why leave your family? You of all people have felt what it's like to have no one."

"Perhaps he hasn't figured that out yet."

"He'll be alone. There won't be anyone." It's almost a squeak, and with her face down in her lap she looks too small for the chair.

"He'll meet the best people in college."

She jerks her head back and runs her fingers through her hair. They get stuck and she consciously drops them to her side, a quick wince from either pain or irritation, I can't tell.

"Well, hell."

"Maybe he needs to go in order to figure it out."

"Figure what out?" Her hair frizzes on the sides, trapping light. It bounces around.

"Everything. Life. Choices."

"Can't he do that closer to home? Ok, maybe not here, but what about Philly or DC? There's good schools in DC. There's got to be. It's the capital," she says with a no-duh inflection common with pre-teen girls.

When I was growing up, I would watch people have conversations with themselves like this. Nice, clean couples would visit the orphanage and meet with every boy, including me. Of course, they had already chosen one of the toddlers. Yet, they would have these flagellating conversations through the most polite faces, about the joys of parenthood and the virtues of each of the young men they were meeting, while I posed with my hair desperately parted.

Ruth's nails gallop on the table. She looks at me embarrassed. "What am I not getting? I know I can be like that."

Her eyes are a blue that I wish could cover the walls of the rectory.

"I think Peter has so much in his head that he doesn't know what he wants. Maybe he thinks if he gets away from everything he knows, it'll make things clearer." I am astonished by how emotional I feel saying this. How can I say this? I've never left. I've never left anything in my life.

"That sounds so easy, you know, Brother? Who thinks that easy?" She folds her wrists in her lap, picks at them like a schoolgirl. I don't like it when she calls me "Brother." It makes me feel further away.

"Ruth, I think Peter needs to feel like he's making his own life. If he didn't, he would resent, well, everyone and everything." Again, there is something more than what I'm saying here. I believe it in such a profound way that it shakes me.

"Oh, Lord, Thomas, he already does. He speaks crazy every other day." She laughs, touches her neck.

"We want what we don't have," I say, almost unaware of my words.

Her painted lashes flick up to the ceiling and back to my face. "That's selfish, don't you think?"

I actually consider the platitude. Things like this seem to slip out of me—appropriate, but without specification, like they were coated in wax. A quick, generic remedy. I hear myself say them often, and Ruth Cryer's sharp eyes pierce their safety. I've seen her angry. I've seen her full of laughter. But even in these quieter moments, she is a pistol, always on the verge of something.

She doesn't know what a platitude is. Not because of any lack of education, but because she can't know it. She is that rare species that poises herself behind her words the way a bullfighter does with his red cape.

When I look back at her, I wonder two things: One, if her gaze has been fixed on me the whole moment. Two, if this is the kind of woman I would have married if not for choosing to join the order.

But what choice? How did I choose to enter the order? I don't remember ever weighing the pros and cons of a religious life. Was it faith that gently pulled me, I absently consenting? Did I consider never having love? Did I know it existed at eighteen, when I joined the order? I never kissed a girl, never had a girlfriend in my life. The orphanage was small, and all boys. I never met girls when I was growing up. In fact, I remember being scared of them, what they could do to me. There was one moment in my junior year when we had a mixer with an all-girls orphanage from Hartford County. The days before the dance, a lot of the boys were talking about conquests, what they would do to their respective dream girls, really graphic details. Mind you, I had similar fantasies, and played them out almost every evening in my room after dinner, but I had never spoken of them. The dance was a little disappointing, or I should say the girls were, for most of the boys. There were more of us, and only a handful of slim, pretty options. Most of us weren't dancing, and we planted ourselves against the wall, on all sides. I don't think the girls were any more impressed. There was, however, this one girl—her name was Lydia, I remember—who talked with me. She was plain, but had big eyes, and I liked her. She was shy like me. We both enjoyed school, that I remember, but conversation sputtered between us, short sentences, and long silences. Nevertheless, she asked me if I would enjoy a walk, and it was on this walk that I believe, in retrospect, she wanted me to kiss her. She even asked me if I had ever kissed a girl before. When I said no, she stopped walking and looked out facing the moon. Oh, the moon, so seductive in its soft light, smoothing all the lines of the world. And Lydia, with her long lashes and small pointy nose, slowly faced me, I believe, to kiss her. And I wanted to kiss her, desperately. But I remember this great awning of fear paralyzing me, and I couldn't make a move. An indiscriminate thought somewhere within me kept pronouncing that I would be rejected, would be left as soon as I kissed her, as soon as I gave her my heart—that is what all women do; that is what all women do.

I didn't kiss Lydia, but it wasn't because I chose *not* to. Soon after that, I joined the order, and I don't remember that choice, either.

Ruth Anne was not Lydia. Ruth Anne was a fiery, red-headed, full-bosomed, disarmingly blue-eyed pistol. Maybe if I were ever able to marry, she would be the woman, all the violence and beauty, so often a symbiotic phenomenon, one begetting the other in some mysterious way.

I smile at her.

"What?"

"Peter loves you, Ruth. It would be impossible for him not to."

She touches her hair, moves it in no particular direction. "Then...why?"

"If he stayed here, he might think this would be it. This would be all he ever knew. He would feel like he's settling." She is quiet beyond a loss for words. I continue, knowing to be careful. "That leaves room for a lot of regret, settling."

She nods her head slowly, as if listening to a lawyer giving council on what must be done to win the case. "So, if he stays, he'll feel trapped."

"I think so. Maybe. Settling for something when our dreams are elsewhere makes us bitter."

She sips her coffee again, slowly. My nose itches. The tips of her arched fingers are white, as if she's afraid of the cup slipping away. The sip is long. I quickly scratch my nostril.

"Is that why you joined the Church, Thomas? To get away from settling?" She taps her fingers on the mug. I notice a hairline crack running up the entire side. Nothing has leaked. "To get away from regretting something, maybe?" Her face is wide. I can't read it, but there is definitely some shadow in there somewhere. I'm not sure if it's a sadness that is uncomfortable with itself or if there is a history to the word I don't know. Regret. Something else entirely. Or me. A fear, a flush, lurches my insides.

"Do you realize we've been talking about Peter this whole time? We're two adults with lives of our own, right? There is more than Peter, right? How about Ruth, huh? How are *you*?"

*

The rectory is almost quiet when I open the door. August is creaking the desk with an oversized eraser diligent on paper. Then, the whoosh of hand across the page to clear the tangle of graphite and rubber. He looks up, tongue pressed against the inside of his cheek with always a cheery smile. "Afternoon. I hope your day is going well."

"So far. You?"

"Blessed. I'm trying to make some notes for the meeting. I think it appropriate that they're having it in the school auditorium, don't you?" The ends of his questions rise so high I imagine his lips flying off his face and up the chimney.

"I'm not sure if it's going to be much of a meeting, August. They're tearing the school down, regardless of what is said tonight." I hear a bitterness in my voice. August doesn't seem to notice.

"The meeting is more than that, Thomas. These people are trying to work together, to assemble in a proactive way. Maybe a little too late, but... that's why it's important we go. We're seen as leaders in the community. It'll give 'em a push." His hands swish up in front of him not so much in the gesture of a push as a cheerleading move.

"I'm not sure I agree, August. None of them go to our church. We serve a different community." I turn my head. "Besides, what will they think of us being there? Didn't we just give testimony to support the demolition of their school?"

"No! We gave testimony to the state of the neighborhood. That's different."

I can't see the difference that apparently August has been able to discern. I am annoyed by his ability to rationalize this. Even if he was remotely bearing a sound argument, these people wouldn't buy it. "But won't they see us as opposition? Won't it be an insult to them if we go?"

August drops his pencil. "How can you say that? This is our *community*. Well, granted, our congregation is *different*, but we live here, and our church is here, and that makes us a part of it. Besides, we are the Community Outreach Committee. We have to go."

He grips his pencil again and writes. It seems to splinter lead. His tongue returns to his left cheek. I have time for a shower. Maybe grade some papers. A to-do list before we go.

"What did *you* do today?" His face doesn't leave the page.

I could tell him I went to see Ruth Cryer. I could tell him that we've been friends ever since first meeting. Once a month or so, we meet at a coffee shop, or a diner, sometimes just for a stroll. We often find ourselves in Fells Point. Some food and coffee on a patio, facing Market Square. Then we walk to one of the benches along the original cobblestone streets. The gulls mix with the pigeons, harass people coming out of the novelty shops and pubs housed in the tiny pre-Revolution colonial rowhouses. The smell of hot dogs and pizza mingle with the brine of the harbor, and maybe someone plays guitar next to the empty wharf that now serves as a lookout point over Middle Branch.

I could tell August that she and I are great friends, as much as we are allowed to be. He would smile and congratulate me on making the human connection, for being so devoted to my students and to the *community*.

"Not much. Strolled around," I say, and leave the room, August's pencil grinding in my ear.

*

King Middle was built in the twenties, when it was still O'Donnell City School and everyone north of Patterson had a red front door. Before that, the land was part of a slaughterhouse, a tavern, a grain store. All of the school's brick was made down the street, one hundred percent

Baltimore made. The burnt orange color gives it away, darkening with age, like liver spots. It probably was cheerful once upon a time, but now it seems to loom over Orleans Street.

August is cheerful, though, even in his gloomy trenchcoat. He hums "City of God" as we walk up the steps to the double doors of the auditorium. A sign, in red and black marker and arrows, says "Emergency Neiborhood Meeting." August points at the sign and harrumphs, bemused.

The auditorium is all brick and tatter, a bold and cavernous ribcage without flesh, both permanent and moribund. It smells dusty. There is a scattering of people, forty or so, swallowed by the immensity of the room. It all looks helpless. I wonder if the students who go here feel lost in such a big space.

We stick out almost comically as we sit near the front aisle, not only because we're white, but because of our pair of identical black uniforms, like funeral attire. Large eyes stare at us from their corners, then quickly look away, then look back, this time squinted, frowning.

August flings his arm up, points to my right and says, "That's Pastor James standing over there. He's at All Friends Baptist down the street. He helped organize the meeting. You know him?"

"No."

August raises a little out of his chair and waves feverishly. The pastor is short, about my height, with very calm eyes. He has a horseshoe of peppered gray hair. I recognize him from the hearing at City Hall. There is a nobility about him that makes August's waving out of place, ridiculous. He notices us, nods softly, and turns back to a large woman talking with her hands. I shift in my seat.

The meeting begins with a woman who declares herself a former teacher at King. She explains briefly to the audience that the school was condemned by the city just before Christmas break and has since been vacant. "They are requiring us to have everything moved by the end of term, when the wrecking ball comes."

Most people already know this, their heads nodding and mouths forming shapes of discontent. As she continues, her voice gets louder and stronger, as do the sighs and agreements of the rest of the room. Most clap when she says, "We are a community, and the city has no right to kick us out. We never said we wanted to leave." August joins in. He won't stay still. He scoots and jiggles like he's buffing the seat with his butt-cheeks.

Another woman stands in front of the group and tells us her home was condemned by the city as well, and she and her two sons are being forced to move. I immediately recognize her as the woman I saw in the picket line at City Hall the night of the Council hearing. She is wearing the same gray and mauve pantsuit, which is too big for her and the shoulder pads slope down over her arms. The tendons in her neck are long and pronounced. It makes me think of the ancient carvings of royalty in Egyptian tombs. She wants to cry, but she doesn't. Instead, her left hand grips into a fist as she tells her story, which appears to be familiar to everyone but me. No money to move. No desire to leave. Forced to leave everything she's ever known. No choice. I keep vigil on her hand, anticipating her palm to open and with it a stream of pent up anger and tears. She is beautiful, even in this moment.

There are plans made. Pastor James announces a group sit-in, a protest, for every day until "the day comes." For a bleary moment I think he refers to the Second Coming. "We will prove our strength as a community by assembling on the steps of this beloved school and proclaiming our rights as Baltimore citizens."

The congregation leaps to their feet. They shout, cheer. The room that seemed so cold suddenly fills with an electricity that sits me up. August is also out of his chair, clapping, a hummingbird.

No one leaves right away. They stand around talking to one another with a familiarity beyond what I even have with my students. They touch often, something I always hesitate in doing—even this kind of platonic touch—with all the news coverage and scrutiny. August is wild with excitement, introducing himself to virtually everyone in the room. They treat him with a contrasted solemnity. He doesn't seem to notice. I can hear him saying, "They're so polite."

When Pastor James, mingling through the group, comes within arm's length, August leaps. "I think what you're doing here is terrific, Pastor. May God grant you advantage." The word "advantage" sounds so strange, a Medieval Crusader in line at the 7-11 buying a chili dog.

The Pastor deliberates over August's animated face, nods. He says plainly, "Thank you."

August speaks again before James can turn away. "I have confidence that whatever happens these next few weeks, it'll turn out fine."

The pastor turns slowly back to August, the edges of his mouth slightly turned up at the corners, perhaps. "Of course you do, Brother." His eyes don't waver. They show no excitement or disdain. They are even. He holds them for only a moment, and then turns to the others waiting to speak with him.

August seems to notice something odd in the pastor's demeanor, but the look is quixotic. I imagine the impression will roll off quickly, with the next distraction.

I'm about to suggest we leave when I see the woman with the mauve pantsuit standing with two young boys—presumably her sons—watching the others. I walk over to her. "Hello. I am Thomas."

She looks me up and down with no subtlety. "You with St. Mary's, huh?"

"Yes. I'm afraid I am."

"Why you afraid?"

She is very dark, making her eyes appear brilliantly white. Everything about her face is unique—her nose, her lips, her eyebrows—like they belong on different people, but they all work together. Her ears sit delicately in the bed of her close-cropped hair.

"I'm not sure," I say. "I guess I feel out of place here."

"Mirabelle," and extends her arm. Her wrist is very thin, her fingers long. My own appear discolored and hairy in hers.

"What are your sons' names?"

"Where are my manners?" She wipes the thighs of her slacks, as if rubbing off whatever has made her unmannerly. "Thomas, yes? Thomas, this is Torvoris, and the young one is Kevin."

The boys mumble a greeting as their eyes shift around. They're hand-some kids, a resemblance to Mirabelle but I imagine more so with the father. I want to ask about the father, but I know not to. Mirabelle shifts a bit, touches the shoulder of her eldest. I cycle through a rolodex of questions, but none feel appropriate. We both feel the pause. We could both turn to go, to mingle with others, perhaps from our own communities, but I want to keep speaking with her, and she probably understands this.

"Where do you live?" I ask.

"Behind King, just over there, right on the corner of Orleans. For now, anyways."

There is something oceanic about her, even as small as she is. I want to know her.

"Have you found a new home yet?"

"We're gonna stay with my sister for a while. Then, I don't know. She don't really have that kinda room for us, you know?"

I nod. I've never had to worry about a place to live. I don't know how to speak of it. "I hope this isn't inappropriate, but what did the city give you for the house?"

She shakes her head. "It's not mine. Was my boss' mother's house, but she got shit for it. That was after they condemned it, because before that, it was worth more, she said. I don't know, it's all fucked up."

Her nostrils flare.

"I'm sorry," I whisper.

"It's not your fault. What you sorry for?"

"It's unfair."

"Shit, ain't the whole damn world?" She bites her nail. "And my house shouldn't a been condemned neither. I took care of it. It was clean. No windows broken. Nothing like it. It was clean. You know what I'm saying?"

"The city probably did it to get the price down, so the developer could buy it cheap."

"You got that right. Crooked bunch of assholes, what it is."

"I just can't believe the city is willing to throw away homes that have been there for so long. There's so many stories in those homes."

"Well, Mr. Thomas, I understand what you saying, but I could give two shits about all that."

Her fists return, and she swallows as her nostrils flare again. Watching her attempt to stifle her vulnerability, her raw emotion, inspires a reverence, a compassion in me. "Excuse me," she says, and starts walking away. "Sorry."

I think to say, "What you sorry for?" but I never was good at being quick-witted, and she is already gone anyway.

August is still talking, this time to an older couple. I stay back, but can make out the words *pray*, *bless*, and *Lord*, clumped together in a quick string of words. He is not insincere. He believes what he says. Maybe that's what is so unbelievable about him. I head towards the door and wave.

We walk home, August talking the whole way. The people he met. Definitions of community that he has read. The role of the Church, "in times like these." He is more exuberant than usual. "This is why I joined the order," he says.

So, August remembers his choice, at some point consciously deciding he would become a religious for the benefit of community. I believe him. And yet, I also want to grab him by the shoulders and tell him that nothing he did tonight was going to change a thing. That those people in there are still going to lose their homes, their school, their community. Mirabelle and her children will have no home soon. Their community will fail them. Actually, that's not quite right. The community has been failed is more the truth.

14

Peter

Mr. Janke has been droning on about the role of the father in the modern Catholic family. We are in the Values section of Religion III. As he lectures, Janke brandishes the yellow armpit stains of his plaid shirt that doesn't even remotely match his pants.

Father. The breadwinner. The protector. He points to the words as if the class can't read them, over-enunciating through his grisly, patchwork teeth. From the third row I see renegade nose hairs sway with the jounce of his flapping mouth. Mr. Janke is married amid all of this, and I'm dying to see his wife. She must be a real winner, he only the bread.

I pretend to scribble notes in the workbook, etching shaggy facial hair on the rudimentary illustrations of the perfect family, standing side by side. Father, mother, sister, brother, and baby. I work on the daddy until he satisfactorily resembles Charlie Manson with a bowtie, then move to brother. I give him a concert t-shirt, a thin goatee, and a pair of Sketchers.

"A family that stays together, a two-parent household, gives children a concrete sense of commitment. Statistically, there is a better chance for their children to grow up without falling into a life of drugs, crime, premarital sex." These last words he emphasizes with his right index finger tapping the board. The way he says sex is humorous, like he's uncomfortable and hesitates in the middle of the vowel until it becomes two syllables. "It is typical for children in a single-parent household to embrace these vices as a means to fill a void they can sense but maybe can't identify."

Se-ex.

I look around to see if anyone has fallen asleep yet. Jimmy's on his way. Frank is picking his nails and then chewing them off. Jude is tapping his pencil to a slow beat. I bet it's the Bauhaus. He's been listening to it non-stop, and I've heard it a couple times in his car. He catches my eyes and rolls his own. I smile, he smiles back, and drops his head back to his song. Hair falls a little over his ear and eye and he slides a finger slow to tuck it back. I will one day wake up in the morning, the sheets twisted between our legs, and the first thing I will do is turn on my side and push the hair away from his face, lightly touch his eyelids, his lips, the side of his neck, softly nestle my body closer to his, and then gently slide down and wake him up with a blowjob.

I notice Tony watching me with his furrowed unibrow, and swing my head back to Janke, whose own is tilted in that feigned listening-with-interest pose, this time to Orlando Menccio.

"So, wearing a condom is kind of like murder?"

"Well, yes, Orlando, in a way, yes."

Mumbled commentary.

Janke continues, "Think about it. When a woman has an abortion, she is preventing her baby from being born. Murder. Yes?"

The class nods or stares.

I plant my hands on the edges of the desk and promise myself not to move them.

"Well, when a woman takes a birth control pill, or a man wears a condom during se-ex, they are preventing fertilization, which eventually leads to pregnancy, which eventually leads to a born child. Therefore, birth control is a more preemptive form of murder."

The audience is frozen.

"So that makes jerking off murder, as well?"

The class is bewildered with nervous snorts, and until I see Janke's emblazoned eagle eyes preying on my face, I don't even fully realize I said it. I mean, I know I did, but in a way I don't fully know. I check my hands. They are still on the desk. I feel my lips twitching up into a snarl. I lick them.

"Is that supposed to be funny, Mr. Cryer?"

His face looks like it's riding a dolly, moving closer to my own without the normal bobbing of movement, sliding right up to my eyes until the only air I'm breathing is a mélange of his mouth: coffee and corpse. I dig my hands into the desk until they hurt.

"No, sir. I'm sorry Mr. Janke."

I take a deep breath through my nose, and hear the erratic squeaking. His face is still close, trembling, ready. When he sees that I've conceded, there is a look of surprise that, mingled with his rage, reminds me of Grant's orgasms. It takes a really long moment for him to back up. The classroom is silent, except for my breath. I feel the beads form on my forehead, and feel a drip from my armpit hair fall to my flank.

I repeat it. "I'm sorry."

He straightens up, walks back to the blackboard, and continues his lecture without labor.

The class relaxes into their chairs with a barely audible groan. I can feel their disappointment, the scorns against my back, from my sides. I'll be a "pussy" for the next three school days. *Cryer wimped out, licked Janke's buttcrack*. I don't give a fuck. I can give up any earned respect from these assholes for the Ivy League. And when I'm a famous whatever-I'm-going-to-be, I'll make sure to piss on their heads from the balcony of my high-rise condo.

Except for Jude. I want to look back to see if his eyes are slitted into contempt, but I don't dare move my head.

There are at least five times I worry that the bell is broken. When it finally does ring, I shuffle my bookbag until most everyone has left. As I walk out, I nod to Janke in deference, extend the hand that I just prior scratched my balls with under the desk, and apologize again, hating every humble moment of it.

Jude is lingering in the hallway.

"Nice show," he says.

My throat is still full of heat, so I only toss up my eyes and shrug.

He continues, "You got anything after school?"

I have Yearbook. "No," I say. We start walking.

"You know Martha Grimes? Joe's girl? It's her spring dance prom thing, but Joe has to go to some open house at George Mason the whole weekend. So, he asked me to take her. Feels better me taking her than some dude he doesn't know."

"Fun, fun," I say, deadpan. Proms are horrible. Everyone is dressed uncomfortably and they dance to bad music and eat frozen finger food. Maggie asked me to go to hers, and it was a torrent of anxiety and bad lipstick. The fact that it is the big deal in high school is more than revealing.

"It's Joe's girl. It's a favor."

"I know Martha."

I am suddenly tired. I don't know if it's followed me from the classroom or if it's knowing that I can't ask Jude "Do you like her?" without sounding like a cuckolded wife.

"Anyway, you wanna come to my house and help me get ready? I gotta pick up a corsage and stuff and get the tux, you know, make myself presentable. I'm not good at that shit."

"Why is it important?" I say.

"I don't want to embarrass her, or anything. And you're good at that stuff."

I don't know what he means, but I nod.

"Anyway, we can listen to the Banshees bootleg I picked up. It's cool. Drink a couple beers."

"Okay."

"Wanna meet in the lower lot after the bell?"

"Yeah, cool."

He cups his hand on my shoulder. It warms through my shirt.

"Thanks, Peter, you're my savior."

He walks off, the weight of his backpack pulling his shoulders back. I watch him disappear into his Math class as his fingers smooth through his hair. The moment would be perfect if he looked back one more time just as I lose sight of him. He doesn't.

*

We drive out to Ellicott City. It's cold, but the sun is out and Route 40's asphalt glitters. The clanging of electro serves as an adequate soundtrack. Jude's car smells like dried leaves, and only a faint trace of the grease lingers since I helped him clean it out. He is in a light mood, prattling on about the teachers at school, the road trip he and Tony Farissi took to Atlantic City last summer, beaches, bikinis, funnel cake, confection.

"We should go camping on the beach when it gets warmer."

That is a nice thought. A commitment, of sorts. A future.

"I've never been to the beach," I lie. Not too much of a lie. I've only been a couple times. "Is there one that we can go to outside of Maryland? How about Rehoboth?"

"Where's that?"

"In Delaware. I heard it's cool, good for people like us."

"What you mean?"

"I don't know. Just, cool."

We round one of the small hilly streets in the old part of town and swing into a tilted parking space in front of a window stuffed with color. From here it doesn't seem like there is room for customers.

"How much do you think a corsage usually runs?" he asks.

"Twenty, twenty-five bucks for a good one."

"What's a good one?"

"What's she wearing?"

"A dress." Dimples.

"Hopefully. What color?"

"No clue."

"Do an orchid and baby's breath."

"Are those flowers?"

I snort. "Yeah."

"Wait, don't guys usually get roses?"

"Why go roses when everybody's going roses?" I say.

"You know what would be cool? A sunflower. Those are cool flowers."

"Sunflowers?"

"I don't know. They're strong, just, so bold, and bright. Like, I'm fucking here and you can't stop me." He starts garbling some punk song, or what sounds like a punk song. "Take a look at this sunflower/standing so tall…"

"But…they probably won't go with her dress," I say.

He looks at me, a really intent look, like he discovers something new in me. I'm taken a little off guard, but I like it. I allow him to look, and I allow myself to look at him while he does it. His eyes are so light, the grin so…easy.

He laughs. "Yeah, I guess you're right."

I clear my throat. "Orchid for sure."

"OK. Do they smell?"

"No."

"Good. How much you think it costs?" He leans up and pulls the wallet from the back pocket of his smooth black slacks. He opens it, examining the shaggy smudge of bills, and frowns.

"Hey, Peter?"

I am already reaching in my pocket and take out a ten. I put it before him in offertory.

"Thanks, I'll pay you back," he says, with a deep, cul-de-sac look of thanks. My right arm twitches with the tingle that runs through me as he gets out of the car.

From behind, Jude's hair swishes side to side as he walks. It's kind of a waddle. He has no ass, and if it wasn't for the grab of his belt, his pants would probably come right down. He disappears into the folds of flowers.

"Awesome idea. This is cool," he says when he returns.

He hands me the corsage. "See, you're good at this," he says.

I open up the plastic box and let the corsage pet my nose.

"You know, I wasn't looking forward to this. I mean, the whole prom thing. But I don't know. I think it could be fun," he says as he pulls out onto the street.

"Martha's a nice girl," my face still in the flowers.

"She is, isn't she? Strange."

"What."

"I don't know. Fillmore's a lucky guy. I mean, Martha is beautiful. And Fillmore's just…"

"Fillmore?"

"Exactly!" He slams his palm on the steering wheel and looks at me.

Joseph Fillmore is the guy that possesses nothing remarkable, and yet everyone wants to be him. He's not incredibly good looking, fairly dumb, at most a mediocre athlete, and yet he is showered with good fortune. He is the perfect average, and comfortable with it. Maybe that's why he is so likeable, and maybe that's why Martha Grimes and all his classmates and good colleges, like George Mason, gravitate towards him. Even *I* like him. He poses no threat to anyone. A safe, unthreatening average.

"We can never be him," I say.

Jude's eyes are fastened to the road. His look is pensive.

Not another word is said on the drive to Jude's, which means not a word is wasted. And though I am a little uneasy in the beginning, a familiar calm gently envelopes us. We are both present, no doubt. He sees me looking at him. I feel a soothing energy drift from my body towards his. We are soulmates who have spent one thousand years together and have now only recently found each other's physical complement in the material world. There is an openness in our silence.

As the station wagon creaks to the curb lined with beige Chevys and shapeless minivans, Jude gives the sigh that signifies the end of all good drives. He is out first, the door slam severe behind the settled and lazy afternoon quiet.

It is not a big house, but it feels like a cavern. There is one huge space that the living room, dining room, and kitchen share. The air is dark, limp, and cool—a welcome sanctuary from the blaring orange epilogue of a surprisingly warm late-winter afternoon—but it is more than that. The walls, though by no means bare, are decorated with empty things. A huge acrylic clipper ship, a poster-sized watercolor beach scene that I swear hangs in my dentist's office, and some air ferns potted in ridiculously precious, miniature, wood-carved watering cans. There are no pictures, at all. I've never met Jude's mother, but I'd hate to see what she wears. I mean, hanging up tiny, crudely carved watering cans with white painted flowers smeared on the side? It doesn't get more precious than that.

Jude points to the cans on his way to the kitchen and mumbles, "My dad made those, about a year before he died."

I stop in front of them, and swallow my judgment in shame. They aren't that bad, I guess. Actually, there's quite a bit of detail in the painting. You can almost see the definitions of petals.

"Where's your Mom?"

"She won't be home for a while. Out trying to keep herself sane by joining clubs. Single-parent-bereaved-widows-don't-know-what-to-do-with-themselves, Anonymous."

"I hear that one has quite a membership."

"You want one?" A hand and a beer bottle pop up from behind a black lacquer refrigerator.

I walk into the kitchen, making sure to touch his fingers as I take the neck of a Natural Light. The house is shale and burgundy, with dark gray leather sofas and chairs, a sparse wood coffee table. Again, it's cluttered, yet empty. It could be a psychiatrist's waiting room, the office of a paralegal.

I bring the neck to my lips. I'm beginning to like beer. "Where's your room?"

I'm first greeted by a Keep Out sign, and then the smell of damp cotton. It's in shambles, a soupy blend of blacks and reds. There is an outline of a desk heaped with forgotten fast-food fodder and sketch books. The far wall is a window covered reluctantly with a zebra striped sheet. Clothes, some tousled, some folded, are indiscriminately strewn in anarchy, draped over furniture in randomly captivating arrangements that I'm sure could be regarded as art in the right context. Jude's room feels dated, and I like that. In the corner, next to the equally buried bed, towers an extensive collection of vinyl. Posters of Morrisey, Frank Black, and the Cure glare at me with Rock n' Roll suspicion—*Are you cool enough?* I almost defend myself to Robert Smith. *I'm allowed to be here. Jude likes me.* I try to ignore the other posters, the ones of generic boobalicious models in barely-outfits—pouting like they actually have something to be sad about—and maneuver over to the album collection. I clear a space in front of them with cautious hands, and begin to sort through the titles.

Jude walks in and goes straight for the closet. He pulls out his tux, uncovers the plastic, and lays it slipshod next to me.

"This is my life," he says. "Look."

It's as if someone took a crimper to it. There is not one smooth square of fabric.

"I don't know how this happens. I got it dry-cleaned, and it's been hanging in my closet since, but somehow…" He grins.

"You're a mess," I say. "You need someone to take care of you."

"I'll be right back to give you your first duty," he beams and disappears. He can tell me I'm a piece of rat shit if he keeps smiling like that.

I fondle the lapels.

He reemerges with an iron. "Do you mind?"

I shake my head and take the iron. "Where do you want me to do it?"

He darts around, then crosses over to his desk and bulldozes half of it clear with a sweep of his arm.

I turn back to the vinyl.

"Choose whatever you want. I gotta jump in the shower."

The shower. Of course. It hadn't crossed my mind. Jude is going to take a shower. Of course. He has to get ready for a prom. Yes.

He crosses to the closet again, grabs a towel hanging from the door. "Just do whatever to it, and I'll be back." He exits. I realize he means the tuxedo. "You're the shit, Peter," from the tinny echo of a bathroom.

I hear the sound of the water come down, muted behind the bathroom door. He is taking his clothes off now, slipping into the warm wet comfort of water. He's letting it run through his hair, sopped against his back, paths traversing his skin, rivulets, like when earth first rained, and the canyons were not cut into its flesh. He's taking the soap, gliding it on his arms, his legs, his neck. What does he start with first? Those shoulders, working down, I bet.

I stand up and lay the tux on the desk and begin. I iron everything, slow, dragging the time like summer. Go over spots that are perfectly smooth, iron around the buttons of the shirt, scolding the appliance when it lets off moans of steam that interfere with the music in the bathroom. I barely—but do—hear humming. His fingers are going to be pruned.

The water ceases with a long squeak. The silence is abrupt. I hear clinking against porcelain. A toothbrush. The sink.

My ear searches for sounds. I hear the door open and approaching feet on carpet. He's coming.

The room rushes with fresh skin and Irish Spring and shampoo. His hair is everywhere, limp and black, water running onto his shoulders and neck. His chest looks thicker, nipples dark, blanched skin, faint hairs sprouted around them.

"Look," he says to his stomach and pulls some skin up, "they're disappearing." He traces the faint lines that were twice as red even a week ago. There is a sandy line of hair from his navel disappearing under the rim of towel.

"No music?" he says to me, rubbing the back of his neck, the line from armpit to hip one lean sweep.

He grabs a record off the bed, and drops the needle. Siouxsie. I appreciate him filling the room with something besides himself.

Jude sighs, his hands on his hips. He is lingering. Does he want to merely exhibit? I keep my head down, only glancing up when I think he's not looking. He continues darting around, gathering things. It all seems frivolous. *Peek-a-boo.*

"I need to look good, tonight, you know? I don't want to embarrass Martha."

"You won't," I say, with the most casual tone I can creak out.

He paces.

"I'm afraid to shave," he says.

"What?"

"I need to shave," he says, rubbing his hand over his lightly bristled face, "but I always cut myself. I never get it right."

"Shaving's easy," I say.

"You do it right, huh?"

"I don't cut myself, if that's what you mean."

"I don't know why I can't get it right."

Jude lingers, still rubbing his face, as if he can buff the hair off. I take a sip of my beer, clear my throat. "You want me to do it for you?"

"Actually, yeah. That's not a bad idea, Peter. Thanks. The last thing I want to do is bleed all over Martha."

What actually happens when all that is corporeal floats out of you? Where does it go? If energy is finite, then how does it manifest when emptied out so quickly? Why not a gust of force, or a flickering of light-bulbs, something to signify such a bold pulse.

I follow him to the small bathroom. There is barely enough space for our bodies. Steam hovers in white veils, hot and almost sticky.

He is in the towel. And nonchalant. In a towel, dripping.

And opens the mirror cabinet, takes out a Barbasol can, fills his cupped hand with foam, and presses it to his face. The white beard is unnecessarily thick.

"Oh, here's the razor," he says.

"Yeah."

He takes both hands and collects his hair behind him, elbows in the air, my whole line of vision the V of his torso. His ribs are small, and you can see them all. Three dark moles wink just above the towel, next to the vein that prowls down and disappears.

I rinse the blade. Is this what friends do, Jude? Don't you know? Was this your way of toying with me? Is that what I am? How much is known, how much is wanted? Fuck. He tosses me in the air, he rolls me on the floor, he swims with me in a shallow pool, he cleaves my lips with his own, his fingers light up my back, my freshly charged gears jerky and fast. Breathing is a hard thing.

"Are you sure you want me to do this?" I ask.

He spreads in a closed smile, looks off, and waits.

"Hold your face still." I have to wrap his neck to get foundation. I begin below his cheekbone. His eyes wince a little. I'm holding the razor too far from his skin, pulling instead of cutting. I press deeper.

I try to loosen my body to absorb the tremor. I need to have something to hold onto. My hand slides down to his chest, surprisingly dark next to his white, white skin.

He laughs, the faint smell of beer. "Imagine if the guys at school saw this."

"Don't laugh," I laugh. He is warm. His skin is softer than I thought it would be. He has a small scar on his chin I never noticed before. He probably doesn't know it's there. I don't say anything. His chest, though, is surprisingly sturdy, stronger than *thank you, I love you, I want you*. I could build a house.

I go slow. Follow the razor's path, running down his cheek, slicing the stubble from his face.

"Are you all right?" he asks. "You sweating?"

"Shhh." These few inches between us.

And that's when the razor tells me. Desire is a fruit, and it ripens in the absence of language.

I nod, and look directly into his eyes, let them remain too long, keeping them while I slide the razor down in a fluid drift, from his full shower-stung cheek, along his rounded jaw, down the warm scoop of his neck, smooth and fluid, liquid stroke. My play, and something about it is just right. He shudders.

I take my finger and lift his head up. I'm in control, now. Again, smooth, from his chin to the Adam's Apple. A sentence.

I go to the other side. I sneak an inch forward. I feel his breath on my neck, feathers grazing a pillow. It's erratic. A pattern of three: an escape— a passion—then two apologies.

I don't try to cover up my hard-on.

"One more side," I say.

I've never been this close to his eyes. They are darker now. Not a wolf. Something more aquatic, cooling. They meet mine for a moment. What is it, Jude, tell me something. They close, and he swallows.

He sweats too. There is something about the whole of his face, haloed by steam, rimmed with wet, black hair. Eyes shaking, getting paler. He is a chameleon, transforming, blending into my want, my wordless story. The sweat on his chest licks my fingers.

Look down. *Look down*, Jude. I want to say it without speaking.

He is shivering, though the bathroom is so warm.

There is no stopping this story. No pause for my heart.

Fresh, clean. Only this. Everything else is gone. Disappeared. My hands on his *face*. *My* hands on his face.

And then he pulls away, suddenly, and turns. "Okay, I think that's good." At first, his body is sort of balled up, crouched into itself, like a squirrel, but then he softens, stands straight. He looks in the mirror, pushes and pulls around the skin around his jaw. "Hey, pass me that." He points to the razor in my hand.

"You have a spot? You want me to…?"

"No." It's hard, urgent, but then he looks at me. "Nah. It's cool." He grabs the razor and quickly scoops it upwards along his neck, checks his face one more time, and drops the razor in the sink. "Thanks, man." He walks out of the bathroom, his back still wet. From the shower? From sweating?

I feel I could faint I'm so lightheaded. I take a deep breath.

I hear him yell from his bedroom, "You want another beer?"

15

Ruth

I come right over to Sarah's house after Peter goes to school. She's free and Mr. Pass has no more work for me yet, so why not? I asked Peter while he ate his cereal if he wanted to do a movie night, watch one of those old black and white comedies he loved so much, and make milkshakes with vanilla ice cream and Hershey's chocolate sauce, like we used to do all the time. When we used to share a bed, when all we could afford was that studio on North Avenue, we'd make an adventure of it—play games, watch movies on the bed, eat junk food. We were broke as the Liberty Bell, broker than now, still feeling the sting of all hell broke loose, but it somehow didn't feel so bad when we played rummy on the bedspread, or sipped our shakes under the covers watching *Bringing Up Baby* for the hundredth time. But he said he was going out again after school, hanging with that Woolsey kid, Jude, the one he's been going to the Point with these past few weeks.

I like that Peter has a friend, but that kid gives me a bit of the creeps—all that black hair and pale, pale skin, I mean really white skin, like *Interview With a Vampire* white. I hope he's not in a cult or nothing like that. He seems nice enough the couple times I met him at Peter's school. And it's just awful what happened to his daddy. I feel really bad for him and his mama. Maybe Peter is trying to lift his spirits. He probably sees something in him like his own self. That's how we come to make the bonds we do.

Sarah's house feels good. The drapes are nice and lacey, the furniture is all wood, and the stripes in the sofa match the forest green carpet. I haven't had matching furniture and drapes in forever. Sarah's lived here for ten years now, and it shows. She's made a nice home here. It feels cozy, and safe. With Peter gone, there's no reason to be at home. It's always better to be somewhere with matching furniture, anyway. And this couch is cozy. The wine doesn't hurt, either.

"Sarah, don't give me that shit."

"All I know, girl, is that your face is looking like piss in the flesh," she says.

I laugh. My skin *is* getting a little dry and like it's got no light to it. I've been getting into the craziness again, and every sound is Isaac and every shadow is Isaac, every phone call may be Isaac.

Sarah reaches behind and lifts the jug up over the sofa and tips it to my glass.

"Vino," she says.

"Maybe that'll help."

"Gives you color for sure." She raises her glass and clinks mine. "To beauty."

"That's something I can't toast to."

She gives me her look and says, "I might right smack you if I knew you didn't believe that, Ruth Anne."

I laugh again and cup my mouth, too hard, and I start to fall backwards. The wine jumps out and on to the carpet. I gasp cause it is such a surprise, even though I see it happen like slow motion. I sit up and look around for something, anything. My eyes are wet. It feels nice to not be so jumpy. Maybe Isaac was jumpy, about something he didn't feel he could tell me. Maybe that's why *he* got into the liquor. Maybe he was too embarrassed to tell me what made *him* jumpy.

Sarah waves her arm back and forth, flipping her wrist. The tops of her arms flap a lot more than mine do. "Don't worry about it. The dog will lick it up. It's pink anyway. Ruff! Hey, Ruff, get in here and do something useful with that tongue."

I look at Sarah, she at me. "On second thought Ruff," she says, "come over here next to *me*."

My cackle comes out croaky and too much. I laugh some more at that. I am on the floor. Sarah falls, too. We're sitting on the floor laughing, her pulling the dog's head close to her crotch, Ruff trying to wriggle out of her bent fingers. I start laughing when I don't need to, but I keep going. I don't want to stop. This is good. Sometimes I hear myself laughing after everything isn't funny anymore, and for that reason.

"Girl, you can't handle your drink to save your life. I can't believe you're kin to Daddy."

Sarah wipes her thick hair back from her face. The lines of Mama are coming onto her like knives in butter. The pinched nose and the thin lips and the crow's feet, both Mama and Sarah. Mama was all lines, and it's uncanny how Sarah is the same. It's not wrinkly as much as it looks like a folding in, a giving up, like the flesh knew there was a fight in this face it couldn't win. I won't tell her that, though.

"That's cause I don't drink like you and Daddy, is all."

"Well, maybe not now, but once upon a time. You had your days."

"I just gotta be with my wits right now."

"What." Sarah leans in.

"Well, you know, paying attention, not getting all fuzzy."

I rub the back of my neck.

"Girl, don't speak in riddles. What ya mean?"

"I don't really know, Sarah. I don't know. Peter's leaving. He's going to be going off to college soon, and nowhere close."

"Shit, girl, that's not for a while. Why you thinking about that now?"

"Cause it's in five months."

She doesn't say anything. I look at my hands, the nails all chewed up like madness. It's been getting worse these past few days. I have my fingers in my mouth like I got no food in the cupboard. Maybe I could ask Sarah to help them out some, put some polish on and make me look like a woman again.

"So, he's definitely going," she finally says.

"To college? Oh, yes. He's dead set on that. And that's a good thing. I mean, he's gonna make something of himself. More than I could say about Joby."

"Shit, or any of my kids," she laughs.

"He just wants to do it far away. I mean far."

"Like, how far?"

"He's looking at New York."

She erupts, "Why the hell would he want to go to New York? Doesn't he know that the whole damn thing is gonna sink, with all those buildings on it? And why the fuck would anyone live in a place where you have to go underground to get anywhere. That place is too crowded."

"I don't know, but I sure as hell can't stop him."

"No," she says, "that's true."

"I heard that's where Joby went off to when he first ran away. He was always talking about New York," I say.

"Makes sense. That boy always had a scheme. Probably got right into the hustle, there."

When I had found out and imagined it all, Joby seemed to be too small for New York, but I've never been there, so who knows. I could only imagine him driving into the city with those big wrap-around sunglasses he wore behind a glaring windshield with the skyscrapers reflected on the sides. I could see him scowling over the steering wheel, in the car he stole from his cousin after he ran away. Sarah looks suspiciously at me from over her wine glass.

"You think that's why Peter wanted to go to school there, cuz Joby's been there? Petey would do something like that, you know, just to be where his brother had been. That boy was Joby's shadow."

She's got a point. "The college he wants to go to most is there."

"Harvard, or some shit?"

"No. Columbia."

"Haven't heard of that one."

I nod. I take my wine glass and stare into it. My pride is short. Whenever I've been thinking about Peter, about college, about New York, I can't let go of it, and it makes me not want to talk anymore. There doesn't seem to be nothing more to say, like a sidewalk that just runs out. There's nothing. Not another road, not a big mountain, not even a wall. There's nothing.

"What are you going to do?"

If I look over the edge of the sidewalk, it's something really big, I know that. It goes on forever, but I can't see. Something might be there, but there's too much nothing to see it.

"I need to move. I was thinking about coming down here by you."

"Why you need to move?"

"Well…"

"That place you got now is pretty cheap."

"I can't," I say. My wine has a little black speck floating in it. A fruit fly, so tiny in a big space. I bet the glass looks like a see-through planet, and the wine is a pink ocean. The bug probably thought it would be a good time.

"What you mean, you can't?" Sarah looks like Mama again when she brushes her hair back, knowing.

I don't say anything. When I hear that sound in people like they're talking down to me my voice runs off to somewhere between anger and embarrassment. They've been two faithful pillars in my life and I always seem to be stuck between them. The speck is moving. I get my nose to the rim of the glass. Tiny little ripples barely making any raucous, but the fly is giving it his all, all six legs and the wings, pushing and flapping.

"Ruth Anne…"

"I won't need two bedrooms any more, soon enough. Peter'll be gone."

"Then you could rent out the other room, make some money. Better than spending more to move again."

"I can't."

"Why not?"

I know my face is reddening, can feel the flush. Sarah backs off, leans her back against the couch. She waits until my shoulders come down, like every time since we were teenagers. It means she doesn't want to fight, and I'm happy about that. As we have gotten older she is more willing to sit back. I place my glass on the coffee table and lean next to her. I take her hand, staring straight ahead. We must look like mirror images of each other, a plate of glass right between us.

She sighs. "Why?" The question is soft, almost too soft to be a question.

"We're getting kicked out. That Crabtown thing they're building. I got the notice that my landlord is selling the rowhouse."

"Damn, Ruth Anne. You didn't tell me."

"I'd be leaving even if they weren't kicking me out."

"Now, why is that?"

I massage my lips with my teeth. "Isaac knows where I live, and…Sarah. Sarah, listen to me. Whatever he's doing, it'd be stupid for me to stay there *and* live alone. I might as well be a neon rabbit in a fox field."

"Ruth…"

"I know, Sarah, I know. He could be full of the Easterly, but I can't take a chance like that. He damn near killed me once, and I'd be stupid for pretending that didn't happen."

"Then move in with us, here."

"You don't have room for me, girl. Besides, then you'd be in all this mess, too."

"Yeah, that's true, but I'm family. We're all supposed to be in each other's shit. There's not many of us worth a damn, and those ones have to stick together. You know I'm right about that."

I pick at the bottom of the sofa's fabric.

"Oh." Her hands fling up to the air and fall down like they practice. "So, what? You're fine with running around the rest of your life, looking over your shoulder?"

I take the glass and a sip before I remember the fly. Sarah scoots in closer.

"Look, Ruth, how many times have you moved since it all *happened*? A whole lot. And I'm not trying to bust your balls right now."

"Okay."

"It's been a while since you saw him. Yeah, he's called and he's tracked you down, and done stuff…"

"Like the time he left that note on my doorstep. Remember? How can you argue that? Remember? What it say? *I have faith.* That's not an apology, you know? Fucking crazy."

"But don't you think if he really wanted to do something to you, he would've by now? I mean, no offense to Petey, but he's not exactly the bodyguard type. I think you'd have a better shot roughing Isaac up yourself than he could."

"I don't know. It's harder for him to do something with Peter there. If I'm living alone, I'm easy. Maybe that's what he's waiting for. Maybe he's waiting until he can have me easy."

"Now you're talking crazy, Ruth. Do you really think that dumbass would think about anything that hard? For Christ's sake, girl, he didn't have the sense to change an oil filter." She stands up. "Look at me. I know I'm your little sister, but you need some sense knocked in you. Look at what he's done to you. You're moving all the time, you can't hold a job; think about what it's doing to Petey. He can't do nothing but go to school and work. Does he even have a girlfriend or anything? I never seen him with one."

I feel small with her hanging over me like that. I could never share with her that I think Peter's a fruit. That's a whole other conversation. I pick my glass back up. This time I see the fly. It has stopped moving, and I shake the glass until it sticks to the edge, above the wine. I drink from the other side.

"I know what he's capable of, Sarah. Not you. I shared a bed with him."

"He has you talking crazy, girl."

"What, crazy enough to cover my ass?"

"No, Ruth, having you tuck your tail between your legs, scared shitless."

"Goddammit, Sarah, you've always been ignorant with me since we were kids. You want me to play tough? Fine. But it's on your head when I'm laying next to Daddy and you're smelling the daisies I'm pushing up."

Sarah shakes her head slowly, looking down at me. Once, when we were little things, she dared me to jump from the rails of the farmhouse porch. It seemed really high then, and I was scared. But I did it anyway. And when I was laying on the ground, rubbing my ankles, Sarah stood over me looking down with the same face she has now, only now the lines in her face make her look more mean and Mama-like than mocking.

Her voice is lower and calm. "I don't think he's planning on coming to get you, Ruth." Her eyes are right on me, big and pointing. "I think he's already got you."

I can't do anything but look at her. I can't do anything but listen.

"I think he's sitting around, wherever the fuck he's at, and just praising his goddamn self. I think he's doing exactly what he's aiming for, and you're playing right into it. What life have you lived since all this began? Not much of one, for sure. It's a damned shame."

I bite down on my teeth. "I'm no sucker, Sarah."

"You're entertainment for him."

"I am nothing for him, and he's nothing to me."

"Then, darlin', you're scared of nothing."

She turns and disappears behind the kitchen door. It swings back and forth, back and forth, less and less, until it stops.

My wine is almost gone and the fly is still stuck to the edge. It probably was flying around all hungry and smelled the sugar and saw the pink ocean and thought it stumbled on the great fucking luck of its life.

Peter will be gone soon. It's funny how you can take care of something for so long, and then one day you're not needed any more, just like that.

I wipe it up with my finger. It's flat, its wings tucked into its side and its legs sticking straight out, almost like it knew it was about to drown, like it had time to prepare its little body. Maybe since they don't live too long, fruit flies also think faster, like a second for us is an hour for them, and they have time to ready themselves when they see a wave of white zinfandel coming to spoil their fairytale buffet. Maybe it was looking for something, the fanciest sugar speck in the whole glass, the perfect pink swallow, that made it get too brave for its own little bug life.

In two weeks it'll be me and Isaac's anniversary. For our first, he took me for a nice dinner out by Locust Point. We had rockfish and a nice bottle of wine. After, we parked at the dock's edge, right by the Domino Sugar Factory, and made out with all the city lights across the harbor facing us. He held my face in his hands, picked me up and held me with one arm while he lowered the passenger seat with the other. He laid me down so gentle before he rolled over and pressed himself into me. He was strong then, but in the way that was so nice. Was there anything else I loved about him, other than those wide shoulders and big hands? I remember feeling so safe, I could trust my head on his chest, and I believed it a good thing. A certain thing. I never would have thought, then, what he is, now.

When my granddaddy was still alive, I would play hide and seek with him and the Jefferies kids the next farm over. The farm was still really big to me then, and when he said "I'll count to thirty while you go find a hidin' spot," I'd squeal and yank at my dress. The pressure of finding a spot just did my little self in. While he was doing the counting I'd be frozen as an ice cube. So many choices—the trees, the steep walls of the creekbed, anywhere in the barns, the tall grass between the silos, the corn. But I stayed right where I was, and when granddaddy was done counting he'd open his eyes and see me still standing there, wringing the devil out of my ruffles.

I don't know what it is about all that space. When things are that big and wide open, you can't see any one thing. And even if you wanted to, you'd get lost looking for it.

16

Thomas

Dinner is all knuckles. Knuckles tapping the colonial oak. Knuckles connected to hands gesturing, on the state of education, on Archbishop Keller's new recruitment plan. Knuckles resting between pruned lips. Knuckles clink silverware, silverware made of real silver, shined every two months by Milsia, a good Catholic woman whose only English is yes and thank you and God bless. The silverware clinks more silverware. It clinks the china plates that were hand-painted in Turin forty years ago. The silverware clinks the antique silver tea service with its Latin engraving, *Fidelis, Fidelis*, and scrolled edging. It clinks the wine glasses, their stems blown the girth of swizzle sticks. The glasses clink each other. A thick cabernet from Tuscany lops to the wood, and goes unnoticed.

All twelve of us sit around this well-crafted dining room table made of solid oak. There is a centerpiece that I've never really paid attention to. It's a ceramic basket. There are silk flowers in it. Some daisies and snapdragons and a lot of other ones I don't know the names of. All harvest colors. On one side is a bird nestled in the flora. It has white feathers specked brown, black plastic eyeballs, and a spoke rammed up its ass. It looks tense.

I can't help but watch the hands, flipping this way and that, grabbing. You can see the carelessness in them. The fingers are soft and plump and comfortable. They aren't nervous. They aren't twisted with the collected little angers that life stews up. They don't shy away from the fork or the butter dish. They grab them. They grab the salt and pepper shakers only the way a master of the house, only the way a man, confident in his ownership, can grab them.

I always sit across from Father Frank. He always sits left of Brother Charles and right of Brother August, who sits next to Father Matthew, across from Brother Simon. He sits next to Brother Saul. We were never assigned a place at the table. It happened that way, since the first few times we came to dinner. It happens that same way in the classroom. On the first day, the students find a desk and silently claim it for the remainder of the course. We claim our little territories that settle us into routine. And before we know it, we're sitting across from Father Frank for over twenty-five years.

All twelve of us sit around this dining room table, eating and talking and grabbing, all Caucasian, in the particular equation of this life. A lot of hair is thinning, most is graying. Some streaks of hair glint with the sheen of metal. Father Mike's hair shines as if it could, indeed, clink. If it wasn't for our black starched shirts and white collars, we could easily be mistaken for a Congressional luncheon.

A series of similars who enjoy routine, the place at the table set, and that is where we stay. We may rearrange the silverware, or perhaps slide the wine glass to the left side of the dinner plate, if we like.

"You're awfully quiet, Thomas. More than usual."

A polyphony of clinks. Half of the faces suddenly look with their foreheads at me, half with pruned lips at Charles.

I understand the need for all of them to participate in my grief. By suffering with me in some way, they don't feel as guilty for their own good fortune, and the intense pocket of emotion becomes more evenly distributed. At the same time, they avoid the topic to include me in their community, their routine, their sameness. They don't want to publicly recognize that my mother's dead. They want me to be a part of their consistency. Perhaps that is what community attempts, consistency where chaos and impermanence and disappointment prevail. But as they scold Charles with stealth eyes I can't help but laugh.

*

"Don't be so certain," August says in his schoolmarm voice. "Sure, people will misinterpret, but they should know the 'Bounce Back Baltimore Festival' isn't meant to do harm. If anything, it's supposed to make people feel better about their city."

"I don't feel that we should assume them to understand that. They're losing their homes," says Brother Simon.

The living room is filled with smoke during the ritual of after-dinner social hour. One half of the house always light cigarettes in this leisure time, the other half slowly die from them. Ultimately, the smoke reflects the voices of the brotherhood—it floats up, curls over itself, and thins into the air.

"But in the name of progress," bites Brother Charles, from behind his pipe. He resembles a bulldog so much I want to throw him a chicken leg and see if he'll fetch it. We joined the order the same year, but because he came in a couple of months earlier, he still considers himself the elder, the more experienced.

"If you think an amusement park is progress," Father Mike says, fingering through a book.

"Well, sure it is," says Brother Charles. "It'll clean up the streets. It makes the neighborhood safer. That's what people want."

"But the people who want safer streets are the ones being kicked out, too," Brother Saul croaks. "They're not the problem. They're just poor." His sincerity mixed with a couple bourbons comes off as desperation in his gravelly voice.

August starts waving his hands in front of him, shooing the conversation like it's caught in the smoke. "Okay, everyone, you're bringing up two different situations. The Bounce Back Festival is not celebrating the demolition of homes. It's celebrating Baltimore heritage. It's trying to build confidence, hope."

Father Mike closes his book slowly, and looks up with a graceful show of cynicism. He is short, closer to the ground than the rest of us. "Confidence in what, August? The continuing decline of the city?"

Some laugh.

August clears his throat. "It's not all decline. The Inner Harbor looks great, and it's brought people back to the city. I remember when there was nothing there but broken docks and warehouses. The only people walking around then were youngsters and hooligans."

"That's true, August, people do frequent the Harbor. But when everything closes up they all drive back to their cozy homes in the counties. The Inner Harbor is just a shopping center," says Simon, "and Crabtown will be the same."

August jumps up in his seat. "But in all fairness it's brought confidence to the area. Look at Canton, Federal Hill, or Fells Point. I'm sure the Harbor had a lot to do with those areas cleaning up. Do you remember how bad off they were just thirty years ago?"

"Then what about Patterson Park, Ellwood Park, and over by Greenmount? It's up the street from the Harbor, and it's *bedlam*." The elders look at Simon with a dismissive, though mild, scorn. Being the youngest at the rectory for the past four years has made it hard for him to be taken seriously, even though he's deep into his thirties, maybe forty.

"*Well*," August laughs, "I wouldn't say *that*."

"I would," Simon maintains.

There is a silence. Some men go back to smoking. The room doesn't fill with discomfort as much as lazy frustration, all but Simon and August, who still sit up.

"These things take time," August attempts to smooth. "The city can't convince people to move back overnight."

But Simon doesn't relent. "I don't believe they're trying to bring people back, August. They're tearing down homes, that people *live* in, and filling in the void with a gigantic joke. Come on, an amusement park *about* Baltimore, *in* Baltimore? It's ridiculous. It's Swiftian."

"And the houses they're tearing down, that architecture, that's what makes Baltimore, Baltimore," Saul mumbles, staring at his empty glass.

"Why don't they fix the houses up?"

"That's an easy one," says Father Mike. "It costs too much. All the building codes in the books now make it hard for older buildings to comply. Takes a lot of money to restore them to code, so it's cheaper to tear them down and build something new."

"I guess that is progress, whether we like it or not," says August. "If the people aren't moving in, then you have to find alternatives for the space. The park will be something useful, at least. Everyone needs to have fun."

I wince at August's optimism, his ease to which he forgives efforts in the name of progress. When else has "progress" brought calamity to a society? I could mention various modern instances of this, warn of campaigns—largely colonial European—that annihilated cultures and peoples in the name of progress. I fear my mention, however, would be accused of hyperbole.

Simon's fire is up. He was brought into the brotherhood for that very reason, to jumpstart the blood of the order. His elegies were passionate and vibrant, if not sometimes overstated. I like him, and the others respect him I think, but they do roll their eyes from time to time. Foolish idealism, they say, untethered by experience. "But tearing down homes, August?"

"If a home isn't lived in, Simon, then all it *is* an empty house," August says. "It doesn't really exist. It has no use."

Simon's hands open flat and in front of him, his face looking like it will burst with tears. I can't help but be caught up in what he says with this face. Many at Mass, especially the women, gasp or clench their hands with this face. "Some people *do* live in those houses. What about them?" He throws his hands down. "August, I'm sorry, but I can't be a part of this festival. I understand why you think it's a good idea, but count me out."

August opens his mouth, closes it, and adopts a breathy, soft whisper, like Lana Turner in *Imitation of Life*. "All I'm going to do is set up a table for the Church. Have a sign-up sheet and talk to people about our service. The festival is already happening. The least we can do is represent our community. A *table*, Simon."

"August, do you know who's organizing the festival? Not the city, not the neighborhood council. MacAllister. MacAllister! Don't you wonder about that? Just days before the wrecking ball hits King Middle. It's a slap on the face."

I get up. The smoke, the frustration, something else that feels more leading. I need some air.

"Where are you going?" August asks.

"Just for a walk," I say. "Excuse me."

"Well, Thomas and I are the Outreach Committee, so the two of us will be there. We have to. Right, Thomas?"

I pretend not to hear him and leave the room. Fucking Outreach Committee. Outreach for what? Who are we reaching? Certainly no one who needs our help. What about Ruth Anne Cryer? What about Mirabelle and her sons? What are we doing for them?

I hear Father Frank behind me, "Leave him be, August."

"But he's on the *committee*," August whines.

The cold is a relief. It gives definition to my weariness, somehow, crystallizing the borders between thoughts that heat typically blurs, and isolates myself from the rest of the world in a way that clarifies things for me. I am distinct. It is distinct, like words demarcated in sentences with punctuation. Cold is the period—the exclamation—and lessens the question mark.

Sound rises up in the city, from the solid ground to the ambiguity of the sky, everything is vertical, rising. I can feel and understand most the click of heels, the pounding of boots intent on destination, knowing something, the scuffle of enthusiasm ascending from the asphalt, mixing with the screech of tires, the cough of exhaust, further up to the slam of doors, the labored pull of elevators, the whisper of handshakes over power lunches, the flush of the abject, rising along the slices of very real brick and metal and glass, of the more implied fortune and desperation, and into the blue, thin, cold air—the cloud of sound popping somewhere high above our heads—our lives, the life that we push down, step on, drop, leave behind, evaporates and reassembles into the soundtrack of at least a new opportunity. At least that.

It is dark along the street, but the giant Crabtown sign in front of me is bright and glossy, and even the most distant light source catches and illuminates the laminate surface. I am not comforted that it is the only visible thing, the rest of the neighborhood shrouded in shadowy disregard. The image is one of those computer-generated aerial architectural renderings. I recognize the street names surrounding the subject, an unnaturally green Patterson Park peaking and disappearing along the bottom of the graphic. In the center is a massive map of pavilions and windy walkways, clusters of perfectly round trees, fountains, parking lots. Silly names like Revolution Square, Chessa Peak, Haunted Harbor, and Ricky's Rockfish & Seafood Shack mark the indeterminate geometric shapes that dot the landscape. Above the map, in bold, happy lettering, "Future Home of Crabtown: Baltimore's Premier Entertainment Experience! Coming Soon!" It reads like a jingle aimed for children, a Saturday morning cartoon.

The distant sirens blending into the folds of city life oddly make the neighborhood feel more quiet. There are few people walking along Baltimore Street, Patterson Park dark and empty on my left, the line of rowhouses on my right staring blankly at that emptiness, the marble stoops climbing to each residence with such orderly and civilized perspective. I turn up Milton Street, for no reason, really. Immediately I see the change, the gleam of particle board nailed in doorways and windows. Some are filled in with concrete blocks, some are shells, eye sockets without eyes. The whole street is still, ominous, without hope, not a single sign of hope, no small flower blooming in the expanse of concrete, nothing like that.

But the homes. They are from an industrious era, a reminder that man has pride. They are brick, brick that was fired, hauled, laid, made to last. Many of these homes still have marble steps leading to the front door. They were built before cranes, before pre-fab houses, before McMansions, before Suburbia. They possess a sense of permanence, of perseverance, when mankind still foolishly believed that what it did, what it constructed, could last forever, could be legacy. But that foolishness bore some undeniable beauty. Now, these new developers, these new architects, see the need for legacy—to make forever—as arrogant. Their goal is only making the most money. They fabricate things cheaply, intentionally impermanent, anticipating the death of their structures before they even bring them to life. It is cynical. They say it is arrogant to think that anything bears permanence, for buildings to bear the signature of legacy.

It may be, but this arrogance made beautiful things, long-lasting things. These were choices made, choices made that built this beautiful city. And what is a choice, if it is anything but driven by the need to survive?

I'm flooded with a pure love for Baltimore, even this Baltimore, struggling with America's current abandonment of history. These empty rowhouses, themselves an artifact from the era concerned with history, embody the struggle. Struggle means there's something to live for, and that's exactly what I haven't been considering all this time. I haven't had a struggle. And now I know I need one. I need to make a choice. I have been complacent, dislocated, for so long.

I walk swiftly down Orleans Street. There aren't that many occupied homes behind King Middle, and only four corners, and if I get there early enough in the night, people will still open their doors to my knocking. I walk faster to shoo away reticence. How could I be so dim? I have a house. I can offer something, I can offer a home. If I hurry, I'll find Mirabelle.

Two rowhouses at the intersection have lights on in their living rooms. The first door I knock on is the southwest corner rowhouse. A man cracks open the door slightly, sees me, then creaks it further with a look of curiosity, perhaps bemusement. "Yes?"

"I'm sorry to disturb you, sir, but I'm wondering if this might be the home of Mirabelle."

"Mirabelle who?"

"She lives on this block. She has two sons."

"What do you want with her?"

"I need to speak with her."

"Why you think she'd want to speak to *you*?"

The question rocks me out of my focus. I don't know if she will want to speak with me. I don't know if she'll think I'm a nut, or insincere. What if she thinks I'm a showboat, that I'm trying to be some kind of white savior? "I don't know. I'm not sure she will."

The man looks me over for a few seconds, scratches his neck, turns his head from me. "That one on the corner," and closes his door.

I can hear muffled sounds coming from Mirabelle's house, which boosts my confidence. They are awake. The door is painted navy blue, with a black Ravens doormat at my feet. When I approach to knock, however, I am overcome with doubt. Why would this woman trust me? Why would she even consider my offer?

I hear the kids raising their voices, either playing or arguing, I can't tell. It sounds like they are tug-of-warring with a toy, something plastic and breakable. Their feet stomp around the floor, dull thuds, a carpeted living room. And there, in the background of their talk-yelling, Mirabelle's much softer voice, muffled by the door between us.

I'm not sure if my knock is loud enough, but within seconds Mirabelle's face appears at the door. "Mr. Thomas?"

"Hi Mirabelle."

"How did you...?"

"I have a proposal for you."

Once inside with a glass of iced tea, I tell Mirabelle about my mother's death, her house, and the rules of the order. Torvoris and Kevin are half-watching some sci-fi show with tin-can sound effects.

"What if you and the boys move in? There's plenty of space, three full bedrooms, a finished basement." Torvoris' head perks up at this mention, looks to his mother with guarded expectation.

Mirabelle leans on the armrest of her faded floral couch, fingers wrapped around her iced tea glass. "How much?"

"Utilities. Water and power. Gas I guess, too," I say. "Those the main ones, right?"

"That's it? No rent?"

"No rent. The house is paid off. There's no mortgage to pay."

"But you could easily rent out a house in Little Italy for serious money. It's nice over there."

"It is. The street is small and well kept, feels homey."

"And you can't sell it, can't rent it out cuz you're part of the Church?"

"Well, I'm not supposed to own it at all. Oath of Poverty."

Mirabelle stares at her tea glass for several seconds, glances at me, then back to the tea glass.

"You can stay as long as you need," I add.

She nods slightly, then lifts her head to her boys. "Kevin, T, can you go to your room for a minute?" The boys slowly gather themselves and stand, Torvoris searching his mother's face, and disappear down the hallway.

Once she knows the boys are out of earshot, Mirabelle crosses her arms and looks me dead in the eye, "You're gonna have to leave."

I can only look at her, surprised.

"What the fuck is this about, really? Huh?"

"I know it's an odd proposal," I manage, surprised by her sudden tone.

"Fuck yeah, it's odd. You come over to my house—you don't even know where I live, you come looking for me. You don't know me. This look shady as hell."

"I know."

"So, what am I supposed to make of it?" Her face is charged, pointed, like a mongoose. "You meet me once, and now I'm supposed to believe you gonna basically hand me your nice house to live in for free? You expect me to just roll over and say yes?"

I adjust my seat a bit, and pull at the buttons on my shirt. I take a sip of tea. I'm not sure how to answer these questions.

She stands up. "You think I'm that desperate?"

I shake my head, but I can see that she is—at least somewhat—by the way she stays fixed on my gaze.

"Thomas, I'm not looking for handouts. I work. I take care of my kids."

"I didn't presume otherwise, Mirabelle."

"It hasn't always been easy, but I manage, and I'm proud of that."

"I'm sure. Your boys seem like fine young men. Should I leave?"

"So, what do you want? What do you *really* want?"

I sit my iced tea down on the laminate coffee table. The surface bubbles in several spots. "Mirabelle, I've lived in Baltimore a long time, been with the order for a long time. I thought I was doing something good all these years. Well, I wasn't thinking about it, really. That's the thing. I haven't done much at all. I haven't even paid attention. Where have I been?"

She sits back down. "So, what, this some guilt thing? You wanna be one of those fucking white folks that get on Feed the Children telethons and some shit, so they can feel better about theyselves?"

I laugh at the image of Sally Struthers and late-night TV, Reagan-era charity shows, Hands Across America. All that bullshit.

"Well…?"

"Maybe," I say.

She clicks her tongue, shakes her head.

"If you're asking if I need to do this for me as much as I'm doing it for you, the answer is yes. I see what's happening with the neighborhood, it's unfair, and the order is ineffectual…they're not doing anything but going to meetings and offering prayers…it's not enough. I have this house. I feel I can use it for something. It can be lived in."

Her head is turned away. She's looking towards the hallway, beyond the hallway, her two boys sitting in their shared bedroom probably trying to make out what we're saying in this living room that she will need to vacate soon. The silence feels long.

Mirabelle sighs. "Why me, Thomas?"

"Why *not* you?" I ask, and my heart floods with knowing she will accept my offer.

17

Peter

I'm not sure why I bought the sunflower. Well, I know, but I don't. It was simply there in a small bucket on the counter by the register. I didn't search it out. It wasn't why I ran into the 7-11. I bought some water. That's why I went inside in the first place. The sunflower only happened to be there. It was bright yellow with the bold brown center, just the way Jude described them. It felt like one of those perfect coincidences, and I needed to buy it. And why not? We are friends. Friends give each other gifts sometimes. And he'd get a kick of the fact that he had just mentioned that he liked them, and there one is, at a 7-11 of all places.

The two rows of petals are open, firm and outstretched, perfect, like they were made of plastic. There are two simple leaves, one just above the other, unfolded on either side of the stem, robust, almost brawny. It is simple vitality, a fresh young cut flower with nothing to do but open out to the sun and stand beautiful.

I haven't seen Jude since the prom on Friday, which isn't that long, really, but feels like an eternity. The bathroom, the steam, all of it kept coming into my head. The whole weekend I was foggy. I couldn't focus at work, kept on getting orders wrong at the drive-through. At home, Ma would be talking directly at me, and I'd drift off, to Jude's wet back, the sweat on his chest, and then the why of it all. Why did he want me to shave him? What did that mean? And even more, why did he break away in those last moments, when it all seemed to be moving towards something, the steam, the scar on his chin, the inches from each other? I walk through the double doors of the school, the abysmal main hall. I am immediately embarrassed. Why bring such a lively creature into such an *institution*? I curve it into my hand and walk with it by my side. I didn't even think about it really. I did notice how much faster I was walking, with it in my hand, towards school, but didn't think about it actually being here. I don't want to be seen as I slink to homeroom. Is that where I would give it to him? Of course not. Surrounded by a dozen morons who heckle about an untied shoelace? I'm a little late, and it relieves me that there isn't the usual swarm in the halls. Perhaps his locker is open. I could slip it in the top compartment with a little note. *Thanks for being my friend.* No. *Had a good time the other day.* Stale. *What's up?* Not interesting enough. He would expect something at least clever. *When you get a whiff and a bee stings you, think of me.*

The sound of my cackle ricochets off the empty walls and bounces back.

Mondays are an example of what I hate the most: beginnings. The beginning informs me that I'm furthest from the end. It is when a journey is at its longest. Sitting at a desk in the classroom, the hours are becoming weeks and I'm pushing them instead of them pulling me.

Jude wouldn't have wanted me to shave him if he didn't want something else. I mean, besides getting shaved. No one does that. It's so…intimate.

But then he pulled away. Was that because he doubted what he was asking for? So, he feels something, but doesn't know exactly how to act upon it? I mean, fuck, his father died recently. His whole world has flipped; maybe the last thing he can do right now is also deal with the fact that he's in love with a boy. That is a lot. Maybe that's why he pulled away.

But obviously, he feels something. You don't allow another guy to shave you, wet with a towel on, unless there is something. God!

What if I gave him the impression that *I* didn't want anything? Maybe standing there, so close, my hand on his sweaty chest, our faces so fucking close to each other, maybe he wanted me to make a move and I didn't, and so he thought that I wasn't interested. And if he thought I wasn't interested, then the whole scenario could have seemed really awkward for me. Maybe that's why he pulled away. He didn't think I wanted it. God, Jude, I *wanted* it.

His locker is protected by a combination. It is a small, shiny enemy, its round face hanging dutifully from the metal lip. The thick air in the hall gives me sense. I can't slip him the sunflower in homeroom. I can't give it to him in the hall.

I see him twice today. I can't give it to him now. But that means I'd have to wait until last period. Perhaps I can slip it to him as we walk out of homeroom. Then what? Everyone would ask him why he had a sunflower in his hand. He'd be embarrassed and look down at the floor. The idiots would bug him until he made something up. His girlfriend gave it to him, or his mother wanted him to put it in the offertory as a prayer for his dad. Or maybe he would tell them the truth. Maybe he would be relieved that here I was acknowledging that I, too, was sweating in that bathroom for the same reason he was; that I, too, was afraid to make the first move; that I wanted to keep sliding my hand down from his sweaty chest and press into him.

And the sunflower, and that it was me who remembered what he said that day, that they were his favorite, for their boldness, that I listen, and that I gave him one, and he wouldn't care what the other guys thought. Maybe his feelings could be that strong, to break out of some chokehold of ignorance. Bold as the sunflower. Him and me, and Jude takes the sunflower in his hand, cups it to his nose, and leans forward to kiss me. Everything else begins to disappear, the rest sucked into a black hole of gasping and wagging tongues, and neither of us care. He leans forward to kiss me, and the room opens up with light, and the sunflower stretches its petals to full bloom. He leans forward to kiss me, and we both realize how small the world is but how great the space is between our lips.

The bell rings, its needle of sound exceptionally invective in the empty hall.

Which fills up quickly. I need to do this.

*

I could put it on his desk just before third period. I know where he sits in History. Second from the door. He always sits by the door. To escape at the sound of the bell, as soon as he can. After Calculus I could slip in, drop it off, slide into Latin. No one will know. I could write something intense and ambiguous. *This is Genesis.* Or maybe one word that means everything. *Bloom.* I can imagine him wrinkled in confusion while Brother Thomas drones on about the Crimean War, staring at the sunflower as if face to face with an archaeological discovery, the truth hidden in the marrow beyond its delicate membrane.

So, it's a little ridiculous, I know, and why would I be prone to such intimations, such thoughtless platitudes. But that's just it, you wouldn't expect it of me, and so it becomes something else altogether. This is about intentionality, not outcome. Who cares about the sunflower, this is about me giving it to Jude, the joke and the not. It shows my complexity.

Tony Farissi walks by, "Word up, Oreo," and bumps his shoulder into mine, a Neanderthal gesture common to the student body.

"Can I help you, Tony?"

"You got nothing I need, Freebie," he says, and I'm perplexed by his meaning, and at the same time impressed he can be so enigmatic. Seems like he developed some nuance along with those muscles.

"I wasn't offering," I say. Yeah, take *that.*

"And by the way, neither does Woolsey." He keeps his eyes square on me, a warning.

"Fuck off," and I turn just as the heat comes in me. I want Jude to remain my secret, off-limits to this fuckwad.

"I know what's up, Cryer," slowly shaking his head. "You're not fooling shit."

"Okay, sure Tony," and as I walk off give him no indication that anything he said phased me, while my gut sinks down the long hallway. I make my stride longer, my legs farther apart, and put my hands in my pockets so they don't swing. I'm sure he's watching me leave.

Out of sight, I unzip my backpack enough to see the sunflower. A couple of the petals have knocked off. There is a tear in one of the leaves. I lean down and snap it off. It looks too asymmetrical, so I pull at the other one. A thread of green flesh holds and runs to the bottom of the stem.

When the bell rings I carefully lift my bag so as not to incur any more damage.

"Peter?" Brother Thomas' voice sounds like a calculator. His tongue clicks softly like fingers on a keypad. "Would you please take this envelope over to the counselor's office? I don't have time before my next class."

*

I could run down to the cafeteria on my way to Journalism. He might even be sitting alone, hovering over a peanut butter sandwich. Jude always brings his lunch, in white paper bags. It pissed me off when we didn't get the same lunch period this semester. It pisses me off even more, now that we are friends. I could've had someone to sit with who didn't bore me, didn't talk about sports statistics or the girls they really didn't hook up with.

I could walk by the table, chat for a second, and move on, leaving the sunflower on the table. I'd be gone before he even realized I left something. It is all so Victorian. Glances in the parlour. Notes under the tea service. Passions in the courtyard.

In that case, I'll write something like *Thought you could use a boost to get you through another Monday* or even more benign and distracting like *The Evangenitals are playing at Hammerjacks on Thursday*. I can't decide which one, so I scribble them both.

At the sound of the bell, I leap down the stairs to the orange linoleum and rank of Salisbury steak. Just before I enter the hall, I fish in my bag and pull it out. A few more of the petals have fallen off and the head is drooping. I cup the stem in my palm and hide it behind my back.

He is sitting in the far corner of the room, alone, by the door that exits to the parking lot. Perfect. I can walk over, do my business, and slip out the door. I walk. He is leaning over a Tupperware bowl, listlessly forking

its contents. He doesn't see me. I fondle the stem. Voices mingle with the
dull echoes of plastic and formica. I didn't choose which note to leave.
How will I attach it? Maybe I should not leave a note at all.

"Peter?"

Paul Rose in front of me. His face is oily, catching the florescent light
on his forehead. He's always so fucking excited. If he had a tail, it would
break everything in a room.

"Are you going to the LIFE meeting?"

"LIFE sucks, Paul. I don't go anymore." I look past his face. Jude's
head is still drooped down.

"Oh." Paul's oily forehead wrinkles. "I still like it."

I move to get around him. I'll be late.

"Can I use your Bible, then? I left mine in my mom's car, and I...hey,
is this your lunch period? I never see you here."

I pull my bag around and retrieve the book to shut him up.

"What's the flower for?" he asks.

"Here." I thrust the Book in his face.

"You got a girlfriend?"

"You want the book?"

Jude is bent over searching in his bag. His hair is hanging feeble. He
could be leaving.

"Who is she?"

"Who? No." I push the book at him again.

"Are you *giving* it to her?" His face looks sinister and even more
greasy. "Are you *really* giving it to her?"

I throw the book down on the floor with a crack and I turn back.
Jude's walking out. I walk fast but not so fast as to stir any heads. I see
some of the petals peel off with the whoosh of the cafeteria's swinging
doors. As I go through I hear Paul yell after me, "What's your problem?"
And the bell rings. I miss my chance.

I run up the stairs. I want to hit each one of them. I grunt and slam
my feet down on the linoleum. I want to fill the stairwell up with the
sound. Fill it.

I punch the wall with the side of my fist, and walk on. I remember the sunflower and put it back in my bag.

Mr. Roy greets me as I walk late into class.

"Mr. Cryer, so glad you could join us."

*

I could've dropped it on his chair during Religion, before anyone came in the room, but Mr. Roy kept me after to discuss my tardiness. The class was half full by the time I got here, and Jude was dropped down into a book, anyway.

Janke is ruthlessly praising some new student philanthropy organization. I can't decide what to write on the note. I take some tape and wrap a tidy piece of paper around the stem. But I don't know what to write. I'm going to give it to him at the end of class. I could write...I don't know what I could write. I'll just give it to him. He looks sad today. If I just give it to him, maybe something. Something must be wrong. He hasn't looked over at me, or made a face at Janke's prophetic rambling. He won't even think too much about the sunflower. Maybe I don't want him to think too much about it.

The bell will ring soon. I make sure not to stir attention. A lot of the petals have fallen off and more are ready to, so I pluck them. What's left is mostly the small, brown center, like a little burnt out sun.

I look back at Jude. He's staring at the desk, picking his cuticles. He catches my eyes, but looks away immediately.

Something is definitely wrong. Maybe on the note I should write *You have someone to talk to.*

The bell rings. The shuffling of bags and shoes and books and Janke yelling over all of it feels dizzy. There is a void in my stomach as I get up. Jude has already left.

I run out of the room. He's already turning down the main hall. I maneuver past the exodus, weaving through backs and bookbags, and out the main doors. He's in the parking lot, unlocking his car.

"Jude."

He must not hear me, because he doesn't even look up. I run closer and call again. He slips into the beat-up wagon and closes the door. I knock on the passenger window, out of breath. I beam my best effort for a smile.

He flings open his door and raises himself up. He looks at me from over the top.

"What, Peter?"

His voice is hard and final. Something is definitely wrong. I want to ask him. His mother? Maybe even the prom with Martha. But whatever it is, his annoyance is too pressed for him to talk about it now. I'm clever enough to be patient.

"What's happening tonight?" I ask.

"I'm busy." It's the voice he uses on the phone.

"Oh, what're you doing?"

"Stuff, Peter. Homework."

I laugh at the joke, but his eyes don't move.

He sighs. "I gotta go."

He drops back into his seat and closes the door, cranks the engine. As he pulls away he signals goodbye with a still hand. There is something so much like an end in the gesture. The car swings back and turns onto Baltimore Street.

I forgot to give him the sunflower. It's wilted, loose, barely any petals left at all. I should have put it in water at some point, wrapped it in a wet paper towel. It looks about as heavy as Jude's eyes just then, dismal through the dirty windshield. There was an apology to them, but they also looked guarded.

I'll call him later. Maybe he'll want to talk then.

I walk home with the sunflower lopping in my hand. When I get there I fill a drinking glass, drop in what is left of the thing, and rest it on the kitchen table. It looks defeated, and lonely.

18

Ruth

I'm doing it today. We always said we were gonna follow her. I told Peter I was going to go, thought we could finally have a nice time together, but he was all floaty and "huh" and "did anyone call me?" So fine, I'm doing it without him. That seems to be the way it's going to be for now on, anyway.

Mrs. Gabriel walks out of her house just after eleven, with the feathery hat and fur wrap swallowing up her face. In that dainty way, she pivots on her heels and locks the door behind her. I grab my pocketbook and do the same, keeping some space between us, just in case she turns around. Course, with all that animal around her, I'm surprised she sees much of anything.

She walks like a woman who was taught how to do it right. Even in those heels she kind of crosses her feet as she goes forward, which looks real classy with those stockings that have the line going up. From the back, and if this was fifty years ago, she would turn heads with that walk. Her body is still small enough to look good walking the way she does.

She stops at the corner of Eastern and sits on the bench. She's catching the bus. If I'm going to follow her without being seen I can't get on the bus with her, and I definitely can't wait for the next bus. That could be an hour. I think to give up and go home, but now I'm more curious than ever, her all dressed up like that and getting on the bus. I may have time to run back and follow her in the truck. It's worth a shot anyway.

She's still on the bench when I roll up, sitting there, her head raised like someone might take her picture any moment. I bet people have, come to think of it. There are now a couple other people sitting on the bench, but none of them give away how odd it is that this real fancy lady is waiting for the bus with them.

When it comes, I jump in right behind it, giving me just enough room to see who gets off when the bus stops. It goes down Eastern, past the park, past Broadway Market. It continues through Little Italy, barely squeezing through the narrow streets.

When it hangs right on President Street and then left on Lombard, I figure she's headed downtown. Traffic gets crazier, and a lot of cars get between me and the bus. I need to swerve every time the bus makes a stop just to see who gets out. Lucky enough, it'll be easy to spot her.

She gets out at Howard Street and walks north. When I turn I make sure she doesn't see me. If I follow her in my truck, I'd be creeping along the street, and even if Mrs. Gabriel didn't see me, everyone else would, and get all jumpy. I parallel park and walk behind her, about a block back. I haven't been drinking or nothing, but I'm a little dizzy, loose in the arms and legs, and really cheerful. Maybe it's the spying, or the secret that spying has to do with. I hum to myself to cool the nerves. It's exciting.

I'm not sure what brings her to this part. I've only come down to Howard a couple times since I've lived in Baltimore, but there's a reason for that. Right here there's a couple pawn shops, liquor stores, and the like, but nothing that you'd have to dress up for. Most of the buildings are boarded up or closed with metal doors. There's no restaurants or soda pop shops, but I do see a Kentucky Fried Chicken in an old bank building. Maybe Peter's right, and she is part of a society that meets up and plans all sorts of things no one knows about. I'm ready for her to turn into an alley and knock on a small door, give a password, and slip into her secrets.

But she just keeps going, walking with that classy walk. She walks past a statue of John Eager Howard, some politician from the old days. He is dark brown, holding his hat at his gut, his foot turned out. Birdshit makes him look polka-dotted.

I think she might try to catch the light rail, which goes north to the Meyerhoff Symphony Hall and the Lyric Opera House, or to any other neighborhood that would be nice to dress up in, but she doesn't. Instead we keep walking, past more boarded up stores. And it's a damned shame, because all the buildings on this street are really nice, could have been classy at one time. Some of them have fancy doors made of gold or something like it, lots of iron, marble, but now they're all empty. I remember Brother Thomas saying something about Howard Street being the Rodeo Drive of Baltimore, once upon a time. Well, that was definitely once upon a time because, now, as we keep walking, it gets more and more like more of the same. There's a couple people walking around, but they look like zombies, like the drugs and alcohol got them. It creeps me out.

After we walk forever, I start to see some antique stores, smack dab in the middle of nothing else. Now, these are all nice, and even though it still seems a little funny for Mrs. Gabriel to be dolled up for some old furniture, at least it's something to go to. About five shops on either side of the street are back to back, all on the 800 block. I wait for her to choose one. I can stay outside and grab a smoke. Besides, I'm as tired as a hooker in a cell block. That old woman's got some legs on her.

But she doesn't stop there, either. I mean, she looks in the windows and all, but then crosses the street and keeps strolling on.

I cross the street, cut in behind her, and follow along. She walks under a sign at the corner of Lexington Street that says "Buy War Savings Bonds and Stamps." For a moment, I feel like I'm back in the 40s, with Mrs. Gabriel's outfit and the sign and the buildings. I wonder if this was a street she used to walk down in this getup back in the day. Maybe this is where she shopped. Maybe she met her husband here. I can almost feel the way it was, with music and people walking and real nice horns honking—not to yell but to say hello. Men smoking cigars together, waiting for their wives to get out of the shops. Everyone's tipping their hats and wearing long thin gloves and tilting their heads back when they laugh.

After several more blocks she finally stops, at a sidewalk bench in front of an empty building that used to be a Hutzler's Department Store.

Judging from the fancy façade, I bet this one was high-dollar. The stone-
work in the doorway is enough to make you feel like a movie star. All the
lettering has that same feel as old Hollywood posters.

She just sits there, her head raised up, her neck long and skinny like
the herons in Gwynns Falls. She looks nice and classy. And that's it. She
doesn't do much else but sit there, and look classy. Her face freezes in
this real nice pose, with her neck all long and stretched out, like those
white birds. She could almost be one of the statues that line the street,
old and dignified and still. I wish I could walk over to her and ask what
she's thinking, but I don't feel like I belong in this part of her life. I don't
know if anyone does.

Four or five bums, or something like bums, sit in one of the archways
of the Hutzler's building. A woman is with them, looking right nasty.
They're drinking from a paper bag, wearing those sleeveless t-shirts that
show the hair under their arms, which I always thought was just tacky in
public. They're sitting, standing, not too far from Mrs. Gabriel. One of
them points at her and they all look and start laughing. They get louder
and louder and now I can hear them talking to her. "Hey, lady!" one of
them yells out. Another says, "What you got on your neck, old woman?
I think that's my dog." They all think that's the funniest thing in the
laughing factory, slapping their legs, and they keep saying things. I can't
tell if Mrs. Gabriel hears any of it, because she doesn't pay attention to
them. Instead, she pulls something long out of her purse, puts a cigarette
in it, and lights up. And that takes the cake for classy. Mrs. Gabriel looks
like a movie star.

And then I get real sad. My neighbor is sitting on a bench in the middle of a part of Baltimore that looks like it was forgotten by everyone,
all dressed up going nowhere, living something that isn't here anymore
except the signs and the buildings and her long cigarette. Her husband is
dead, she is old, and some drunks stinking up the street are making fun of
her. I want to go over to them—pretending to smoke with their pinkies
out and laughing—and shove that imaginary long cigarette down their
throats. I want to take a river and run it straight down the street, and

wash away the nothing left that's here now. I want the buildings to open back up and people of all kinds—lovers, families, all the fancy people—to crowd the sidewalks with shopping bags and feathered hats, greeting Mrs. Gabriel as she smokes on the bench. I want her fancy outfit and her classy walk to feel right in this place.

But it doesn't, and those drunks know it doesn't. They look more right, here, in the now. And that makes me grab my chest, like the sinking of my heart will keep going down to my belly and fall out my ass if I didn't clutch my shirt.

*

I figured the sun would get so tired it'd just fall out of the sky. Driving back home I half expected it to and kept my drizzled head ducked down a little. Some rain came, and so did a surprise hangover. Maybe it was all the sadness that brought it—the rain, the aching. In care of the thinning brakes I drove slow, which didn't help my head none. It throbbed. I remember the bottom string of Daddy's banjo when he would sit in the kitchen, plucking drunkily with no good sense of how to make nothing close to music. I never remember him making a fuss over his head after those whiskey nights, but every time *I* did, hell. It could be a message to myself: "Girl, you know better than all this." I wish sometimes my head would shut up. It's always talking, in some way or another.

Patterson Park is full of people, wrapped in a semi-circle around someone speaking into a megaphone. Looks like a rally, or something, some chanting, something about Crabtown. As the car gets closer I try to see who it is, a politician, singer, a comedian. It's getting late, so I don't slow down too much. I continue on to Mickey's Corner Market for some tomato paste. I left a note this morning telling Peter to come home for dinner. I was going to cook up some jambalaya, his favorite. After how I've been acting and being on edge and all, I thought it'd be good to have a nice dinner. Besides, I had to butter him up, somehow. I didn't know what I was saying to him tonight, really, but I knew some jambalaya couldn't hurt.

When I get to the corner, I see a For Lease sign tacked on the bay window facing Eastern Avenue. Mickey's is empty. I throw my arms up and drop them back on the steering wheel. This is the third corner market to close since I moved to Highlandtown. They're all running. The one that was right around the corner from our house, the cramped one owned by the Greek widow, moved into Anne Arundel County across the street from Marley Station Mall in a brand new shopping center. She complained that most people who came in the old store only bought gum and lottery tickets and that her produce was turning before she sold it. I told her *I* bought it, but I don't eat beets, is all. It was foolish, but I wanted her to know she had some kind of support, that she was appreciated, even though I didn't care much for her. She never was very friendly. I just cared about something else, something bigger than her, and definitely bigger than her cramped little grocery. She looked tired and said moving out would be good. She wouldn't have to worry about the guys who spent their day drinking outside her store and scaring customers away. The brown baggers, smelling sweet, talking sweet, all sugar and glassy eyes, not like the assholes on Howard Street hassling Mrs. Gabriel.

Instead of driving out to Dundalk, I gamble on the 7-11 a little further down Eastern. Sure enough, Hunt's tomato paste, priced twice as high as anywhere else I've seen it. What the hell, though. Money's like water in my hands, anyway.

*

I walk into my room, throw my coat on the bed, and return to the living room. My CDs are in a milk crate under the brass bookshelf that I've had since my first marriage. Abe didn't like wood, so he bought this instead, claiming it to be "real" brass. The frame was turning a dull yellow and rusting in spots all over. I like the way it looks now over then. I rummage around the crate, passing Metallica and Journey, Rush and Joan Jett. I know what I need, a lot of guitars and drums, and I need it loud, to blow everything out of my head. Sure enough, there's Asia. If I was a girl I would've squealed. I run to the living room, and slip in the

CD. It still works, but I have to fast forward through power ballads and zingy guitars. And there it is. *Heat of the Moment*. I turn it up. When the chorus starts I sing along, and the tight knot in my gut eases. The music takes away the feeling of bad news. Things will be all right. We'll move into a new spot, maybe this time in a better neighborhood, live close to Sarah, have dinners with her and Delia. I'll get a job and do Mr. Pass' books on the side, save a little money.

My arms do their thing to the song, real Stevie Nicks-like. She was so beautiful to me when I was a kid, with all the fabric on her dresses floating around her, what a picture. I was always called a "musical girl" in school. I keep dancing, into the kitchen with the tomato paste.

And there, I freeze, I really freeze. All the warmth from moving around drops right out of me when I see it on the table. A droopy sunflower with a long stem stands in a drinking glass smack dab in the center. There is a note. The harmonies and guitars, the music, crashes together all of a sudden.

I first mull over leaving. My head rings *under the bed, in the closet, Peter's room*. But there's something that makes me know he's not here, some kind a gut feeling, and I remember what Sarah said. Listen to my gut. Only be scared if you got the time to be.

My back pops out in sweat, though, as I look at the note. It's taped to the stem. It says nothing. It's blank.

It's just like him to let me know he can get in. I don't know what the blankness means. The future is blank? Being dead is blank?

I run through the house. I lock the doors. I look out the windows. I call Sarah. She may think I'm crazy, but she'll still come over.

There is something about no words. That note and no words scare me more than a note and all the words in the whole world put together.

*

I wait until after Peter finishes the last bite of jambalaya. He's so into the food that he doesn't notice my tapping fingernails on the table, which usually gets him crazy. There's a lot on his mind. He has this way about him where he eats too much when he's full of thinking. His father was the same way. I wouldn't tell Peter that, though.

"Put up your coat and stay awhile," I say. "You look like a frog in a music box."

"Sure." He drops his fork down on his empty plate. It sounds loud and alone. He leans back in the chair and puts his hands up on the edge of the table like he's about to push off. "I'm here, Ma," he says with a little roll to his eyes.

"I know you like it in this apartment, now that you have your own room and all..." Listening to my voice, it sounds teacher-like. I try a small laugh, but it comes out more as a groan. "Right?" I add.

He nods slowly, but keeps his eye on me. That same face I had as a teenager, that I still have when men give me flowers.

"I like it fine enough, too," I say. "But I was wondering... me and Aunt Sarah been talking. And, what with me always going up there, and Delia about to have a baby, Sarah would like us to be closer, to help out. So I was wondering if it might be a good idea to find a place up by her. Sarah's already found a little townhouse a couple blocks from her place. It's only a little more than this place, and I think it'd be worth it to get out of this neighborhood, anyway. It's safer there. And it's a little bigger and has more windows. And a little yard. Nothing *fancy* fancy. Maybe we could even get a dog."

"No," he says.

I laugh. "At least I know how you feel."

He looks straight at me, unwilling to flinch. I recognize the face, but it's a little more than stubborn Peter. Something else is going on.

"I remember when I was your age, we all ran around in the fields outside of town, having a ball. We could see stars, and there was room to move. We didn't have to worry about people shooting us or beating us half to death for a pair of sneakers."

"When you were my age, you were already a mother," he says.

"Well, I mean a little before then. It was healthier than being right in the city. It stunts your growth."

"Yeah?" He folds his arms and makes his face look bored.

"This neighborhood's not doing too good. Everything's moving out. There's not even a good market around here, anymore. And Patterson Park is being overrun…" I stop, think about my words, "…with drug dealers."

He shrugs. Normally, he'd press into me, asking what I meant.

"We're not moving, Ma." His face is solid, his mouth serious. He looks almost like a man. I forget sometimes that he's going to be one. "At least wait until I go off to college."

"There are things that we should do even if we don't want to," I say. I feel trapped by the way his eyes don't blink or move.

"I am not moving again, Ma."

"We've always promised to look out for one another, Peter. Right now I need you to work with me, here." I look around to see where my purse is, to show him the relocation letter.

He leans up to the table. "How many times have we moved because he called, or made a threat? That's it, isn't it?"

"Well, it's actually not that, really. I mean…"

"No, Ma."

"You know that theme park they're building…"

"*No*, Ma."

"Peter!" His look is so stubborn that I fluster and can't keep sense. "You'll still be at St. Mary's, you'll have the same friends."

He stands, his voice cracking, but his height frightening. "What friends, Ma? I don't have any friends. How can I? We're either moving or you're telling me I can't go out because of Isaac."

"You went to Fell's Point just the other night." This is beside the point. I want to show him the letter.

His eyes dig into mine, and fill with hurt and a bunch of other things. Adult thoughts. They're sharper than they should be for this talk, something else wearing him, but I can't ask, not right now. He's waiting for me to give up. "I don't have any friends, Ma."

"That's a lie, Peter, and you know it."

"What are you talking about?" he says. But I know he knows.

"Don't." I put my hand between us like a stop sign. There's something in the way his voice goes up when he lies that I can't stand. "You know what I'm talking about."

He's angry, but only stares at me, half waiting. Most times I think we are two pluses in a math equation, but now we cancel each other out.

"Peter, I've heard you sneaking out of the house, the past few months."

He looks straight at me, but with trembling eyes, the something else that troubles him. "Have you been spying on me?"

"Oh, Peter, that's ridiculous. I hear you leave. So don't tell me you have no friends."

He snorts, lines curl up at the sides of his mouth. There is something in the leaving that must be what is behind his face, the trembling. He speaks slow, saying each syllable sickeningly slow, seething through his teeth. "I don't have *any* friends." His fists ball up. I can't place his voice. I've never heard it before, and I don't know what has happened to him that could make that sound, something I've never heard in him. And I grow angry, with the not knowing. That his life has things I don't know, the only thing I do know. And his face looks so awful right now. "Do you want to know the truth, *Ma*?"

It's just so mean, the way he says it, the look he's giving me. I slap him as I think it, to cut the wickedness. I feel his cheekbone hit my palm. Through my shock, I see him as a boy, when he would dance to my bluegrass records with his chubby arms waving the air to the beat, only now the picture has edges, sharp lines in it. Spit hangs from his mouth.

The slap felt right. It is clear, in the way words can't be, words I don't even have room for. He touches his face and I still feel his skin on my fingers, the impression of his cheekbone cupping my palm, stinging. And Joby, *in Hell. I am*, he said. I had to cut the mean-ness.

Peter laughs at me with his eyes, looking at me through lowered lids. It startles me. I'd think he'd be shocked or ashamed. But this is ridiculing, something I've never seen from him, another newness. He looks like Peter, some kind of him, but I don't recognize this face at all, and I know that something very large has happened to my boy. What has happened? What have I not seen?

I want to say *Peter, I didn't want to do that*, but I can't. His eyes don't allow me. The way he looks at me gives me no room. I lower my shoulders. We're fighting for the same square of linoleum in our kitchen. I want to tell him about the relocation letter, about Isaac's flower with no note.

His hand still touches his face, his eyes stillborn. "When I sneak out of the house, I don't visit friends." His voice is calm, but creepy calm.

I look at my hand, then back at his face. The air feels like it's going out of the room. I know that I will be hurt by this son, too. "It doesn't matter, Peter." Joby said he was *in Hell*.

"I go to a bar."

"Peter, I don't care. I didn't mean..."

"Where I meet men and I go home with them, and we *fuck*." The eyes he gives me. I know them, a memory far off. He walks towards the stairs. I smell the metal in his hair, as he passes. The sound of his large feet on the stairs is a slow heartbeat.

From the top of the stairs, I hear the tears in his voice, screaming down to me. "I have no friends!" His door slams.

There is no air in me, I can't even open my mouth to explain. The relocation letter. Isaac's flower and no note. To have Peter understand. All of it is stuck way down my throat.

I'm fifteen again, in that old kitchen I grew up in, the green and orange kitchen, a man looking at me from behind a refrigerator door. I am struck by something I hadn't prepared myself for, and should have known possible. Peter was looking, becoming, looking like them all, all men, a likeness to Hollar, to Abe Ewing, a likeness to Isaac Hibbs.

19

Peter

Through Him, in Him, with Him, in the unity of the Holy Spirit, all praise and glory to you Almighty Father, forever and ever.

The auditorium is packed with invisible ice devils playing hide and seek behind our rhythmic puffs of white breath. And despite it being an all-school Mass, filling the cavern with microwaved hormones, most of us are clutching our forearms. They won't let us wear coats during service because comfort implies disrespect. And certainly we wouldn't use each other. Boys aren't supposed to be sensible, only dignified. Men are islands. No touching.

Tony is picking his nose. Paul is biting whatever's left of his nails. Jimmy is sleeping again. Almost like clockwork, the death wheeze of his snore plays Lazarus between Proclamation and the Creed. Someone in the row behind me farts, followed by pressed giggling. My stomach is empty. Father Mike is homolyzing how it feels to be filled with the Holy Spirit while I'm filled only with methane.

But none of it matters, and I don't care.

When I saw Jude's empty seat in homeroom, I thought he had ditched again. I thought just for a moment maybe he wasn't calling me back because something serious was going on at home. But I see him. On the stage, in the heavy white robe that pulls his shoulders to the floor. He's holding the dented gold bowl of wafers while Father Mike lumbers through the blessing. His dyed black hair, the bruised moons under his eyes, the sharp edges of his bony shoulders—tent poles, the look of pain. Wincing during prayer. Who would have thought that a Catholic school boy posing as an altar assistant is a staunch Atheist. Must admit, it's a good cover.

I want him to get over the shock of his feelings, leaving me to stew in the uncertainty. Hurry up, Jude. I want to be with you.

Christ has died, Christ has Risen. Christ will come again.

We slog in line for the Eucharist. I'm behind Paul, who's still biting his nails. He told me last year that Communion makes him nervous because he's never had the guts to reveal in confession that he once spooned peanut butter on his dick and had his dachshund Lipshitz lick it off. I don't tell him about Grant or any of the other ones, the hairy chests, the bulky middle-aged man-bodies, the thick hands clutching my waist, the smell of their experience, none of it. The only thing I'd be able to confess about what I did with them is that I liked it.

Jude. He looks like a stray mutt scrubbed and perfumed for a dog show. None of us feel comfortable in that robe, and me and the others have worn it many times. But there is something that looks almost right about it on Jude. It's not the length, nor is it the color. If it wasn't for the black underlines of his pallid features, he'd disappear into the shifting light that haloes the crucifix behind him, the same light that beams in the periphery of immaculate dreams or the struggle to remember. Tony flicks my earlobe.

The organ drones on solemnly, sounding more like a eulogy than a celebration. I wonder why it ever became such a chore to endure Mass. I can imagine how fun it was back in the day. John would gather everyone around a secluded seaside group of trees, the fish and bread and tossed jugs of wine all at his feet. Everyone hugs and sings. They would dance and drag their linen through the salt water, their stomachs filled with the good old Blood of Christ, until they saw him, their grief painting memory tangible. Their eyes would turn back into their heads to see the past clearly. And there he would be, standing on the beach with his body

glowing from behind, his arms outstretched. The daylight would drift
below the earth, and fire would take the place of their glory. They saw
the Lord again. A flame for his presence.

Jude. Though he appears uncomfortable, he manages to administer
the manna with remarkable conviction. He enunciates each syllable,
"The Bo-dy of Christ," with the right mix of authority and shame, and
places the wafer slowly in cupped hands, in sleepy mouths. He didn't
wash his hair today. It pulls against his scalp.

As Jimmy cups his hand, I hear him mutter to Jude, "Nice dress." Jude
doesn't even flinch. His thin jaw, skin stretched like alabaster muslin,
clenches only slightly.

"The Bo-dy of Christ."

His ears are small. I wonder if that means he hears less, or picks up
higher pitched sounds; I could make high-pitched sounds, in those ears.

"The Bo-dy of Christ."

His fingers are long and hairless, unlike Grant. Grant had dark brown
sausages with tufts of black hair above the knuckles. They tasted like a
sharp and meaty beef bouillon. Jude's would be smooth in my mouth.
They would slide in slowly, and taste like meringue.

"The Bo-dy of Christ."

His fingers pick up the wafer so delicately. His wrist floats over to the
waiting hands in a languid half circle that reminds me of summer heat.
His voice is certain, a Doric column.

And it makes sense. It's not the robe that looks right on Jude. It's the
role. Standing alone, distinguished in white, haloed by light, presenting
with conviction the symbol of a doctrine he doesn't follow. This whole
getup, the circumstance, suggests that nothing is truly certain. A boy may
lose his father to suicide, another may desire only other boys, and a non-
believer may serve Communion, but that is what they are given. So with
our own hands, with our voices, we fashion a response of certainty. That
we will take what is given us, and simply deal. So if he is willing to possess such certainty in giving, I will as well. My ears, my groin, grow hot.

"The Bo-dy of Christ."

His eyes don't acknowledge me. Of course they wouldn't. This isn't the time for friendly chatting or smiles. He can't tell me why he hasn't returned my calls, avoided my eyes since Martha's prom; he can't tell me why he's made me feel like my skin is being peeled from inside out with those fingernails by his silence. This is the Body of Christ, and it is what we are given, and it demands all our attention, and we must make the enduring of it our certainty.

I move towards him and open my mouth for the manna. I wonder if he will sense the warmth emanating from my lips. My tongue first grazes his thumb, and then I close my lips around it entirely, just up to the knuckle, just enough so he knows I want more than Mad Dog in the car, that I want more than peeking at his stomach when he lifts his shirt, that I want him, and to also let him know that it would feel good. *It would feel so good, Jude. It would be me, for you.*

And then I taste him. His thumb is a sting of oil and sweat and salt. It's not meringue at all. It is merely a smoother version of sharp and meaty beef bouillon.

My eyes open with his deep squeal, and just in time to watch the dented gold Eucharist bowl sail from Jude's hands, bits of light shimmering like the glint of a disco ball, and hit the red carpet with the clang, the gong, of something hollow. The Body of Christ spins through the air like Frisbees. Jude follows with grabbing hands, silly enough to think he could catch them. I drop to the floor with him, to help him collect the manna, but before I can even fully bend my knees, his face whips up and dares me. All of his features, usually so delicate, now look old, bitter, pursed into the center of his face like a sphincter. I remember where my mother slapped me last night. I feel it again.

I stop, and turn. The auditorium is corpse quiet, hundreds of teenage boys wearing the same clothes, wearing the same wide eyes, open mouths, staring at me, staring at Jude, who is scrambling to collect the Eucharist, the robe slumped around him on the floor. What else can I do? With the wafer safely stuck to my tongue, I bring my index finger to my forehead, to my sternum, then shoulder to shoulder, and walk back to my seat.

20

Thomas

Ruth makes me nervous with her fidgeting, scratching the sides of her hands, pulling on her fingers, biting her nails. The amazingly fitted jeans swish each time she crosses her legs, uncrosses, crosses them to the other side. Her eyes have a tired red ring around them and her makeup doesn't look as careful as usual, but Ruth is still beautiful, beyond decorum—she is the architecture.

When she appeared in my doorway I was in the middle of Gettysburg, one of my favorites. I get particularly excited about it. The kids seemed more interested, too; they always do. I can think of two reasons: the gore, which is always a way to pique interest, and the fact that it took place only miles away, a battle that virtually occurred in their backyard. And today I was feeling lighter. I had more energy. I was keeping their attention.

When I saw her, I must have held her image a little too long. The kids started turning their heads to follow my gaze. She was standing there, pulling herself up to be noticed, on her toes. She looked pleading. I was surprised, of course, but I immediately thought of the incident in Mass, with Peter, something about him doing something lewd to the altar boy. The talk of it ran through the halls, already, speculations and typical gossip.

I don't think I had ever seen Ruth in the school, let alone in the middle of classes. There was a lot of shuffling at the desks, the boys hardly ever seeing a woman, except for Mrs. Bell or the lunch-ladies, and definitely not one like Ruth. They began whispering to themselves and giggling. I wasn't annoyed, though, not today. I walked over to the door as casually as I could and told her to meet me after class. She nodded frantically and apologized. She was overly anxious, and I felt sorry that she had to wait.

She pulls a letter from her purse, opens it up, and hands it to me. It's Columbia University. I can't help but smile, and look up. Ruth is biting her bottom lip.

"This is terrific, Ruth. Congratulations."

"Yeah?" Her eyes are big and watery, her fingers keep touching her mouth.

"Absolutely. This is a full ride. This is where Peter wants to go."

"He talks about it all the time. *All* the time. Well, he used to."

"I can't tell you how difficult it is to get in, and to get a full ride?"

"We know he's smart." She is not present, her words coated with a gloss, something distracted. Her voice sounds more quick and girlish, and her body is hunched and small in the chair.

"Of course." I want to ask what's wrong, but if there is anything I have learned, it is not to ask that of a pleading mother, that she will come to it.

She pulls her fingers from her mouth in a quick tilt of her head, rearranges herself. "What does it mean, Thomas?"

I feel confident that I can explain it, to provide this service to her. I put my hand on hers, feeling the wetness on her fingers. I haven't touched Ruth very much in the time I've known her. I'm aware of that, because though her face has become familiar to me (even now), to feel her fingers crowds all of me to that sensation. They are both soft and bony, thin and alive.

I expect her to say something more, but she only chews on her bottom lip. We will tear our own flesh in moments of anxiety, chew, a ripping away of ourselves, and eat.

"That he has choices." I rub her hand a little and smile. "He's on his way to great things." I wonder if she minds the moistness generating in the heat of our touch. It might be wise to remove my hand, but I don't want to. And, today, I feel more confident in doing what I want and don't want. I feel purposeful, more so than I have in years, maybe ever. And it makes me feel wily, youthful. What is it about confidence that aligns itself to youth? That is just it, I feel younger in this cloud of confidence I possess. Mirabelle and her family are in my mother's house. I made a choice.

"You think this is where he'll go and all? To New York?"

"Columbia? I'd be surprised if he didn't." I stroke her hand a little. "He will, I'm sure."

"Is it everything? Will he have anything to worry about? At all?"

"You mean money?" I ask.

She nods. I smile, but she doesn't. Her eyes hardly waver while the rest of her body does, small uncoordinated movements.

I look back at the letter, examining it, more for her sake, to appear sure. I can tell she came only for this certainty. It's a little disappointing that the visit is all for Peter, but today is a good day, and she's here. "The scholarship covers tuition, room and board... yes. It covers everything." I look up with a grin. "Lucky little bastard." She doesn't play along. I remove my hand. "Ruth, you came here on a school day."

"It feels like the Post Office."

"What do you mean?"

"I don't know, the floor, the way the place echoes." She twists her fingers, pulls them away. I imagine what St. Mary's looks like to someone from the outside. The speckled linoleum is indeed institutional, its copper framing, the loud clack when one walks the halls. The walls are large and a smudged white chosen years ago, the offices all fake wood and swivel chairs, the classrooms more linoleum. Yes, I can picture it as Ruth may see it.

"You know, Thomas, why I never come, you know, to those parent meetings and things? I know we're supposed to and all...'cause I'm not that kind of people, and those kind of people make it clear that I'm not." She smoothes the denim over her knees. "I sit down with those kinds of people and all I want to do is stand up. They're not with me. They're looking at me, but they see something real different than what I am.

And I hate being all around that. I don't know to put my hands at my sides or fold them in front, for Christ's sake. And my nice dress all of a sudden looks stupid next to them. And I *like* my dress. It looks just fine. But when I'm out here eating the cheese and all... I don't know. I might as well smoke long cigarettes and wear a fur coat on Howard Street."

She lowers her head and nibbles on her bottom lip. Her hair falls to one side. She needs to say more, whatever it is that she means, and I want to give the space for it. I have learned this much from my service in the order, that confession, all communication, requires space for most people. Fear—all this time I believed that by listening I was helping absolve their fear. Instead, I was avoiding my own. Knowing this fills me with an empathy directed outward that I haven't felt in so long, that pure good openness, like when the sun peeks through after a rainstorm. It also embarrasses me. I want to tell her that we are part of all the choices we have made, and St. Mary's was a choice, that she chose to be a mother of a St. Mary's student. I want to stand up and say it, that we can be anything with our choices, but I know it's foolish to proselytize something I am only beginning to understand. I want to tell her about Mirabelle, about what I've done. I could tell her all of this, and much to my surprise I really want to. I want to talk to Ruth, as a person who shares fear, as a man who has been living inside it for so long, and not even knowing why. But I am keenly aware that she comes to me for something else, not for my humanity, but something I represent to her, a role. I am not really a man to her, maybe I'm not a man to anyone. I am a brother in black cloth, a counselor, a listener. I am made heavy with a sudden feeling of loss.

"There's hardly ever been a time when I didn't feel like that, you know, around people that I'm not from. I mean, I have my sister Sarah... and she's so ignorant of how other people think that it doesn't bother her. All the rest of my people are down in Tennessee and I hardly ever see them. I've told you about my family."

The first time Ruth told me a Tennessee story we were in the cafeteria at Hopkins hospital. Peter had fallen down the steps outside of the chapel and fractured his wrist. We were sipping coffee while waiting, and she told me about the green hills, the washboards and jawharps, her Grand-mother and cabbage, the way her Uncle Bo couldn't even read but played the fiddle faster than "a dog could piss it out hearing the dinner bell."

"Tell me. I forgot."

"Thomas, they are real good people...surely have some rotten ones in there, but most have a good heart. I always felt like they had a life that was real sharp and clear, like they made the air cleaner, and seeing was more important somehow. That doesn't even make sense. They have to work real hard when it's time, but they don't work when they're done. You know what I mean? And it seems here, you're always working a little bit all the time. There is never rest or any real feeling. It's like being half alive. You can hear half of everything or only half-taste food. And even in how everything looks. Like out there, it's all clear. Everything has a shape and color. Here, things all squash together, like they're no real lines in anything. You know what I mean?"

The battles outside Bristol, Tennessee were probably full of gun-smoke, war smog, but that was a long time ago. Smoke from a violent instant can clear, but the constancy of city life gives no reprieve. It is a violent continuity, a faithful blurring of lines. I find that beautiful about the city, the melding of things.

"Oh, Christ," she says, and throws her arms up.

I realize now she doesn't come to me for counsel. She only needs my ears to hear, but I'm fine with that.

"You know, I look around the neighborhood, and everything is what I know. Right? I've lived here a long time and there's nothing wrong with it, really. But I don't know anyone anymore. I got some neighbors who're real nice, but they can't know me...I'm not their kind of people. Even the ones who live in the same kind of place. They might even have a kid or something. But we're different. And I'm not saying that 'cause they're all Black. It's something else. I try to tell it to Peter, but he just thinks I'm being racist. I try and tell him I don't mean people like blood only. They can be any color and still be your people. I don't know. I'm speak-ing crazy now." Her laugh is phlegmy, and she clears her throat quickly.

I can listen to her speak forever, with that round rolling language, that language meant for the hills. I think of Mirabelle, who speaks like the trees, a more flat, yet rich, fecundity.

"Peter'll be in New York soon," she says like a snap. The weight of the words is extraordinary.

I can't even feel my nod. But I do feel her.

"You're beautiful," I say, and immediately become limitless.

Ruth looks pointedly at me, not accusatory, but almost admiring, perhaps at my honesty. Her eyes well, her mouth sputters with too much feeling, and she turns outward. I understand. "I'm gonna do this right," she says. She pulls my fingers into her palm. The white nails press deep into my tan skin. It feels like a final touch, but she doesn't try to get up. She sits with me, firm but unwilling to move. Perhaps she thinks she'll fall over, afraid to stand up with her own heavy words, her heavy thought. We sit there, quiet for a long while, both unaware of what to do with so much certainty.

*

Mirabelle has cleaned up my mother's house. I notice the front porch has been swept and the door scrubbed. Even the brass knocker is gleaming my bent face back at me. There is something lighter about the house. I almost feel a sense of betrayal creep up my legs at first, this new house, this updated history, but after seeing her satisfied face, hands folded in a dishtowel, it is supplanted with a warmth.

She nods, a tremendous power in the small movement that I can't identify, except that it belongs to her. "Thomas. Just in time for some lunch. Hungry?"

"What are you making?" I smell herbs and melted butter and meat.

"Hog's ass and hominy," she says with a straight face, and waits. We share a slow smile until she turns back to the kitchen. "Give me five minutes," booms from behind the wall.

The air is clear of dust motes and light pours in through the windows. The house always was a dark place, blanketed and cloistered. Now it feels exposed in a good way, cheerful. The walls of the living room are distinctly a color: winter green. The brass clock above the fireplace accurately tells time. Mirabelle has transformed this house into a home.

She returns with two plates of corned beef hash, each topped with an egg over-easy. The yolk is a perfect yellow dome.

"I'm kinda still having breakfast," she says.

"It looks great."

She hands me a fork. My mother's silver. Its age is given away more in style than condition. The scrolled handle has her initials engraved with flowery cursive. There is something about seeing her life continuing in such small detail, a legacy wrought in a pencil-thin trace. She probably imagined this fork in the hands of children that would come after her, the expansion of progeny, in a kitchen, perhaps in Omaha, or Savannah, or maybe even in this same house. They would ask with huge innocent eyelashes whose initials stared back at them, and the stories, illuminated bits of my mother, would unfold around a dinner table. She'd become a great curiosity, her stories forever larger than her small Italian body. I would have gladly passed stories like that on to my own children, and delighted in the way they told them to their children, the exaggerations, the misrepresentation, the unintended lies. I would have gladly done this.

"Your mama had some beautiful things," Mirabelle says softly, acknowledging my blurry stare.

"It seems."

"Hmm." She takes her fork and cuts her egg quietly.

"How are the boys adjusting?" I ask as I take a bite of the hash. It is very salty, but good.

"I don't tell 'em too much, s'all. Better for me to worry about things than them. They just think we moved. Love the house, though."

"As long as they are fine."

"They fine." She smiles. "You like the hash?"

"Very much."

"Everybody like hash. S'good for you, now. Can't go wrong with hash."

She eats slowly and carefully, as if she's afraid she'll wake up some alien element of the house, perhaps my mother's ghost. Her fork never clinks against the plate, and she puts it in her mouth with precision, no scraping, no smacking lips, and chews silent, absolutely silent.

"Mirabelle, is it fine if I pop over like this, sometimes?"

Mirabelle's head bobs as she looks at me incredulously, and swallows. "It's your house. You can do what you please."

"Think of it as your place, too…"

She nods quietly, with gravity.

"I feel good that someone is putting this house to use… and takes care of it." I look around to show her I've noticed.

"It needed some cleaning. I hope you don't mind. I touched nothing 'cept to dust. Ooh, dusty."

"You've only helped," I say.

"Would you rather stay in a house like this, Brother, you know, rather than living with all those other men?"

"Maybe. I don't know. I'I haven't thought about it."

"Got your own room?"

"I do."

"Well, see, that could be good, right? Got your own room but you got people, too. Could be good. How many you live with?"

"There's twelve of us," I say.

"Just like the Bible," she says.

"Sometimes it can be a little much living with that many people. Don't you think?" I ask.

"Like a family, sounds like."

"Well, not really. We're all grown men."

"You live together, right?"

"Well, yes."

"Then it's a family. Sounds like the best kind, too. No screamin' kids runnin' around, no wife tellin' you you got to cut the yard, no rotten husband sneakin' around on you while his babies sleep. You get to go in your room when you tired of 'em. See, that sound good to me." She laughs from her hips, a rich rocking that I feel as much as I hear. Its low volume defies its power.

"It's different, though. I respect them, very much actually, but I wonder about having a family, a real one. Something more tied together." I never would have said something like this before, but it's somehow part of the lightness I feel, the escaping of words. I am not afraid of this.

"I'm tellin' you Brother, you got the best kind of family. Who say anything 'bout family bein' together? My husband just got up and walked out after I had Torvoris. I don't think he felt tied to nothin', to get up and walk out the way he did. We coulda been strangers for all he thought. They ain't no ties left, none that you can't cut up when you feel like it. Least you bound to your house by somethin', bound by your religion. Most people got nothin' like that, even if they got a husband and kids."

"There's not much community left," I say.

"You got that right. That's why you lucky. You got people that gotta help you if you in trouble, at least. That's what it is." She motions to my plate with her chin. "Eat your hash, now."

"Trouble," I say.

"Like what's happening up in Ellwood. No one said two words to each other three months ago. Now, it's meeting here and meeting there, and *we're all in this together*. And I say, where were you all this time? And that's why these days your husband will leave you just like that, abandon his own kids," she slaps her hands, "like they nothin' to him." She gets up, sits back down without a pause. "He got no one to answer to no more. No one on your street give a damn." She looks off, out the window behind me.

"Things used to be different," I say. "Growing up in the county, everyone knew everyone else in our neighborhood. I remember when my mother left—I was really little—I remember women dropping food by for us. They made whole dinners, good ones. Meatloaf, parmigiana, meat and potatoes. They'd drop by, check on us, help us out with the house. It seems like fantasy now."

"That's real nice." Her words feel genuine, but there is something removed and bitter in them, as well.

"Maybe that's what we need now, to bring that community back, give each other that sense of responsibility," I encourage.

Mirabelle pulls her head back, the flesh of her neck pinching together, her eyebrows high. "I don't know about all that, Brother. There was problems with all that community, too, know what I'm sayin'? People all in each other's business. When you got that kinda pressure, you made to do things that maybe you don't want to do. See, people only want community when somethin' go wrong, but when we makin' good money and everybody happy, they don't want people all in they business. They's a pressure to havin' community, know what I'm sayin'? And people don't want it unless they need it. People talk about the good old days and all, but that's a bunch of horseshit."

Suddenly her eyes widen and she cups her hand over her mouth. "Brother, I'm so sorry. That wasn't me talkin'." She shakes her head, looks down, grabs her hips, as if her words physically hurt her, somehow, the shame of them.

I laugh, and she's confused. "Mirabelle, it's all right. I cuss like a sailor, all the time."

She looks up, dubiously. "You allowed to do that?"

"Well, it's not recommended, but they're just words."

"True, and I don't mean no disrespect."

"I know. They're just words."

She continues, after a few comfortable moments. "Anyway, now, all that community s'good sometimes, but it ain't good all the time. That's what I'm sayin'. Here, let me take that plate."

"Thank you."

She rises, her legs like tree trunks, and moves into the kitchen. I follow. It is small, not nearly the size of the one in the rectory, but cheerful. With Mirabelle rinsing the dishes and the light gleaming off the stove, something feels perfect, and I want to stay here. I already want to be in this room again, even though I'm here now. This kitchen, this whole house, felt more like a museum, an artifact, when my mother was alive. It was a mournful, colorless place. I look forward to Mirabelle, who is handing me a towel. I take a plate and start drying.

"Do you think it would have helped you if the community was together, you know, to keep your home?"

"Nah, not really. People are good to keep each *other* in line, but this was the city. They a different story. I mean, believe me, the people are *angry, real* angry, but they pissin' themselves cuz they can't keep the city in line. The city above all that. So, what can we do? The plates go in that cupboard."

I didn't know where the plates went, and am glad, now, that I do.

"That doesn't seem right to me. They should be the ones finding ways to make the people happy."

"I don't know about no government, Brother. They always comin' up with ideas, and I think most the time they mean good, and maybe that's me bein' nice, but it don't matter anyway, cuz what it's about is no government knows what I need or what you need. Only your own people know that. Your family, your friends. Problem is people don't know if they wanna be they own island or live with each other. But no matter what, we need people at least some of the time."

I am suddenly filled with something like pride. This woman is a home all to herself. She continues drying.

"I will never have children, Mirabelle. My family line ends with me."

She stops, gives me her kind, full attention. She drops her head down and looks up at me. There is wisdom and joy and pity and confidence and quietness. Her arm comes to my shoulder, like we are old comrades.

"You can't predict the future, Brother. But it worth tryin'." She folds her towel on the counter and puts the last plate away. "Don't you think?"

21

Ruth

I walk into the police station on Eastern Avenue. It looks like a post office, except there's lots of desks and the smell of old coffee. I didn't even bother to call ahead, since sometimes you'd be on hold with 911 until after you got pregnant and had the baby on your kitchen floor. I'm pointed to the front desk. A woman with real short black hair and no makeup leans on her elbows, reading a magazine.

"Hello. I was wondering if I could speak to someone."

"Sure, ma'am. What is it regarding?"

"Well, see, there is a man I have a restraining order on and…well, he's my husband. But anyway, he left me a flower on my table yesterday with a note, but it wasn't a flower I wanted. You see, he had to break into my house to give me the flower."

The officer woman pulls out a form. "Let me get your name."

"Ruth Anne Cryer. That's with a 'y.'"

She begins to write. "So, Mrs. Cryer, your husband gave you a flower?"

"Right, but not in a good way, y'know?"

"He wasn't supposed to?"

"My husband…you know, I don't like even calling him that. He won't sign divorce papers, and it costs too much, anyway. His name is Isaac Hibbs."

She writes that down too. "Okay."

"Isaac doesn't live with us. A couple of years ago he went all psycho on me and my son Peter—I had another son, Joby, but he's dead now—and me and him got out of there. Only, I should have left before I did, because Joby wouldn't have run away. But since then he's been calling and coming over and leaving things like flowers on my table with a note. So I got a restraining order." I wonder why the officer didn't write any of that down. Isn't that the story?

"How long ago did you get the restraining order?"

"Almost two years now."

"Has he violated the restraining order before?"

"Oh, yes."

"Have you called us before?"

"Well, no. I was never at the house when he broke in."

"How do you know it was him?"

"Well, sometimes he would leave pictures of himself. Naked porno pictures. Or notes. Things that gotta be him."

"Are you sure?"

"Definitely. And he used to call all the time, and creep me out by knowing where we live and all."

"Unfortunately, Mrs. Cryer, the restraining order doesn't protect you from phone calls unless he calls and threatens to violate the order by coming onto your property."

"Right."

"So what is the note on this flower he gave you? Does it suggest that he is threatening to violate the order?"

"Well, the note was blank."

"Blank?"

"There's no words on it. It's creepy."

She writes that down. "Was there anything else with the flower?"

"No. Just the note."

"The blank note."

"Yeah. It's creepy."

"How do you know it was your husband?"

"Isaac? I just know him. It's something he would do, you know?"

"Mrs. Cryer, is there any proof it was him?"

"I know it was."

"But if there was no note with his name saying he was coming over..."

"There *was* a note. Just cause there's no words on it doesn't mean it wasn't a note."

"I understand, but..."

"Look, I know."

The woman puts her pen down, real soft. "Ma'am, this is what we can do. If your husband calls and threatens you or your family's life, or if you see him violating the restraining order by coming on your property, you can call us and we'll send someone out right away. But we can't check on every suspicion. I wish we could, but we don't have enough patrol cars for that. Now, you can always file a harassment report if you like, for the phone calls. Here is the form. Fill in boxes one, two, and four. You need a pen?"

The form is a bunch of boxes and words, and I don't want to fill out any form—that's not what I need right now—but I take the pen in my fingers, anyway. My nails are a chewed up mess. Two of them are red from bleeding.

"Look, now, I'm telling you that blank note means something a lot more than nothing, and my gut is telling me that he's gonna come and do something. It means he knows where I live and he has nothing he wants to say but he has a lot he wants to do."

The officer pauses, moves the magazine off to the side, and folds her hands. I know the look she's giving me, like I'm some kind of charity case, like I'm a child. "I'm sorry, Mrs. Cryer. You know how many calls we get concerning domestic disturbance? It's a shame. We get there, and the girls' faces are banged up and they're crying and bleeding everywhere and scared, and we know these assholes have been hurting these women. But then we start handling their man, and the women pull a one-eighty on us and freak out, screaming 'get off him' or 'don't hurt him.' I know it's not always like that, but that happens most of the time. It's a shame.

And those are the cases where there is a direct violation: a threat, defying a court order, something like that. We get there, and there's nothing we can do."

I pull hair away from my face. "I'm not some girl," I say.

"Of course," she says.

"It's not like that this time. I won't get in the way. You can shoot the son-of-a-bitch for all I care. I'm not some pansy-ass."

"No, ma'am," she nods, and glances over to the magazine.

"I've been running from this asshole for two years. You can stick dynamite down his throat for all I care."

"Because you're married he needs to specifically make a threat to you in order for it to be a pursuable violation."

"What do you mean?"

"It's not enough for him just to be on your property. Not really."

"But I got a restraining order."

"I would advise you to get a divorce, ma'am."

"I got a restraining order!"

"You'd have more ground if you got a divorce."

"Divorces cost money." I throw the pen down on the desk.

The officer breathes deep and blinks real slow. "You give us a call if you see him, as soon as you see him around your house."

"I need help. I got a real bad feeling."

"OK. Maybe we can have a patrol car circle around your block tonight. What's your address?"

I can tell by the way she looks at me that they won't send no patrol, and she is just saying whatever it takes for me to be gone, to not bother her no more, to get back to her stupid fucking magazine. I feel like she's sending me back on home with a box of Rice-a-Roni. "You all can't do a thing, can you?"

"What's that, ma'am?"

I look around at the station. It's quiet, nothing like I imagined a station to be, with criminals being pushed into jailcells, hookers being booked, interrogation rooms, phones ringing in every corner. The ceiling lights are ugly. "So I can only call you to protect me after he's broken in and done chopped me in the gut. That right?"

"Ma'am, you give us a call if he threatens you, you hear? I'll send someone over right away. Okay?"

"Crazy…" I turn back to the station's front door, where I came in. Pointless. I can't get a divorce, I can't get police support, so what can I do? I can fill out more forms that do nothing. And wait. My Mama always told me "rely on no one." And though she was a the queen bitch of hellfire, she got this one right. She truly did. We're all on our own, truly.

"Ma'am, you didn't finish your paperwork."

What can I do? We're all on our own.

"Miss, Miss Cryer? Miss Cryer."

*

When Peter came home, he didn't say two words, pulled down like the life had just gone out of him. I know our fight didn't help nothing, but I know there's something else, too. I wish I could do something, to make fried eggs and chocolate shakes for us and sit with him, but there is a sting between us that only time will pour milk on. It's still too tender. And, to be honest, there's been sting for a while. I have to admit that now. It really hasn't been the same between us since Joby left. Not so much what Isaac did to us all, but that Joby's gone. And I stayed. I stayed with Isaac, even after what he did to my kid. And Peter saw that. Peter saw it all. How could he have any respect for his mama after that? How could I let this happen to my own children? No, how could I *choose* to?

I killed Joby. All I wanted in my life was to protect my children, but I killed him by not leaving that night in Cherry Hill, that night in the rain. I should have grabbed Peter, his terrified eyes big as saucers on that couch, and walked out of that house without so much as packing a bag. I should have said to Joby, "If this is Hell, Joby, then we'll all try to get out, or be stuck there together." But I didn't. I stayed. And though I finally did leave Isaac, the beating I give myself for doing it too late is far worse than any hand he ever laid on me.

Peter's reading in the living room. I'm sure he hears me walking around, but doesn't look up or pay no mind. The lamplight comes across his face in a nice, warm way. Somewhere along the line his nose grew more manlike. It's not the two dark holes and a bulb of skin, anymore. Since he was a baby he had more the likeness of me. When the kids and I visited Granny the few times before she died, I'd walk in the door and she would start and clutch her saggy boobs and say "Damn, Ruth Anne, if that child ain't the spittin' image of you, no matter how pickaninny his Daddy."

When he was little he complained about his nose. Sarah called him Puggy Petey. I told him it would change. I told him he had a long way to grow, and his nose would follow his legs and arms and shoulders. And it has. But I didn't see it change, not really, with all that warning. It just did and I never thought about it and it happened, his nose changing right under my own. What was it that kept me from watching this happen?

The look of pure mean that Peter gave me, the way he said *Ma*, with so much hot spit in his mouth, that's something I'll never shoo out of my head. I know he was hurting and he wanted me to feel his hurt, that's why he said what he did. And it's not *what* he said that made me a long-tailed cat in a room full of rocking chairs. I've known Peter was a fruit for a while now. Who gives a rat's ass who he likes? That's his business. I'm just sad he told me the way he did, like he was throwing an arrow into my heart. I wish he could have told me while we took a walk along the harbor, or over a crab cake at Faidley's, something nice.

Really, the only thing that worries me about him being a fairy is that he'll have to deal with men in his life, with their hiding, that weakness, with that hot burning deep inside their churning guts that you never know when and how will rise up in them, like a volcano. And the AIDS. Peter will never be safe. Or maybe he will know how to deal with the men because he is one, knows the churning because his guts do the same. He'll know how to deal with them better than me, I'm pretty sure of that.

I remember the time we went to the aquarium in the Harbor, me Joby and Peter, must have been ten years or so ago. Peter loved fish and used to sit in front of Sarah's tank and watch the guppies and tetras whenever we would visit. So he and Joby and I took the bus to the harbor. By then the Harbor was safe and it was fun to go down there and people watch. The aquarium was huge and they had everything imaginable from the bottom of the ocean, and then some. Joby ran off on his own, and that was all right cause he was pretty big by then. But Peter stayed with me. We walked deeper and deeper into the building, Peter's head bent so far back you'd think it would pop right off, his eyes and mouth open wide. His face was fixed, swallowed up, like he was in the water himself. It seemed the only other thing he was aware of in the whole world was his hand wrapped around my fingers, which he squeezed real tight.

When we were by the dolphin pool, Joby ran up to Peter and stretched out his hand. "Hey Peter, come here. I gotta show you something." He looked at Joby, then looked up at me. I was smiling. He tightened his grip on my finger, turned back to Joby, and shook his head without one word. He always followed his brother, so this was special to me, that he wanted to be with me. Maybe that's why I remember it so well.

And now he looks out the window, his book on his lap, and doesn't even turn to me. We're in the same house, but we couldn't be farther apart.

I go into my bedroom, pull the letter out of my pocketbook again and read.

Congratulations Mr. Peter Cryer. We are pleased to extend you an invitation to be...

New York is far away. I'd hardly ever see Peter. But that wasn't it. I look at the letter again. Mr. Peter Cryer. Mr. The letters seem to take his name and close it up, make it stand all on its own instead of being a part of many names. It is not Peter Cryer, student at St. Mary's; not Peter Cryer, Baltimore teenager. It is not Peter Cryer, son of Ruth Anne Cryer. It is all itself. It demands its own spot, a bigger spot that is full of other Mr.s and other names that have letters at the end: MD, PhD, Esq. New York doesn't feel nearly as far away as that.

I take myself into the living room and lean against the wall. Peter is still glowing under the window, looking at the whole world. I close one eye and hold the letter up to Peter's image, seeing how it fits. The typed letters run across the page and disappear into his pale blue pajama top.

I know he will take the offer, and now I know he should. He is leaving me. If I was more a mother and less a woman, I would only say he is leaving. He is going up to New York City to pursue dreams, ones that I don't even know about, and he will be a Mr. among a whole slew of Mr.s. He will leave and begin a completely different life. It strikes me funny that someone can do that, get up and leave and start a life inside a life already, just like that, by choice. Granddaddy didn't choose to die. Daddy didn't choose to lose the farm and move to Baltimore. Granny had no choice but to stay in Tennessee her last years. And me, well, show me where the choice was in any of it. Yet, it can happen, a new life inside a life that's been living. Any fool could keep all the things they like about their past and carry them along, while dropping the ones they didn't, anywhere between here and there.

What would I carry with me? Not Peter, not Joby. There is no career or anything. I have no lover in my life. I'm not sure what I can take with me. It seems all these things are tied down to a place.

I could take my strength, if I had it. I believe I do. I can take all the things I've learned about love. I can take my love for Peter and Joby. I can take my pride and I can take courage. I can take knowing I have lasted this long and I have a lot of living left. I'm sure I could make something of all that. It's just a matter now of doing what needs to be done. I will soon take with me the knowing that I made things right by my children, that for all the bad I did to them by staying with Isaac, for all that I put my children through all these years, I made up for it in the end. That Joby didn't die without some kind of justice, that Peter can see that his mama isn't just a woman who's afraid, and that she's sorry for all of it. And she's not going to be a pansy-ass no more.

It's funny. I keep looking for signs to make sense of what I already know I'm going to do. Maybe this is why choice is so scary, because it's running in the dark, without anyone telling you what's out there. The future is like a place that only comes into view when you get there. There can't be signs, because no one else knows where it's at, either. Yeah, maybe they've been near there, or around there, but not *there*.

I walk back into my bedroom and pick up my cell. My fingers are stiff as I dial his number.

"Hello?" The voice is dull and loud.

"Isaac, it's Ruth Anne."

"Ruth Anne." He says my name like it's his. I want to slam the phone down over and over and pop his eardrums.

I clear out my throat and make my voice even. My ear sweats. "I want to talk to you."

"Ah."

"To have a talk."

"My wife wants to talk to me." There's a pause. There's something in his voice, like he expected me to call, and I hate it.

"Are you drinking?" I ask.

He sighs real dramatic. "I don't believe in divorce, Ruth." He is too calm.

"No. I was wondering if we could talk."

"That's nice." I hear him laughing deep in his chest. I squeeze the phone until my hand hurts. My lower lip stings from my teeth. I'm not sure how to do this. I don't know when would be the right time.

"Ruth Anne?"

"Yes."

"You called *me*."

I flip my head like I'm shaking something off. "I was wondering if we could talk."

"You said that already," he says.

"You could come over and maybe we can make some lunch. I've just been thinking about a lot, when we were together, and…"

"You lonely?"

There is a slimy coating over all the words. I can imagine his tongue hanging out of his mouth and shaking like a rattlesnake tail, slowly traveling up my leg. I want to confront him about the flower and the blank note, but I don't need him being defensive. I need to make sure he comes over.

I close my eyes and pretend I'm talking to someone else. A woman is asking if my hair color is natural, or if I know the recipe for cornbread. My grade school teacher is asking if I did my homework and if I remember the capitals of all fifty states.

"Yes."

"You're inviting me to come over?"

"Yes."

"Ruth, I would love to see you. There's a lot to talk about."

"Yes."

*

Isaac hung up minutes ago but my hand is still gripping the phone, pressed and numbing my ear. My elbows dig in to my thighs.

The moon has moved out of the window frame. The only traces of it are the reflection on the tree next door and the faded blinking of all the stars. But its sureness hasn't left me.

With Isaac gone I can make things right, for Joby, for Peter, even for me. I can have thoughts in front and behind me and I won't be crowded in. And when I kill him, he will be gone, and this will be my apology. Joby being dead won't be for nothing. My life won't be for nothing. And, Peter. He will leave and I will be alone, but I will be more than alone if I live every day regretting my life. Above everything I don't want to live in this regret. Not anymore.

22

Peter

They were talking. During Calculus the only thing being calculated were words. I heard the whispering, the urgency, the knife-tongued gossip. There was a heft to their breath, and they would come to my name—*Pe-ter*—and it would cut through all the other whispers. *Pe*, and the pocket of air would pistol into an ear like a sneeze. *Ter*, and the lips would peel back revealing the snarl underneath. My name said everything.

There was more talk in Honors Latin, and the level of whispering increased. Father Frank had to threaten the class twice to shut up. I bleared at the blackboard, the conjugations of *venari* commingling with chalk smears and dust, the letters appearing as indistinguishable curves and lines, as if I didn't understand language of any kind. Except for my name, *Pe-ter*, that puff and snarl.

Fuck them.

The bell rings and I'm the first to stand. I'd rather hear the whispers at my back than see the faces, the teeth. I try to look unaffected as I move through the hall. Jude will go to his locker to change books. I concentrate on getting to him, whiting out the rest of the hall, the adolescence, the ringing in the ceiling, the whispering, the rows of dingy locker doors, the fluorescence painting everyone's skin the color of an illness, the crass daylight silting through the windows, the thick dust, the thick faces of the teachers standing guard at their classrooms, the shrill shrieking scuffing of the fucking linoleum.

He is not here. He's always here. This is where he's supposed to be.

I am afraid to turn, but I have no choice. I can either bury my head in my chest, or wade through with dignity.

I face the loudness behind me. It all comes in, the weight of it. It collects at the back of my throat. I walk towards the door that empties to the courtyard.

Sanders is first, his thick neck, head that looks like a helmet. His barrel chest swells from his small hips and reedy knees, a giant sail fastened to a kayak. He always looks so stupid.

"So, Cryer, heard you were giving Woolsey's finger a blowjob this morning."

A group of juniors huddle around him, look at me with wide eyes, and wait. My throat is chalky and I swallow. I know I have the words to whip around his witless chiding, but nothing. I'm not all here.

"I don't know what you're talking about." I move past them. The staleness presses into me. I want air. I keep moving towards the door. They're laughing. I should have said something.

I push open and light floods me. I wind around to the porch outside the cafeteria. I thought the fresh air would feel good, but everything is still heavy. My eyes adjust and I see a whole crew lounging on the picnic tables. Some of them point and say my name, puff and snarl.

Jimmy, with his own thug duo, hops up and crowds into me. The scratchiness in my throat moves deep into my chest and pulls down hard.

"What's up at Mass today, Peter?" begins Jimmy, loud enough for the porch to hear. "What did you do to Jude? You sucked on his finger?"

I try to keep my head up, but my chest is so scratchy. I take small breaths. My lungs are filled with wood shavings. I have to keep clearing my throat. Why am I so full of retreat? Dignity, Peter, dignity.

I don't stop walking. "That's what you say." It hardly comes out. My lungs are swelling, like an allergy. I run up the stairs to the grotto to get away from them. I wheeze as I climb. My chest is full of sand, full of wood shavings, full of salt. I suck in air like an old man. I cross the grass to get to Mary, who stands helpless. My head pounds. Blood is going to burst from my head. I try to clear the flames from my throat. When I reach her I can lean against her. I can get a breath. I will spit up the shavings and the sand. I'll retch it all out of me. Mary, the whole world is writhing around us, a bunch of tails and tongues, wagging the light, falling out of focus, swirling within this moral cataract. Mary, if only I can reach you. Something will happen. Something will be lifted. Your constancy, the life of a statue, far outweighs the mobility of my slipping in and over. You are safe.

Tony's voice chases me, all laughs, in between and outside. "Where you going, Freebie?" Little torments all around me. The air is cold, stinging. But the sun is hot. It beats on my head. Mary can't help me breathe. I need calm, while my body betrays me. I need a glass of water. To sit down and be still. My chest is so thick that breathing makes my eyes water.

"Where are you going?"

I want to spit my lungs at his face. To have it all come up and out and all over him. All these years I've been carving out my own niche, making a clear path for me to walk through, just enough to survive and just enough for me to stay firm in who I am. And now, it feels not like a path, but a see-saw, straddling two worlds. I have been wrong. I am not viewed as bold to these idiots, but something else. Look how they close in around me, like the weak link of the species, ready to pounce and feed. I have gone too far, have gone from bold to something else. Simply because of a mouth and a finger? I can't run, but damn. The running, tails to snap, tongues to snap. The pressure has to stop.

I turn. "I don't know what fucking happened!" It takes the rest of my lungs to get it out, and my face flames where anticipation and moment meet, where the shame of lying, of not being able to stand square and strong and say *oh, yes, I did it*. Not this time. I look only long enough to catch legs, bookbags, huge eyes, all parts of them, but not connected.

I twist away and run, past Mary, over to the street. I keep going, across, leaving the school, little bursts in my chest. I lurch down Baltimore, but the street is so narrow; there's no room for me on this road. I stop and my legs give way against a stoop where a woman and her two kids sit. I cough. It's deep and painful and dry, but there's nothing. There are no wood shavings or salt. No sand or olive pit. Not even words. Nothing comes up but a sharp, high-pitched hack that sounds like a rooster, a cock, a crow.

"You all right, honey?" the mother asks. I look up at her, obviously poor, rather fat. Her kids furrow their brows at me. The girl has a white Barbie doll in her hand, absently stroking its blonde hair.

I have lost my ground. And then I realize that if my classmates know what happened, then the teachers and the administration might know what happened. And if they know what happened, they might call me into the office and that will be it: expulsion. No high school diploma. No college. No escape.

Why did you do it, Peter? Why did you have to open your mouth, your fucking mouth? And Jude, what has he said? Of course he was freaked out. I sucked his finger during Mass. Why did I think that was the way to tell him anything? And now I may be expelled and may have ruined everything because I love that boy so much. Fuck.

There is nothing to do but run. I run all the way home. I could have run to Rome.

*

The train makes me feel like I ate a ton of eggs, the runny ones, that butter and yolk queasiness. I haven't eaten anything since I got on, my meal only the slight rocking motion on a giant machine barreling towards New York. The guy next to me doesn't seem to mind, his head dropped back, mouth open, a Pez dispenser. His nose hairs are Greek.

This feels right, the only thing I can think to do. If everyone pushes me away, then away I'll go, I'll leave.

I tossed *Catcher in the Rye* and *The Prophet* into my knapsack, along with some clothes and the rest of my money, but I'm too glued to the window. The world whirls by in gray and white lines, telephone wires and washed out houses. Nothing much to look at, but I keep waiting for a single image, something, that will announce my leaving, a trumpet to this new journey, a man holding a cardboard sign that says "On Your Way," something I can see that will become the affirming symbol of this whole thing.

I am not going to feel like I belong anywhere. All the slapping—Tony Farissi, Grant, Janke, school, the cafeteria, sunflowers, Ma, fuck—won't do anything if it can't even reach me. They can swing their arms out, waiting for palm to strike cheek, bone to bone, waiting for the sting to get me, but I'll be long gone, and the arc of their arm will keep on, nothing to slow its intent, until it comes right back round and nails them in their own head. I won't be there, and they'll realize how they only hurt themselves more than me.

I don't know what I'm doing, how long I'll be gone, or if I'll ever come back. It's the leaving that matters.

The age, the darkness of train, feels romantic to me, and not in the way girls use romantic—I mean the right way. Wrapped in my coat, legs curled into the seat, looking out at the whizzing world, knowing it will slow and stop once I'm deep in the belly of New York, the greatest city on earth. There is a truth to it. I can see what I look like right now, can imagine the music playing. Something with vibrating guitar, a constant synth note in the background.

A woman gets on at the Trenton stop, and sits across from me, her bags bursting at the zipper. She is nice-looking, for an older woman. All of her skin fits her face well; even the wrinkles have a kind of purpose to them. And she doesn't smell like a bouquet of cheap flowers, like many old women do. I mean, why would an old woman insist on the desperate need to be associated with a blooming flower?

She suddenly asks me, "Do you have Irish in you?" I guess my face gives away some of my feeling for such a stupid question, because she quickly adds, "Your hair, it's sort of red, very unusual for... my daughter's hair is red. Her father is Irish."

"I am," I say. Yeah, it's a stupid question, but she's elegant, with her knees together, tilted towards the window. She still has delicate ankles.

"My Ma, she's white, Irish, it's even redder, like that coppery color. And she has more freckles. My dad's why I'm…"

"You're lucky. That hair color is recessive. And it's so nice." I don't like the word recessive—it stings somehow, but I can tell she means no harm. She seemingly acknowledges her envy by scooping behind the ear her own gray with two fingers, eyes down in humility. I don't like her doing that, because she has such nice fingers and the rings on them are sensible and lovely, nothing too gaudy.

"I like it. My brother's hair was typical and black, so yeah, I'm the lucky one."

"Black Irish," she giggles.

"You can say that," I say.

*

New York's Grand Central Station is way bigger than Penn Station in Baltimore—huge. People are everywhere, zipping feet and briefcases, echoes and all at once. It takes me many seconds to get hold of everything. But man, it's what I want, to be in the middle, have the electricity all around my head. I go up the marble steps to the mezzanine, turn, and then back down, into the sea of people, descending slowly, a movie star at his opening, everyone below, everything wanting. I could do it over and over, but I know I'd look like a freak. I search instead for a kiosk, a person with a uniform on. The first thing I want to do is go to Central Park. I've always wanted to walk in Central Park, alone, maybe with a cigarette puffing from my pouty lips, the only living boy in New York thing.

The girl in the information booth looks like I asked her the dumbest question ever. She rolls her eyes and points, like no one ever comes to New York for the first time and wants to see Central Park. Her makeup looks desperate, so I don't feel like she's one-upped me or anything like that. I shrug it off and follow her finger. I even say thank you, in my sweetest voice. I've heard plenty of times that New Yorkers are rude. I don't blame them. Most people *are* stupid. But they shouldn't assume everyone is. If she would have given me a chance, she wouldn't have been so dismissive. We may even crack each other up, be friends.

I'm almost out the revolving doors when I realize I left my bag at the booth. I look back. I don't see it. It would have been right next to the booth, under the girl's scowling face. I run over, search around. Gone. The bag is gone, just like that, with my clothes and my books. I twist around. How could it disappear so quickly? I am about to ask the girl if she saw anyone take it, if she saw it at all, but I know she didn't. You can tell she's one of those bitches who thinks nothing is interesting beyond her own manicure. I don't even ask. The adrenaline courses through me.

I look again, around the booth. I scan the bobbing heads of people in brisk walk. The bag, anywhere. But I know it's not worth it, even though most of my money and my clothes were in there. I don't even know why I packed what I did. Whatever fit in the bag, I guess. It wasn't really a plan, more a need, and took all of ten minutes.

Fuck it. I'm in New York for the first time, the place I've dreamed of being forever. If I have no clothes and little money, I'll figure it out. People lived without currency and denim for thousands of years, before we had sewing machines and capitalism and sweatshops. We ran around with calloused soles, skin bare, took what we wanted. New York is merely a concrete version of the wilderness, you could say. Buses ride like mastodons, the mountains here a perpendicular steel eruption to the heavens. There was no money in the hunt, in the blocking of the sun, shelter in caves. And didn't all the great artists, the great writers, the musicians, show up to New York young and filthy and poor, and it worked out for them. Besides, Central Park is free. I researched.

Gray, loud, crowded, soaring towers that bleed right into the color of the sky. Who cares about a bag? The cold wind, the pushed sounds of car-horns, the syncopated beats of heels on sidewalk all slice through the air, penetrate. So much is going on. It becomes very easy to figure out how you must walk. I don't stop, make a choice, and head to the right. You can tell it's important to keep pace with everyone else. I adjust my scarf and work it. Arteries, platelets, the healthy flow.

And like destiny, a collective seeking intuition, all that jazz, there it is. It has to be Central Park, butted right against the most majestic of

buildings, a splay of late-winter trees, their naked branches swallowing
people in black pea coats, coffees in hand, horse carriages. I found it
without the need of a map, or trial and error. One decision, and *voila*! I
can believe in omens. It feels so good to be far away from everything in
Baltimore, even if I don't know what the fuck I'm doing.

The park dips down into itself, a recess of land as well as city, a nurturing pocket. The pathway meanders, curves this way and that, urging the
walker to get lost, forget about their job on the other side of the trees,
the straight lines of human ingenuity, of the city grid. How clever, the
park an antidote to the logic of the city.

Patterson Park is nothing like this. I heard they cut down many of
the trees because it was easier to spot the shady dealings of what Highlandtown had become. Maybe that's where that term came from, shady
dealings, under trees, shaded from the eyes of the law. All of Patterson's
open space doesn't feel like much of an antidote to anything, as if Baltimore bleeds itself into the park, no reprieve. People aren't walking in
Patterson to get lost. They walk their dogs so they can take a shit, or
maybe play Frisbee, until it gets dark, and then everyone flees for their
life. I bet people walk in Central Park at night. With so many people
around, how can anything happen?

I don't even see buildings anymore. Imagine when the trees have all
their leaves, how dense it would be, how one could easily disappear, minutes from their own neighborhood. What an awesome thought. Only
to reemerge into their life as if nothing happened, and the day resumes.
That is what I want my life to be, a series of disappearing acts, to descend
into anonymity, to be harbored by trees when actions have exposed me.
How can I ever go back to St. Mary's, the snarling mockery of students,
the tsk tsk of teachers who rely on faded seminary walls as their moral
compass? So, my mouth and his finger, what the fuck of it? Why does
the exposure already close my life like a box? That life is so fucking tight,
small, like a fist. And Ma, her hand, she was so scared. I can't even be
angry, exactly. But I can't forgive it, either; the slap—the pathetic gesture. It's disappointing that she didn't do it with full intention, that she

didn't own it, or at least think of something else, something less Lifetime movie-of-the-week. At least I mean what I do, at least I meant to blow Jude's finger.

I am alone among the branches, deep within. Where do I go? In the park, in the world, same thing. The familiar parts of my life are being erased. I am made unable to return. I think of that amusement park they're going to build in Highlandtown. I am the neighborhood before the wrecking ball, before the roller coasters and funnel cake, so what am I supposed to do other than move on? If there's nothing to return to, why go back?

How can Jude be so afraid? I saw his trembling body as I was shaving him. He asked me to do it! He had to know what that was going to lead to. He had to feel the heat he was generating off his body. He wanted me. Why didn't I just go for it then? Now, he turns away from me, lowers his eyes. I can't tell what it is. I was tired of anticipating, playing up the maybe. I had to suck his finger. Weird, I know, but it just felt like what I was supposed to do. I don't know why I thought that, of all things, would be what he needed.

There is a guy sitting on a random bench under a tree that still has its leaves. His posture is familiar, a slouch that seems to protest verticality. The loose fro, the skin tone, the dark black eyes, even from here. He sees me as I see him, and there is this moment of recognition, that certainty. He leans forward.

"Joby?"

My voice surprises even me. I haven't made those syllables out loud in a long time, once so familiar and now erased. Impossible, but it becomes my entire mind, the shock of it. I quicken towards him.

"Joby!"

He stands up, body sprung into alarm. He looks both ways, like crossing a street, and takes off.

Absurd as it is, I follow him. There's nothing else to do, a fullness in the follow. He walks fast, but not as fast as someone running from something in fear. He doesn't walk as fast as I know he can, because I'm able to keep up. Joby was lightning, always running from something in fear, even on the track that went round and round, getting him nowhere. His fear burned ruts in the pavement. This pace is a leading, not an escape. I follow.

"Joby?"

I push harder. We are deep into the park, running, dead leaves stirred in the speed. A road appears through the bramble, an openness. He runs across. Cars zoom past. I see his blue jacket getting smaller, but the park opens up. There is a terrace, or something, steps. I finally cross the street. I don't see him for a moment, and think he has disappeared. But then, by the statue, a fountain. He stands there.

"Joby! Wait!"

What an absurd order to make—wait—the whole thing absurd, stupid. Wait for what? Joby, for what? I am fully aware of the impossibility as I run to catch up, his blue jacket getting larger, the black of his eyes clear and tight as winter. This is not Joby, of course it isn't, but it is Joby, and why does it matter? Joby left, too.

I catch a stone on my foot, and flail, arms and hair, and hit more stone, face first. It is a groan of pain, slow moving and large. Blood on my upper lip. I stand up, the pain all in my face. I look back to the road, on the sides, the pathways. No trace of him. I walk up to where he was, the fountain. I know he isn't Joby, but he looks so much like him, what I remember. I don't know. Blood is running from my nose. I wipe with my sleeve, a long smear slowly seeping into the fabric. I fully understand the pointlessness in calling his name. There is a statue of a woman above the fountain. The blood keeps coming, I feel it drip onto my shirt. I clamp and hold my nose up. The woman has wings. An angel. She has a lily in one hand. Under her feet are cherubs, seeming to marvel at their placement, between angel and the water.

I can't understand why I needed to call that guy Joby, why I was chasing after him. Of course it wasn't Joby. But he looked like Joby, moved like Joby.

After walking straight for however long it takes, the screaming city comes back, the buildings all line up to greet me with their multitude. It seems impossible to really get lost in the park. So long as you go straight, the city will find you again. That feels comforting, sort of.

I am aware of how I must look, blood on my face and shirt, which is of course a very light, very stainable yellow. Fuck. I find a restroom in a deli and at least rinse off my lips and chin, pull the brown crusts from the rim of my nostril. The shirt is definitely ruined. I have no other with me. I squeeze the paper towel I'm using to rub out the blood, until my knuckles turn white. I want to hurt something. The foolishness of running after Joby's doppelganger, the way I look, that I ran after him at all. Joby. The same result, a different circumstance, that I know well. He runs, I run after, I fall, he keeps on. Joby. The name is out, I said it aloud, and now it is all back, and that pisses me off, because it hurts.

Columbia. It is in Manhattan, that I know. I could go there, all that New York will be in the future, nothing of the past there, the way it should be, the New York I've wanted. I look for a kiosk, a subway station, something, and soon find stairs that descend into the underground. I ask a man coming out of the subway how do I get to the school, and without sizing me up or anything he tells me to take the line up to 110th. He didn't even look at me funny for having blood on my shirt. I like that. People don't look at you funny when you ask for directions in New York, even if you have blood on your shirt.

I go down, struggle to figure out where to go, people every which way, music reverberating off the tiled walls, the crush of the trains rolling in. It's dirty, but no one seems to care. I love it.

We all pack into the train. I am a part of them, easily, though I speak to no one. Every kind of person is packed into this thing—Black, white, brown, Asian, and a lot of in-betweens, the not-sure-whats, like me. Nothing of it, here. Everyone doing what they're doing, too busy to care or pay attention to anyone else. I look for signs that tell me how many stops I take before Columbia, but it's too crowded to move over to the map, so I pay close attention to every stop, the tiles on the subway walls. The numbers move up—79th, 86th, 96th. I anticipate 110th. The next stop says Central Park North. I marvel that a park can be so big that it traverses that many blocks. A lot of people get out at this stop, and I wonder what's up there. An older Black man keeps staring at me, but not in an alarming way or anything. When our eyes meet he asks, "Mother or father?"

I immediately know what he means, and answer, "Father."

"Me too. You're so light."

"You're not."

He laughs.

The next stop says 116th. I start. What happened to 110th? I hurry through the crowd, try to get out, but the incoming passengers sandwich me in. I could always double back. I squeeze out at 125th. I can simply walk back the fifteen blocks, and see some of the city, rather than smash myself back in the train. And the walk would do me good.

A totally different place, but this one looks familiar. The buildings are lower, older, the sidewalk isn't as crowded. It's more run-down, mostly brick, grungier. It looks a hell of a lot like Baltimore.

And there he is again, only he has changed clothes. He wears a black coat, jeans, and the famous grin, the one that hooked everybody when he was younger. He could seduce girls, teachers, people's kids. Everyone was hooked. Everyone loved Joby, even when he got busted for drugs, or stole money out of your wallet. *He's in a phase, he'll snap out of it, he's a good kid, don't worry, he's got potential.* This Joby appears to be waiting, for what I have no clue. For me? No, never. I do not call his name, or approach. I simply watch, as people pour all around us, he and I the two constants on this sidewalk in New York.

My prominent memories of Joby are—like all memories—pointless, things that fill the mind, and take us away from what's happening in front of us. Most are of him displaying some big-brother meanness. He used to love to strip me of my clothes, force me outside, and lock the door. I was little, so it wasn't *as* embarrassing as it could have been. I would wrap my hands around, trying to cover as much of my body as I could, and cry. I would feel so hurt by him. I'd let him hurt me every time. Stupid.

We were visiting my grandparents at their farm, one of the rare times we went. I was about six or seven. Joby got a BB gun for his birthday, which goes to show you how crazy redneck Ma's Tennessee family was. I mean, Joby couldn't have been more than ten. I was laying around on the porch, feeling the summertime, when Joby said to me, "Hey you have ten seconds to run." I didn't know what he was talking about, but when I saw him cock the gun, the fear overtook me, I remember. And, instead of bolting out of there, I ran straight to his legs, hugged them, and begged.

He counted, "Ten...nine...eight..." I remained at his legs, only my pleading grew louder, more desperate, filled with tears, "Please Joby, please," my hands clenching the fabric of his shorts. It wasn't until he got to the last seconds that I knew he wouldn't relent, and in terror I finally began to run. I heard *one!* and a moment later the pop of the gun and a searing pain in my butt. He got me. I went down, clutching my ass, screaming. It only took several seconds for someone in the farmhouse to run out, my Uncle Arthur. When I turned toward him as he picked me up, I saw Joby. He was standing in the same place I left him on the porch, with that grin on his face, the one that seduced everyone, and then slipped into the dark of the house behind him. That was the first time I remember hating that I loved him so much.

I did love him. So much.

He hasn't moved, still waiting for something, maybe nothing, this Joby who is obviously not Joby. He scratches his leg, adjusts his stance. I stay put, staring. Why does one love their family so much, even when they don't deserve it? How much is it the animal in us? How much is evolutionary, some kind of tribal fitness? And how much is the opiate of culture, the brainwashing of *well, that's how it is*, something like that? How could I love someone who scarred my left ass cheek for life?

He finally moves on, disappears into the sidewalk, the street carts, the goings-on of the neighborhood, not even looking back. Why would he? He never saw me. And it wasn't Joby, anyway. So absurd. This is what memory does to people, to Ma, it haunts us. Fuck it.

The sun is waning. It's too late to really see Columbia, and I don't even know where it is from here. I've lost the desire anyway, feel so tired. I go down into the subway station and back in the direction I came from. The faces are everywhere. I could probably see Ma, Jude, maybe even another Joby. I keep going. Perhaps one of these faces is my father. I know what's going on. I'm not stupid. I keep going.

The Statue of Liberty. That would be an appropriate spot to visit, the gateway for so many new lives, a giant green welcome mat for those seeking. Joby and I planned climbing to the top and mooning the world.

New York will be no boys who are afraid, no mothers who are afraid, no fucking people all running scared. New York will also be no Joby.

I look for maps, find out how to get to Liberty. Above ground, newer skyscrapers soar through the gray air. A wind picks up and bites into my chest, but I walk into it. I believe Ground Zero is somewhere around here, but that is not where I need to be. I don't need to see any more absence today. A big hole where once there was teeming vertical life, business in the sky. I don't need to see what was, what will never be again. I'm sure many people crowd around, stare into the absence, use that time to reflect. There are many that think they need that. I feel that's been my whole life, though, staring into the absence, the promise of something. What if Ma stuck around with Abe? Would we have been a steady family? Would we have lived in a proper house, stayed in one place, had dogs and a badminton set and normal family problems? Would she have never met Isaac, been so desperate for love to have fallen for someone like Isaac? Would Joby have stayed? Would we have fought like brothers, but looked out for each other, the way brothers do? Would we have come to New York together, like he promised? Would he have kept his promises?

And I wonder what about that is so desirable anyway. So what if I had constancy? I'd probably then complain about how boring life was. Look at all those films, TV shows, novels about the malaise that coats the American nuclear family, stressing the evils of stasis, that staying put, the effect inevitable change has on that kind of life. Maybe I'm better for how I came up, constantly moving, running, looking over my shoulder, more resourceful or something.

But there's something about it that grips my heart. I can try to reason how ridiculous the desire is, how it plays like greener grass, a stupid platitude, fine. It never shakes off me, though. What is a life that moves constantly, never settling into an understanding of what is around, that only looks toward the next place and the next place? Ma never stops moving, and look at her. She has nothing, really. How could she, always ready to run? I want something. I want to go forward into the world, and then let it gather around me.

And wait, here I am in New York. Aren't I running?

As I approach the ferry post, a sign tells me that the Statue of Liberty is closed for maintenance. The ferry isn't running to reach it. I can see the statue, out there, like it's rising from the water, in the distance, but I can't get there.

The welcome mat has been pulled out from under. I can't help but play the metaphors in my head.

The dimming light of the sky isn't exactly welcoming, either. The buildings block the exact location of the sun, so the muting of light is dull. I feel an overwhelming sense of loneliness, even while people cross all around me, taxis honk, and neon lights switch on.

I walk, I don't know where. Everywhere seems to be open, yet closed, so much life and yet nothing. Almost every block is a subway entrance, inviting me to go down into the belly of New York, only to be spit out somewhere else that will say, quite simply, *no*.

A small café with a blinking sign advertising coffee and pita sandwiches beckons me. No one's inside, the walls are a dingy yellow, and somehow its pathetic existence feels more comforting than anything else right now. I walk in. The man at the counter first greets me with the plastic *hello can I help you*, but quickly looks at me with a screwed-up face, even takes an unconscious step back.

"Can I get a falafel?" I say.

"Hey, do you know you're bleeding, man?"

"Hey, do you know I'm hungry?" I snap back. What business does this guy have asking me anything but if I want fries? Look at him, with his yellow shirt with red stripes and stains, looking like a one-man hot dog stand. Why does he need to tell me I'm bleeding? Everyone's got to say something. Everyone has to make their little judgments. Why can't we all leave each other the fuck alone? Coney Island hot dog fuck.

I grab the falafel, sit at a table, and stare out the window, at a world so different and similar to my own. It's New York, but it's anywhere, cold and damp and unwilling. The salt of the hummus almost stings my tongue. I realize it's not too late to get on a train back to Baltimore. There is just enough cash left in my pocket, taunting me. Isn't that the way it works? At least my *failure* can be followed through.

*

I need some power, something affirming, so once I get back to Baltimore, I head straight to Benny's. Even though the men are gross, at least they want it. I could have any of them, and right now that's what I need. And I can't stay at home right now, anyway. I can't. I need someone to want me, to not push me away. I know it's a band-aid. I know.

The bar is almost exactly the same every time I come in, from the music playing to the men lining the counter, and, unfortunately, even to Grant sitting at the far edge in his cocky smirk and sideburns. He sees me, gives me a quick head nod, and goes back to whatever trick he's picking up tonight, one of the pale-faced underage kids who frequent the place. I think his name is Kyle, something like that, another fucking pasty-ass white kid.

I go to the other end and say hello to Derek, spark up small-talk, very outside-my-body like. I don't want to sleep with him again, or anyone tonight, for that matter. I just want them to shower me with their affections, at least show the desire through their beady, grateful eyes and the way they rest their rough hands on the small of my back. Derek talks about his job and his house, the dog that's too stubborn to die. Others chime in with their own dog stories, house stories, bland job comparisons, each taking turns touching, rubbing my shoulder, my back, running their fingers on mine. I have met all of them at one time or another, have even slept with a few. Sometimes, more than one has their hands on me, and it feels a little claustrophobic. A couple more saunter over from the pool table, say hello, everyone chatting about trivial things while touching, smiling, touching, laughing, touching. I look over at Grant, who is tonguing Kyle now. He looks up and I immediately look back to one of the guys, smile as wide as I can to show I'm enjoying myself immensely, with all the attention, the knowing I can go home with any of them. I even laugh, at nothing, but no one will find it awkward. Everyone here is laughing also at nothing in particular. They all can hear the emptiness of the sound, no matter how loud, as if it comes from somewhere else in the body.

I look over to Grant again. This time he looks up to me while he is making out with Kyle, and keeps his gaze, steady while he licks the boy's neck. The fire courses all through me furiously, and I'm not sure what it will turn into. My body pulls back instinctively, and I stumble through the men surrounding me, almost fall if it wasn't for their hands grabbing, rubbing. I quickly pull myself out of the tangle, practically climbing over them, their mouths shaping O's at the sight of my sudden movement.

I break free, and storm to the door. This was a mistake, the needing of anything, as if this place could ever be a sanctuary. How pathetic I am for having only this to go to, much like these men and their empty laughter and desperate hands. There is no power here. I move farther away from the middle-aged men calling my name in so many tones, "Pe-ter" a concert of apology, incredulity, surprise and—what would you know—clear as day, even a puff-and-snarl.

And yet none of it comes close to that feeling, coming back from New York. That was supposed to be a beginning, a real beginning. And within hours, I was back on the train, retreating back to Baltimore, blood on my shirt. Just enough money for the return, to the dollar, even more humiliating. New York was like everything else—unwilling to have me.

What is it that I do, that I am, that makes for this constant rejection? With everything: school, home, Jude, this city, now even New York, maybe everywhere. I can't blame everyone else anymore, as if somehow

everyone else is the problem. I'm not an idiot. I have to accept that I
am a factor in all of this. I have to figure this out because I don't want
to be standing, alone, in the middle of all the nights in my future with
nowhere else to go. I need to find my way to enter, something.

I walk to Mount Vernon, where most of the homo bars are. I know
they card, and cops patrol the area, so never come. I don't really know
what I'm expecting by going there, anyway, but I don't want to go home.
I just need to walk, to be somewhere.

Charles Street is the main thoroughfare to Mount Vernon. I forget
how magical it is, especially at night. The buildings are all lit at their
cornices, every one different from the next, and well maintained, a storybook, perfect little lines of the street grid. For a moment, I feel like I'm a
character in a Dickens novel. There is a warm glow to the restaurants and
shops, people walking quietly about, like a movie set, maybe of *A Christmas Carol*, or some PBS special. I come to the cobblestone of Mount
Vernon Square, Peabody Conservatory nestled on the right, Walters Art
Gallery on the left, stately wide brownstones all around, light peeking
out their windows made lavish with expensive curtains. I walk through
the square, past the Washington Monument. You'd never know it was
the twenty-first century. Usually it annoys me how obsessed with the
past Baltimore is, but here it feels right, even comforting. Lovely.

Eager Street is entirely different. It's pumping techno, neon signs,
and men only slightly older than me prancing together, holding each
other, tight jeans and t-shirts in the winter, so much activity in such high
contrast to the stately Square only a few blocks away. The men seem to
be going back and forth to the few bars that ring the intersection: Grand
Central, The Hippo, The Stable. I stand back, take it all in. I'd love to
walk in, grab a beer with someone closer to my own age than any of the
guys at Benny's, maybe even have a conversation that's worth something.
But I can't. Not yet, anyway. The last thing I need right now is to walk up
to one of the bars, have a burly doorman ask for an ID, and get turned
away in front of a line of hot guys. Another push away, another slap.
There's been too much rejection already; I can't take any more. I lean

against a brick wall and watch this world move along in front of me, the playful freedom, what could be my own future, if I wanted. They look so happy, and that makes me feel more alone, because I don't know how they do it. I could be one of these guys, if I tried. If I allowed myself to...what? What are you going to do about it, Peter?

I begin going back towards the general direction of home, or at least the closest Ma and I have gotten to home. We've moved six times in the last three years—Cherry Point, Greenmount, North Avenue, Curtis Bay, Brooklyn, now Highlandtown. I could write a guide to living in Baltimore, have pictures, testimonials, except they'd all have to be from me, because I'm back to having no friends. So, what, home is where your family lives? I have half a family. That gives me Ma, and that is it. Maybe there is only home, maybe there is only this one point where we belong. That sounds so depressing, and how does it explain why I have a sting across my face that throbs when I go home? Why is it so important to belong, anyway? But I know how empty that question feels. I know I don't mean it even as I think it. It might be weak of me, but I want to belong, to something. I want to belong to something.

There's a coffee shop on the corner that's still open, even though it's late. Red Emma's. I have nothing better to do than go home, so I walk in. It's tight and long, but packed with people, lots of chain-wallets, ripped clothes, piercings, topiary hair, punk. For a moment I think this to be the modern-day Lost Boys (and Girls who look like boys), like all Baltimore teenagers who have no home and no love come here to wane away their youth, mark themselves, piercings for pain, tattoos as belonging. It's a real surprise. I didn't think there were this many alt-kids in all of Baltimore. I wonder if Jude knows about this place. There are books everywhere, and really good music coming through the speakers that I don't recognize. I go to the counter, feeling very tall and plain-looking, for a change. A guy and a girl lean against the counter, talking.

"Who is this band?" I ask.

The girl flicks her head annoyingly, turns to me. "Well, hi."

"Hi."

"Would it be alright with you if we finished our conversation? I know the coffee's important."

"I didn't realize…"

"I know that," she snaps, and I'm sure I became a blotch of red, the heat rising straight from my neck.

"What do you need?" asks the guy, sort of laughing. I can't even look at or respond to him, being so embarrassed and amazed at the fierce face of this girl. She has bleached hair, shaved close to her scalp, like a pretty boy, with intensely royal blue eyes, half lidded. I can't help but stare, she's so intense.

"Uh, I just, the band. I like the music."

The girl rolls her eyes, turns, and disappears behind a wall. I watch her leave, mesmerized by how much power she takes out of the room with her. I could have that kind of power. I know that I possess that same intensity. I wonder how she harnesses it. If I could tap into mine now, I'd still be in New York, I would have Jude next to me right now, I'd go home to Ma without the distance between us.

"Social D. It's an oldie but goodie."

"Huh?"

"The music. Social Distortion. You asked."

"Oh, yeah." This guy is so soft and open, in contrast to the girl. He almost looks blurry, indistinct.

"Have you heard of them?"

"Well, I wouldn't have asked."

"My name is Max." He holds his hand out. I am confused. I'm not sure what I'm supposed to say, still warm from being called out so pointedly by something so, well, cool—that girl. Some kids in the coffee shop are playing chess. I've never seen young people play chess. A lot of the kids are reading and talking. I hear buzz words: capitalism, holistic, reciprocity. It is both wonderful and so heavy. I suddenly feel very tired.

"I think I need to leave."

"You're welcome to leave whenever you want," he laughs, and lowers his hand. "What is your name, handsome?" I keep looking for the girl to come back, afraid she'll yell or give me another eat-shit look, and yet I want to see her again, the power of her. She's so young, with that power.

"Peter. I need to go."

"I hope you end up where you need to go," he says, and I'm almost to the door. I turn around, and the guy is watching me go. He waves, shrugs. He has smooth, dark skin, almost the color of Grant's. This boy's name is Max. I wonder if he's Maximillian or Maxwell, or just Max. St. Paul and the cold comes back to me then, crisp and demanding me to go home and sleep.

23

Thomas

Simon is pacing around the parlor, a thin veil of sweat on his brow reflecting the lamplight. He mutters not quite like a madman, but a man who is mad. Indeed, he is. The fire of his passions builds in the tips of his ears, now the red of freshly split brick.

"How can this happen?" he spits, in mid-mumble.

"You know this city, this government," I say.

"Yeah, but this? How is no one saying anything?"

"Maybe they don't know."

Simon stops, looks accusingly at me. "*We* do."

"Yes," I say. I want to tell him what I now know, but I can't think of a way without giving away Mirabelle.

Simon keeps his gaze on mine for a second longer than is comfortable, the pupils of his eyes shaking ever so slightly. Is he *that* furious, or is this passion, energy, one of his many emotions that look too similar, bound up in a moment? Sometimes it's hard to differentiate with Simon. He appears on fire when he's arguing and when he's teaching, but also when he's watching the news, eating, gardening. It's hard to read, and that's why the rectory will never fully relax around him, never quite like him. Simon believes it to be his outspoken nature, but that's not the case. Several of the religious are passionate. However, we can read balance through their actions, their words; they can be read. With Simon, one can't tell—everything is urgent. I understand why many think him exhausting.

"What are we going to do now?" he asks with sincerity—not a drop of irony—to the grandfather clock in the corner.

The night came quick, and I am searching for a way to tell Simon what I know. I wish Mirabelle was here.

"Something," I say.

*

Simon had tapped me earlier that afternoon. I barely had time to put my teaching materials down.

"Thomas, you need to come with me. You'll appreciate this."

"Appreciate what?"

"Just come with me."

We were out the door five minutes later. The day was at its most intense; you could almost hear the buzz of the afternoon all around. Had Simon asked me a month ago to investigate dealings concerning the Crabtown development, I would have shrugged my shoulders, lifted my hands in that *whaddyagonnado?* gesture. But now, with Mirabelle and her family in the house, I feel more awake somehow, more aware and wanting to be aware. It feels good.

"I'm glad you're doing this with me," he said.

"Just don't tell August. He'll think I'm somehow betraying him."

"That's absurd."

St. Paul Street beamed with the glory, the reverent heart of the city with its restored brownstones softly looming over the street, large mature trees that nestled into the coarse grandeur of stoned walkways, everything civilized, settled, now bathed with the amber of the setting sun. If the rest of the city, hell, the rest of the country appeared this way, all would make sense with the world. Dusk, gracious in its perpetual dying.

The Maryland Historical Society was appropriately adjacent to Mount Vernon Square. Peabody Conservatory and the Washington Monument peeked over the tops of the dramatic cornices that capped the stately rowhouses on the west side of the street. The entry was dark wood and gilded ornamentation, lavish yet perfectly suitable for the space. An oil tycoon may have lived here, a man who, by virtue or greed, wound up significantly contributing to a Baltimore history. That is the purpose of the rich. Now, his home is frozen in time, his legacy, in death, an organization devoted to very living tourists. Or, is it more a sarcophagus? Do we preserve the spaces that people have lived in to bring back the dead, or to pretend they never died?

A gray-haired woman led us down the long hallway to an office in the very back. Sitting there, with his head down, forehead almost to the desk, reading from a pair of thick glasses, was a bird-faced man. He had to be around sixty, but in an unhealthy way that made him look older. He reminded me of my middle school science teacher, Mr. Lingus, skin the color of pig feet in formaldehyde. Probably a smoker, and it's too late to stop now.

He was not startled when we walked in the room, as I had expected, with those pointy features. "Please, come in. I'm just reading an obituary." He smiled, unaware of himself.

Simon immediately launched into his questioning. It concerned Crabtown. Apparently, two buildings that were listed on the historic registry were part of the site plan, and slated for demolition. Simon had discovered this at a neighborhood meeting, much like the one August and I attended at King Middle. I picked up that much, and little else. I was too interested in this man, this Mr. Thuza—his skinny, old man smell wafting from across the large oak desk—to really listen to much beyond particular inflections. I could hear the distinct puncture of sound whenever Simon cried *why*, and the slow, careful croak of Thuza's *well*, that began most of his sentences. What a man he was. What had he wanted to become as a boy? He seemed so entrenched in his oldness that I couldn't imagine him young—the glasses that would start a sudden fire in a sunroom, the rumpled shirt, the thin shoulders and bloated belly, the resignation. Granted, his voice rose when he spoke of a unique Victorian factory on Read Street, or the Beaux Arts remnants of North Charles. Light glinted from behind those absurdly thick glasses, almost lit up the frames, when he discovered we lived in the rectory at St. Mary's, and he quickened while relaying the history we already knew so well. Hadn't I been excited about that same history? Aren't I still? Did I look similar to this man when I pointed out the rectory's old doorbell, with its long, wrought-iron lever, and the dumbwaiter in the kitchen, and the leaded glass in most of the first-floor windows, his fingers skeletal to my hairy stubs?

However, everything else appeared banal to him. Simon's questions of government authority and municipal politics were answered in monotones. When not talking of historical this and historical that, the man went limp, like Michigan J. Frog when put on stage in front of an audience, *Ragtime* to croak.

The *present*. The details of the present bored this man, and his entire attention was consumed by that which remained after the people who had made them—lived in them, worked in them, loved in them—had died.

"Can you believe that?!" Simon yelled. "Eminent Domain my ass!"

"Do you have children, Mr. Thuza?"

"I beg your pardon?"

"Are you a father?"

"Thomas, that's an odd question."

"Oh, no. I'm not married."

"Were you ever married?"

"Thomas?"

"No. Why do you ask?" said Thuza.

"Excuse me. I'm going to get some air. Excuse me."

The chill of the new evening was welcoming. I sat on the marble steps, the polished smooth wealth of the Baltimore that flourished in that Old World way when steel was everything. The tight and cold grip in my chest was nothing alarming like a heart attack, but I held a small panic just the same.

And what, in the next twenty years, would be my moment of sad recognition? Would I have one, or would I sit behind a desk and devote myself to preserving history by denying that which *becomes* history? Isn't

history a series of very present actions, and *only* very present actions?
And of those great actions, was there happiness, merely in the presence
of them?

My greatest happiness in recent years has been the recent violation
of my vows, my harboring of an unwed mother in a home I am not supposed to own. I need to face that realization. My life is changing.

There is something about the choice, something definitive that I now
own. Nothing as base as owning the house, but something else. This presence. The action without knowledge of the future, what *will* become history. I feel that has something to do with happiness. The present action is
what makes history, and those who live only in history can never be present. The man. Thurza. Him and me. Me and him. My life is changing.

Simon was flagrant when he came out of the building. "What was *that*
all about?" I stood up and brushed myself off, with no way to explain.
Fortunately, Simon wasn't really interested, and broke into explaining
his and Thuza's conversation.

"Eminent domain, Thomas. Eminent *fucking* domain, pardon my
French."

"The buildings?"

"Have you heard of condemnation?" Simon asked.

"Well, certainly, but..."

"I mean in the sense of city planning. OK, so there's eminent domain,
where a city can demand a private owner to forfeit their land for the
greater municipal good, of course for its market value, right?"

"And the owner has to comply."

"Right. Apparently, the city can declare eminent domain, but can also
simultaneously deem the property unfit for habitation."

The brownstones in the streetlight were storybook, and I loved looking up as we passed by each of them, the slow graceful loom. Horse
and carriage had belonged, hoof to stone soft and lovely in the night,
echoing off the facades of the square. If only the horses were still here.
Almost comically, headlights then blared out into the dark night from
a line of cars.

Simon abruptly stopped, an exasperated look when I turned. He must be terrified of growing older, seeing age as a cancer of apathy, himself so youthfully righteous. "Thomas, don't you see what's happening? The city is condemning a lot of the private properties as unfit, which reduces their value. They're getting appraised *way* lower than what they're worth so the city can afford to buy them back, and then hand them over to the developers of that amusement park. I *knew* it."

"Knew what?"

"That there were dirty dealings here. The city's broke."

"And they plan to up-sell to the developers?"

Simon paused, looked out at St. Paul Street, as if this was the doomed neighborhood and he was surveying the land before the demise. "No. They haven't."

"That would scream corruption."

"They're selling the properties at cost."

"So, they are practically giving it to the developer? Why?"

"They are *that* desperate." Simon sighed. "They are hoping for the tax money generated by the amusement park."

"Wouldn't all this be too transparent? I mean, if they lowered the value of all those homes? There are a lot of homes, a lot of people."

Simon looked gravely at me. "Transparent to whom, Thomas? The City Council? They're approving the condemnations."

I remembered the first time I met Mirabelle, her fists and oversized mauve pantsuit, what she said about her own home. I hadn't considered the information then. I wanted to affirm Simon's suspicions, but I couldn't mention Mirabelle. I'm not sure what side of virtue he would choose. "Wouldn't the people want to do something? They know, right?"

"They *are* doing something."

"What do you mean?"

"They've been having rallies uptown. You know this place called 2640, up in Charles Village? Non-profit community space. They're meeting there with some organizers, talking strategies. We've been trying to find a legal way to contest some of the demolitions, to at least buy time. If we can even stall some demolition, maybe the historic buildings, then maybe we can…"

"What do you mean, *we*, Simon?"

Simon, again, with the grave look. "Look, Thomas. I've been going to these meetings. They need someone who can help them out. Why do you think I came here today?"

"What would the brotherhood think if they knew…"

"The brotherhood isn't going to know."

"Won't they find out?"

"Will they?"

"Well…"

"We all have some secrets, don't we, Thomas, some things we can't share with the others?" His eyebrows arch high.

"What do you mean?" I ask.

"Thomas, I know," he says, with the finality of a knife chop. "So, are you going to help me, or what?"

How does he know? I had been so careful whenever I left the rectory, and usually left from school to remove suspicion. He knew I wouldn't tell on him, because he knew I had an even bigger secret than he. Did he know *everything* about the house, that I was harboring a family there? Had he followed me? Did he watch from across the street, through the window, watch us eat dinner? Did he think she was my lover? Did he spy on me? I'm afraid to ask these questions.

"I am going to help you," I say. With this knowledge, the extent of the corruption, I realize Mirabelle is only the beginning. So much more must be done.

One day, I had come over to the house and, as was becoming the ritual, I helped prepare dinner. Mirabelle was assisting Torvoris with his math homework while I peeled potatoes for boiling. I never had the chance to cook at the rectory. Milsia, the rectory housekeeper, grew suspicious whenever we came in there to fix ourselves anything, perhaps thinking we were undermining her position, or threatening her job security. The kitchen was hers alone. It was nice to come over to the Exeter house and feel domestic for a change.

After dinner Mirabelle and I took our coffees out to the stoop while the boys watched TV.

After a few sips, Mirabelle filled the pleasant silence. "Why did you join the order, Thomas?"

I was not surprised by this question. I had been asked many times, by lay people who grew to know me well enough. I had my prepared answers. I wanted to serve God. I wanted to give myself to service. I wanted to be in communion with all of humanity. But now, the lightness I'd been feeling lately has helped me see my real reason.

"I didn't want to be my father," I said.

Her mouth opened slightly, the coffee steam mingling with her breath. "Why would you say something like that?"

"Married. Then divorced. My mother left him, and he wasn't the same after that. He loved me and did his best, and he was good man, but he was only half there after she left."

Mirabelle tilted her head, but the way she did felt sincere, as if everyone mimicked the gesture from watching how effective it was for her. "So, you were afraid?"

"I think so. Of being left, like my father."

"You know, your mother left *you*, too."

"I suppose, yeah."

"You never wanted to get married?" she asked, softly, into the air.

"No." I looked into my coffee. "No marriage for me."

"You ain't... uh..." Her eyebrows were arched so high I thought they'd launch off her forehead.

"You've been reading too many tabloids. No," I laughed.

"Brother, I'm sorry. I didn't mean to. I mean, it don't matter to me, no way. To each his own. I'm just saying, you know, all them things you been hearing on the news and all." She stood up, waving her long dark arms like she was sweeping the space of misunderstanding.

Again, I laughed. "No harm. Sit down."

"Well, I'm a fool." She buried herself in her mug.

"I guess I didn't want to fail at marriage."

"You think your father did?"

"I don't know. Maybe I didn't want to be the one who disappointed his wife."

"Oh, Thomas. Now how's *that* gonna turn out? Everyone disappoint everyone at some point. You human." Mirabelle rested her hand on my thigh. The warmth immediately seeped through my cotton slacks. And, the wonderful strangeness of it flooded through me, and I was a teenager again.

"I was quiet growing up. I wasn't a popular kid, kept to myself most of the time." I was aware of the growing erection, and tried to soften it by tightening my sphincter. It worked for me before. Beautiful women sometimes touched me, and my penis often responded.

"I'm sure there were a lot of people who liked you." She patted me a couple times, and I thought she was going to remove her hand, but it stayed there. She was looking distantly off into the neighborhood, and the streetlight caught the smooth cliff of her jaw, the clear brown cheek, and my erection resumed. I couldn't tell if she was aware of the slight movement in my slacks. Thank God they were black.

I laughed. It was awkward, but gave me a chance to shift a little without making it too obvious. I hoped it played off as being shy. "I had a couple of friends in the orphanage."

"Any girlfriends?" Her hand was still there, and her eyes seemed to be closer to me than before. I couldn't read them for a moment. I became very aware of her breasts, the power in her legs, how beautiful her skin was.

"There was one girl who could have been, maybe. Lydia." The erection was full-on now, and there was no way she couldn't see it. My whole body broke out in a sweat. I wanted to jump up, but I also wanted to stay right there. At that moment, the best feeling in the world would have been for her strong hot hand to wrap around it and squeeze with all her might. My penis pulsed now.

"Lydia," she repeated softly, as if blowing dandelion seeds into the air. Her hand sliding ever so slightly closer, with each stretch of breath.

"But it didn't happen," I said, and softly took her hand, slowly placed it back on her own leg. I breathed in deeply.

She bowed her head. I remained quiet, not really knowing what to do.

"What do you want, Thomas?" She was embarrassed, and I had not expected that. I didn't know what to expect. How could I? I wanted to clear this up right away, sweep the awkwardness, maybe even shame, under the stoop and start over. This will not be ruined, not this feeling of purpose, of worth. Maybe this is what home could be.

"Nothing. Mirabelle, nothing." I meant it. She had already given me plenty. I didn't know if she'd understand if I revealed that to her. "No, not exactly. I don't know what I want."

She kept her head down for a full minute, what felt like forever. I didn't know how to rectify this, and I felt helpless, probably as helpless as she felt. With all the scenarios I had encountered as a teacher, this was not one of them. My arsenal was depleted, and I certainly didn't want to sooth with platitudes, half wisdoms, not with her.

Eventually, I said what seemed to be the plain truth. "I understand the confusion. This is a strange circumstance. But I am happy, with exactly what this is."

She sniffed, rubbed her nose on her arm, a thin ribbon of snot darkening her shirt sleeve. "Yeah, well, I feel like a damned fool."

"Yeah? Well, so do I."

We both laughed, relieved, the air back to its chill.

I repeated, "These are strange circumstances."

"No shit," she said.

After a moment she got up quickly, grabbed my empty cup, and with the gesture was able to completely change the tone. "You know, there's talk back in the hood. Some shit going down."

"What do you mean?"

"I don't know, talk. Big talk." She pulled the door and we headed toward the kitchen. "The people are getting real mad, Thomas, talking like they've had enough." I watched her large hips swing the way they do, and marveled at my self-control. Maybe I was made for religious life. What other man could have withheld? "I'm glad I'm outta there, my kids and all."

"Of course," I said, habitually taking up the dishtowel as she washed the cups.

"No, I mean like there's talk of some serious shit going down. Real bad, I think."

"Like what? What are they saying?" I asked. Simon flashed across my mind, the rallies uptown.

"Bad things. I'd be careful being over there, with your students and all. The pot is boiling over, I swear. The talk is getting violent."

"Really?"

"Really." She lidded her eyes with threat, and I got the message. Time for serious talk.

I grabbed a coffee mug. "Tell me what you know."

24

Peter

The mornings are getting warmer. My room is always the first to feel any heat, and it's a little toasty today. The rest of the house is still as I quietly get ready. I celebrate the small triumph that today is Friday, relief, surviving another week without any confrontations—no calls into the principal's office, no pink slips, no sit-downs with Ma. The weekend is booked with double-shifts, so that's covered. I just have to get through one more day. I've been silent, keeping my head down in school, at home. I went to all classes, every day. I made sure to get to homeroom just in time for the bell, so no one—Farissi, Wilkinson, any of them—had the chance to lay into me. I went the long way to every class, used the back stairs, hid in the basement bathroom during free period. Everything feels combustible, and it'll explode if I say or do anything. I didn't raise my hand in English once, didn't even answer problems out loud in Calc. I picked up extra shifts at Roy Rogers, closing shifts. The smell of chicken fry was deep in my fingers, but it was better than eating dinner at home, across the table from Ma. If I say two words out of turn, the whole world will flip upside down—I'll get called into the office and expelled, Ma will reel out something else she doesn't mean, Jude will angrily shove his finger in my face, still smelling of my spit. *You did this, you did this*—everyone screaming at me—*you did this*.

I slide down the stairs, grateful for the carpet, the muting of feet, and aim straight for the door.

She's at the kitchen sink, staring out the window, hair all over the place, in her pajamas, the ones I got her for a birthday some time back. I can tell she's chewing her fingers, smoking a cigarette. I can't pass by with her right there, so I make a quick beeline to the refrigerator, and open the door between us. It helps to speak with a shield. I conjure something benign. "Want me to go to the store?"

She doesn't answer, so I peek over the door. She doesn't hear me, her face still lost in the world beyond.

"We need eggs and stuff. I have money. Ma?"

"What? Sure. Wait." She jerks a little, starts to face me, but turns back out the window, like her body decided to do one thing, her mind the other. "I don't want to fill the fridge now...I mean, you don't need to get anything. I will go." She lays her left hand flat on the counter and takes a long drag on her cigarette.

"What's out there?" I ask, trying to lighten up the look on her face. It's almost scary how not there she is.

"Baltimore," she says, with the finality of a butcher chop.

I can't ask her what's wrong, not yet, because I know at least part of what's wrong, and I can't go there. But there's more, and I'm worried. She is pale and tossed, like I would imagine a tweaker to look. Her eyes glow translucent blue from the morning light, even from my side-view. If we can just get through this week, this weekend, maybe then I can talk to her.

There must be something to say, something that will acknowledge the divide but not address it head on. I certainly will not apologize, even though I feel sorry, for something. Maybe her. I feel sorry for her. "You need anything?"

She continues biting her nails, but her shoulders loosen a little, grateful yet worried. The ring around her eyes is fire red. There is so much anxiety in her that I'm not sure if she will break down in tears or explode into fury. She breathes in and says, "Peter, not now. We'll talk later."

*

I'm normally not a sweater, but all this week I go right through my undershirt, big wet circles at the pits of my button-ups. Why heat? Does our body mistake anxiety for illness, and heat up to push it out? I haven't even gotten to homeroom and already the sweat is dripping from my pit hair. The bell rings just as I sit down, like planned. No time to respond to eyes, no time for shit-talk.

Jude is morose, as usual, unresponsive. Not like I'm going out of my way to talk with him, but I try sneaking glances his way, communicate through eyes. I've tried the wounded raised-eyebrows and the pensive, apologetic furrow. Nothing. He may see, but immediately turns away. His denial is strong. I'd rather him get angry or bullyish, shoot me a vicious dart with his wolf eyes, something. But, nothing.

Everyone else does, though. Lots of snickers, lots of pantomimed blow-jobs, wagging tongues, all towards my bowed head. I barrel through the hallway to each class, taking the back routes, avoiding the majority of chiding smear, but some filter through. Farissi is the only one who still audibly asks, "What's up with the fingerjob, Freebie?" I say nothing and keep barreling, to Physics, to English, to Calc, to Religion. Free Period has become my sanctuary, and into the bathroom I go.

"Mr. Cryer?"

My name spoken in formal address. The time has finally come. An official voice to officially discuss my very unofficial behavior, my moment of indiscretion, and during a religious ceremony, no less, Mr. Cryer. I turn. Brother Thomas. I am confused for a moment—would *he* be my disciplinarian? The only one I'd trust enough in this entire school to *not* find ways to bring me down?

"Will you come with me for a moment?"

He looks very stern, his already thin lips tight, taut, I can't think which word more appropriate. "Yessir," I croak, and clear my throat. We go right through the main hall where my peers would crack on me, but Brother Thomas' presence mutes their taunting.

He closes the door. I brace for the talk, order myself to speak soft and without flourish, as little as possible. If I'm going to get through this without being expelled, I need to be all apology and no excuse. *It was a stupid mistake* will be my mantra. I may need to beg, and I have to be ready for it.

"First of all, congratulations."

My turn to make my lips taut. "For what?"

"Columbia. It's quite a feat, getting a full ride."

Immediately, New York plays across my mind. The subway, Harlem, the Jobys, blood. I didn't make it to Columbia. I want to tell him I didn't make it there. I got off the train too late. It was getting dark. What ride?

But then it begins to make sense. I haven't even thought about college this week. And then it registers what Brother Thomas is telling me. How does he know and I don't? The guidance counselor? Do colleges announce their acceptances to the high schools before the applicants? I'm pruned with questions.

And then everything clears and I see at the end of the confusion my mother, standing in the kitchen window, bitten nails, frenzied face. Slowly, a coldness wraps my chest, snakes along my body and fills me with something like the sound of moaning metal. I feel my eyes well, but swallow the whelm, of this news and Ma at the kitchen window.

"Peter?"

I nod. I'm afraid anything else will deceive me. I look at Thomas, consternation all over his face. I nod again. I can tell he's uncertain, but I know he won't press too much. It's one of the reasons I like him. He allows people to be whatever they are, whenever. He sits against his desk, folds his arms, the fabric struggling over his belly. Dark hairs peek out from the space between buttons.

"I wanted to talk about your mother. I saw her last week. She seemed stressed, more than usual. Is anything wrong?"

I don't even know where to begin. The possibilities spin around my head, I mean really make me dizzy. Should there be an order to the list? Shall I present them like ingredients? First, you take her baby-daddy, Abe. Then, Isaac. Throw in a fag for a son. Add a dash of no steady job. And Joby. Voila! A shit sandwich. Is there a package that I could fit together, wrap it up neatly, and hand to him? *Here's a little something about the two of us.*

I'm shaking my head and softly laughing. That's my answer. That's all that can come out. Poor Brother Thomas looking at me with concern, pity, confusion, his face changing gestures wildly. His arms come out a bit, like he's preparing to wrestle an opponent, like some male instinct, to hold together the breach in decorum. That makes me laugh even more. At some point I can't tell what I'm laughing at, that I'm even laughing at all, but I know I'm not crying. And I will not. I will not do that.

*

I head over to Red Emma's, the coffee shop on St. Paul, after work. There's nowhere else to go, nowhere I want to be. What, Benny's? Score a booty call on a twink app? None of that appeals to me right now. I wish I could call Jude, ask him to meet up with some Mad Dog, go back to life chats in his beat-up station wagon. I wonder if that'll ever happen again. I felt like I belonged to something, then, for just a moment.

I just want to be away from anyone who knows me.

It's busy again, with the same young college-age crowd, reading and talking, a small group in the back having what looks like a meeting. The fierce shaved-head girl isn't around, but the Max guy is at the counter. He's wearing a loose-fitting tank top. I can see one of his nipples, trusses of hair peeking out the sides of his slender but toned biceps. He's got the faintest crop of curly black chest hairs.

No one knows me here. It feels good to escape the hot breath of all my current fuck-ups. I think I'll stay here until it closes.

"Do you have anything other than coffee?"

"We have tea and Italian soda." Max presents a row of brightly colored display bottles behind him a la Vanna White. "Want me to play some Social D for you?"

"Huh?"

"Social D. The band you asked about last time. I remember you." He says this with a grin that is so open and beaming but also like there is some secret between us. His skin is smooth and dark brown, his teeth effortlessly white. The word that comes to mind is *fresh*.

"You're not from here," I say.

"Wow, is it that obvious? No, I'm from the midwest. Well, the Dust Bowl, actually." His hair is longish, in tight corkscrews that crown his head, like he gets up every morning and twists with his fingers. It looks clean, enough for me to want to bury my nose in it right then and there.

"So how did you end up here?" I ask.

"In Baltimore?" He says Baltimore by pronouncing with the T. Definitely not from here. "I go to MICA."

"The art school?"

"Yeah, I study painting."

"Cool." I wonder how much older he is than me, if the shaved head girl is his girlfriend. "But why Baltimore?"

His brows furrow. "What do you mean?"

"Why not New York or Chicago or San Francisco? You know, art cities."

Max's hands flail in excitement. "Baltimore *is* an art city. There's lots of artists here. For one, it's cheaper than those cities, so artists can afford to have studio space. And have you been to Artscape?"

I don't know what he's talking about, and I guess my look reveals that, because he asks, "You live here?"

"Yeah. Born and raised."

Max looks at me like I'm a golden egg, a unicorn, and though it's a goofy face, almost stupid, it's really adorable. "Awesome," he says.

Max tells me about MICA, about coming to Baltimore for the first time, about his studio mates. His love for Baltimore is almost comical. "I mean, this coffee shop couldn't be in *any* city," he beams.

Max is naïve. I want to pop his Baltimore bubble, tell him about the abandoned rowhouses, the murder rate, the detritus, about the assholes at school, about Jude the Obscure, how this coffee shop is like an island in the middle of a sea of misery. But this guy is so earnest.

"Who is Emma?" I ask.

He almost jumps, "Emma Goldman!"

The way he says the name makes me feel embarrassed that I don't know who that is.

He breaks down her history for me, the anarchist ideas, the activism, and then he points to the back of the room. "See them over there?"

"Yeah," I say, and lean onto the counter a bit, to get closer, catch a bit of what he smells like. I follow his finger to a dozen or so people—different ages, different ethnicities—huddled together in rapt conversation.

"They're a fair housing coalition. They've been meeting once a week since I've been working here, like two years. Lately it's been more frequent—that Crabtown project in East Baltimore."

I almost tell him that I live there, but I don't want him getting the impression that I'm just another poor Black kid from the hood. "What about it?"

"They're protesting the demolition. It's already started, but they're trying to stop more of it from happening."

"Why?" I ask.

"What do you mean?"

"Why are they protesting the project? Have you been in that area? It's fucking ratchet. Why are they upset about the demolition?"

He simply says, "The people living there. It's wrong," his lips comfortable, his eyes gentle and open. When have I ever possessed such pure, simple conviction, or compassion, for anything?

He brightens up. "See? Where else in the country are you going to have a coffee shop like this? Baltimore's rad! You want a soda? I like the strawberry."

"Yeah, sure," I say, marveling at this genuine, fresh, kind, hot boy, the loving way he looks at the same city I hate so much, the group in the back organizing some kind of social justice, the intelligence of the place. And even more, none of my recent drama exists here. Not a soul knows about Ma or Jude or sucking fingers or me losing my mind and chasing ghosts of my dead brother. This little coffee shop is everything right now.

"So, you want me to play that Social D record again?" Max leans his elbows on the counter. I see down the opening in his shirt to his lean torso, his belly button. His exhale tickles my chin.

"Sure," I say. "I'm Peter."

"I know," he says matter-of-factly, and grins.

25

Thomas

From the outside, MacAllister's home appears quite modest, a three-story rowhouse across the street from the entrance to Federal Hill, the old battlement that now peacefully overlooks the Harbor, with the best views of the city's skyline. Thirty years ago, this neighborhood was only beginning to feel the effects of the Inner Harbor's rehabilitation from broken-down wharfs to shopping plazas. Before that it was withering, many of the old dock-workers pushed out with the industry, and those left behind showing signs of struggle: lots of drug-dealing, lots of men in dirty wife-beaters hanging outside of the corner bars, lots of sirens, day or night. Now, with the bleed of the Harbor, and the old dock workers long gone, the neighborhood has found its feet again, with white-collars who want a short commute to the medical campuses and biotech firms.

The formstone that probably once plagued MacAllister's house has been blown off, the gray and brown artifice chiseled away, like an apology, to reveal the true stately brick beneath. A lot of Federal Hill was now doing the same thing, a whole neighborhood sorry for the formstone folly, making amends. The result is handsome. His rowhouse has simple but clever accents of green and white around the windows, the brick all repointed.

A girl of about thirteen opens the door. Her womanly features belie her still-small face, but it looks like she will be lovely when it all comes together. She wears pink, and has a charming smile. "May I help you?" she asks.

"Hello. I'm here to see Mr. MacAllister." I give her my name. "I'm from St. Mary's."

"I know that school," she says. "Are you a teacher?"

"I am," I say.

"Cool. I want to be a teacher."

A smaller child ducks under his sister's arm, squeezes between us. He can't be older than six. "Hi!"

"Hello, there," I say.

"Look," he says, sticks his finger in his mouth and begins to wiggle a loose tooth.

"Sean, go get Daddy," the girl commands, the beginnings of that motherly tone she will one day use on her own children. She poses her face, no doubt, in a copied gesture from her mother.

"Okay." The boy runs back into the depths of the house, yelling "Daddy, Daddy, Daddy." The sound is bright and pure, and I can't help but feel an immediate love for the family.

The girl opens the door wider and asks me to come in. The inside of the house is deceptively big. All levels have been gutted in the center, in an oblong circle, to allow a complete sightline from the entrance to the roof. It is very dramatic. A gorgeous Edwardian chandelier descends down, crowned by railings on both floors above.

"Do you like teaching?" asks the girl.

"I do," I say, still looking up.

"I'm Rachel."

"Thomas."

She investigates my clothes. "Are you a priest?"

"Not exactly," I say. "I'm a brother." The house is lovely, a mix of clean, modern lines with enough curl, enough warmth to feel comfortable. Just enough hangs on the walls to feel sophisticated without being pretentious. Many places around here go too far, stripping away the essence of the spaces, installing recessed light and box moulding. This place, I'm afraid, is quite balanced and lovely.

"What do you mean?" Rachel asks.

"Kind of like a priest in training, only I don't want to be a priest."

Rachel is polite enough not to press further, but I can tell she is absolutely mystified by the absence of logic. Luckily, MacAllister arrives in time to save me from the explanation. He extends his arm as he walks towards me, the Vaseline smile that I remember.

"Hi. Can I help you?"

"Mr. MacAllister. I'm Brother Thomas Manilli. We met at the City Council hearing several weeks ago, about Highlandtown and Ellwood Park."

He shakes my hand, the smile fixed, searching his databank furiously. I can tell he doesn't remember at all.

"Of course, of course. Come in please. We were just finishing breakfast."

"I'm sorry to bother you on a Saturday."

"No, please." He ushers me to a room next to the giant, open kitchen, an anachronistic family room, yet magnificently decorated with antique navigation maps. The couches are leather, but the coffee table is a contemporary metal cross-base. More of the same balance of chic and homey, yet pristine. Another boy, perhaps nine, helps a very attractive woman in her late forties take up plates from a light wood farm table that straddles the rooms. How do they manage to keep a home so tidy with three kids, maid or no maid? I presume there is a maid. I take a seat.

"What can I do for you, Thomas?" he asks.

I look over to the family, the children help load a dishwasher. I turn back to him, and he reads my concern. "Oh, no, my wife knows about the project. She's even helping plan the festival next weekend." I keep quiet, my gaze steady, and he understands. "Hey, honey, I'm going to go to the office for a minute. I won't be long."

His wife acknowledges curiously, and MacAllister leads me up the stairs to a dark but spacious room, loaded with plaques, certificates, and bookshelves with texts, mostly planning codes, architectural jargon, some history books. I notice *Things Fall Apart*, the orange paperback spine dwarfed by the thick monoliths of urban planning.

He sits behind his mahogany desk, assumes the position of alpha in that relaxed way of a veteran businessman. Do they take classes on gesture, on posture? Is there a required Acting for Business course in most MBA programs? Or, does the business become the man?

"What is this about?"

"I'm here about Crabtown, the demolition."

"I presumed that," he says.

"I'm afraid there is some talk, and I'm concerned."

"Concerned about what? What talk?"

I adjust my chair. How do you warn a man who seems so confident, who has a perfect house and perfect children and isn't too much of anything in particular? How do you convince him to take heed? I can tell he is used to managing crises. He takes it all in stride. He wears a blue shirt and khakis on a Saturday mid-morning for breakfast. Who does that? He is a just-in-case man. He probably has a carry-on and toiletry bag fully packed in his closet *just in case* he has to travel at a moment's notice. Do I speak urgently, do I overstate to get through to him, or does he read exaggeration like a pulp novel—with a smirk?

"Some people in the neighborhood, the ones who are relocating for the demolition. I heard some are planning an action."

"You mean the march, the protest?"

"During the festival in the park."

"I've heard some things," he says. "It's to be expected."

"I'm afraid it's quite serious, Mr. MacAllister."

"Call me Ponty," he says, and takes out a cigarette, lights it.

"I'm not sure what, exactly, but it sounded threatening enough for me to see you."

"What have you heard?" His attitude is so relaxed, I can't help but be irritated. I didn't expect him to be a captive audience, necessarily, but with this long lean back in his chair, smoking a cigarette, he might as well be laughing at me. For some reason it makes me feel feminine.

"Some people in Ellwood Park are saying threatening things. Only some. Most have just been assembling, nothing more than that. They are planning the march. But some of them have heard that a group wants to lead the march right to you, to your house. They know who you are, know where you live."

"People talk all the time, Mr. Manilli. You and I are talking right now," he says.

"I'm not speaking merely of the march, Ponty. I have word from a reliable source that they are targeting you, specifically, and I'm afraid it might get…"

"Who is this reliable source?" The very ends of his mouth curl just enough to spur a pip of white-hot anger in my gut. I'm not sure if the question does it or the dismissive tone. Am I mad because he asks that question or that he asks with no interest? He offends me; he offends Mirabelle, he offends me.

"Mr. MacAllister, I'm coming to you with a sincere concern," I manage, the white-hot spreading through my belly and chest.

"Mr. Manilli, I'm sorry, but if I hesitated every time one of our planned projects was threatened with some kind of action by the people, I would never get to build anything. Nothing would get done. I don't know if you're aware of how the people work in this town, but they don't want anything new."

"I don't believe that is what fuels the ire of these people."

"What fuels their ire, then?"

"Their homes, the condemning. The people know about it."

"Ah, yes. I see." MacAllister fiddles with a tin of pencils for quite some time. Perhaps he thought no one knew, or maybe he didn't expect someone like me to expose it so frankly. He leans back in his chair. "Have you seen the shape of the homes back in that neighborhood, Thomas? They would have been condemned anyway."

"Perhaps, but the way it is being done is what angers them."

"That might be what they *say* angers them, Mr. Manilli, but that is not ultimately what it is. People resist change, we all resist it. They say, 'what will happen if we build this, tear this down, change this, vote for this new politician? What will happen if we leave this job, move to this town?' But the fact of the matter is, Mr. Manilli, Baltimore *needs* this development. I mean, look at this place. I have lived here all my life, and it breaks my heart how much it has gone to shit." He stands up. "Do you know that we have less people living here now than we did sixty years ago? We used to be one of the biggest, most beautiful, most promising cities in the nation, the *world*. One million people lived here. Now, one in every four homes is empty, in some areas over half the homes are abandoned. It's like Warsaw after the evacuation. What is that? This is *America*."

"I don't know if Ellwood Park sees what's happening as a form of progress," I say.

"Of course it's progress! You of all people should know. You live right by that cesspool! Have you driven on Fayette lately? Try doing it at night. It's like a bunch of zombies wandering around. I've seen fires on the street, Mr. Manilli, burning *mattresses*. Even the police are afraid to go in there. It's out of control. How can an alternative, any alternative, be anything but progress? What else could we do?"

He is convincing, not in what he says, but the way he says it. He means what he says. For a moment, I forget why I am in his home. A lovely home, a lovely family. This is what all cities want to be, he is what cities want to be. A healthy family life. A strong tax base. Revenue for the city to then spend on civic improvements, parks, balustrades, clean sidewalks with trees planted in rows, civilized. Why am I here, then? It was to warn him, yes, of the possible threat to him, to his family. Yes? Then why do I want to argue? Why am I angry with him, for his sincere love for the city? What is there to argue? Aren't I here to warn him? Where is the argument in this concern?

"Look, Mr. Manilli, I understand that you come here on good principle, and I appreciate you going out of your way to tell me. But it is part of my job. I'm trying to make this town a better place, to improve it through this development. If that means I get threats, I'm willing to accept that. All change is a struggle."

I am disarmed, this word struggle. We are all struggling; even he, in his own way.

"What if you just talked with the people of the neighborhood?"

"Do you think those people care about their neighborhood, care about the city? If they did, why would they let their neighborhood fall apart like that? How do you reason with drug addicts, with criminals?"

"Not all of them are criminals, Mr. MacAllister." I look down to see my hands in fists. I think of Mirabelle.

He relents, softens, knowing. The fire in his eyes settles. "Of course. No, you're right." He sits on his desk, deliberate. "But answer me this: what good would that do? Yes, there are probably many good people living north of Patterson Park, some families, old folks. But does that make the neighborhood salvageable the way it is? Should we abandon plans to make a place better because a few good ones are opposed? Would we ever move forward? And these people, they make up a minority of the general consensus. You have to agree with me, there. And sometimes, Mr. Manilli, there are casualties to progress. Think about it. When Crabtown is built jobs will be created, the neighborhood will be safer. Folks will move back in, maybe fix up some of the abandoned rowhouses around the park. Do you know that only *half* are occupied in the whole neighborhood? People might use Patterson Park again. Imagine that."

"You may be right, but is there a way to bring everyone together to discuss the plan? Maybe if they heard you speak on the project?"

"I have learned from my experience in this business to not get close to them. You get to know them, it makes it more difficult to get the job done. More conditions, more red tape. I know that sounds callous, but it's the truth." He stubs out his cigarette.

I can only look at him with curiosity, with a dull anger, an annoyance, and then a realization that he is right, in some way. Isn't that the most effective way to make change, to proclaim from afar, from atop the hill? The less specific the people, the less of a people they are. Don't we close our eyes, just briefly, before we make a decision of consequence, this instinctive need to erase the world that will be affected by our choice?

I stand up, and I fully know that this man, Ponty MacAllister, is my enemy, but not because I hate him. In fact, I understand him. He is the

Machiavelli to my Thomas More. He is the ends to my means. And, both kinds of men are necessary, both justified. I can recognize this, walk out of his house, and still know that he is my adversary. We will be civil to one another, even ask about each other's lives at a dinner party, if the opportunity ever arises, and it probably will because we have the same interests. We are enemies, though. There is policy, there are plans, made at the top of the hill, and then there are those at the bottom. Sitting in this very tasteful office, listening to this man believe in what he does, I understand my place. I belong at the bottom of the hill. Maybe I knew it already, but this feeling settles through me in a resounding way. This man is my enemy, and I respect him. There is a sword hanging above his chair, mounted on the wall, the blade slightly unsheathed, just enough to see the glint of metal.

"You are in danger," I say. "But you already know that."

"I want to make this city a better place, Thomas. For our children. I really do." He stands up from the desk and now pleads with me, like a teenager asking the prettiest girl to go with him to the dance. *I want to treat you the way you deserve to be treated.*

"I know you do," I say.

*

I hear August's voice booming through the rectory even before I put my coat on the parlor rack. Other voices lead me to the study. A handful of the clerics are sitting while August and Simon stand, facing each other. It is almost comic how the men are perfectly staged. Give them pistols and a Tombstone, the dust roiling along plank and desert.

August is very high-pitched, "How can you do this without consulting all of us? We are a *community*. We make decisions *together*."

"You weren't doing anything, August, and we don't have time to deliberate. By the time we all agreed on something, there'd be nothing left of the neighborhood."

August moves close to Simon, his finger pointing. "How can you say I haven't been doing anything? I've been to council meetings, I went to..."

He notices me. "Thomas. Did you know that Simon here is helping organize a protest rally during the Bounce Back Festival? At the *exact* same time. It plans on going along Baltimore Street, right where our booth will be."

Simon, underneath the heat of argument, looks at me, pleads silently for alliance.

August says, "Well?"

"What?" I ask.

"Don't you think that is a conflict of *interest*?"

"Whose interest?" I ask.

Father Mike and Brother Saul look more entertained than concerned. They shift their seats to take in the third factor to the fight. They both take sips of their coffee in the momentary silence.

August says, "It'll look ridiculous if you and I are manning a booth at the Festival while Simon is leading a protest opposing it at the same time. Shouldn't we be unified on the issue? What will the neighborhood think?"

Simon snaps, "What do you mean ' what will the neighborhood think?' They don't care about us. We've done nothing for them, except be a big, beautiful private school while bulldozers park in front of their homes. We've done *nothing* for them."

"Oh, Simon, you are so dramatic, and that doesn't excuse the fact that you went behind our backs. Thomas, you have to agree that is bad form, to be so clandestine."

Father Frank stands up. "He is right, Simon. You should have at least consulted with us before you assumed action. You have every right to believe what you do, but now we are divided in the public eye. The last thing the neighborhood needs is more division."

Simon opens out his hands. "We don't have time for this. And we *are* divided on this issue. It is wrong, what MacAllister is doing. Thomas, tell them."

The men turn to me again. I get the faintest whiff of Brother Saul's whiskey.

I am surprisingly calm. "There is a lot of corruption surrounding the Crabtown project."

Simon slaps his thighs. "See. We have been investigating the developer, even the city. This is a bad deal for Highlandtown, and we need to stop it."

August looks at me with the innocence of a wounded animal. "Is this true? Have you been helping Simon on this crusade?"

"I've been researching the project, August, yes."

"And we have discovered that the city and the developer are engaged in severely unethical practices." Simon continues, about the condemnations, the reappraisals of land, the back-door dealing. The men sit captivated, whether due to the information or Simon's intensity, I have no idea. "That is why we can't be a presence at the festival," he says.

"Simon, we all agreed to be a presence at the festival, remember? We had a *meeting* and, as civilized gentlemen, we *discussed* it, and then we *voted*."

Father Mike suggests, "Should we have a meeting again to discuss this, now that there is more information to consider?"

"We could do it after dinner on Tuesday," Brother Saul says.

Simon shakes his head. "I don't have time to wait for you all to deliberate. My commitment to the order is to do what is right, and this is what is right in my heart. I am assisting in the march on Saturday."

August snorts, "And are you going to lead your march right through the booths at the festival, right past me and Thomas? Are you that arrogant?"

Simon laughs, "August, do you really think Thomas is still going to help you at the festival?"

"Is this true, Thomas?" August asks.

"I don't think I can," I say.

August moons, looking so betrayed. "But we're the Outreach Committee."

"But this time it doesn't feel right, August," I say.

Father Mike clears his throat. "August is right, Thomas. We selected you to represent us at community and city events, whether you agree with the politics or not."

Simon interjects, "But this one... Mike, we have to make an exception. Aren't there exceptions?"

There is indistinct mumbling from the men, glances.

"You know, Thomas, we don't always believe in what we commit to, we religious serve as impartial supporters of people. You of all should know that showing up is part of the job," August says.

"Maybe that is our problem," I say. I think of all the things I've done but didn't believe in, the things I've been impartial to, been noncommittal of, the times I've ignored or dismissed or paid no mind. I think of Mirabelle and her sons. How many times have I overlooked a situation that I could have helped, made better, by using my meager resources?

"Fine. I'll man the booth alone," August says, and storms out of the room, but not before throwing me a look of pure disappointment. The apology bubbles compulsively to my lips, but I keep it trapped behind my teeth, and manage not to respond with anything beyond my eyes.

Simon grins as he watches August leave, shakes his head.

"What?" I ask.

Simon says, "I just can't believe he's still going through with it. Where's his backbone?"

My nose wrinkles. "I think his backbone is very much there, Simon. August believes in what he's doing."

"Which is what, exactly?"

"Serving the people, in the way he knows how."

"You're not defending him, are you, Thomas?"

"I think we can disagree and still support one another."

"Yeah, well, at least we know what's right." Simon's face is smug, so self-assured, so arrogant, just like Ponty MacAllister. I can't help but wonder whether Simon identifies as a Thomas More or a Machiavelli.

"Do we always?" I ask, and head to my room. There's a protest to prepare for.

26

Ruth

I get over to Sarah's not too long after Peter leaves for work. I do it fast. My hair is in tangles and I'm a shaky mess from drinking coffee all night. Peter didn't even notice when he woke up this morning, or at least pretended not to notice.

I drag myself up to her porch just as she opens the front door. She is wearing a thick bathrobe with pink squares all over it. Her hair is pushed all on the top of her head. It really does look like a nest. Her eyes aren't fully opened.

"Christ. Why you calling so goddamned early all the time?"

"I need you to do something for me, Sarah."

She holds up one flat hand, lowers herself down on a porch chair and says, "I think maybe I should be sitting before I hear whatever's about to come out of your mouth."

I take the chair across from Sarah. "Look, hon," I say after a breath, "I was wondering if Peter can stay with you for a bit."

Her head perks up. I wish more coffee could do that for me, right now.

"Peter?" she asks.

"Yeah."

Her eyes look at me like one of those hologram puzzles. The wrinkles in her forehead are real deep. I don't have time to read them, and even if I did it wouldn't matter.

"For a little while," I add.

"Why?" Her face reminds me when Paw-Paw died and I had to explain it to her under the oak tree that was growing into the back porch of the farm. I was just getting used to death myself, still didn't really know what it was, but I explained it like I was an expert. *When our bodies get old, we die, and then become invisible and go to a place in the sky and we live on top of clouds. That's where Paw-Paw is.* I remember her, all puffy and red. She looked at me, looked over to where Paw-Paw was all dressed up in his Sundays, laying in the box with roses and carnations all around it, looked back to me. She wanted to believe me, I could tell. And I kept my eyes on her, like a big sister should. I had the gumption to believe in what I was saying, and she could tell. But, still, it was Sarah. "Why?" she asked then, and in the same way, asks now.

I know I can't answer her. If I try to I'll be here for twenty Tuesdays getting an earful.

"Maybe run by my place tomorrow so Peter can grab some clothes?"

"What's wrong?"

Her face breaks my heart. I know the girl loves me and I know the way her eyes get all round that it is all love. Of all that may be, I am certain of love.

"I have to take care of some things."

Sarah's face firms up. She grabs my shoulder. Her eyes move side to side, but each time say something else. After a moment they settle, and rest on my chin.

"Sure, Ruthie."

"One more thing. I need Eddie's gun."

Sarah's eyes get large as moons. "Ruth Anne!"

I don't have time for explanations, I just can't, so I fix my eyes onto her and set my mouth like the line of a pencil, and steady my gaze. Please, Sarah.

It takes her own face a whole bunch of moments to settle down, her thinking about all the possibilities, but she knows me, and knows if I could say something I would. And, as if she's been told that she lost the beauty pageant by one point, she starts to nod.

"Thank you," I say, with all the gratitude I can muster.

She clears her throat. "You going somewhere?"

I wonder why she asks that question when her face has already readied itself for the answer. The face of her could never hide her insides. She never needed to hide much because she didn't do anything worth hiding from. Her words were the same as the mouth that made them, her choices the same as her footsteps. This I understand. Everything about my sister was whole, all of her could be written down on one page, but the page would be clear—not white—and you could see everything the page was through the page, on the page, like it all became part of the page, too, but only when it was there. This was something I hated when I was younger, loved when I was older, and now envy so much that it hurts to look at her, how clear she is.

"Yes."

"Today?"

I nod.

She grabs my hands together, wraps her own around mine. "You feel sure about whatever it is you're doing?"

"I do," I say, and I mean that more than I've meant anything in a long, long time.

"Well, then." She brushes hair from her face with a quick finger, her eyes slowly reddening but staying with mine. "Let's get on with it."

III

Or Does it Explode?

III

Or Does it Really?

Prelude

April

The morning sky was a single, flat layer of matte gray. There was no betrayal of a sun peeking through, no suggestion of blue. The halcyon haze compelled the brick to crackle the air with its fire color. Matter, indeed, made of fire.

On the front steps of King Middle School, beyond the plastic orange safety fence that surrounded the soon to be abandoned school, residents of Ellwood Park assembled—with posters, with signs made of foam-core and rulers, broomsticks and duct tape.

Some of the protesters thought at first it was their own burning that rendered the brick so alive on this particular morning. Of course, the art teacher, one of the first several hundred protestors of many more to come, whose studio classroom faced the street on the second floor of King Middle, knew that this was the ideal light for photographing the city. The soft, even gray of the sky acted as the perfect white balance for the camera, for the eye, and made all other colors more manifest. She would have shared this insight with eighth graders in her 2D Art class during third and fifth periods in the fall term, if she had not been reassigned to a middle school in the county, if King Middle had not announced that this spring term would be its last.

Reverend Arnold James of All Friends Baptist Church emerged at the top of the steps. He waited for the crowd to lower its chatter, its

early-morning excitement. He wore an olive green double-breasted suit
with a tan checkered tie, like a high-class camouflage. The crowd settled
even more when they heard him tapping the microphone attached to
the portable amp.

"It is so good to see so many folks out here on this gloomy day. Hopefully, the march to Patterson Park will warm our bodies up." The crowd
clapped and whistled, began hoisting their signs into the air:

Housing is a Right!

Save Our Neighborhood!

Crabtown Is A Joke!

Would This Happen in a White Neighborhood?

More people arrived. And before churches opened their doors for
first Sunday session, the crowd had grown to over a thousand. Two of
the protestors, Brothers Simon Royer and Thomas Manilli, standing
ever-so-slightly apart from the larger crowd, would normally be preparing for Eucharist at St. Mary's, sorting the sacrament into shallow bowls
and goblets. This morning, however, they stand, somewhat awkwardly,
in this growing assembly. If one saw this particular congregation from
above, they might mistake the image for an ancient Greek amphitheater
during Dionysia, a radial band surrounding a single man. And the chorus
between them, evenly spaced apart: six uniformed police officers, standing stoic between James and the protestors, between the orator and his
audience, a thin white line. People began practicing their chants:

No Justice, No Peace!

Impeach the Fools, Save our Schools!

Soon, a new wave of participants arrived, a younger group, mostly
men. They stood on the fringes of the crowd, their gaze sideways, shifting
stance from one foot to the other, an energy in their bodies that seemed
uncontainable, that pulsed in their veins, that could escape and break
brick. Pastor James noticed these men during his rally speech, and if one
was particularly perceptive, they would have heard the slight change, the
minute hesitation in his voice, not quite as resounding in its conviction.
If one had been more perceptive, they would have also seen the alarm in

the police officers surveying the crowd as James roused the rally, would have seen Officer Nathan Borofsky glance at his squad—each of them nod in return—and subtly tilt his head towards the left and speak into his shoulder microphone. And, if one were especially perceptive, they might have discerned by the movement of his mouth that Borofsky had requested backup under the auspice of a potential 10-34.

The news trucks rolled up, a new layer to the throng. The reporters and cameramen and grips and boom operators scurried around the crowd to locate a spot, their best angle, sometimes interrupting those on the fringe of the rally, running into their signs, tripping on feet, protestors vocal in their annoyance. One of the cameramen said to his assistant, "This is way bigger than we thought." The assistant nodded, seemingly transfixed by the closing remarks of Pastor James.

"Are you ready to march for our community?"

The rally cheered, and with that, several crowd leaders ushered the protestors to move along Lakewood Avenue, towards the park, among them Simon Royer.

Feet shuffled, pushed forward, searching for cadence amidst the dense lot, arms raised to hold signs high.

No Justice, No Peace!

Arnold James followed behind. He kept an eye on the boys, the young ones with their sideways glances. None of them looked familiar, had never attended the neighborhood meetings, the town halls at the school. Were they even residents of the east side? He watched them lurking the edges of the march, their limbs less purposeful, too loose for James to feel any comfort in their presence.

No Justice, No Peace!

Not even two blocks into the march, Borofsky's backup arrived, eight vehicles, directly ahead of the mass. The screech of the tires on asphalt, the hurried exit of the officers, made the marchers instinctually jerk back, and then, with even more conviction, press forward.

Borofsky flinched and muttered a small "fuck" under his breath. Couldn't the cars have parked further up Lakewood, out of sight of the march, been in position by the time the crowd passed by? He knew the conspicuous entrance would appear confrontational. He hoped the new officers would quickly fall into formation, line Lakewood as they had been instructed, before any fear or agitation could sweep over the crowd.

No Justice, No Peace!

But it was too late. Stray cats on the corner could taste the metal in their back teeth. The air was crackling with stares and wound-up bodies. The anger harbored deep in the hearts of the crowd—an anger that was so entire and encompassing that none of them could see its origin—surfaced, rising from their organs, through ribcages, creeping through muscles, and into the thin layer of skin, all nerves triggered, alight and charged.

As the crowd approached the scrambling officers, their chants grew louder. Some marchers now faced sideways, towards the cops, instead of forward. For a few, the chants became something else, closer to a cry. They chanted for something more, beyond the neighborhood, something that bore a history older than the brick that surrounded them. And one woman, thrusting her sign like a shield instead of a flag, added to the chant:

No Justice, No Peace. No More Racist Police!

Quickly, the modified chant, the desire so great for something larger to channel the pain of the crowd, surged through the rest of the marchers.

And then it happened, as it does, the great need for the laden current to jump circuit, the crave for discharge: from crowd to mob.

A woman threw her sign at the police officer in front of her, tears in her eyes. She cried not for her neighborhood, not at this moment, but for her fifteen-year-old son, who now lived paralyzed on his entire left side from being beaten by police for resisting arrest during a random street check. Almost immediately after the woman hurled her sign, two officers grabbed her, wrenched her to the ground. The woman scratched at the officers, the fury a fluid, something to fill. Several protestors shrieked at the sight.

"Calm down, ma'am," the larger officer said.

"Don't you call me ma'am," the woman yelled, waving her arms in hopes to connect to something, to scratch, to catch, to grab at retribution. Her son had been hanging with friends on a stoop during the street check, and refused to be humiliated in front of his new girlfriend when police ordered him to get on his knees. "I've done nothing wrong," he said. Three batons made contact with his spine before it was over.

The officers struggled to keep hold of the woman, her arms flinging. The larger officer restraining her—perhaps in a moment of frustration, but also something else that was lodged deep in him, that summoned his father's voice, news casts, stories around BBQs, ridiculing laughter, that twitched the muscles in his crisp blue uniform, a metallic bite of feeling from somewhere hiding behind his guts, that slid out of the shadows of his organs, and rose up to his mouth and pulled his lips into a snarl— hoisted the woman up by the back of her hoodie a full six inches off the road and slammed her back to the asphalt. Upon doing this, the metallic bite abated, his fear and regret immediately flooded him. "Now," his voice trembled, "keep it together."

A voice, strident and clear amidst the inchoate cloud of noise, exclaimed, "She's bleeding!"

Indeed, she was. The crowd saw. And many screamed at the sight.

The officers surrounded the scene, faced the encroaching crowd. "Get back," they yelled. Some pulled out their batons, lifted their elbows in preparation. A woman was pushed forward, a baton met her shoulder. A scream. Men in the crowd began to ram through, their hands collapsing into protective fists, fists for their wives, their children, for their homes, and their history. Another baton raised. More screams. Then a rock thrown, a piece of metal.

And this is how it ends, and this is how it begins.

27

Peter/Ruth/Thomas

I throw the covers off and clean up quickly. I want to leave so it looks like any other day, and don jeans and a plain t-shirt. It pains me to go out like this, but I don't need Ma questioning me when I come down the stairs. Besides, I'm not sure how long I'm going to be. I could arrive and Jude not even let me in. He could have security watching his house, looking for a tall, slender mixed kid climbing up the ivy trellis, calling his name in desperate yelps.

I want some power back. I want some closure, I need to *know*. And with everything constantly denying me, what am I supposed to do? I'm a teenager, for Christ's sake; this is the time to feel powerful, full of youth and stupidity. That's what all the movies say. So what? We can't take risks when we're older. I might as well get them out of the way now.

Ma is already awake when I come down the stairs, but barely, her hair mussed into a sculpture of abandon, her fingers twitching. She looks almost scary. Her shoulders are hiked to her neck. Something is wrong, but I don't dare to ask. She knows so much now. I remember what Thomas said, about Columbia. I want to ask her about it, why she didn't tell me, but I already know why. I guess I just want to hear her answer. But, no, not now.

"I'm going to work," I say.

"You get off this afternoon, right?" It is high-pitched, but not cheery. And strange. I would press some questions, but right now it's more important to get free from the house.

"Yeah, at four."

Now I had to stay out late, at least for the length of a work shift. I didn't want to even explain coming back early. But I had this covered, too, planned to meet Max at Red Emma's.

"Wear a jacket!"

My natural instinct is to raise my voice in ridicule. She is in the kitchen when I slide the thing over my shoulders.

I watch her for a moment. She is walking back and forth through the rooms, completely lost. It's almost comical, with her fingers crooked and her mouth drawn down and her eyes a little too open, but there is also something sad about it.

It's fucked up, really, devoting almost twenty years of your life to raise a child, only for them to leave. All that sacrifice, only to be alone. What is the purpose? I will not have kids, even if the possibility would ever come, and that comforts me. Maybe that's what being gay is all about, some kind of social evolution to rid the world of child-rearing and all of its pointless sacrifices. But the word: gay is such a stupid, simple word for something so big and complicated in the world. Maybe I'll come up with a better word; that'll be my contribution to faggots everywhere, a word that reflects more resolutely their condition. There's a lot in a name.

I go straight to Jude's through the tight early spring air. The trek is long, two bus lines and several blocks. The city is still quiet, more so than usual. At Light Street, the harbor on one side, the empty office buildings on another, something feels artificial. The towers could have been paintings, the USS Constitution a hollow model floating in the dredge. I feel like it was all mine, like an amusement park before it closes. I wonder if the Crabtown park will be like that—crazy during the day, scores of people with cameras and plaid shorts and fanny packs, then desolate at night. Funny, much like the area is now, in some ways.

On the first bus, there is a man, mid-thirties, sitting across from me. He stares out in that common blank way that people do when riding on the bus, for fear of resting their eyes on each other, even though that's what they want to do, stealing glimpses in hopes of discovering something, to compare themselves, looking for a clue to confirm their status. Or, maybe he's just another guy trying to figure out what I am, trying to check the race box on the form in his mind, so he can make his presumptions, and has been stumped. But this guy stares out differently, and my own stolen glance tells me he isn't in love with his life. His presumable wife, who sits next to him, and not so next to him, knows this. She is looking away, more than looking away, because she isn't looking at anything, not even at the reflection of herself or her husband. They haven't talked about their unhappiness, and instead sit next to each other but not next to each other, saying nothing at all. Maybe they fear what talking would do, change things that they aren't certain they want to change. He glances at me with envy, the idea of me. He can smell my freedom, my mobility, and he hates me for it. I keep my gaze on him long enough for him to see me. It is electric to feel his envy, and then to reply yes, I have freedom, you have every reason to envy me. I feel even more assured and want more than anything to be off the bus and at Jude's house.

It looks like it might hail, the sun hiding. The gray film seems to overtake the sky, only a constant and dull ambient light, the waiting room of our worn-out heaven.

*

Choosing what to keep isn't too hard. Much of it isn't any kind of stuff I ever wanted anyway. At the time it seemed to be stuff we needed. Ironing boards, frying pans and jackets, candle holders, a gardening book I never opened, baskets to put nothing in, and where did I get the money to buy all these things when I've never had any money to begin with? What was mine I could pack into the pickup with no more than a little pushing. The back of the truck sinks a little, but nothing it can't handle.

I keep walking into the rooms like I'm making a checklist for nothing but remembering. I see parts of the house that I didn't pay no mind to, day to day. The dirt jammed in the corners where the floor meets wall seems like someone else's. I have to stare at it long enough until I know it's mine. I'm not sure why, though, cause it's not like I've lived in this house my whole life or anything. I look at the countertop in the kitchen, the one I was just getting used to. I knew in the morning not to look at the plaid lines printed in the Formica or my headaches would fire up. I realized only a week ago that the sink leaks into the floorboards.

When I take my baskets off the walls there isn't any kind of dust line or sign that it had been there at all, except for a tiny hole in the wall. The time has been filled with short-term leases and visits and all these things that don't really stay with you. Nothing in my life has been with me the whole time. Not my home, not my men, not even my body. It changes, everything changes, and I never understood that. I've been trying to have some sameness, but it wrings out wrong every time.

Mrs. Gabriel's gone out. For the first time I feel good about that. The place on the other side of us is empty, but I go over to take a look. It's a shell of a house with nothing but bricks and walls. The windows are shattered all over the floor with the spray paint cans and trash and splints of wood. Looking down, the whole place seems to be a lost cause, something left to die slow as a snail, to have to wallow in its own salt. But when I look up I see the walls, straight and strong and made like they were meant to stay. The moldings around the corners must be six inches thick on either side. The fireplace reaches all the way up the back wall and reminds me of my Paw-Paw when I first remember being scared of how big grown-ups were. All this rubble scattered around these perfectly laid bricks brings to my heart some big sad failure.

Peter will be fine. Better than he has ever been.

Standing still makes my hands all sweaty. There's no one in the park. The wind slices me up pretty bad but the walk is better than standing around in the house. I got everything done and ready. Now all I need is Isaac to come over.

The truck shouldn't be parked out front. Anyone can see that it's packed full. I should've thought about that. He'd know I was up to something.

It turns over as good as it can. I swing it around to the alley out back and park it out of the view of any of the windows. Just in case.

It's nice being outside. I don't want to be in the house any more than I have to. The wind is cooling my armpits.

The box in the passenger seat is half open. I don't want that stuff to blow away, pictures and letters and all. I need to clean up, but I don't want to go back in just yet. I pick up the stack on top. Letters from old friends, Christmas cards from family, pictures of Mama and Aunt Ginny, of me and my cousins who all lived down the road, and who now live all over. I pick up the photo, smeared with god-knows-what on the top edge. We're smiling, Junior, little Tommy, me and Turk, teeth wider than our faces, probably just done with egging Mr. Hawkins' new blue Ford, or at least thinking about it. Mama used to snap away those thoughts all the time with her wet dishtowel. I'd be sitting in the kitchen watching a bug crawl across the window or nothing at all and all of a sudden I'd feel the whap across my back. I'd say, "What was that for?" and she'd say, "Just in case you were thinking about doing something ornery." For the longest time I thought she could read my mind. But if that were the case then she would have whapped my cousins all the time, cause they were the real trouble-makers. They were rotten little sons-of-bitches. Good fun.

Underneath my cousins is a Polaroid of me and Joby and Abe and Peter. I quickly shove the other photos on top of it and close the box. If I look at it, I'll get selfish, I know, and that's not what I need to do right now. I get out of the truck. This is a good place for it. The slam of the door sounds somehow perfect in the winter wind, like a good decision.

*

I've been in front of Jude's house for I don't know how long. I know he's in there. His curtains move.

I don't understand his cowardliness. What he has been through, you would think an innocent romantic interlude wouldn't have him so walled up. I assumed it would be fairly expected, with the way we had come together so quickly. But for some it requires patience, time to grow into new things. I was too disappointed, hurt, to see that he needed time and patience. I was selfish in being upset. I realize that now. It was yet another thing for him to go through. Again, the word gay doesn't feel like the category, hard to accept that word for something so much larger. It's such a little shit of a word, nothing noble about it. This is why it's so important to see him alone. To soothe his fears and give him the chance to allow his desire, allow it to go beyond the word. I need to be confident. I at least have to know.

With every step I feel sure. It's a blessing. If every snot-nosed teenager possessed my sense of reality, they wouldn't fill their own with the ridiculous mistakes commemorated in after-school specials. We don't have to be slaves to our age. We just have to think.

My knock is soft. I'm disappointed. I should have rapped on the door like a police officer. I'm confident of my presence and purpose. I have to be.

The door creaks slowly. I push down the rising flush in my chest. Seeing him gives me that drained-out weakness, but this visit is far too important. I'm the teacher today. I need to be steadfast and confident. Today I am releasing him. He needs me to be unwavering.

"It's early," he says.

I stand silent. I make it a statement.

He opens the door wide and stands aside. "My mom's here. Let's go in my room."

We slink down the hallway; I concentrate on his shoulders. He goes right for his bed and slumps against the headboard, pulling a pillow to his lap, and stares, first at the floor, then at me. There is a small curve to his lips. Standing feels best for now, having physical height over him, commanding the space. The words I'd rehearsed last night, this morning, on the bus—now they won't come. I push through the silence with a cough to signify the beginning of my planned speech. Maybe the words will rise with the sound.

But there's nothing. I recited something on the 81 bus. I saw myself lighting a series of lanterns illuminating a path to understanding, words that led to discovery. There was something about something. It was everything. I mapped out all the great and relevant truths and why they brought us together, but now I can only see the vague outline of where the words were going to be. His stare is awful.

He throws up his arms. "What?"

I say his name.

"Why did you do that?" The question is so abstract it takes me a moment to realize he's talking about Mass. I can tell he's afraid to talk about it, because his eyes are trembling, and his voice is angry.

I don't know how to answer him. I don't know why I did it, really, other than I wanted to taste his finger, I wanted something to happen. I could say that. It doesn't seem like the right thing to say right now. He's angry, and I'm surprised how that deflates my fortitude. It wheezes right out of me, and then that cold stone in the gut.

"Peter, you always have *something* to say."

Still nothing. I'm frozen in the unknown of this.

"I don't think we should hang out anymore," he says.

The term "hang out" hurts. Hanging out is when guys get drunk at parties and smoke pot and watch buddy action flicks. Hanging out is a way to bide the time. Hanging out is not communicating your deepest feelings, revealing the dark parts of yourself, making yourself vulnerable. I mean, talking about death? I want to say all of this, but I can't. Not now. He wouldn't listen, with his face so angry. There has to be a way to get through, to disarm the meanness. It needs to be something off guard, to surprise him, make him listen. That's how I disarm Ma when we fight. It has to be hard-hitting.

"I've seen your scars."

"Yeah, you have," he winces, and his face softens a bit. "They're almost gone."

I think back to those nights in the car. Only a handful, yes, but they play out already like a central part of my life, moments where connection was certain, where it was just the two of us. If only it could always be just the two of us, and there were no suffocating boundaries, no words thrown at us from the flicking tongues of teenagers, from anyone, and we could merely exist together without anything but our own words, or maybe no words at all, better yet. Like right now.

"I love you," I say. That's it, simple and direct. That's right.

Jude's face doesn't move, respond in any way. Perhaps he didn't hear me. I say it again. The second time doesn't feel nearly as good.

He looks at me as if he knew I would say this. I didn't plan on saying this! His face has a premeditated bracing to it, his lips pursed, his eyes looking down as they look straight at me, like one of those plastic Jesus sculptures. He looks at me with pity! And says nothing.

"And I think you love me." Another grasp, an empty grasp. And this one doesn't feel good at all, not at all. I went too far. I went too far, again. If only I could believe in what I know. If only I could believe that words make stale all things of desire. I know it and yet I don't.

"Peter, I'm not...."

I pull myself closer to him, move onto the bed. I need to explain, really make him understand. I know he is scared, of what it means, of whispered words that would, that will swirl around, the immediate future. Please understand Jude, please; it is about what you *are*, not what you *aren't*. He recoils, but not as much as I thought he would. "It's not about that. It's about us."

He shakes his head slowly, with something weighty, like resolve, like power. I have to show him with something other than words. They've been failing me. They fail everyone. I went about this all wrong. If desire ripens in the absence of language, then words kill it, make it rotten. Words, that attempt precision, yet never absolute, like science, like religion, never in full agreement, always slightly askew from exact meaning. If desire ripens in the absence of language, then words kill it.

I close my eyes and move in to his lips. The distance feels farther than I thought, the want of it lengthening time and space, just like in my dreams of it happening, as if each time our lips are about to touch, the scene rewinds just the moment before.

The punch doesn't hurt as much as make everything loud. There's a ringing in my head and it comes out of me and fills Jude's bedroom. I'm on the floor at the foot of the bed. My eyes blur from the pain or shock, and Jude smears over to me, his arms waving apologetic.

"Fuck! Peter, man. Are you all right?"

It's not until I say I love you again that I realize I'm crying. He kneels down on the floor, looking helpless. "I'm sorry, man. I didn't mean to do that. It's just…"

"You had to," I say. It feels right to say it. I want to apologize for him, make it all right. I want to be on his side.

"What do you mean?"

"To change things, make them okay. Hitting, it changes things." I understand this, Ma understands this. Joby understood this. I want to tell him about Ma, about Joby. I taste a little blood in my mouth, nothing too bad, not like my nose in New York. I want to tell him about New York.

Jude shifts. "Peter, that's not what this is."

"We can only do things—some things—saying them is wrong." I lean forward the smallest bit. This feels right. This is the moment. First, it didn't look like it would come, then it does in the wake of the violence. There needed to be a force to blow the pressure out. This violence wasn't one of refusal, but the fear of realizing the truth.

"Peter."

I lean in further, inches from his face, and whisper, "Listen, Jude." I hope that when his mouth opens, he won't taste the blood in mine. And what if he does?

*

I run directly to Patterson Park. Once the police began clashing with the protest, it would only be a matter of time before it spilled to the festival. I'm panting so loud I can't hear anything else, but the shock of adrenaline keeps me running. I haven't run this much in ages, and I feel the burn in my lungs, but I have to get to the festival before they do.

Patterson Park is flat and yellow. And the worry has taken me from tired to tight. Every loud noise triggers my nerves, a series of circuits

connected together. MacAllister's arrogance in the face of a death threat.
Simon's constant berating. Ruth Anne's strange visit. Every time I hear
one of the clerics whispering, I swear I hear my name. *Thomas harbors
a Black mistress, a concubine.* Now this protest gone wrong. Everything
is on the very edge of the life I know, everything tossed into such fury.
I don't know how far behind the people are, so I keep running until I
reach the edge of the festival.

The clear chill gives everything around me a speed. Volunteers are buzz-
ing this way and that with clipboards and t-shirts. Vendors are serving
wieners and funnel cake to a small-ish crowd. A cover band called The Fish
Mongers is playing a speedy rendition of "Whole Lotta Shakin.'" The cars
on Baltimore Street seem to move faster, despite the random red brake-
lights blinking as their drivers investigate the activity at the park. Even my
hands appear faster as they move in the search. And August, he really is
moving faster. The Church is taking up three tables side by side, one for St.
Mary's, one for the L.I.F.E. program, and one mostly empty. He's arranging
pens and pamphlets there when I finally reach him, gasping for breath.

"August, we have to go," I croak.

August is high-pitched. "Thomas! Did you come to your senses?" he
asks cheerily, adjusting one of the table covers.

"The protest. It's coming," I say.

August ignores my plea. "The festival got off to a slow start, but more
people are arriving. I got two people signed up for our newsletter already,
and…"

I grab August by the arm, and his arms stiffen. "Now," I say. "We have
to go. Something happened."

August shakes his head. "Thomas, what are you talking about?"

I hear a low rumbling coming from what I think to be behind me. Not
one distinct sound, just a constant colorless thunder. I turn around, but
see nothing. I think it may be the festivities dully echoing off the brick
facades that surround the park, but that doesn't seem right, and the air
isn't right for a storm. "Whole Lotta Shakin'" continues. But then the
sound gets louder, sharper, there is more definition. I can tell other peo-

ple in the park start to hear it, too. Their heads cock to the right almost in synchronicity to the birds on the telephone wire above them. The sounds become more and more distinct with every second, the sound of wood, glass breaking. Others are almost human voices, maybe angry voices, yelling. And the low rumbling, I realize, as it articulates closer, is feet on asphalt, lots of them. They're already here.

A young kid comes from out of nowhere and pushes me hard. I fall back as he grunts something with hot breath. He looks up, licks his lips. And with an explosive energy, slides his arm across the table. Flyers, pens, August's fan of pamphlets scatter to the ground. Just as quickly, the kid grabs one of the tent poles and pulls. The tent falls in. I scramble underneath it, find the edge, and look up. The kid is gone. Other tents are fallen over, and at first I wonder how this kid could work so fast. But then I see several boys repeating the same assault.

Some people are trying to reset their tent. Most are standing around bewildered. And that's when I hear the scream, from a woman two tents down.

I turn behind me. Hundreds of people are running up the street. They are throwing rocks. Some have sticks or bats in their hands. The sound is louder now, the yelling, voices in chaos. The woman screams again, this time followed by a low moan, clutching her chest. The angry crowd is coming right towards us.

*

The farm had these beautiful hills. It looked like God threw a green velvet blanket over the whole countryside, everything was so smooth. There was always a breeze that moved over things real light and never pushed you or whipped you or anything. It would touch you real soft and make you feel like you could move with it. Whenever Granny and I would go walking up them I would take the ribbons out and swing my hair back and forth like the movie stars and let that wind come all over me and through my hair. I always felt older and prettier, like I had the makings of Natalie Wood, Maureen O'Hara, even Katherine Hepburn.

I wouldn't want to talk and I would walk real slow and steady. I made sure not to trip over myself while still keeping my head up and into the wind. I was a horse riding through the hills and my hair was my mane. But I wouldn't let anyone ride on my back, never. I would be strong and beautiful and never trip on myself or talk any nonsense, or listen to it either. I wanted nothing as choppy as talk.

I was sixteen when I got pregnant with Joby. And it wasn't that I wasn't ready. I was pretty mature for my age. But Joby came way before there was any want for a baby. He rushed me in all ways, even in the white bed on the day he was born. He gave me no notice and pulled my guts the whole way. And so I hated him and at the same time loved him, from the beginning. When they first put his jelly-covered skin in my arms I was filled with the amazing thing I had just done, but cursed him for the done-ness of it. I would pull on his legs a little too hard when I changed his diaper, all the while singing "I'm a little teapot" with a smile that I could have sworn was real. I would take him to the park and play games and sometimes when he chased after the ball I would watch his little legs run and I would all of a sudden get this fist in my heart, a great big sadness. It weighed me down and sometimes I hated myself for it, and sometimes I hated him for it.

When Peter came along I already knew I had done wrong with Joby. I think I mean to say *to*, not *with*, I'm not sure. He was three years old and already mean. Soon enough, he would spend all his time outside with the neighborhood ruffians, getting into trouble, especially after Abe left. He broke a windshield when he was barely eight. A year later, got caught stealing an armload of Mallo Cups from 7-11. By the time Peter was in middle school Joby had been in Juvie Hall twice. And then Joby started running away. He came back, then would run again, come back, every time a little taller, a little skinnier, a little more hair above his lip. Usually there would be a new tattoo uglying up his arms or legs. Every time he'd show me the new crossbones or dragon I swear I could see the words, in the outline of the bones or the belly of the snake, "I hate you." I know it wasn't really there, but I could see it. Joby would smile with all his teeth like he just won something, yet his eyes would be sad at the same time.

And then he ran away for good, and it was all my fault. Now, it's time to make it right.

*

Jude is against the bed. I slightly hover over him, my hands almost touching his thighs, and I close into his face. He doesn't move away. The initial touch of his lips has me shudder with heat, the beginning of some great moment, the dream, the fantasy played out hundreds of times, celebrated with my eyes closed. Aren't all the perfect moments? I open my lips for him, ready to take everything in, say everything in the poetic gesture of a first kiss.

But his lips don't move. They are there, very much there, as soft as I imagined them to be, but nothing moves. Perhaps it is fear. I move my mouth more, to assure him, let him know it's all right, let my tongue move over him. But, nothing. He doesn't accept me. He neither pushes me away or retreats. Nothing. I open my eyes to his filling my vision. They are open, still, and resounding with pity.

I pull away. He looks at me with more resolve than I thought possible. It's plain what he says with the stubborn face, the thin dash of his mouth. He seems so sure of himself. This isn't the Jude I ever saw. This face is something secure, firm in its knowing. It's what *I* am supposed to be. He very slowly shakes his head.

Snot, saliva, shame all come out hard, and the clear unnerving calm of a strange but strong Jude smears through my tears in an instant. I continue to smear his room, smear the hallway beyond, the truly unfamiliar house and the light of a daytime Baltimore that is the same still gray as Jude's icy eyes, the color of refusal.

I am running, again.

*

Isaac's Malibu pulls in right where my truck was a half hour ago. It pulls in slow and he's looking out his window at the house. It takes him a while to get out and I hear the familiar squeak when he slams the door.

His clothes are different and he's buzzed his hair real short and I think maybe he's joining the Army again. His belly's a little bigger. I can tell, even through his loose striped shirt. He doesn't look half bad all dressed up, even for a son-of-a-bitch. He carries a bottle.

I don't meet him at the door. I walk into the kitchen, I sweep some crumbs off the counter. I push in a chair. I wait for him to knock.

I open the door slowly and try to be relaxed about it. I'm not as nervous as I thought I would be, but I catch myself biting my bottom lip and I lick it.

"Isaac."

I don't want to sound too excited, but I don't want to sound like I don't want him here, either.

"You look nice, woman."

I'm wearing the black skirt and red blouse I wore often when we went out for dinner. I thought it'd be a good choice. I nod, but I don't smile. "Thank you," I say.

He doesn't smile, either.

"Here," he says. The bottle says Gallo, a blush.

I give him room to come in. He smells like car grease and aftershave.

"It's empty in here," he says. "A lot of your things are gone."

"Yeah."

"You moving again?"

I hear the nasty little grin under all his talk. I hear him telling me how much he knows, how much he thinks he still has over me. I look towards the desk drawer. "I'm just getting rid of some things."

"Downsizing. That's good," he says.

I lead him into the kitchen, and follow a few steps behind.

In the kitchen he asks me, "How is Peter?"

"Fine."

He scratches behind his neck. He looks to the chair and back at me and shifts his feet. "That all? Fine?"

"He's doing real good. He got into college, in New York. A full scholarship."

I don't know why I tell him. I guess it doesn't matter.

"Oh good, that's good. Hmm. Good," he says real quiet. He scratches behind his neck again. "That's great. New York," he says much louder.

I put the wine on the counter right where I had swept off the crumbs.

"You look beautiful," he says, and shows a little teeth.

I ask him if he wants a glass of wine. He says sure as he sits at the table, but then I back away and grab the bottle and put it in the cabinet. It wouldn't look good if we were drinking wine.

"You're nervous," he says, tilts his head in that grinning kind of way, and crosses his legs like he's staying awhile. I pull at some strands of hair clinging to my cheek. If there wasn't reason I would tell him all kinds of ways to rot in hell and beat his face, but now isn't the time for that, or anything. I'm close to the gun and I could pull it out and do this now but it doesn't feel right just yet. I'm not sure what to wait for, though. I'm not sure if it's nerves or fear that I won't do it fast enough or if it is the weight of killing. Maybe it's God's invisible hand, the one you see in the way of a dove in those paintings in church, but not a dove in this case; an invisible hand, something in the heart that shoots through the body and takes the choice out of it. But what do I do if God is keeping my hands held? Would God forbid me to do this if it meant protecting my son, myself? Eye for an eye? Wouldn't this be the best doing? Couldn't I be God's hand, and somehow He is suggesting something slightly different than what I planned? I don't even know if I believe in this shit, anyway. I need a moment. There's sharp feeling in my head.

"Do you still carry your tool box in your car?" I ask, the idea suddenly coming to me. "Can you go bring it?"

"Why?" he asks, sitting up.

"The hammer. I need to pound back in a nail in the basement steps. I almost tore my damn toe off this morning." It's true about the nail. It's too perfect and true and I believe God sets things up to help us out once in a while. "Come look." I get him up, making sure not to touch him, and point.

He gets up and I show him the nail. He runs his finger over it real slow and looks over to me and keeps rubbing it.

"We can fix this," he says.

I give him a quick smile that makes me want to take a shower as he rises and stretches his hands over his head. He wants me to see his erection. I make sure he sees me curve my lips at it.

He smiles and walks out to his car. Smiles, smiles, and I hate him and it seems like smiles mean hatred more than any other thing, if I added up all the smiles in my life. I go to the desk drawer and open it quiet and quick. The gun.

*

The bus is a coffin, already far from Jude. Even though I'm curled up on the seat I want to flail all my limbs. Push. Punch the stale air. Bite the window and shatter the glass, chew it in my mouth. I want to be something besides defeated. Defeat, defeat, defeat, my whole fucking life, a pushing against the world, the small world I've had to live in. It has enveloped me for so long that it lingers, the small world lingers even if I left everything I knew and moved to a bigger world, a cloud of smallness and defeat hazing the clear picture of me, reducing me to a single insignificant blur. Fire is in my throat, my hands, vibrations all over my body.

And what else can I do but sit on this fucking bus and have the defeat fill me? I think to go to Red Emma's, to see Max and his cheerful face, but I'm worried he'll see me like this, the defeat, and think differently of me. There's nowhere to go, even though I'm moving, slowly, through Baltimore. So what is the coffin, the bus or Baltimore? Where does the real containment begin? The tagged-up metal of the MTA? The brick houses, every single one its own cask of Amontillado? The roads, the zip codes, what?

A sharp crash. The window becomes glass and liquid, beer splattered. I can almost smell it, that beer smell, though the window isn't open and didn't crack. I'm surprised by the beer bottle, by the window not cracking. I look beyond. There are dozens of people. No, hundreds of people, running around, running forward and around the bus, yelling. The bus is in the middle, the running people an ocean. The bus looks like it's sinking. The bus rocks. People on the bus rise in panic, shock. Some look innocent. Back and forth, like a cradle, a big metal cradle, the bus rocks. Everyone stands up, sits down, bobbing chairs, their arms fly backward, they lean into their knees. One woman screams at the bus driver, "What do they want?"

More and more people, mostly men, pour through the crowd around the bus. They move all ways, some stop. Only a handful rock the bus. Some bang the side of the bus with their fist as they run by. Some high-five the ones rocking the bus. Some wave to us, flash menacing grins. Others look like they will cry. Women on the bus begin to scream, ask stupid questions like "What is happening?" I ask the same thing in my head, but not out loud. The surge of people generally moves in the same direction. Some are definitely angry, waving bats, rocking the bus. Most are not, though, and seem focused on something else. It's not altogether unfriendly, actually. And most move on. Where are they going? We are not their target, it seems, but merely on their way. Their eyes are blazing inside their sockets. The street isn't visible anymore, just the wild eyes of something between anger and intoxication, maybe that is what fervor really means.

I know it. I feel it. They want to punch, flail, let it out. What is it? Anger in a box, something bigger. I want to run. I want to scream with them, beat against things, too, but not here in the bus. The eyes inside the bus are large moons. The eyes outside the bus are stars, hot fiery balls. Like my brother. It's a whole lot of fiery eyeballs, like Joby's. I want to be angry with them. I am angry with them.

"I want to get out!" I storm to the front. "Open the door!" The driver looks at me, back at the crowd, back to me, his mouth open.

"Open the door!"

"They'll come in!"

"I need to get out!"

I grip his hand and plant it on the door handle, and pull. His mouth is still open, staring at me, as the door unfolds into the boom of sound that fills the bus. I run out quickly, almost stepping on the people in the street. The sound is now beyond loud. It fills the entire space, the city, the early spring, humanity, earth. Every crevice is filled with sound, filled to the cosmos, full and explicit. I look out and I feel I recognize these people. It's not their faces, it's something else, like all of these people are Joby, every one of them, something so electric and full, so angry but not empty. Definitely not empty. I am surrounded by this fullness, and I move among it in this slow and pregnant way, and I don't know how much longer I will even know myself. We all move together, towards what I have no idea.

It seems at first that the crowd moves with me without concern, that I easily take part, a snowball headed for the bottom of the hill, each of us a single flake, compounded. The push of it feels so whole and entire, all of my body full, no other desire anywhere. Only some kind of fury. Everyone looks innocent, in a strange furious way. I saw it in Joby when I was a kid, I see it now. It's scary, but I'm not scared.

But then I see a few of the faces turn towards me, furrowed at first, yelling at last, but not at the whole world, or whatever it is larger than all of us that compels them. I haven't even thought what this was about. But these few are somehow angry at me, I can tell, only some, but yes, at me. They seem to say with their furrowed faces, *Why are you here*? I can't understand why. I move with them. I, too, am furious, uncontained. Joby was, too. I, too, want to feel my body push as hard as it can, to flail, to fill the space infinitely. But they don't see my face, nor my expression, not the push-pull. And then I get it. The sea of people, all furious, are Black, and I am more aware than ever that I am, indeed, half-not.

*

The park is full of screaming people. This is how war must look, the environmental noise louder than thought, and then the senses attempt to shut down for fear of overload, a numbing of sound. Many run. There are men colliding with crunching force. I can't tell if it's intentional. There is no way to tell who will run past me and who will strike me. I can't prevent any of them. I just need to go. It's better to keep up with the speed of everything than stand still. I think I hear gunfire and I definitely hear screams of pain.

August is already down, bloody. I pull his arm. He is weeping, his face streaked with dirt and shock. "Get up," I say, and he obeys. I pull him close, check for anything severe, but it looks like only cuts on his face and hands.

"They started kicking me," he cries.

"Can you walk?"

"What is happening?"

"Get up, August."

I hope that August's wounds garner sympathy, because we're moving against the crowd. I'm afraid they'll do the opposite, the way nature feeds off the weak, kill the chick that falls out of the nest. He is walking on his own, but weighs heavy on my shoulder.

On the street, people run in pattern-less angles. Car horns and alarms layer over the voices, over the crunching of glass and metal. A group of kids rock a truck until it turns on its side. I'm impressed by the feat more than horrified. Some push, others pull, back and forth, and when it begins to tip, a couple of them jump in the back, and it crashes to the side. They emerge triumphant, pumping their arms. I'd be kidding if I pretended not to understand why such an action would be so satisfying. It goes back to childhood. Breaking icicles off the eaves of houses. Throwing rocks at bottles. Demolition derby.

Something metal flies, almost hits August in the head.

"They're trying to get me, Thomas."

"Everyone's trying to get everyone," I assure him.

"I didn't do anything."

I keep moving, faster. I can see the rectory.

"Thomas, I've been trying to help these people."

The hurt in his voice invokes pity, but the contempt in it confirms my thoughts of August all along, that though he is a kind person, his convictions run very close to the surface. Often that kind of philanthropy is more dangerous than not caring at all.

"The rectory will be safer than this," is all I say.

*

The eyes are more yellow than white in their anger. I try to move away from them, but I am surrounded, most focused on something bigger than me, but a few see the something bigger *in* me. That I can tell. It pisses me off, and I am cold in my fear, that I can't keep with the crowd, pushing my anger out like them. Does anger really have a reason? Isn't it pure energy, built in the gut, like friction that has no relief? I, too, have no relief. I am angry too. The eyes looking my way are angry, too. Can't we recognize the same feeling in our trembling faces?

One punch in the side, awkward, more a push than a pain. But another comes, and another until, like energy, a chain reaction. There are a few taking their aim at me. The stomach, the back, the shoulder, and a kick in the leg. None of it hurts exactly, but it's fierce, a sharp *no*. I want to insist our half-sameness and our full-sameness, to urge them to look at me and see, but everything is too quick and without words, and I know they won't stop until I am beat, energy released, me a bloody revenge. I understand it's so personal that it's not. One guy tries to knee me, but another stops him, grabs his shirt collar, and points beyond, to what I don't know. Arms in front, I push through. I know a place I can get to quick.

The walls to the grotto are high and no one thinks to scale them. You'd have to know it was there. And the one entrance would be closed, the iron gate locked. The rest of the school shows itself so easily, with its windows and furniture aching to be broken, and nothing but Mary waits in the grotto. And so they are drawn to what they can break. The shattering glass already chimes the afternoon. I worry if I can leap once and over, quick, without too many witnesses. I have to try. The gruff stone, the chalky mortar, and I pull my arms hard. One leg on the top of the wall. I pull with everything I have.

"Hey!" My foot stops, an arm, a man. An angry man. He has my foot, his eyes rapturous from the catch. I make a sound like an animal, my eyes on his.

My father. Abe. Would they see him in me if he were by my side?

I push the leg that he pulls as hard as I can—an awkward labor— and it releases from his grip. I look ahead. Our bodies are clumsier in the crowded violence than I imagine. I scramble, scrape the wall, my knees and the stone, my feet paddle in the air, but they are free. The cold ground and the sting of my legs, and I make it. The sound is still loud, but is muffled by the wall, by the emptiness in the grotto. No one else is here, only some junk, some wood, a baseball bat, maybe thrown over from the street, so much a contrast. Mary quietly poses. I take in breaths, but can't satisfy the rise in me, the need to push out.

I got hit, strangers, kicked, strangers, I got punched, Jude, slapped, Ma. Peter, oh Peter, a hit for every heart. All of this, the violence, the love, the end. I want to push out, push it all out of me, hit something, hurt something. This is what Joby felt, I know it. He wanted to push out. I grab the bat. I swing. Is this what Isaac felt, too? Ma slaps me. I hit the tree. The bark chips. I swing. Jude and his face. I hit the ground. A soft thud. My heart. All of my muscle, my body. Do not deny me, do not deny me, do not deny me. Do not deny me. I swing at Mary's head.

She breaks, jagged, right at the neck. Her head sails, and hits the ground, one more crack in the back, and rolls in the dirt, rests about three feet from me. Her face is intact, lies on its side, looking right at me. And even though it is stained with mud and grass, a piece of nose chipped away, so far from her body, Mary's eyes, crusted with earth, remain pious and forgiving.

I drop to the ground, all of the fury released, spent, now shock and a calm. She stares at me. I take deep breaths. The bat has splintered, looks silly in my hands. I never played baseball, can't remember ever having one in my grip. Joby played baseball, really well. There's blood on my arms and shoes, and I don't know whose it is. Mine? Some of it, I'm sure, but not all of it. Mary keeps looking at me, and what else would she do. I lay down on the cold grass, almost thawed, lay down and face Mary. I catch my breath. I wipe away some of the dirt with my thumb.

The laughter begins in my abdomen, almost like a deep, rising cough, slow and punctuated. Yet the more I let it come, the faster it gets, until I am in a full-blooming fit of laughter. I roll over on my back, the trees and the sky fill my vision, rocking on the cold ground, uncontrollable laughter. I am filled again. I turn back to Mary. There she is, still pious, still forgiving, even when beheaded, and that makes me burst, laughing even harder, full cackles, so full-out, pushed out, and feeling so awesome.

*

I hear Isaac come in. He's in the hallway fast. And then in the kitchen. The hammer is long shiny silver and black. Isaac is large and blond, tall and muscled behind it, the blond hairs clutching the handle. He stops.

"Why you sitting down? Let's do this," he says.

The pistol is already in my hand under the table. My finger is on it. Quick is all. I'm afraid I won't know its weight right enough to aim fast. I might hit the table when I pick it up. I might take too long. Mess everything up.

"Ruth?"

I might miss. My sweaty finger might slip. I want to say something to him. Before. A final word.

He moves closer and his mouth opens.

It takes so long to lift the gun up and aim it with both hands. My fingers move so slow. He moves so slow. I pull the trigger and the sound moves slow. My hands pop up. My fingers hurt and he suddenly falls back. The grip kicks out of my hands and the gun sails into the air, round and round. It comes down slow. It hits the table. The vase tips, the sunflower falls out, and water darkens the tablecloth.

He screams and that punches through and makes everything faster. I watch him fall on the floor. His arms pay no mind. One crunches under his back. He screams again. I don't know what he means. I get up and stand on the other side of the kitchen, excited, something freed from my hands. I feel ridiculously tall.

He still looks big but it's all broken up. He moves around so clumsy and strange and the strangeness of it is shocking. He spits out some mean words, horrible words. His face is so many things. I can't look at it. It's ugly and even worse than him.

I grab the gun from the table, cock it, walk over, and aim for his face. To quit it. I hold the grip tighter this time. I pull the trigger and his face becomes something else. Once his face and thrashing and then something else.

Isaac's eyes stare open, unblinking. I clutch the gun tight to my body. It's warm through my shirt. He sees though I know he can't. I want him to. I want him to know I did it. I wish he'd see it's me who stands up, that I'm holding the gun. I know that I'm alone, but not his kind of alone. It is so much and I'm so alive that I can't even stop shaking or crying or laughing. My body does everything it can at once.

*

Almost all of us are looking out the windows in the parlor and library, through the high wrought-iron gate that keeps us relatively safe from the looting. Its spear-like points at the top give me courage. We can't see the park, but the street is erupting. A small car is on fire. Bodies run all over in frenzy.

Simon holds his head in his hands, still stunned. "We were marching, peacefully. I mean there were signs, and chanting. Normal stuff. Some people were pumping fists in the air, but peaceful. We came to a police barricade, I guess they knew we were coming, and said we didn't have a permit. They ordered us to disperse, and I don't know, it was tense but quiet. And then all of a sudden there was a scuffle, something happened to one of the protestors, someone had thrown something at an officer, and they started using their batons. And then some started screaming and punching, and it was a rage. So much rage all of a sudden. Fighting, and more police. And then, it just went… haywire. So fast. It happened so fast."

Everyone listens, but no one responds. What is there to say?

Brother Saul is already drinking, as every occasion outside the typical garners cause to dip into the whiskey in daylight. He looks through the window with sad amusement, and is silent. Father Michael watches him from the Second Empire high-back chair, slightly away from the action, much like everything in his life.

If anyone speaks, it has nothing to do with the nature of the riot, but is merely an abstract response. No analysis, no critical evaluation. The events outside signify something well beyond that. Brother Charles says, "Will you look at that?" or Father Frank will let slip a single adjective like "amazing, unbelievable," the descriptions of sublime incomprehensibility. There is no room for reflection in such a present phenomenon.

August is now bandaged up, a Band-Aid on his temple, his face washed. He looks out the windows with the rest of us. Even he is quiet, but his is prompted by defeat. The sadness he wears all over his body moves me, yet I'm not sure why. Much of him is naiveté, which I find inexcusable for someone his age. Perhaps it is the child I see in him, and wish for that in myself. I'm not convinced of this, though. It seems too neat, too simplified.

More and more fill the street, and now the park no longer seems to be the destination. There isn't one. The urgency spreads all over. More and more glass breaks, the sidewalks littered with refuse. Despite the growing numbers and alarm, I keep my face at the window. I'm embarrassed by my fascination, feel like I should be doing something helpful, but I'm not sure what can be done except wait it out.

It gets worse. Things are cracking. There is heat. Wrinkled air from fire coats the asphalt grunge. Within the smolder are the streaked stains of people running, every which way. Articles fly, boots, bottles, bodies.

August says with his hands clutched by his heart, "What is all this for?"

A man, not much older than my students, but a man for sure, runs close to the gate of the rectory and stops, as if he knows we are looking out at him. The turn of his head reveals wide white eyes, whiter than white, especially against his dark skin. He looks directly at us with those huge, brilliantly white eyes. And stares. The contrast of his stillness to what goes on behind him is unsettling.

Simon gets up from the chair, quietly mutters something that pulls me away from the strange spectacle. His light eyes reflect one of the car fires on the street. Simon is not saying anything as much as scowling. The shuffling of his feet and the seemingly unconscious mouth have him appear delusional, especially with the fire reflected in his eyes.

Even when a fire truck arrives to tend to the burning cars, the man at the gate keeps on us, not yet wavering. The yellow hoses snake along with the oversized men, and then the water. It licks the burning, wets the screaming on the street. The man stays, with a slight part to his lips, daring.

Simon sees this. That is where his face goes, not to the buildings that shrug the heaving ground, not the fear slobbering on the street, but the man. He growls, Simon actually growls, it cracks his chapped lips, and his low voice slowly rises the way magma would if it were sound. The shapes of his mouth and face grow more and more distorted as his growl gets louder. The man outside keeps intent on this.

More than the chaos in the streets, the fire, the screaming, the pain that prompts the screams, is Simon and this man, staring at each other—one growling, the other stone-faced—and I realize somehow that this, this is the riot.

The growling gets louder, and now we hear. Simon's fists are balled, sweat on his forehead. The growling pulls from his chest to his throat, higher pitched. His chapped mouth trembling, his watery eyes fixed on the figure outside. A white ball of heat. Simon looks like he will explode with hate, like he will actually burst into pieces.

As if anticipating this, the man suddenly has a brick in his hand. He throws it. It gets bigger and bigger.

A cracking. Glass, and then a white crystalline web of cracks. Once the outside, now a reflection of our faces, each sliver, cracked.

Simon screams, at what I don't know. Some have been hit by pieces of glass, clutching their faces while Simon screams, looking through their fingers at his spectacle. He is outside of himself with anger.

He yells at August, "You did this! You did this!"

August recoils in the chair, too stunned to even protest.

He leaps over towards August, like he's going to attack. "This is you!"

Simon's fury is so total, I can't manage it. Suddenly, I run between the men, Simon's screaming face in my total view. I become mucus and tears instantly. I want to shut his mouth. My forearm clenches, my small knuckles, my hard knuckles. And I fight. My fists go, keep going. They hit Simon's flesh and I don't care. They keep going. Simon screams, then moans low in the throat. His arrogance. I hit flesh, and then I hit blood and keep going. His arrogance. I keep going.

I hear August's high shrieking voice, "Thomas! You're going to kill him!"

Many limbs come and hands pull me, drag me away from Simon. He is a pile, a ball. His face appears from beneath his arms, no longer fierce. I turned off his fury, and I am at once satisfied electric and sorry. His eyes were recklessly angry, and now they are exhausted, helpless. My own eyes are hot and wet, the clerics holding my seething, my struggling body. It is staring at Simon, old clerics all around us, blood on his clothes, this explosion of a man, that I see, somehow, Baltimore itself.

Baltimore is shards of itself. And glass, in its newfound violence, the soundtrack.

28

Ruth

The dark here is just fine. Everything about it is clear and simple and the way it is. I could drive ten hours more and not even feel it with this kind of night. The truck is rolling along, the cab is warm, and I am away. I am awake. I know it won't be for long, and it's a little crazy coming back home if I know I'm gonna have to leave again. But I felt the need to see it, at least one more time.

The Blue Ridge Parkway is a snaky road around the mountains. The mountains are soft and large and I think of an old woman's boobs, like she's laying her body down in the trees and the mounds spread out with that slow rise. On my right, out the window, the sun finishes up and it has everything far in the distance all purple and orange, but it's not a crazy orange. It's the nice orange, that some girls wear on their lips. On the other side is a ribbon of cliff and a valley below, the cliff white-tipped with the hint of snow, but now it's black, with a couple lights here and there. The moon is hiding.

I have the window open, just a crack, the air here is so much thinner and nice to breathe. In front of me is a broken yellow line, each dash sliding into the truck with a rhythm that I move my shoulders to. Behind me is everything I took. When I first started driving I looked back every minute, afraid to see a box fall, my underwear fly off in the wind, or worse, something coming towards me. But now it's not a worry.

When you're on the road for a while, or anything really, you settle into it and start paying attention to other things. When I get antsy I smoke a cigarette. I only stop for the bathroom and gas.

An old-timey song comes on the station I found outside of Roanoke, banjoes and a friendly voice, and I sing along in between puffs of my Virginia Slim. It is a song for the road, one that me and Peter and Joby would have sung together when we drove places and lived a little, back when I had the Impala and Abe was still sober. I would be smoking a Slim, Joby in the front seat, Peter swinging his chubby legs in the car seat, picnic packed for Gunpowder Falls. It's not like we picnicked all that much or nothing, but it feels like we could have. That's how memory does. A whole chunk of time will be put into the box of one moment, and that one moment really shows what that whole time was like.

This is what I miss, not something that's gone, but something that won't ever be. There'll never be my boys going on a picnic to the Gunpowder or anywhere else. There'll never be grandkids in my truck singing along with their daddies, swinging their legs. There'll never be grandkids. Maybe, but it don't seem to be in the plans for Peter. And Joby, well, he will forever be nothing more than a child, a teenager, nothing more than memory. He already lives in a box.

*

The rest stops are few and far between, so I pull in when I see the blue sign. The parking lot is mostly filled with trucks. I relieve myself and go to the pay phones. Sarah will still be awake.

"Where are you, girl?"

I tell her and she laughs like she knew all along. I tell her about the road and the chimneys in the valley, the clouds that settle below the mountaintops, and she sighs out the wanting to be there. I ask about Peter. She says he's in the basement, but hasn't gone down after him. "I'm giving him room to do his thing."

"What do you know?" I ask.

"The police called. Peter told me."

"Is he all right?"

"Never know with that boy. Could be a lot and nothing at all, at the same time. He's the spit of his mother, I'm telling you. Is there snow on the ground?"

"Just a little. It'll still be cold in Bristol." I give her further instructions, about the house, Peter, as much as I can think of.

"God dammit, Ruth Anne, you crazy bitch."

We both laugh.

*

I didn't know what to think when I saw Peter just before I left. While all those people were running up and down the streets breaking things, he raced in the house, wild-eyed. I was still sitting at the kitchen table, getting my body to come back together. He looked at the empty house, the blood on the kitchen linoleum, Isaac. He kept his eyes there, but didn't seem surprised.

"I had to," is all I said.

He nodded. "Are you in trouble?"

"Not anymore." I wasn't sure about that, either. I had called the police. I told 911 what I did, told them he threatened me, told them about the restraining order. They were so busy with the commotion from the park I knew I'd have time to get out before they came. I told 911 where to find Isaac, told them I was leaving and could not stay, that I would call once I knew where I'd be, and gave them Sarah's number. They told me not to go anywhere, but seemed to accept it without a lot of questions when I said I had to.

"There is a riot," Peter said.

"I know."

He looked down at Isaac's lifeless body again, out to the living room, then back to me. His face was worn out, but not upset in the typical way, and was filling with tears. "Are you all right?"

"Yeah," I said, and that did it. Both of us let it all go, and it felt like some kind of boulder left my body, like I was made of air. He came over to me. His head felt heavy and warm in my lap, my hands immediately into his hair, and even now I know I will always remember that moment when I think of relief. There was all sorry and understanding and love wrapped up in the quiet of it. I was grateful we were quiet and just crying. It felt so good to touch his head, for him to allow me. That simple, the love between a mother and child, that big and simple.

When he picked up his head and looked at me, I said, "You're a man." He nodded.

*

Now it's all night, cold, clear, full dark and stars all over. Granny used to say there was a star for every memory you made, and every time something happened that would be worth remembering, another star would pop up and squeeze into an empty spot. She said the good life was lived when, once you were a granny, you could look up and there were so many stars you'd pee your britches.

Which ones are you, Joby? Are you that big white flickering one? Maybe the cool blue one that hums? You have to look hard to see that one. Come to think of it, that would for sure not be you.

My best and brightest stars shine on in Bristol, just before we moved to Baltimore, that short but slow time when it was all of us together, right after Paw-Paw died. Not that I wasn't sad about Paw-Paw, but we all moved in together, Daddy taking over the farm. Granny and I became the girls in the kitchen. She taught me how to make hoecakes, the fresh biscuits, how to cut the venison so it slid along the knife. In summer we must have spent half the day in there, and not always doing kitchen things. This is where the stories came, the telling of family and folks in the valley, Paw-Paw's kin trekking from Charleston to the mountains, staking the land around the holler, building themselves the farmhouse. Growing anything and everything that would keep the land, mainly cabbage and green beans. Granny always shook her head when she recounted Paw-Paw's mantra: "A man is nothing without land." I asked her once, what's wrong with that?

"The words are a little mixed up is all, honey," she said. "A man don't need to own the land to become something, is all. He is the land already."

I always hoped I'd meet a man the way Granny met Paw-Paw. It was the Sullivan County Fair, I bet a barn-dance. I can't remember if it was Granny's story, my own, something between them, but I see Paw-Paw, quiet and lusting after the girls, lined on the other side of the wall, blue-grass wiggling their butts, looking up through their hair in that flirty way we all learn so young. He walks over, she shrugs, the light so nice on her cheeks, which is why he went to her first, and holds out his large and rough hand. What would Granny have thought of him, then? Was he a dreamboat, or was his manners what aimed her to accept his offer to dance? Maybe she just liked the song, and wound up marrying him soon after and forever, straight out of an old-timey romantic movie, the ones Peter got all dreamy in his eyes over.

*

Daddy's name was Adam Cryer, and I always thought that had the ring of a movie star, or some character in a fat book. He was the one who named me and Sarah, told the stories of the Bible that we were named after, and that made him so big to me, all by itself.

When he died, Mama called me first. I was already with Abe at the time, bouncing Joby on my leg after supper. I remember blurting out *no* as if the word itself was powerful enough to stop it and turn back round what God had done. Joby slid off my lap and Abe cocked his head like a dog seeing himself in the mirror. I said, "Daddy. Oh, God. Mama. I'm sorry." I was already starting to cry, and Abe was holding my waist. There was a grunt on the end of the phone, and Mama said, "Ruth Anne, you always say the stupidest things," and hung up.

Daddy worked. That's what he did. If he wasn't working, he was drinking, and if he wasn't doing one of those things, he was sleeping. But he was mainly working. He had moved around a lot before I was born, riding trains and taking jobs in God-knows-where. He wandered around looking for work, in the way people could do back then. He would get work in carpentry, and he also worked a long bit for a demolition crew. He built things some times, and then broke them apart others, "like a damned fool," Mama would say. That's where he got his swollen, hard hands. That, and the liquor, I bet.

I can't even keep myself together when I think about Mama and Daddy meeting. There couldn't be any magic about it, but I guess everyone has their own at some time. Daddy never talked about meeting Mama, and she would tell it so bitter, so I put together my own version from what I knew. He was laying down road right outside of Bristol, was hanging with some of the other workers in town on a Saturday when she passed by. Now, I can see how Mama would have attracted him—she had her charms, one being her figure, and she was dressed for the market. It was important for her to always look better-dressed than everyone else in town, even to go to the market, something I knew was connected to how cold people were to Mama, even the people she had known since she was a little girl. It seemed she liked it that way, because I never remember her being upset that she didn't have much in the way of friends.

Daddy thought she was the classiest thing and followed her down the block. She knew he was doing what he was doing, if I know Mama at all, but she knew she always looked better from the back, so let him keep on. Daddy, on the other hand, had a nice face, and he had strong arms, so it only seems right that she was in front, and he followed. "Excuse me, Miss," he said to her. She smiled before walking across the street, swinging the hips only that much more to keep his eyes, but without making people talk.

They got married in the same church I was christened in, a small yellow building on State Street, that much I do know. I think Granny and Paw-Paw would have approved, probably relieved that Mama's piss and vinegar didn't keep all the men away. Mama had her figure, and Daddy had his smile, and that was good enough for everyone to be happy.

We lost the farm soon after Daddy took it over. According to Mama, it was all Daddy's fault, and it was from that time on that all of Mama's words were said with hot spit, the meanness creeping up in her until she was as hard as an unboiled bean. He didn't manage things very well, I guess. He was a worker, but maybe the farm was too big for him. He was used to the work being in front of him, not all around, not the land itself. I'm sure he tried. And then he got the job at Kennicott, and we moved, and Baltimore killed him.

When I got word that Joby died, it was a full day after it happened. His body was found next to a fence. We couldn't give him a proper funeral, because we didn't have the money and he couldn't be viewed, anyway. He had been shot twice, once in the face.

I had to call Abe and tell him. He was living in Poppleton at the time with another alcoholic he met at a bar. He was so far gone in his own misery that he said nothing, just cried. I would have felt better if he was crying for Joby, but I knew he wasn't, and that's why I wasn't with him anymore, and why my boys took my name again, no more Ewing than needed to be. So I sat there and listened to my ex-husband cry into the phone. It was raining outside—the last time I saw Joby it was raining—and his father was crying. That's why when I think of you, Joby, you always disappear in the rain.

This is the whole story, when we meet and when we part, when we begin and when we die. And now, I feel like I have the open place in my heart to tell it all.

*

Bristol is silent and asleep. I ride through State Street, looking for a gas station. Nothing is open. It's been ten years since I came to visit with the boys, but not much has changed. Quiet and empty, with Tennessee to my left and Virginia to my right. It's funny how each side looks the same but they are real different in the way things are done. Makes you know even though a state ain't much more than a bunch of lines on a map, the lines do something anyway. I wonder if any of the shopkeepers on the Tennessee side wish they could cross the street for lower business tax, or if the liquor stores all line one side of state, so they could sell on Sundays, something funny like that. I can imagine Peter rolling his eyes and saying, "How ironic," in that smartass way of his.

One Chevron light on the edge of town. I pull in, and a tall, skinny teenager with pizza-face comes out of the little office, walking quick and all business. At first I wonder if he's going to tell me the place is closed, or that my kind aren't welcome here—whatever that means—or that the cops are looking for my truck, I don't know. Just the jitters of everything, I guess. As I shut off the engine, he pokes his head in my window.

"Good evenin', ma'am. You need a full tank?"

"That would be good, a full tank," I say, really feeling that word *ma'am*, like I am respected, something decent. I keep my chin up just a little.

He goes to the tank, does his thing. You can tell he's done it thousands of times with how quick and easy he moves, without even looking. Grabs the handle, flips the lever, unscrews the gas cap, like one single move. No gas attendant would even dare to pump gas for a customer in Baltimore; God knows what crazy ass is inside the car. This guy doesn't even know the danger.

"You need some help gettin' where you goin', ma'am?" he asks.

I can't help but love this kid, because he speaks with the accent that brings me back to bean soup and corn, to screened-in porches, to the sway of a life in me. *Ma'am.*

"No, I'm good. Just getting home, is all."

"Well, you be careful. No telling what kind of people are running around out there at night, and whatnot."

Well, that just does it for me, and I crack up, just let the nasally sound rock the truck and fill the empty quiet street.

"Ma'am, you all right?"

And I'm crying. Why wouldn't I? The tears are filling my eyes and falling, but it's a good clean cry. I'm not heaving or hurting. The weight of me already left, anyway. Sometimes everything can be so much that crying is it, the only thing to do. The freedom is as big as the Blue Ridge, and just as scary if you're not used to it. But at least I'm willing. And I know why I'm crying. That's real important.

This is where my new story begins, anyway.

29

Peter

Soon, fireflies will begin their lusty throbbing.

They may have already begun down in Tennessee, the slow float of blinking yellow in the thick air, the warmth of the South, of summer, of sex, kids innocently pulling the glowing abdomens off and decorating their fingernails, innocently murdering—to only be a kid. There are no kids in the photo, no bugs and not much summer, but the settling after a change is there, an ease.

The photo was taken some time just before her arrest. She is lightly smiling in the photo, the setting sun glinting her eyes, that pale yet intense blue. Her skin is evened by the warm colors of the sunset. That's probably why she chose the photo. She always hated her skin, loved her eyes, and the sun this way flatters both—head tilted, a light squint to match her smile, at ease. She is leaning against a porch, scratchy wood planks and a screen, with a swing on the right. Behind her lies a small yard, and the dark of a thick grouping of trees.

"She had just planted a garden," I say. "Cabbage, green beans, radishes."

"She looks good, here."

"Yeah."

"Who took the picture?"

It's a good question. Whoever it is captured her in glow, no pretense, no pose, a moment within a longer moment. The way Ma's head tilts, the easy confidence, looking straight into the camera, I have a feeling it is a man. She hasn't told me anything, probably won't. She's still too raw for that kind of reveal, knowing her, especially now.

"We have a lot of family down there," I say. I'm not sure why I lie, but it felt intuitive, and harmless enough. I could have said "had a lot of family" and there'd be no questions. It's not like Brother Thomas will go down to Tennessee to make sure.

He keeps his gaze on the photograph, searching, admiring. It's worth admiring. Everything about her face had softened, a change had been made, so quickly. It seems the same is true for him, but in a different way. His eyes are dark and tired, but he doesn't look sad or upset, maybe quietly resigned, or relieved, something like that. He has lost weight, at least in his face. A different kind of change. It's always worth gazing. He keeps his eyes on the photograph. "Poor Ruth," he says.

"Yeah," I say.

"Your mother is a survivor."

The platitude only mildly annoys me, really. I mean, what do you say? In lieu of everything, what wouldn't come off as insensitive or overly sympathetic?

"She's lucky, though. It could have been worse." My own platitude.

Brother Thomas picks his fingers, slowly. With each pull of the nail he shows his concern, a mélange of shredded cuticles, mangled fingertips. And even though his face reassures me not to worry, there is plenty of worry within him. I am touched by how much he's willing to fake it for me.

"So, how about you, Mr. Cryer? How are *you* doing?"

Graduation was quiet, and much like the remaining days of the semester, moved along politely. We wore the long black gowns, turned our tassels, listened to endless suggestions for our future, ate cake during the reception. It wasn't a somber occasion, but sober. Ma wasn't there, she couldn't be. I wasn't upset, even when they called my name and no one cheered as I crossed to grab my diploma, shake hands with Ducee, only the empty clap of sympathetic parents lifting the weight of a moment I was sure I would forget.

And school. The halls were clean, efficient in their shuffle, amidst the cleanup outside the walls, the recouping of losses. A maturity settled over St. Mary's. Underclassmen weren't as loud when they talked, didn't absently slam lockers. Homeroom wasn't the flurry of jokes and jabs, scurries between scootching chairs. Even the teachers were more courteous, less fervent in their admonishments when they had to assert discipline, which was also less frequent.

I never got in trouble for sucking on Jude's finger. There were no visits to Ducee's office, no after-class conferences with admin, even the student mockery ceased. It's like they all knew I could have cared less. Ma's arrest pushed that fear far out of me, and I immediately viewed it as the trifle it was. There's nothing like a little time and fugitive arrest to find perspective, recognize the life in miniature that high school has you shrink into.

The remainder of that final semester went by like it hardly happened. There was prom. I didn't go. There was the Senior ring ceremony, I obediently partook. There were baseball games and Spirit Week and other things I ignored, red ribbons thrown across the rafters of the auditorium, exuberant bubble-letter signs on doors. No one gave me shit, besides incidental snickering here and there, for having my fly down or getting meatball sauce on my tie. I made no new friends among my classmates, nothing like that; and it wasn't like I became feared or respected, nothing quite so satisfying. The riots had somehow tempered the masses. Perhaps it created a humbling of sorts. It was as if the entire school was controlled by a radio console, and someone turned the volume down. Some days I wanted to yell in the cafeteria, "My mother's committed manslaughter," but no one would have heard me. I was grateful for that.

Jude and I only spoke once after the day at his house, the day of the riot. We were preparing for the Latin final, and I asked him for a pencil. He reached into his bag, and gave me one. That was it. All the pressure of him, the love for him, all of the build-up, the anxiety of high school, just fizzled. Granted, I still saw him as something I *could* have loved, and his gray eyes remained stricken with longing, maybe even for me if I allowed myself to fantasize, but that was all. The craze, the drama, it all receded as smooth as emptying water from a bathtub.

I don't know if many of my schoolmates knew about Ma, Isaac, the murder. Murder, what a big word for such a small woman. Some of the administration knew about it, Brother Thomas knew about it. They had to, because of the address change, moving in with Aunt Sarah, the days I missed for court. Brother Thomas would have told someone. They wouldn't have found anything out from the news—not a single story on it. The murder. Everything was devoted to the riots and their aftermath—the National Guard, the curfew, the random outbursts in other parts of the city, a particularly violent aftershock in West Baltimore, Molotov cocktails in the towers. So even if someone did know about Ma, I didn't notice. There was no inkling of reveal, no special treatment, no tilt of sympathy, and I said nothing. Funny, in the wake of the largest riot in Baltimore history and my mother killing her husband, life became quieter for me than ever before.

Brother Thomas still holds up the photograph. Those close-set eyes of his pull in tight, like he's remembering something that never really happened, but that maybe he wanted to happen, or could have if the world gave him a break. That's something I'm not willing to discuss, really. I say, "I started working here a few weeks ago. I quit Roy Rogers. No more grease and ketchup. Now I smell like coffee grinds and milk. I'm moving up in the world."

"A barista, then," in a soft, patronizing way.

"Very Italian, huh?"

He scratches his nose. "I would assume that to be more pleasant."

"I like the people."

Max worked with me two days a week, and we probably hung out at least two more. He lived at the edge of Mount Vernon, just before North Avenue, on Guilford, really close to Red Emma's, so after work I would spend the night at his place. He offered, knowing the bus to Aunt Sarah's in Curtis Bay took a long time and was unreliable in the late hours after we closed the shop. At first, we talked activism and politics until we fell asleep—more him talking and me listening—me with a pile of blankets on his floor, amazed at all the worldliness he had for a boy living in Baltimore. But after two nights of that, he told me it wasn't a problem sharing the bed with him—I didn't have to be uncomfortable—so I crawled up. Within ten minutes, we were slowly moving our hands over each other. I loved how gradual it all was, not the immediate business of the men at Benny's. After we were finished, Max and I would hold each other, the sweat of one drying on the skin of the other. There were no quick showers or sudden realizations of commitments, the guilty need to get back home to the wife or girlfriend or other source of guilt now that bodies were spent. The sex was a little awkward and fumbling, not as desperate, and sometimes Max and I didn't know what to do, but I loved it. We laughed. I felt like a boy, and I liked feeling that way. I liked him.

I walked into Red Emma's a week after Ma left for Tennessee, a week after the riot, days after the National Guard circled Highlandtown. The city had been absolutely silent, everyone waiting for a recurrence, afraid of vigilantes or more looting, and though I appreciated the lull in school drama, Curtis Bay made me crazy with its looming quiet, only the cracked-out hookers making any sound at all. No offense to Aunt Sarah, though; she treated me with calm, gave me space, let me sit in the room she made me for hours on end, staring at the wood paneling. We probably said less than twenty sentences to each other that first week. I really think that helped me more than any shoulder squeezes and heart-to-hearts. But Curtis Bay was so quiet except for the tractor trailers rolling through, the occasional yelling from the street, and I couldn't sleep with all the thoughts *and* idleness. So, I caught a bus, walked into the shop, and asked if there was a way to get involved. The girl at the counter, the one with the buzzed head and bloodshot eyes that caught me before with all that power, laughed at me. "Involved in what?" she asked. I didn't know how to answer her.

Eventually, I talked with the collective, a whole group of workers who ran Red Emma's together, who met at a rented space in Charles

Village. The coffeeshop was way more than a bookstore and café—a whole social justice thing—all about democratic this and anarchy that. I fell in love. Everyone was so smart and passionate and used words that I only read in books. It ripped open all this possibility, and made Baltimore so much more than I ever thought. I hung out there after school, began friendships with Max, Bryan (an International Affairs major at Hopkins), and even the bald chick with the attitude—her name was Trina; she began calling me Nutmeg, and would cup her palm to the back of my neck and lightly squeeze. Before I knew it, I was offered a job, learning about properly steamed milk, neo-socialism, and found myself working alongside—and aching—for Max. He was dedicated to his studies, painted small acrylic scenes of the historical moments before assassinations—JFK in the motorcade with Jackie O, a profile of Lincoln and Mary looking down from their box seats at the Ford, a close-up of Charles Guiteau getting a shoe-shine. He argued the moments he painted were always forgotten.

"Everyone focuses on the moment after, the time of blood. But what about the moment before? We may see a clue, some kind of pattern in these moments before, maybe even learn something about ourselves," he says, his eyes squinting, flirting.

He never told me what that could be, though. I didn't press for the answer, and would burrow deeper into his side, close in the space of our bodies, our two boy bodies, his so much darker than mine. "I'm full-blooded," he would tease.

Baltimore so quickly became a different place for me. I have friends who want to talk about *things*. I feel really on my own, and not just because Ma left. I feel older, like I have walked through a door to a different dimension, an alternate me. Maybe we all do when we feel we belong somewhere. Maybe that's the quiet, some kind of reflection period. Perhaps the riot was a next step in the growth process for the city, like a rite of passage from boy to man, from alienation to belonging.

Brother Thomas sips his coffee slowly. He is relaxed and in good spirits, all considering, sitting at the table, but I can tell he is exhausted. "You seem to be well," he says, a little distracted. I think to ask him if he is doing well, and I realize I probably have never asked him before. Does he accept that as part of the teacher's life, that no one asks him how *he* feels?

We saw each other at the hearings. There wasn't much to them, really. Ma was wearing the sundress I really like, with the red and yellow flowers, navy blue heels. She looked like the photograph, fuller, healthier, only weary from the extradition. There were no sides to be taken, no furious victim or victim's family. No cross-examinations or vitriolic pulpit speeches from attorneys. No one came to provide testimony for Isaac, even. I didn't even know he grew up near the Pennsylvania border, both his parents passed away. Brother Thomas gave Ma a testimony of character, which certainly couldn't hurt, being he was a cleric. He made her out to be a saint, really. And though I had always thought that he wanted to bone Ma, I didn't realize how much he cared about her, too. It's funny what I didn't realize about these people when they were part of my everyday, but when placed in these more surreal circumstances, whole aspects of them surfaced unexpectedly. Brother Thomas was eloquent, and he was a man who possessed love like me.

Ma was very courteous and charming when she spoke to the judge about her marriage to Isaac. She didn't play the victim too heavy, and there was an economy with the way she talked about Isaac's violent outbursts, his creepy phone calls, that seemed to me respectful, that despite him being a son-of-a-bitch, he was dead after all. She was such a superstitious woman, and I wonder if she was taking care not to stir up the bad spirits or something. It worked in her favor, I guess. All thoughts of a murder trial were dismissed. The judge kept telling her she was lucky even after the sentence—one to two years—fleeing an accidental death scene and having no license for the gun.

When Ma finished her testimony, and it was my turn, we exchanged a look that I will never forget. I had known this woman, lived with her my whole life. I thought I had seen all there was to see in her. But as she got up and walked back to her seat, and I got up to sit where she had just been— where I was about to lie under oath and say I witnessed Isaac storm in the house uninvited, that I saw the struggle, saw my mother scramble for the gun in a desperate act of self-defense, saw her shoot Isaac to protect herself and me—Ma turned her eyes up at me in a face that winced and loved, that wanted to send me to my room and yet build that room all around her. I swear, I saw myself in her face so clearly, beneath the makeup and the hair, beyond the color. I saw myself, because it was the same face I had, sorry and grateful. We were somehow equitable creatures, one for the other. It wasn't a balance of power, nothing like that at all, but a mutuality, two equals indulging in their closeness. We were now somehow parallel in this life.

I visit her often, twice a week, usually. The glass between us is filthy, smears of lips and greasy hands. She looks washed out in the beige peels the prison makes the inmates wear. They are quiet visits, with her asking for details to fill her mind. The glow she grew in her face down in Tennessee was fading with the "pig slop" for food and the women crazier than "rabid cats in a chicken-house." Her small half-laugh, a true harrumph, always gives it away. She's gotten into two small fights, but nothing that got her reported or too banged up. She didn't tell me why she got into those fights, but I'm aware of enough *Caged Heat* pulp only to imagine she was the pin-up of the cell-block.

I want, sometimes—when she is sitting across from me with her hair tangled—to ask her if it was worth it, but I don't dare. Besides, from the steel in her eyes, the acceptance of sitting behind that disgusting glass without so much as a sniffle, I know her answer. She did say the first time I saw her, after I told her "nice outfit" and she laughed, after I had nothing to say and she smiled at me, and when I was about to leave: "I'm free, Peter." I believed her, but it hurt in a small fierce way, something precarious about such resolve in the circumstances. Maybe that freedom was from me, too. The glass was so filthy.

Brother Thomas sips the last of his coffee, and slides it on the saucer carefully. "And what does the future hold for you, Mr. Cryer?"

I knew he would ask this question. And I really don't know how to answer him. For so long I had anticipated the future—which school I would attend for college, which city I would move to, how I would get the hell out of Baltimore. I counted the months, the days, so intently that I never gave myself a chance to know what I was going *towards*. All of my plans were about escaping, and none of them were about facing forward.

"I'm not sure yet," I say. "Right now I'm working at this coffee shop. Hanging with these kids. I deferred Columbia for a year, not sure if I'll go, but I have until March to confirm. Probably take classes at the community college in the fall. Not sure. But I'll figure it out."

"Staying in Baltimore, then?"

"For a while," I say.

"That sounds like a good plan," he says, and looks at me pleasantly.

"It's not much of a plan, but I'm happy with that. No more plans, for now."

He quietly repeats, almost to himself, "No more plans."

"And what about you, Brother?"

He abruptly laughs, scratches his beard. "Well, first thing is you won't be able to call me that for much longer."

I startle at that, sure he could see my shock, but I'm not sure why I'm surprised. It's a time for change, for everybody. Why wouldn't he make one, as well?

*

After work Max and I set out towards St. Mary's. It's a long walk, but the air is not too stuffy, and a breeze reminiscent of spring lightens the usually oppressive heat of late Baltimore summer. Max likes walking. He doesn't have a car, and will even walk all the way to Charles Village from his apartment when he isn't in a hurry and foregoes his other love of biking. He's done a lot of it by the looks of his well-defined calf muscles, unexpectedly thick compared to his lean build. He isn't as tall as I am, but we're about the same size. I've worn his clothes, when I forget to bring my own. I leave socks by the bed the nights I sleep over, I can't seem to help it. There's quite a collection building in his room.

"You have everything you need?" he asks. I look in the bag again, even though I know what is in there. I bought the materials yesterday at MICA's supply store—some Weldbond and white putty. He peers in the bag, as well, curious goofball that he is. Max told me what to get. I didn't know the first thing about epoxy or glue, other than the Elmer's I used for my construction paper masterpieces in third grade.

We cut through Lafayette Homes, Pleasant View Gardens, whatever they're calling it now, the projects on the other side of the JFX, trash and weeds and lots of men drinking out of paper bags. Max doesn't seem at all fazed, skipping along, stealing glances at me, even bold enough to wrap his arm around my waist. It feels so good that I don't push him away, but I do keep an eye on the glassy faces that watch us walk by.

"Imagine what this all looked like back in the day. Horse carts and Victorian corsets," Max says. I can't imagine much of anything resembling history when I think about the projects, but I can play out little vignettes in adjacent Butcher's Hill, with its dainty rowhouses and colorful windowsills, the touch of the artists that had moved into the area, and the young families that have since taken over. We pass the quaint sidewalk shops along the slender street, the trees that gently shroud, hide us away from the concrete exposure. Max plays with the underside of my arm. "Romantic, isn't it?" I think to point out the derivation of the word, to correct him, but he's in his whimsy. You can tell he's not from Baltimore, but I like that. He lends me a new set of eyes, a fresh way of seeing the city. Being a kid from a suburb in Oklahoma, he had never seen a rowhouse before moving here for school. He still finds them amazing, endlessly repeating, "They have so much character."

"You're a dork," I say, and he laughs.

St. Mary's stands more alone than ever. Beyond it lies empty brown earth behind fences where brick rowhouses stood just weeks before, remnant rubble scooped into a loader and dumped into giant metal containers. The sign for Crabtown blares across the open expanse, so strange to see such wide-open space where a cramped neighborhood once was.

A tremendous sadness fills me, looking out at the empty squares where city had once thrived, even if the thriving occurred way before my time. I used to look at this same neighborhood with disgust, the gutted-out houses, the dark corners, the abandonment, embarrassed by its inability to thrive. Six months ago, I would have praised the demolition of Highlandtown, Elwood Park, all of it. And yet now I feel the erasure deep within me, a loss, not because it was a place I lived, but that it would happen at all—a feat of…arrogance. I think of Grant, behind one of those wrecking balls, swinging wildly without remorse, and it makes sense. So arrogant.

Max locks his hands to give me a boost over the wall. He looks up at me as I steady myself, open and relaxed, his hair a pile of corkscrews. He squints in the sun.

"Hi," he says, and grins, his smile all gums.

"You're such a dork," I say again.

Mary is standing headless in a sea of leaves. The grotto has long been forgotten, with school closed for summer, and its future unknown. However, someone did place the broken pieces into a crate and sat it by her side.

"How long has she been here?"

"A long time," I say.

"No, I mean, like this."

"Since I did it."

"You?"

"We had a little tiff." I Kewpie-doll my face. "I sent flowers," I say.

There is a moment where Max beams incredulous—that I would damage something sacred, that I would destroy anything at all. Ah, what he doesn't know about me, or at least what he doesn't know about who I have been. He brings his hands to my waist, and leans in, breathes against my neck. "Why'd you do it?"

I pull back and shake my head. "I don't know. To keep going?"

"How is that?" he asks.

I don't answer, and pull the crate over to us, pick up the two large pieces—the face, and the back of the head. I hold them out helplessly.

"That won't be too hard," he encourages. He sweeps his arms fluidly, grabbing Mary's bits, and sits Indian-style in the grass, a slice of light striping across his chest. "Give me the glue."

"No," I say. "Let me do it." I sit down across from him. He gazes into me in that intuitive way he does, allows himself to understand, and nods. Max has a very even temperament, doesn't indulge in reaction. I'm fascinated with that ability. I grew up in an explosive household, from Ma to Joby and certainly me, all of us tangling our furies into one immediate mess of family. Max only responds after his impulse flows through and quits; you can almost watch it dwindle through his body. He has so much patience, even in managing my inability to possess it. He hands me the pieces of Mary, and I take them awkwardly into my own lap.

Baltimore is a broken city, but I have realized that which is broken has beauty, a fierce beauty with sharp edges that begs for repair. Ma, behind the glass. It is in the act of repairing that we fully understand what we can do. Of course, we also are responsible for breaking the very things we mend. So be it. But if we keep running from the things that break us, we'll never recognize what makes us so remarkable: our ability to heal that which we simultaneously destroy—whether it be a city, a family, a friendship, my heart.

I am very aware of the rise and fall of Max's breathing while I match the edges of the head and apply the glue. Once the pieces are pressed together, I stand up and walk towards Mary's body.

"Let me see," he says.

I showcase my work, do a little curtsy. "Like apple pie."

He laughs. "Apple pie." That gummy smile.

I turn back to Mary, nothing much else to look at in the grotto but her graying figure amidst nature's entropy, the unfolding consequence of time. Bees hover around the withering azaleas behind her, their wings glimmering in the afternoon orange, shadow from the huge poplar checkering the stone walkway. Max comes to me, holds Mary's head as I drizzle Weldbond on her neck, the glue sap-like and glinting. He tells me to hurry, it dries fast, and we grab both sides and hoist her soft, tilted face back where it belongs. We stay there a while, letting the glue do its magic, its mending. Max looks right into me, and winks.

The light slowly moves all around the grotto. Sounds from beyond the stone walls grow clearer in our shared silence—the birds in the trees at first, the cars rushing by on Baltimore Street, the machines that tear apart the city to the East, children yelling, the slamming of front doors, their angry occupants.

We gingerly let go of Mary's head. It stays. A brightness opens in my chest, and I let out a small laugh, knowing that I did this, that I broke Mary and then I came back and fixed her, that she will continue to listen to somebody, if not me, and look upon them with pious and forgiving eyes. Her lips are parted ever so slightly, but no words, only the beatific grace.

Max takes his shoes off, kneads the grass with his toes while I look into Mary with all the history I share with her. How can I already look back on this time in my life as distant, like a photograph that has yellowed? Yes, the tint of my high-school life has already changed, that's what it is. Maybe that's what happens to everyone with their memories. Or maybe the change in me colors the memory. I can tell this is something I'll think about again. For now, there is Mary—I remember her in every way, and say good-bye.

Max comes to me, puts his arm around my waist, and squeaks out a small, "Yay." It is just enough.

We allow silence. He rubs my back. It is enough.

Mary maintains her humble gaze, has already forgiven me for hurting her. She knows it's part of what makes a change come, been around long enough to know that. Max's breath is sharp and cigarettes in the air. His hands. The air. Long enough.

I allow it all, the warmth of it.

30

Thomas

The apartment is small, the basement of a mid-to-late nineteenth century rowhouse. Two rooms, a bath, a makeshift kitchen with stove and refrigerator on the far wall. Regardless of its meagerness, I love the damp smell of the porous brick laid during this period, slapdash constructions accommodating the influx of a dirty-hands Europe. It is cheap, just off North Avenue. I have yet to experience winter here, but the dark and dank eases the summer heat of the city above. The family in the main part of the house are Section 8, at least five children, but I can't be sure. The landlord didn't even want to rent to me initially, saying that Section 8 was more a guarantee since the money came from the government, and I had no credit to speak of. She asked through her broken teeth why I was still renting, me being middle-aged, fairly well-dressed, and white. I had to explain over and over again the structure of my former religious life. Her face pruned in concentration, letting out small whistles for breath. After the third full explanation, she shooed her arms, all loose skin, revealing no bra underneath her oversized blouse, and asked, "Why you leave? You kicked out? You one of them kid molesters?"

Mirabelle kept insisting I move in to the Exeter house. I couldn't even call it my mother's house anymore.

"Why rent a place when you own one, can live for free?" she asked.

I could have moved in, had the boys bunk together, or fashion a room in the basement. I'm sure it would have been comforting to have a family scuttling above me, always have company at a time when I was feeling quite a bit of loneliness.

"It's the first time I'm on my own, Mirabelle. I need to do it this way," I said. "I want to."

Mirabelle cupped my shoulder, and gave me a small shake of her head.

"As long as I can swing by for dinner now and then," I said.

"You can't cook a can of beans, Thomas. I'd be accessory to death by starvation if I didn't feed you." We both slid into that knowing grin, that grin between us.

There is a bed, a nightstand, a small dresser, a card table loaded with papers—an application, and my notes, all kinds of notes in my careful Catholic handwriting. Yes, it is sparse, gloomy, a basement studio with mismatched essentials, but it is what I chose. I reside here—Thomas Manilli. Poe's last years were lived in such a way, I assure myself. His were the ending of days, however, and mine—I promise to myself—are the beginning. We crawl at two times in our lives. I am very pleased with this apartment, almost proud of it. It was one of my first real decisions, with many more to come.

I finish the application for City Council. It is long, tedious, and may be fruitless, but I had been encouraged by my work with the East Baltimore Neighborhood Association. We have been staging sit-ins outside the Crabtown site every Saturday—peaceful, small, yet newsworthy. Every week there is something new being constructed, many of the amusement park's buildings already in the first stages of erection, skeletal steel beams gridding the sky. The park has been scaled back a little, one of the historic registry buildings preserved through our efforts, a church on the far east side of the site. Little victories.

I saw MacAllister once during these sit-ins. He had on a hardhat and a clipboard, deliberating with the construction foreman. He hadn't been assaulted in the riot. In fact, the riot didn't make it to Federal Hill, where his house stood. It was one of the few areas untouched in City Center.

That's why the rich go to the top of the hill, and proclaim their words from up high to down below.

The sit-in group was simply chanting, "Bal-ti-more, Bal-ti-more," through our plastic megaphones, underneath one of the many towering cranes with their long arms extending precipitously over the city. And there was MacAllister, working presumably, overseeing his grand project. He caught my eye, and nodded, a purely respectable nod. He understood our roles, as well, it seemed. We both were doing what we felt was right, for the city, for ourselves. What marvels me is how groups of people can be so divided in their singular quest for the common good.

Many think I have a shot at getting a seat on the council, having been a cleric, a teacher, a public servant, for so long. Others are concerned that will be my Achilles heel. Questions could fly about why I left the order. People will make up their own stories, colorful ones I'm sure.

I sign the last page, fold the papers into the envelope, walk to the closest mailbox, and drop it down the chute. No harm in trying.

*

Nothing seemed to change much in the weeks following the riot, except that the whole neighborhood took on the consistent calm the rectory had always maintained, which highlighted how eerie it all really was. I didn't expect it to stay this way, and by mid-summer the city came back around, just in time to buzz alongside my resignation from the order, which I had been part of for my entire adult life.

At first it seemed as if nothing would ever come of the incident with Simon. The rectory had kept silent about the violence—outside, inside, against one another—as if it were part of an ancient purging festival, channeling the pent-up anxieties of men, the running of the bulls or Dionysia, a subversive understanding that whatever happened there was merely the stuff of memory. I'm sure it seemed to them not to matter to me either way. I was already planning my leave. There were lots of chins held high, stoic and restrained formalities. There were lots of silences, respectful nods, a carriage of somber acknowledgement.

After perhaps a month of distance and silence, the first small moment, a fissure of emotion—a reveal—came from August. I was in the garden, under the lilac, weeding. This is not something I did often, if ever, but I had felt the need to tend to the house's exterior, as if in lieu of the city's chaos the simple act of keeping the yard tidy would contribute to some kind of collective healing. I had come out almost every day that weather permitted since Easter. I pulled dandelion and crabgrass, such tenacious renegades to the careful order of our garden. All of a sudden, from behind me, I heard my name. It was more a high-pitched shriek, just my name, "Thomas!"

I turned to see August, red-faced, bordering on tears. I don't know how long he'd been standing there. If not for his paunch and favored hip, for his baggy eyes, he'd have looked like a child on the verge of a tantrum, the frightening uncontrollable emotion he didn't know how to express. He didn't say anything else, only looked at me desperately, afraid to speak, afraid of what the words would commit him to. When he stomped away, I sat on the ground and looked at my hands. Dirt outlined the sinewy crevices in my flesh—a map, a river. I was not surprised by the outburst, and felt some relief in it. I expected it to happen, somewhere in the folds of my knowing. August's behavior reflected all of Baltimore, the fear of what to do next in the wake of such violence, such an irrational break. There were no words in the irrational, and instinct was deemed unreliable. So, there it was. My violence, the city's violence, expressed in a frustrated shriek of a name, red-faced, and that was all. I absolutely knew then that I would leave the order.

It helped when Father Mike came into my room after dinner on a rather uneventful evening, to usher in the inevitable. He wasn't usually sheepish or afraid to be direct; his squat stature demanded he be assertive, or else be dismissed quickly in the neutered yet misogynist world of the Catholic clergy. This night, however, he entered sideways into the room, leaned against the dresser, keeping distance. He had difficulty making eye contact, telling me about rules of the order, violence committed upon another, a series of repentant steps, this is for the preservation, the order of the order, all while fiddling with my books on the edge of the dresser.

"I understand, I expected something," I said, watching him finger the pages of Joseph Campbell.

This seemed to relieve him somewhat, as he faced his body towards me, and nodded. "This in no way will be an action for expulsion. Merely disciplinary."

"I understand," I said.

"You've been with us a long time."

"Yes, I have."

"We know who you are, what you do for the order."

I didn't understand this, and wondered how they could know me when I hadn't figured that out myself. Perhaps this was a naïve realization, but I felt that, among all my history, my knowledge, the thinning hair and protruding stomach, I was indeed naïve, a boy, not much further along now in my forties than I was when I first took the oath. Another wonder that came to me suddenly was what they *did* see.

"Which is what?" I asked.

"Excuse me?"

"What I do for the order. What is it? I do not ask in defiance, I'm curious."

Father Mike stood there for quite some time. He was stolid, not fumbling, but I could tell he was searching through his database of phrase. We all had this amazing ability to recall such great words, as our study had been to read them over and over, such a beautifully classic Western education. One could easily be identified as a purveyor of wisdom if it was spread before you like a lavish, solitary dinner, to feed on the words selected as the most nourishing for humanity, a brush of humanity.

"What we all do, Thomas. Sacrifice a certain kind of life to enrich the lives of others."

I understood this is what he had to say, as I would have said something similar if asked, but his was slightly modified, if only a little, by honesty—a small, tight honesty, an awareness in him that I had lost my

purpose. Yet, despite the presumption, it gave me comfort that Father
Michael only resorted to half a platitude, and meant the rest sincerely. I
could tell. He lived for the sacrifice. And I realized I never considered it.

That is when I told him, about the house, about Mirabelle, and that
I would be leaving the order.

*

There were changes I found very difficult to manage. For one thing,
utilities. Though I had lived a routine life that consisted of chores,
responsibilities, even something as parallel as monthly duties, I consis-
tently forgot to pay my electric bill, which I found shockingly high every
month. I would be rifling through the recently acquired collection of
pans, wondering which most suitable for making scrambled eggs, when
the lights would go out, and I knew once again that I had forgotten.
Imagine, a man holding Teflon and a spatula in the dark?

Looking for a job proved equally challenging. At first I intended to
continue teaching. However, towing minds through history felt too dry,
now. Who knew what was true in history, or even if truth could ever be
involved in the documents that history favored? How would the riot
be rendered in the pages of future text? A race divide? A class struggle?
Something so singular and pointed, a label? A scrawl of chalk on a blackboard, a scratched in period. Next lesson.

I got a job at the Museum of American History in D.C., giving tours
to groups and coordinating events, four days a week. I suppose it is
similar to teaching, only we move through a space as the information
unfolds, and there is something more authentic about that feeling. I
insisted on only covering contemporary history, that which I had lived
through or experienced in at least some peripheral sense, so that I could
contribute stories beyond the curatorial, beyond a yellowed document.

One of the joyous discoveries was public transit. With the order there
was access to cars, plenty to share, and even though the bus ran directly in
front of the rectory—everywhere I went—I had always chosen to use the
car. When I think about it, there wasn't even a choice—I simply never

considered the bus. Now that I ride it every day, I can never think to go
back to a car. I read while I wait for the bus, I read while I ride the bus. I
can average thirty pages on the MARC train, each way to work. I probably have gone through twice as much literature as before. When I'm not
reading, I watch Baltimore move around me, a pointless yet fascinating
documentary, rubber and asphalt soundtrack, brick and mortar, solid
and moving. There is so much more to a city when we're not forced to
focus on its roads.

*

My mother's home is brightened among the other rowhouses; Mirabelle has softened the marble steps with planters on either side of the
stoop. She has scrubbed the window sills. Torvoris plays in the street
with some of the other kids. I imagine Kevin is inside, reading one of his
fantasy books. The tang of bolognese hangs in the humid bloom of Little
Italy. On every corner scrolling signage beckons the hungry to partake
of scampi, authentic pizza, handmade pappardelle. There's been talk of
Exeter becoming a walking street, to ease the car traffic and make it safer
for the kids, but also to encourage pedestrian tourism. It might not be
so peaceful if they got around to doing it, but I wouldn't cringe every
time I saw Torvoris running fearlessly between the cars. This particular
evening is heavy with smell, no wind from the harbor, and just enough
cloud to trap the whole of Indian summer.

Mirabelle is tending to the first-thing's-first of her after-work everyday, making sure dinner is on, toys and shoes are out of accident's way.
I place the small bag of groceries on the counter—some bread, milk,
and butter. She swings the door open and calls out to Torvoris, time for
clean-up and homework. Kevin sidles out of his room before Mirabelle
calls his name—or maybe she doesn't need to anymore—and he immediately goes to the kitchen to set the table. He grabs four plates intuitively.
I feel so damned good when he does this.

"How did it go today?"

"I don't know. I filled out the paperwork. We will see."

"How does that work anyway, Thomas?"

"Not sure if I understand it any more than I did before I filled out the paperwork, tell you the truth."

"Well, it's something noble, any way you look at it."

"And I think I have a first sentence," I say.

"For the book?"

I nod.

She laughs. "Thomas, who is going to read a book about Highland-town? Half of it ain't even there anymore."

"Exactly. Which is why I'm writing it. I have some great notes, there are many stories, too many."

Torvoris storms in, arms and legs going every which way, out of breath. He immediately comes to my side, rubs my head.

"Shiny," he says.

"It's hot outside," I say.

"Mama, will I go bald when I get old?"

Mirabelle snaps around. "Torvoris, what kind of thing to say is that? Apologize to Thomas."

But I am too busy laughing to hear the mumbled sorry.

"Glad you can laugh about it," she says, keeping her evil eye on Tor-voris. The boy goes to the sink and makes himself appear useful.

I look to Mirabelle, giving my most pitifully hurt face, a pushed-out lip, and slowly broaden in the smile that comes to me so easily these days. She fights at first, her mouth pinched in motherly discipline, but we beam sideways at each other with conspiratorial humor, both knowing the absurdity of being angry at anything for too long.

Nobility. Nobility is possessing a true sense of ownership over the circumstances of the world. Nobility is the feel of earning the whole lay of the land, whether it be in the mind, the heart, or the Trust. Nobility is not chin-up silence; it is not stoicism. I thought I had always possessed nobility, if not in my contributions, certainly in the sacrifice of becom-ing a religious. Belonging to the order lent me a status that I didn't earn, however, and though I was immediately respected by wearing the black pants, the black shirt, I earned none of it. My fear of the world kept me hiding behind the order. Now, living in a basement, loveless, working a meager job with little prospects, has me feeling more noble than ever.

After dinner, we wash and put away the dishes in ritual fashion. Mirabelle forbids me to wash because she feels like I don't scrub hard enough.

"You know all about the virtue of cleanliness, Thomas."

I grab the tea she has made and we go out on the stoop, another ritual. The sun has all but gone down, and indigo spreads itself over Little Italy, the tops of the terrace homes. Some have built decks on their rooftops, and are watching the windows downtown flicker on, little squares of light that reflect off the harbor. She pours me a glass. I drink. The street mingles with muted sounds, of mothers calling children for dinner, words ricocheting off brick, cars in the distance.

I spoke with one of my co-workers at the museum a few days ago who was complaining about how the value of community was fading quickly in this day and age. I didn't agree with him. The community I value most I don't ever see fading. I lost my familial community, first when my mother left and then when my father died. I lost the order, but I haven't lost my choice to belong. To belong to what? That is inconsequential. The choice is what matters.

I suppose I lost my faith too, or maybe I never had it to begin with. I tried a couple of times to attend different services at various churches, Catholic, Protestant, a temple on Liberty Boulevard. But even before the sermon began, as I walked into the respective building, I marveled more at the architectural detail, the designer's choice, the being of history that enveloped the structure. The church was an artifact, a museum piece, a ruin. This did not upset me. I saw it as beautiful, and that was enough for me to feel at ease with the discovery. So, where does faith go? For all the walking I do, I haven't thought to search. I'm not interested in finding it.

Mind you, that does not mean I think it has disappeared and sometimes, when I'm walking around the city, whether in kooky Hamden, or briny Fell's Point, or the ever-stubborn Highlandtown, I suddenly spot bits of it. I'll see an old Greek man struggle across a street, and watch a

short Latina with three small children saddled to her legs, run to the man
and give him an arm. Or a large oak splayed out in Druid Hill Park will
loom over my small history and tell me how silly my own thoughts grow,
without root. Once, a dark morning on the D.C.-bound MARC train,
I glanced from my newspaper to the aisle and—several rows up—I was
sure the elderly woman gazing emptily at nothing in particular was my
mother. I kept my eyes on her until she looked my way. I was not afraid.
When she finally saw me, I smiled at her. There was no confusion, only
a pleasant smile back, a long glance. In my heart was forgiveness, a sense
of peace, of connection. I don't know what was in her heart, but her
face was soft and present, as if she understood why this stranger needed
to look upon her. These moments come to me unexpectedly, when my
mind is focused on other things. So perhaps in some mysterious way, I
am keeping eyes open to my faith, or maybe it is openly searching for me.

Regardless, I know it is not something to search for, and when it's
ready to present itself again, or I feel its reemerging tether, I will be there.
For now, I won't be facing it, and I'm at peace with that. If I am to best
the encompassing fear that has kept me from being present in the world,
then I must look life in the face, accept it, and continue. There will be no
more looking only to the past. I have my resolve, for now. Nothing can
shake me from it until I am strong enough on my own.

There was only one time I played Lot's wife since I left the order those
months ago. I heard St. Mary's would be closing, due to immeasurable
damage sustained by the riots and not enough support from its investors,
or perhaps the faltering order itself. I heard so many reasons, and none
of them mattered. The only real true thing was St. Mary's was closing.
I found myself walking over to the school, after a dinner at Mirabelle's.
I wasn't looking for anything in particular. I didn't go up to the grotto,
the front doors, or even walk on the school grounds. Perhaps I wanted to
take a good look before it would become yet another stunning Baltimore
edifice to fall into ruin. I walked around the building quite absently,
watching the trees pan across and in front of the greystone and mortar.
The trees were in full green, the walkways filled with dead azalea flow-

ers and leaves. I could already feel the youth gone from the campus, the impression of the school now cold, ghostly, a mausoleum wreathed with fallen nature.

I then found myself standing at one of the floating docks in the harbor. The neon sign of the Domino Sugar plant glowed directly across the water, the buzz of downtown in the distance. On one side of me were two defunct fishing boats, rusted and tipped towards each other, like leaning lovers. On the other was an enormous fenced-off plot, with a sign announcing the arrival of a luxury hotel and condominium complex. Along the edge of the dock, all kinds of trash had collected—beer cans, candy wrappers, Styrofoam food containers—bobbing in and out of soapy foam. I could even see a discolored photograph hugging an empty two-liter soda bottle, of what appeared to be an older woman and a small boy.

That was the only time, as I stood there, head down towards the scum and water, the wet simmer of fish and foul, that I played out a history that didn't exist. I imagined that there was a parallel life I led on the opposite shore, and that all the debris below was the life I had lived and let go of—enough to float and collect—and not the life I never had the chance to lose. This life wanted to reveal itself—the document, the need for document. Enough to float and collect, this history of a life across the water. I saw glimpses of my father, healthy, reading the Bible to an older version of myself that he was never able to see, in the sunlight by the South River. I saw a group of men, myself included, running through a field together, friends together, a beautiful affection between us, something shared. I saw glimpses of kissing Lydia back at the dance all those years ago, the moment her eyes wanted me to, and I knew. I imagined the photograph in the water to be proof that, in this other-shore life, my mother didn't leave, that she loved me, that someone loved me, that someone deeply loved me. Across the water, I looked for a figure, perhaps standing alone like me, looking for his parallel self, like me, curious about who was finding what he left behind—his lived, loved life, the histories of it faded by the float across the harbor.

I just as quickly let that history fall away, determined to create a new one, and focused on the clear reality of the Domino Sugar sign. And though I was so full of sorrow, there was no deep hurt within me. I kept focus on the sugar factory, its constant neon light, waited until my cheeks were dried by the wind of the Patapsco River, and walked back across the dark, obliterated corners of Highlandtown, to whatever it was my new life would be.

Acknowledgements & Gratitude

Thank you to the Ragdale Foundation, Shuffle, Crosstown Arts and the Hub City Writers Project, for granting me the inspiration, space and support to write this nugget.

To Diane Goettel for her willingness to deal with my diva-self. It's great to work with you again! Thanks to Jared Shaffer for whipping out that RISD degree. Thanks to Adam Prince for showing me all the opportunity. And Jonah Strauss for saying to me over bubbles, "be what you want the writing to be."

To Emma Kuli, who lifts the world with her enthusiasm and love. Thank you so much for the willingness and labor.

To Randall Kenan, who made belief so sweet. I will thank you forever and ever for your mentorship. I miss you.

To Charles Johnson, for all these years, even after the buildings closed.

To the dedicated teachers and readers and cheerleaders during this book's long, long journey: Kazim Ali, José Alvergue, Nicole Archer, Nancy Au, Julia Barzizza, Dana Bean, Syr Beker, Dodie Bellamy, Paolo Bicchieri, Simone Billings, Sarah Broderick, Trina Calderón, May-lee Chai, Maxine Chernoff, Sharon Coleman, Matthew Clark Davison, Matthew

DeCoster, Kevin Dublin, Steve Erickson, Antony Fangary, Seth Fischer, Peter Gadol, Jessie Scrimager Galloway, Katrin Gibb, Heather June Gibbons, Kirk Glaser, Robert Glück, Wayne Goodman, LD Green, Allia Griffin, Jim Grimsley, John Haggerty, Hollie Hardy, Kai Harris, Irwan bin Iskak, Elizabeth Gonzalez James, William Johnson, Maria Judnick, Heidi Kasa, Douglas Kearney, Kevin Killian, Junse Kim, Yume Kim, Cheryl Klein, Peter Kline, Chad Koch, Genine Lentine, Maggie Levantovskaya, Jennifer Lewis, Joanna Ley, Alanna Lin, Julián Delgado Lopera, Susan Mason, Alexandra Mattraw, Richard May, Kelly McNerney, Monique Mero-Williams, Toni Mirosevich, Tomas Moniz, Matt Monte, Ari Moskowitz, Dipali Murti, Tim Myers, Jill Newman, Alvin Orloff, ZZ Packer, Sebastián Páramo, Felice Picano, Baruch Porras-Hernandez, DA Powell, Shobha Rao, Linda Ravenswood, Claudia Rodriguez, Diana Rosinus, Stephanie Sabo, Zak Salih, Noah Sanders, Janet Sarbanes, Kendra Schynert, Maureen Seaton, James Siegel, Norma Smith, David St. John, Chanan Tigay, Robin Tremblay-McGaw, Danielle Truppi, Gaia Veenis, Matias Viegener, Lyzette Wanzer, Jerry Wheeler, Arisa White, Michael Wilde, Stephanie Young, Edmund Zagorin and Maya Zeller. Thank you all for your generosity and support.

To my friends, my family, some already named. To Bridgette. I hope you know how brilliant and kind you are.

To Lambda Literary and to Foglifter, for the spaces you create.

To my students. Keep going! You always have my heart.

To my mama. This is a redemption song, whether for you or I, depends. I love you.

To Baltimore. To Cherry Point, to Poppleton, to Highlandtown, to Curtis Bay. To the Patapsco. To Key Bridge sunrises. To the dancing. To the *DANCING*.

To Antwan Dorsey.

And to Marco. Always to Marco.

Photo: Lemia Monet Bodden

Miah Jeffra is author of three books, most recently *The Violence Almanac* (finalist for several awards, including the Grace Paley and St. Lawrence Book Prizes), and co-editor of the anthology *Home is Where You Queer Your Heart*. Work can be seen in *StoryQuarterly*, *Prairie Schooner*, *The North American Review*, *DIAGRAM* and many others. Miah is co-founder of Whiting Award-winning queer and trans literary collaborative, Foglifter Press, and teaches writing and decolonial studies at Santa Clara University and Sonoma State University.